PENGU
THE SCEN

Kavery Nambisan was bor
Daughter of a former Union
Delhi and graduated from St John's Medical College, Bangalore.
She stood first in surgery and was sponsored by the University
of Liverpool for higher training. She obtained the Fellowship of
the Royal College of Surgeons when she was twenty-four.

Kavery Nambisan has written several award-winning books for
children. Her first novel, *The Truth (Almost) About Bharat* was
published by Penguin in 1991.

The author is married to journalist and poet Vijay Nambisan. She
currently lives and works in Bihar.

The Scent of Pepper

Kavery Nambisan

PENGUIN BOOKS

Penguin Books India (P) Ltd., 11 Community Centre, Panchsheel Park, New Delhi 110017, India
Penguin Books Ltd., 27 Wrights Lane, London W8 5TZ, UK
Penguin Putnam Inc., 375 Hudson Street, New York, NY 10014, USA
Penguin Books Australia Ltd., Ringwood, Victoria, Australia
Penguin Books Canada Ltd., 10 Alcorn Avenue, Suite 300, Toronto, Ontario MAV 3B2, Canada
Penguin Books (NZ) Ltd., 182-190 Wairau Road, Auckland 10, New Zealand

First published by Penguin Books India (P) Ltd. 1996

Copyright © Kavery Nambisan 1996

All rights reserved

10 9 8 7 6 5 4 3 2

Typeset in Palatino by Digital Technologies and Printing Solutions, New Delhi

This story is entirely fictitious. Any resemblance of the characters to persons living or dead is purely coincidental and unintended.

For Amma, Babbu, Thai
and
Vintage

Fire can burn
but cannot move.

Wind can move
but cannot burn.

Till fire joins wind
it cannot take a step.

Do men know
it's like that
with knowing and doing?

Dévara Dāsimayya
(tenth-century Kannada vacana poet)
. Ramanujan's translation in *Speaking of Siva*)

Contents

Contents

Acknowledgements

I thank Tulasi, in Kodagu, for sharing with me her priceless store of information on local customs; the British India Library in London, where I gathered much of relevance from the other point of view; and Mike Michell, June Webb, the Parsons and other members of the Coorg Planters' Association in Britain, who supplied me with delightful reminiscences. My thanks also to Vijay, for reading my manuscript as a friend and editing it as a professional; and to my friends in Kodagu for bringing my story to life.

Acknowledgements

I thank Pulari, in Kodagu, for sharing with me her priceless store of information on local customs; the British India Library in London, where I gathered much of relevance from the other point of view; and Mike Michell, June Webb, the Parsons and other members of the Coorg Planters' Association in Britain, who supplied me with delightful reminiscences. My thanks also to Vijay, for reading my manuscript as a friend and editing it as a professional; and to my friends in Kodagu for bringing my story to life.

A Note to the Reader

Coorg, the region in which most of this story is set, is a small enclave in the hills off the south-western coast of India. It was settled—when, no one knows—by a tall, fair, warrior-like race whose roots and ancient provenance are still a matter for much speculation. They assimilated a form of Hinduism but have many cultural traits and religious rituals with no counterparts elsewhere in India.

Kodagu, as they called their land, was settled by the British circa 1800 and brought extensively under coffee plantation. So valuable did the coffee trade become that the British deposed the reigning Haleri Raja and annexed Coorg—their Anglicization of the older name—in 1834.

Ten years after Indian Independence, the territory of Kodagu became part of Mysore (now Karnataka) State. It is still heavily reliant upon the cultivation of coffee. Its Kodava inhabitants still hold themselves as a race apart. And they still contribute a disproportionate number of the Indian Army's soldiers, of all ranks from jawan to Field Marshal.

Part One

Part One

————————————————————

There was half a minute of daylight left when the boxcart carrying the bride reached Athur. The jackals began their maniacal music in the bamboo groves and the sun bled behind the areca palms as the oxen waded through the stream, pulling the cart up the last slope to the house. The bride's aunt touched the girl's bangled wrist and whispered in her ear; Nanji raised the curtain from the window of the cart and looked at the sprawling, tile-roofed Kaleyanda house.

As the red blush in the west merged with the violet darkness, the lamps inside the house were lit. Bone-thin, nervous and seventeen, Nanji entered her second bridal home five years after she had travelled in the same boxcart to her first. In the semi-darkness she saw her husband—big and eager in white *kupya* and *chale*, the silver-sheathed *peeche-kathi* dangling from his waist. Behind him were the unknown faces of her new relatives and the massive figure of the Rao Bahadur who was her father-in-law. His was a good face, engraved with deep, honest lines and his voice was gentle.

'Sprinkle some rice in the water, my daughter.'

Nanji dropped a pinch of saffron rice into the copper pitcher at the doorway and bent to touch his feet. The Rao Bahadur's face brightened with a momentary smile.

'Music,' he said, and receded into the shadows.

The festive sounds of *kombu*, *kottu* and *dudi* filled the house. Her aunt whispered again in her ear. Nanji touched the feet of her mother-in-law and was greeted with a quick embrace that proved awkward when the crescent-shaped *kokkethathi* of the bride caught in the brooch the mother-in-law was wearing. They disentangled themselves after a brief struggle, but the curved tiger-claw brooch that Chambavva pinned her sari with stayed on the red satin jacket of the bride.

'You can keep it, I have so many,' Chambavva said, establishing her superiority.

Smothered by relatives, sweating inside her silks, jewels and flowers, and exhausted by the journey, Nanji struggled for calm: Boju, the youngest son of the Rao Bahadur, led her into the front room.

'This way'.

The graciousness of her new home filled Nanji with a diffidence that she quickly stifled. The front room was larger than her father's entire house and had a ceiling so high it was invisible in the dim light of the lamps. She stood there and thought back to her first wedding, with its three days of ceremony; she had ridden from her father's home in Tenth Mile shining inside out, jewelled feet restless, the rhythm of wedding music pulsing in her youthful blood. The same night, her dreams were shattered by the toddy breath of her husband, who at twenty-six lived precariously with a peevish liver and rotting guts. Nanji rebelled; she bit and clawed him every night but it wasn't any use. He was a man and she was only a child and she ended up with a contused body and contused mind. A year later, she was delivered from torment when her husband was trampled to death by a horse as he wandered home in a drunken stupor. Thirteen-year-old Nanji was cast back into her father's house in widow's white.

Nanji accepted the colourless life of a widow, but things had changed in her father's house. Shortly after the death of Nanji's mother, her father had succumbed to the insistence of relatives and taken a second wife, who was ripe with her first child when Nanji returned. This second wife treated the girl like an unpleasant excrescence and plied her with endless work. Nanji was so effortlessly efficient, it was impossible to blame her for unfinished chores. The stepmother blamed her instead for every calamity: when a coffee bush withered, a hen refused to lay eggs, a pig developed sores or a snake was found in the well water, it was Nanji's fault. The stepmother swiftly relegated Nanji to the kitchen and backyard, determined to wring maximum work from her for minimum food.

Nanji's brothers Nanu and Anni slipped through a harsh childhood without too much suffering. They whiled away their time in the village primary school. Their father was careless about paying the fee of eight annas a month but they managed to spill over to the next class each year. It was far better to sit on the classroom floor and scratch away with chalk on slate, or stand on one leg when punished, than it was to bear the uncharitable abuses of a stepmother. Nanji and her brothers had the innocent resilience of children in the face of injustice.

Nanji's second marriage was the thoughtful gesture of a father who saw in her eyes a ruthless courage; she reminded him of a wild animal biding its time. It made him nervous; he desperately wanted to find her a groom, but who would marry a widow? No offers came even when he made it known that in addition to a good quantity of jewellery, he would gift his highly-prized boxcart and a pair of his finest bulls to his daughter when she married. Nothing happened. Then one day, five years after she was widowed, the young Kaleyanda vet from Athur was summoned to castrate half a dozen pigs on the farm. Baliyanna was graceful, with grey eyes, magnificent shoulders and skilled, gentle hands. He did his job with six quick neat strokes of his scalpel and when he looked up from the squealing pigs, he saw the girl milking a cow outside.

'Who's she?' asked Baliyanna the vet.

'Nanji, my sister,' said Nanu.

The vet's grey eyes focussed briefly on the long-faced girl in a coarse white sari tied over the right shoulder in a careless knot. She wore no chain or earrings, not even a coloured bangle on her thin wrist. 'A widow, by God,' he muttered and walked away to wash his scalpel and his hands. The following week, a letter arrived from Rao Bahadur Madaiah, asking for Nanji's hand in marriage for his son. Nanji's father accepted without bothering to ask Nanji.

The Rao Bahadur owned three hundred acres of coffee and five thousand *battis* of land; he had sent two sons to England to be educated. He was not a man to be trifled with; when he declared that even though Nanji was a widow, it would be a proper wedding with the attendant fanfare and music, her father did not object. Nanji's stepmother resented the loss of the boxcart but conceded in the face of the prestige the marriage would bring. Those who did not know Baliyanna said he was marrying the widow out of greed, that her father had surreptitiously promised more gifts in an attempt to palm her off before she rusted into middle age. But those who knew him said sentiments nobler than greed made him seek the widow's hand.

Nanji folded away the suffocating sadness of her past and awaited the fearful moment when she would be alone with her new husband. That night she realized that not all men are beasts. In the shadows cast by the lamp she studied her husband's kind face, his grey eyes, thick moustache and high cheekbones, and buried forever the misery of her first marriage. Shielded by his strong shoulders, she lay in the four-poster bed and looked up at the ceiling of smoked black wood. She breathed in the clean smell of the cowdung-washed floor, watched the lights and shadows darting like friendly angels across the iron bars of the window, and cherished the moment forever. As she fell asleep, Nanji sent up a prayer of gratitude to Lord Igguthappa for bringing her to that gracious home.

In the morning, she saw the house flooded in sunlight, the coloured glass windows scattering gems on the walls. In the front room, where the roof was as high as the areca palms outside, Chambavva sat in her armchair, sipping milk from a silver cup. Beneath the massive round rosewood table, her two pet panther cubs frolicked.

'They're gentle as kittens,' Chambavva assured her. 'Come, let me show you the house.'

Nanji walked round the table which was big enough to seat twenty persons for a meal, twenty-eight if closely packed. Chambavva showed her the six bedrooms, the dining room and the large; airy room near the kitchen with an eighteen-foot-long narrow black table and benches on either side. 'For any number of hungry children, and when needed, for non-Kodava guests whose caste does not allow them into the other rooms,' Chambavva explained. The kitchen, store, study and attic made up the rest of the house. The bathroom was at the back, near the well. The toilet, in true Kodava tradition, was a roofless bamboo enclosure around a pit in the middle of coffee bushes.

Chambavva left Nanji to get on with her duties as a daughter-in-law. She was a haughty woman who relegated cooking, the care of children and other mundane activities to her retinue of lazy Yerava servants who maintained the house in a state of genteel disorder.

For Nanji, the house was the sacred symbol of nobility. She, more than anyone, was to make it the strongest fortress of the Kaleyanda clan—even when, many years later, her crippled son who had turned Congressman threatened to convert it into a bustling farmyard of idealistic youth. 'A Kodava woman gives her all for the betterment of her husband's home.' Her grandmother, Neelakki, had told her this one morning long ago while churning butter in the copper pitcher.

The Yeravas were a tranquil race with a genetic determination to resist change. For generations, they had worked as cooks, cowherds, sweepers and washerwomen. When Nanji came, the Yeravas tried to resist her assertiveness but in the end they had to give in. She triggered off a frenzy of cleaning, and the Yeravas, unused to such agitation, had no time to contemplate what hit them.

In the morning, when they appeared at the gate in a lazy

column, she armed them with long wire brooms and sent them off to sweep the front and backyard. That included two-and-a-half acres of land, from the bitter lemon and guava trees in the front of the house, to the fringe of areca palms along the sides, right up to the coffee-drying yard, and along the back beyond the well, the bathroom and vegetable garden up to the pigsty and barn. A dozen brooms moved over the ground in unchanging arcs of monotony; that done, they had to sweep the cowshed, wash the pigsty, fumigate the chicken coop, and clean the granary, the threshing shed and the barn. After that it was time to get out the twelve brooms and do it all over again before sundown. The five servants who had lazed inside the house were now set to wash and polish the roof until the black wooden beams boomed and sang instead of creaking like old, arthritic women. The ceiling lamps were taken down, cleared of cobwebs and dead flies. The great round table was scrubbed with lye, polished with oil, and the floors swabbed with day-fresh dung mixed in antiseptic vegetable juices. Nanji ordered the servants about, polished copper and brass, and climbed up to the attic to rescue mouldy, forgotten furniture from the past. The house of the Rao Bahadur, already very impressive, became the most talked-about house in Athur.

Nanji treated the Yeravas well. 'Like Kurubas and Kudiyas, they too are the children of Kodagu,' her grandmother had said while grinding rice on the well-worn stone. 'Yeravas never think beyond their next meal. They cannot be corrupted.' Nanji cared for her servants. She fed them *thaliya puttoo* with fish, or *akki otti* with chutney made of jackfruit seeds, and kept a pitcher of jaggery-sweetened coffee hot at the fireplace for them. And she showed the Yeravas that it was more fun to work than be lazy.

No one resented the praise and accolades that Nanji received, particularly not her mother-in-law. Fathered by a nobleman (her father had been a diwan in whose memory a village had been named) and husbanded by a Rao Bahadur, Chambavva had no choice but to retain her prestige by doing as little as possible in the way of work. She had the pink, pampered cheeks of a baby. She always dressed as if for a ceremony in a satin jacket and silk sari pinned with a tiger-claw brooch. She wore her ruby-encrusted, serpent-headed choker and three-stringed *ponnumale* even at home. Her sense of grandeur never deserted her and she insisted that she and her husband eat off silver plates and drink from silver cups. The gods, too, were kept in their place. She spared a minute each morning to clasp her hands and say, 'Lord Igguthappa, protect our clan,' and then reverted to her life of gracious sloth. After fulfilling her duty of producing five sons (one had died of brain fever at the age of two), she lavished attention on the pair of panther cubs that her husband brought back from a hunting trip in the jungles of Kiggatnad. She filled her life with weddings, funerals, naming ceremonies and house-warming pujas; she wore heirlooms and sported new tiger-claw brooches as evidence that her husband shot no fewer than two tigers a year. She was queen of the house and knew it; so she did not mind relegating all responsibilities—save that of rearing the panthers—to Nanji.

Rao Bahadur Madaiah was the reigning *pattedara* of the Kaleyanda family, which meant that all important decisions had to meet with his approval. He had studied at the Madras Presidency College, a considerable achievement at a time when most Kodavas did not study beyond the school in Virajpet or Madikeri and were considered fortunate and intelligent if they managed to study in Mysore or Mangalore. The fact that he was unable to complete his BA did not sully his image in Kodagu but Madaiah himself was disappointed. Though he never talked of it, he tried to make up for his deficiency by sending two of his sons to England and two to Madras for their education. In 1903, when Baliyanna graduated as a veterinary surgeon, the Rao Bahadur said, 'My son has a degree that even the British respect. He must have a bungalow to match his status.' He bought the sprawling house, one hundred and twelve acres of newly-planted coffee and five thousand *battis* of land in Athur, and moved out of the family house where he had lived until then with his wife and children and fifty other Kaleyandas. All of Coorg envied him.

But the Rao Bahadur had a problem: the contagion of mental depression that wove its sly web around many Kodavas did not spare him. It was worse than the plague; with plague you were subjected to a short, fierce period of suffering and a dramatic exit but with this depression without cause, the victim lingered between life and death for an interminable period. The worst aspect of this deadly disease was that the victim became invincible to every other illness, so it was more difficult to die. Madaiah's depressions, which had no cause and therefore no cure, had pushed him into the abyss of slovenliness for the past eleven years. He cloistered himself in his study and never went out except on monthly hunting trips, more out of habit than love of sport. Even Nanji's efforts to draw him out of this self-imposed hell were of no use. He ate his meals in his study with the thoughtless, uninhibited gluttony of the hopeless, swallowing unchewed rotis, chunks of pork, bowls of rice, tiers of *puttoos* and potatoes. He ate with reckless, bestial haste; it wrapped him in the malodorous vapours of flatulence and indigestion, increasing his rancour and depression. His unwashed hair turned greasy, his sleepless eyes were bloodshot; he managed the estate only with the help of clerks and *maestry*.

As the years passed, his massive figure shrank until his hips were sucked in, his broad shoulders collapsed, his shoulder blades jutted out through his coat, his neck hung forward and his arms dangled by his sides like the big wooden spoons that Nanji stirred her jams with. His *galle meese*—the white whiskers that met his sidelocks—were unkempt, the eyes held a fire that was destined to die. When in the worst throes of his depression, he curled himself on the bed and refused to get up. The family was determined to hide this appalling shame; they managed to project a bright and dapper

Rao Bahadur to the outside world when occasion demanded and later hustled him back into the study that was his hell and his home.

Nanji could not accept it. She would stride into the study, fling open doors, unbolt windows, get the room washed and scrubbed with cowdung, she would put great red bunches of *rajakirita* in a copper pitcher by the table and light incense sticks to drive away the dyspeptic, farmyard smell that surrounded her unhappy father-in-law. And she would ask: '*Mava* . . . some coffee? Some food?' The Rao Bahadur wanted nothing.

He refused to wash himself. His eyelids oozed, his breath smelt of rotting jackfruit, fumes of decay escaped his nostrils and lice throve in his groin. Nanji knelt before him with a bowl of hot water and tried to work the wads of dirt from the soles of his feet, weeping helpless tears because she couldn't budge them even with a knife. Baliyanna consoled her: 'He's a fortunate man, without worries.' Nanji wondered if her husband was serious or if he was mocking her.

Her new life left no time for Nanji to visit her father's home in Tenth Mile, until she went there for her first confinement seven-and-a-half months after her marriage. In the boxcart she carried two sackfuls of honey-sweet mangoes from the four trees in the compound. After two days of forced hospitality, her stepmother subjected her to a meagre diet and coffee without milk, though it was established Kodava custom to overfeed pregnant women. That wasn't mindless pampering but a wise tradition, because more often than not women succumbed to puerperal sickness. Only the tough survived, and they were so tough that they lived through ten or twelve confinements until menopause rescued them from the hazards of fertility and they pulled on, often outliving more delicate husbands.

Tradition demanded that pregnant Kodava women eat eggs laid by red hens, two ladles of ghee a day and rotis with wild honey, in addition to a *lehyam* made of jaggery, sesame seeds, cashewnuts, almonds and sunflower seeds in the morning and a cleansing paste of garlic, asafoetida, cinnamon and pepper at night. They drank coffee with cloves and cardamom, and milk boiled with saffron, until they passed perfumed urine, perspired perfumed sweat, wept perfumed tears and breathed perfumed breath and their skins gave off such pungent smells that passers-by could feel their nostrils twitch when they came within five hundred yards of a pregnant woman. The women were massaged with coconut oil, bathed in water boiled with herbs and scrubbed with *shikakai* until their fattened limbs resembled succulent raw meat. Women who could read were given the *Mahabharata*, *Ramayana* and the *Gita* in the hope that they would bear a son who would be a saint or a scholar such as Kodagu had never produced.

Nanji had to do without any of this. After two stress-filled months of starvation, she delivered a rat of a baby who gasped thrice and died. The obligatory forty-five days in bed followed, with a woollen scarf round the ears and a bandage round the belly and then Nanji returned to her husband's home. 'Future pregnancies I shall handle myself, without help or hindrance from my stepmother,' she told herself as she alighted from the boxcart and went in to resume her duties. Ten months later, she triumphed with the birth of a boy who weighed as much as ten seers of rice. She delivered him right there in the bedroom on the four-poster bed with Bolle the cowherd's wife rubbing her back and fomenting her belly with hot wet towels. All her twelve live children were born thus.

Nanji was two children and three-and-a-half pregnancies old when one morning she went to the study with a glass of coconut water for her father-in-law and found him retching blood into his brass chamberpot. His incurable depression had caught up with the Rao Bahadur and he had decided to end his life in a way fit for nobility, by swallowing his diamond ring. There was reason enough for his death, had he but known; but the suicide itself was unmitigated by any solace.

Chapter Two

The death became public when Boju walked to the flowering mango tree and fired two shots, choosing his father's favourite gun from the twelve in the gun-rack. Swift-footed Yeravas were already out of the gate and across the ramp to the opposite side of the stream.

'Yajmana! It's Madaiah Yajmana!'

Villagers snaked in through the gate like disciplined pilgrims: women in white, men in their best, most sober clothes. The dead man wasn't just anyone, he had married a diwan's daughter and he had received the title of Rao Bahadur from the British for his loyalty. Such solidity of background. He deserved a splendid funeral, and the family could afford to give him one.

The sons laid Madaiah on the stone slab near the well, peeled off his dirt-encrusted clothes and washed away the slime and accretions of eleven years of decay. Neighbours, relatives and prompters were at hand.

'Bathe him in scalding water!'

'Sit him up! Sit him up!'

'The sovereign on the forehead!'

'The mirror, where's the hand-mirror?'

They dressed him like a bridegroom in *kupya-chale*, with the *peeche-kathi* at his waist, covered his wispy hair with the gold-lined turban and put a mirror in his hand. They stuck a gold sovereign on his forehead and sat him up on a divan in the centre of the front room because the Kaleyanda men never take anything lying down. The round table, so massive that it overwhelmed the room, was pushed to a corner to make place for the mourners. The sons changed into white dhotis, covered their bare chests with white cloth and stood at the door, stupefied by the suddenness of the death.

Chambavva kept vigil near the body in widow's white, with the shoulder cloth knotted in front, greying hair loosened, denuded of chains, earrings and her tiger-claw brooch. Her soft, baby skin was unused to the roughness of the reed mat on which she sat but her grief overshadowed physical discomfort. Her status had slipped from that of wife to widow. Even a decaying husband was better than no husband.

True, the Kodavas treated their widows better than most, but even so, a woman without a husband was a symbol of grief. Though her husband had ceased to exist for God knows how long, his physical death still left a vacuum. He looked so fresh and youthful now, after the cleansing. Chambavva's mind wandered back to the days of his hook-nosed handsomeness, she remembered the strength of his arms, the eagerness in his stride, the precise confidence of his limbs and she bent her head so as to avoid the glances of pity from mourners who pressed flowers and sympathy upon her. By midday, the room had filled with women in white like so many doves of peace. Mourners came all day to touch the feet of the dead man and to drop a rupee coin in the brass plate at the foot of the divan. Near Chambavva stood Nanji, pale and prominent in her advanced pregnancy. She rearranged the garlands, relit the incense sticks, served black coffee and *puttoo* to the guests, and tried bravely to hide her sorrow.

Nanji was the saddest person at the funeral. She was not mourning the death of her father-in-law—his death did not sadden her any more than the felling of a rotting *athi* tree or the withering of a coffee bush—her tears were for the splendid diamond ring that the Rao Bahadur had used as his instrument of suicide. After slitting his gullet lengthways and causing him to vomit a chamber pot full of blood, it had passed slyly into his stomach and it still lay there in his fermenting gastric juices. The diamond, big and perfect, was a family heirloom that should have rightfully passed to her husband; now it was irrevocably lost. Such was the moronic stupidity of men who could not think clearly in moments of grief. Neither Baliyanna, Boju nor any of the Kaleyanda men thought of the possibility of rescuing the ring. It could easily be done. Had she not once, when slitting the belly of a chicken, found a gold sovereign with the royal insignia of Queen Victoria lying face down amidst undigested grains of rice? Had she not washed and rubbed and scrubbed it and added it to the treasures that she kept in a red satin purse between sheets perfumed with sandalwood in the bottom drawer of her wooden chest? Nanji itched for action but any suggestion from her could easily be misinterpreted. So she submerged her grief in the endlessness of her duties, minding her oldest, ensuring that everyone had eaten and pausing to feed the little son who slept in a cradle in the bedroom.

Mourners kept coming; they leaned on the round table, sat on it, toppled furniture and filled every inch of space, like stacked white linen. Many remained standing. Such discomfort was borne with the fortitude that was an expression of their caring; they had come to stay until the body was cremated. There was no single person to direct the course of rituals and these went on till four in the afternoon when ten young men of the village dressed in black *kupya-chale* appeared, their guns ready for the funeral honours. Baliyanna, Boju and four cousins carried the body on a bamboo chair to the half-acre clearing amidst coffee shrubs that was reserved for family funerals, where one dead son had already preceded the father. Fresh stacks of wood had been cut and readied for the cremation. Three times they carried the body around the pyre; Chambavva followed, with a cracked mud pot on her head, water trickling from it over the babyish face that was distorted with grief. The ritual of the cracked pot symbolised the dehiscence of her married life. Nanji walked behind Chambavva, throwing rice into the unlit pyre. When the Rao Bahadur had been mounted on his final perch, the sons, wife and relatives touched his lips with wet *tulsi* leaves in farewell, Boju removed the silver-sheathed dagger from his waist and Chambavva broke her bangles over the body. The ten young men who were lined up before the pyre raised their guns in a slow graceful arc and fired twice. Baliyanna lit the pyre.

Until the eleventh-day ceremony, Chambavva, like the Kodava widows before her, did not comb her hair or sleep on her bed; she abstained from milk, meat and spices and ate only once a day, after offering food first to the spirit of her dead husband and then to the crows. With Nanji, she walked to the backyard with the food wrapped in banana leaves, laid it near the well and clapping her hand, called: 'Ka! Ka! Ka!' The crows were only too happy to feast on the food; death meant little to these realists who believed only in survival. But to the grieving family, the fact that the crows enjoyed the food meant that the dead person too was satisfied. Chambavva did it for eleven days until the soul of her husband joined his ancestors and had no further need for worldly victuals.

At the eleventh-day ceremony, a hundred guests were fed, besides the workers, Yeravas and a multitude of wanderers, beggars and derelicts. The family followed the age-old Kodava custom of a pilgrimage to Talakaveri at the top of the Brahmagiri hill. There they scattered the Rao Bahadur's ashes in the river; when they came home they ended their period of abstinence by eating a breakfast of *thaliya puttoo* with chicken, and coffee with milk. For the first time after the Rao Bahadur's death the family was on its own.

Baliyanna sat in his father's study, intending to sort out matters that needed attention. The first thing he saw was a cream envelope addressed to the Rao Bahadur; it had arrived from England the day he died and Nanji, who had put it on the desk, did not think that any news could be important enough to intrude upon the immediate tragedy.

So it had stayed there, leaning against a jar of water until Baliyanna slit open the envelope and read the three-page letter. He bellowed with rage and Nanji—who was cleaning sardines for lunch—hastily wiped her hands on her sari and rushed to the study.

'What is it?' Nanji asked her husband, who was cursing at the letter in his hand. A photograph slipped from between the pages of the letter and fell to the floor. Nanji picked it up and saw the cause of his anger. Appachu, the star son of the Rao Bahadur, who had been sent to England to study for the Bar, stood with his arm around a large, flat-faced white woman. 'He's married an English whore!' cried Baliyanna. He grabbed the photograph, tore it to shreds and threw it into the chamberpot that had served as a receptacle when the Rao Bahadur vomited blood just before his death.

'*Thu!*'

Appachu had passed his law examination with honours and married one Marjorie Hicks. Neither English nor a whore, she was a fair-complexioned, unfortunately plain Eurasian, the daughter of an undertaker from Tooting Bec. In the same letter, Appachu conveyed the tragic news that Machu, the other brother in England, who was studying medicine at Charing Cross Hospital, had gone for a weekend to Torquay and drowned while swimming. The tragedy of Machu's death did not hurt Baliyanna so much, because death, when it is an accident, is unavoidable. But one could certainly think before jumping into marriage with a half-caste. 'He could have got the most beautiful and accomplished Kodava girl for the asking!' he shouted.

Appachu had committed the unforgivable sin of disclosing both tragedies in one letter. Had the Rao Bahadur read it, he would have had monumental reasons for the suicide. His death was a greater misfortune because the effect preceded the cause; the suicide remained a futile act, without justification. The family was branded by three distinct, permanent tragedies.

Chambavva and her sons tried to keep the shame to themselves but people talked. 'There will be no escaping the anger of our ancestors,' they said. 'Kodagu will be punished.'

The rains were held back that year. The land became parched and the Kaveri ran dry. When the rains came at last, it was nearly time for Kailpodh, when the Kodavas worship their weapons, and too late for the paddy and coffee. The catastrophe affected the economy of Kodagu for five years, and the burden of guilt was borne by the Kaleyanda family.

The humiliation of Appachu's marriage, compounded by the grief of losing Machu, knocked Chambavva out. 'He promised he'd become a fine doctor and look after my gout and colic,' she wept. Her life had been remarkably free of incident; now these multiple blows were too much for her to bear. The greatest shame was Appachu's alliance with an outcaste. The day before her sons had set out for England, she had spent an entire evening counselling them about evil foreigners.

'Keep away from the women,' she had warned. 'They paint their lips like they're spouting blood, they walk thrusting their chests forward—no shame—and morals, they have none. Keep away from them or you'll contract diseases more gruesome than smallpox or the plague.'

Chambavva wasn't religious but she had offered two thick gold bangles to Lord Igguthappa so he would guard her sons. Upon her insistence, the Rao Bahadur had asked an English friend—a Mr Hayes of Pollibetta—to request his older brother in England to be their guardian. The senior Hayes, who lived in Beaconsfield, was horrified at the idea of entertaining Indians, however lofty their background. When the boys visited him, he served them weak lukewarm tea on the porch to express his displeasure. The boys kept away after the first visit and decided to take on London themselves.

London took to the boys. Appachu and Machu were both blessed with good looks, easy grace and a natural ability to adopt English customs without awkwardness. Machu quickly succumbed to the charms of several girls in succession until his untimely death closed that chapter. Appachu tried valiantly to fight his vigorous urges. When he married

Marjorie Hicks, he excused himself by citing the comfortable fact that the girl's grandmother was a Wagentrieber and the great-granddaughter of none other than the famous Skinner of glorious cavalry tradition.

Chambavva roamed the house like a large, white, dishevelled bird, embarrassed at outliving two sons and a husband. Watching her, Nanji feared that she too would go the way of the Rao Bahadur. But the widow surprised everyone by making an announcement one day in the middle of lunch:

'I'm going to live in the Crystal Palace.'

Crystal Palace was one of the many Kaleyanda family homes. It was a splendid house with twenty-eight rooms that were connected by a maze of doors and passageways. Each room had four windows with panes of coloured glass, which made the house look like a jewelled, friendly monster crouching in the green lush valley at the foothills of Kundathbottu. It was said that when invaders had tried to plunder the temple on top of the hill, the Kodavas fought them off with the help of a swarm of wild bees that hung from hives on giant *athi* trees. The buzzing of those huge killer bees was said to be as terrifying as their sting, as menacing as war music. Crystal Palace had been built by Madaiah's great-grandfather as a symbol of protection for the temple. Martin Hojohn, a British official, had been so fascinated by the house that glittered in the morning sun that he suggested it be named after the famous glass house in London, which had housed half the treasures of India for an exhibition during the reign of Queen Victoria.

Any member of the Kaleyanda family had the right to live in Crystal Palace if they could meet the expense of food, firewood and oil for the lamps. The house with its one hundred and twelve coloured glass windows reflected so much light that it was difficult to sleep at night without flashes, squiggles and geometric figures interfering with one's dreams. Perhaps for this reason it only attracted widows. Twelve Kaleyanda women were now there to escape their luckless fate and lived together as a cackling, cheerful, harmonious lot. The widows organized a rota for housework which allowed them ample time for simple pleasures like singing, cowrie games and occasional, boisterous toddy-drinking sessions. When money was tight, the women brewed their own liquor and reached complex and sophisticated levels of inebriation. The revelry could be heard from the foothills of Kundathbottu beyond Kunda right up to Gonicoppa.

The Maplas who came to buy oranges and cardamom hitched up their lungis and hurried home to recount tales to their families in Kerala. 'Oh, the devilry of the Kodava women!' they said, and wondered what drove the widows to such mirth. Thus was truth distorted. The innocent pleasure of the widows was an expression of rebellion that no one had the time or compassion to understand, so the women hid their frustration and wandered through the house, saw themselves mirrored in coloured glass which multiplied their number to one hundred and forty-four. Crystal Palace was also known as the House of Widows and it was a happy place.

Chambavva packed twelve white saris, twelve long-sleeved jackets and four white vastras in her tin trunk and asked Baliyanna to escort her to Crystal Palace. She gave Nanji her twenty-six tiger-claw brooches, eleven tiger-claw pendants and her *kokkethathi*, *gundumani* and *pathak*. The rest of her jewellery, she said, was to be shared between Nanji and Boju's future wife.

Chambavva's only problem was her pet panthers, who had grown into menacing, muscled hulks that lived on freshly killed rabbits, partridge and wildfowl. She couldn't possibly expect the widows to accommodate her pets at Crystal Palace and Baliyanna firmly refused to keep them in the house after she was gone. When it became known that the prized panthers were up for sale, eager buyers clamoured at the house. 'I don't trust any of them,' Chambavva said, and held on to her pets until two short dark men came all the way from Travancore. 'Please let us take these fine animals as a gift for our Maharaja,' they begged. 'Your pets will be ensured a royal lifestyle for the rest of their lives.'

Satisfied that her pets would enter an imperial household, Chambavva parted with them and gave a gold sovereign to the men in gratitude. The same day, the two men (who actually owned a beedi shack in Fraserpet), sold the panthers to a British Range Officer for four gold sovereigns and converted their beedi shop into a hotel. The following morning, the Range Officer finished off Chambavva's pets with great finesse, placing the barrel of his gun in one ear and squeezing the trigger so that the bullet came out through the other ear without staining the animals with a drop of blood. The marvellous, undamaged specimens were packed off to Arthur Fox the taxidermist and the result was two perfectly preserved panther skins that hung on the wall in the Range Officer's bungalow. They stayed there for nineteen years until the officer moved back to England, taking them with him. The panther heads adorned the walls of the pub called 'Courage' that he opened in Wales; and he never missed an opportunity to explain in exquisite detail to his beer-drinking customers how he had shot the panthers in an intrepid hunting expedition.

Madaiah's death, followed by Chambavva's exit, forced Baliyanna to be master of the house. He did not like it. The thought of spending his life worrying about coffee bushes and sheaves of paddy frightened the vet, who loved the smell of animals and the complexities of disease and death. Nanji sensed his despair and quietly extended the domain of her responsibility to the estate and the land. Some weeks later, she asked, 'Do you want me to pay the wages?'

'If you like,' Baliyanna said, his heart leaping with gratitude at her thoughtfulness. 'While you're at it, perhaps you can maintain the accounts.'

'I've been doing that,' Nanji answered, and showed him the accounts written in the laborious scrawl of an illiterate woman who had taught herself to write. They were precise and methodical. Thus Baliyanna was permanently relieved of estate responsibilities.

Baliyanna was one of the three vets in Kodagu and the only vet with a degree. The vet in Sunticoppa was an illiterate quack who gave soap-and-water enemas to cows to induce labour and whose treatment for horses with colic was to wrap a hot wet blanket round their flanks. He was marginally superior to, and several notches safer than the semiliterate quack in Madikeri whose universal treatment for bestial ailments was an infusion of tulsi and castor oil. The exotic remedy was marketed in bottles of different colours, sizes and prices but the result of the remedy was the same each time: a farmyard full of shit.

The sure, calm touch of Baliyanna's hands soothed animals. He was the only vet favoured by the British in Kodagu. Not a week passed without Baliyanna being summoned to cure a febrile calf, to get a nail out of a horse's hoof or cope with fulminant dysentery in pigs. He treated chickens, dogs, buffaloes and bulls with remarkable success and the only reason the two quacks survived was that Baliyanna could not keep pace with the demand. He never took on more work than he could handle at a judicious pace. He refused to see cases after sundown unless they were emergencies. Like his father, he forged a friendship with the British and ironically, he was partly responsible for triggering events that snapped the link and led to the exodus of the white man.

In those early years of the century, the relationship between the ruler and the ruled was amicable. It was seventy-five years since the peaceful annexation of Kodagu by William Bentinck; the majority felt that it was the best thing that had happened to them and set about aping the rulers. The British, as a gesture of courtesy that had more to do with convenience, showed their appreciation by building a local cemetery in Pollibetta for burying their dead. Just as they had done in other parts of India, they changed the name of Kodagu and called it Coorg.

Nanji had an instinctive dislike for anything new and resisted changes that did not spring out of her tenets. In the house, she organized the chores and reduced the number of servants from five to two. She supervised the workers and never lost the chance to show the solidity of her knowledge. From the age of three she had walked in the fields, her feet sinking in soft bubbling earth; at five she had worked alongside her grandmother, sowing, transplanting and cutting paddy. At seven, she had squatted with the Yeravas beneath coffee bushes to prune them before the rains. She had watched flowers bloom and dry into brown clusters and seen green berries stir to life beneath the flowers. When the berries ripened, she had hurried to pluck them behind the fast-footed Yeravas with her bag slung on her shoulder to save her father six pice a day. She was infused with her grandmother's dynamism and shouldered responsibility without fear. She would dart behind a coffee bush and pluck out an errant shoot or point to a patch where the weeding had been indifferent. Maestrys and writers sulked and grumbled but they knew that the only way out was to be efficient.

The workers liked Nanji. They called her 'Baliyakka', which means Big Sister, and salaamed her; they brought her soft bamboo shoots, tender mushrooms, fleshy king crabs, fresh greens and elegant river fish. Nanji returned the courtesy with a supply of buttermilk to pregnant women and jaggery coffee for the workers. *Akki otti* and lime pickle were handed out every morning. If workers fell ill, they preferred Nanji's treatment to the doctor's in Gonicoppa. Nanji had stumbled on the truth that medicines for animals worked quite well for humans and there was always the vet's supply at hand. In the busy month of Dalmiyar when coffee is picked and when paddy is transplanted in Adare, she gave the workers food so that they would not waste time going home to eat. Two years after she took over, Nanji extended her efficiency to the

23

cultivation of orange, pepper and banana.

She did not miss out on wifely duties: in the process of producing four boys she proved there was no need to gorge on pungent food and reek of pregnancy. She stayed active till the last day of her condition until she felt twinges of pain or the trickle between her legs. Then she sent for Bolle, locked herself in the bedroom and finished without fuss, so when Baliyanna came home, she would be sitting in bed drinking coffee.

'Here's another boy for you.'

She had no time for normal feminine pastimes. When she went to weddings, it was only during the *muhurtam* to bless the couple, present a tiger-claw brooch to the bride and come away. At funerals, she only stayed long enough to lay flowers on the body, drop a rupee coin in the *thali* and sit with the bereaved for five minutes. Nanji never let anyone steal a minute of her time; she listened and talked only if she could carry on doing what she wanted. Women came to her for all types of advice. She taught them how to manage a twin pregnancy, how to use a potato poultice to draw out a thorn and how to rid the house of termites. But the best advice she gave was on how to commit suicide. It was a common habit among Kodavas to kill themselves and Nanji had nothing against this so long as they chose the least messy and least expensive mode of exit.

'Hanging from the ceiling or stabbing oneself in the neck is quick and respectable,' she said. 'But the best and most austere way is to put one's head in a bucket of tepid water and stay that way till dead.' She never mentioned the unpardonable method used by her father-in-law.

She managed her boys without fuss, although they were by no means easy to handle. The first child suffered from constipation; his bowels moved only once a week and the stony pellets he passed were like the marbles the boys played with. Her second son ate only at midday, the third slept in a tightly foetal position and the fourth had a musical cry which, once begun, went on and on with an interminable variety of notes that brought cattle, pigs and neighbours' children to the window. An ordinary woman would have been quick to believe these eccentricities to be the sign of unique talents but Nanji realized that more likely they were signs of mediocrity. For her, the trial began when she delivered her sixth child.

Chapter Three

The baby stirred late, after the seventh month. When it first moved, the thrust was so sharp that it jerked Baliyanna's arm off Nanji's belly and he woke with a start. He cupped his hands over the baby's head and it slipped away in the liquid contents of the womb. He laid his cheek on Nanji's belly, then looked at her in alarm. 'You have fever. You must rest.'

Nanji swung her legs over the edge of the bed. 'It's the first day of sowing. I can't trust the Yeravas to plant in even rows, I must show them.'

She went to the field, picked out a sheaf of green paddy and, bending from the waist, began to plant. She loved the feel of soft mud in her hands and the breeze on her ankles. Nanji came from a family where the women were industrious, without the lazy drinking habits of men. They stepped into the field like cranes, worked alongside the Yeravas, planted, threshed paddy and stacked hay. The men were happy with their hard-working wives because Yeravas were unreliable and cost one anna a day and four seers of paddy a week. Kodava women were practical: they wore the sari with the pleats at the back, so when they bent over wet fields, the pleats did not come in the way. They had learnt this from the toddy-tapping Kudiyas who swung back the pleats when they climbed the *panne* tree. The free-flowing end of the sari was brought beneath the left arm across the back and knotted over the right shoulder. The Kodavas followed Kudiya tradition, with a few modifications. The brooch replaced the knot for women with means, the blouse took on incredible plunging necklines, sleeves lengthened, shortened, disappeared and reappeared—frilled, trimmed with lace and embossed with mirror-work. The straight, no-nonsense fall of the sari over the front accentuated curves and enhanced beauty.

That day, when the baby began to stir, Nanji worked swiftly, the Yeravas followed, and by midday she got them working in perfect rhythm. Nanji went home, satisfied that the Yeravas could be trusted to carry on planting until the gong sounded for lunch. She fed the family, cleaned the fish for supper and stirred the pot of banana jam until it became thick and dark and was ready to be poured into jars. That night, her fever and chills got worse and she could not sleep. 'Give me one of your veterinary cures,' she begged her husband. Baliyanna covered her in three blankets, walked the three-and-a-half miles to Gonicoppa and brought Dr. Seshagiri from the Civil Hospital to see his wife.

'Malaria,' the doctor said and prescribed a cautious dose of quinine. 'If the fever continues, she will need more quinine but that's not good for the baby.'

The fever was quelled and Nanji went to the fields next day. Two day later, the fever was back, so she dosed herself with more quinine and worked. Nanji was impatient with illness, inactivity irked her; she swallowed fifty bitter pills before the fever finally left her but she had exceeded the maximum dose. Now she suffered the aftermath: the ground lurched beneath her feet, her ears felt like caverns filled with buzzing insects. She was forced to rest in the afternoons. She battled nausea with gooseberry wine and worried about the baby. 'He doesn't kick in the usual way,' she said to Bolle. 'He batters my womb as if it's a fortress.' Bolle coaxed her to try the time-tested *lehyam* of *thil*, jaggery, cashew and almonds smothered in ghee in an effort to counter the effects that quinine might have had on the baby.

It had rained non-stop for two weeks and the air was heavy with moisture and the fruity smells of mould; Nanji rested, a perforated mud pot filled with glowing coals warming her from beneath the cot. It was the damp month of

Adare when the best heating device was pressed into use: pots of glowing coal that were moved in a day-long procession from room to room. One afternoon, through the monotonous patter of rain, Nanji heard a voice at the window.

'Baliyakka . . .?'

She recognized the voice of the brother-in-law she had never met.

Appachu was handsome, and taller than his brothers. The English climate had whitened his already fair skin and he looked European in his jacket and twill trousers. He bent to touch Nanji's feet—an act of respect for the wife of his older brother, although he and she were the same age.

Appachu was eager to tell her about Marjorie. 'It was God's grace that I met her, outside a grocer's in Tooting Bec, handing out pamphlets on Christ. "Love Christ and be saved," she said as I walked past. One look at her and I decided to be saved. Christ led to coffee, coffee to church on Sundays; I proposed to Marjorie in the midst of a sermon. She berated me for distracting her but accepted my proposal and the fourteen carat ring. Her only condition was that I get baptized, so the very next day I became Appachu Basil Pinto. Did you know, Baliyakka, Christianity is the only religion that forgives?'

Nanji did not know. People forgave; how could religion forgive? His words reminded her of the rancour that his marriage had incited in Baliyanna. She couldn't bear to tell him of the impending tragedy, so she tried to make up for the hurt to come with a touching display of hospitality. She fed him *paputtoo* steamed in coconut milk, chicken curry and the best red bananas fried in ghee. Overcome by greed and nostalgia for childhood favourites, Appachu wolfed twelve *paputtoos*, all the chicken and ten red, ghee-fried bananas. He told Nanji that Marjorie couldn't come because she was in the family way. 'She's busy furnishing our bungalow in Bangalore,' he said. 'I've got my chambers on South Parade. Rich locality, rich clients.' Nanji was pouring him a third cup of filter coffee when Baliyanna came. He took off his muddied boots in the porch and saw Appachu through the doorway.

'Drink your coffee and get out,' Baliyanna said.

Appachu smiled at what he thought was a joke. His smile incensed Baliyanna. 'Get out or I'll shoot,' he said reaching for the gun rack, with its impressive array of six double-barrelled guns and six country-made rifles.

Appachu did not drink his coffee. He tried to smile at Nanji and she saw a face darkened with the indelible sorrow of rejection. He walked out into the rain, his hands still smelling of coconut milk, chicken curry and ghee-fried bananas. 'Don't come back as long as I live!' Baliyanna shouted.

'Must you keep your anger burning for so long?' Nanji asked, surprised by the hardness in her husband, whose nature it was to be kind.

'Kaleyanda men don't forgive easily,' Baliyanna said, as if it was a burden he was forced to bear. They heard that Appachu went to Crystal Palace and Chambavva refused to see him. Only Boju shared Nanji's sympathy for his brother and wrote to him, but he never got a reply. Seething with humiliation, Appachu had resolved to snap all ties with the family.

After weeks of rain came a spell of brightness and warmth. Nanji felt the baby pushing down and she sent for Bolle, heated the water, stacked the sheets and prepared food for her husband. She lay on the bed and with her hands plunged into her lower belly, felt the baby's head jammed in the pelvis. 'Get another bedroom ready for my husband and take the children to the neighbouring Jammada house,' she said to the servants.

The twinges became sharp and her vagina flooded with warm fluid. Nanji crouched in bed hugging her knees; five pregnancies had taught her that by squatting you got the weight of the baby's head to do most of the work without exhausting yourself. When the first wave of contraction gripped her, she breathed deep and pushed down. Bolle came just as the bag of membranes bulged like an opalescent balloon and burst, drenching the sheets with rice-water liquor. The head glided out through the thinned-out lips of the vagina: first the sloping forehead with distended veins, then the fleshy ears with pendulous lobes and a straight nose that had shed the Kaleyanda hook. The baby eased its shoulders by shifting to an oblique angle, chivalrously avoiding the tearing of maternal passages. Once the shoulders delivered, the baby slipped out and Nanji's first gasp of joy changed to a cry of horror. From the waist down the baby had withered lifeless legs. So deep was Nanji's shock that she forgot to cut the cord and her blood pulsed into the baby for a full ten minutes after birth, giving him a permanently sanguine complexion. Bolle cut the cord, delivered the placenta, rubbed Nanji's back and whispered soothing words.

'Call my husband,' Nanji wept. 'Tell him I've given birth to a cripple.'

There wasn't any need: Baliyanna had been peeping in at the window, not two feet away from the four-poster bed. When the bluish-green bag of membranes that was no different from those of cows and horses bulged and burst, the rice-water liquor splattered his face pressed against the window bars. He saw his son at the same moment as Nanji, felt the same elation and the same sorrow. He went in to console her. Turning the baby gently on its stomach, he pinched its buttocks. 'Look, there's good healthy muscle here, he won't be a cripple,' he said, trying to make her believe what he couldn't.

Only then did Nanji notice that the baby hadn't cried. The suffused face lay mask-like in her arms and there wasn't a flutter of movement in the chest. Mindless of her own fragile condition she sprang out of bed and looked frantically for some means to revive her baby with. And she seized the first thing she could find: a handful of the coarse-ground pepper that Bolle had just brought in after pounding, to store in a jar. Pepper had many uses but reviving a newborn was not one of them. Nanji did not stop to think and her husband was too stunned to offer any suggestion. Nanji rubbed a generous pinch of the fiery powder into the baby's nostrils.

The baby sneezed so violently, its body rocked off the bed, and then it started to cry with indignation at the treatment meted out. It screwed up its red face, clenched its fists and bellowed. But the legs remained still.

Neighbours and well-wishers were generous with advice.

'Massage his legs with semisolid, fragrant coconut oil before you bathe him, smear them with warmed peacock fat afterwards.'

'Feed him meat broth, it will strengthen the muscles.'

'He's six weeks. Give him eggs, ghee and cream.'

'Four months. Feed him minced meat.'

By six weeks the baby gave up milk. He pretended to suck but held his mother's breast in his hands and sucked the nipple without drawing milk. He never crawled but learnt to drag himself cheerfully along on one hip. Subbu, they named him; Baliyanna called him Kunta, the cripple.

In spite of his tadpole legs, Subbu had heavy bones and weighed more than any of Nanji's other children had at his age. She carried him to Malethirike, walking the four-and-a-half miles up to the temple for the festival; she promised an offering of two legs of solid gold to Lord Igguthappa, if he made her son walk; at Bhadrakali, she gave a gold-plated crown for the goddess, and at Peggala a six-tiered brass lamp. Nanji believed the gods were human in their needs and desires. The Hindu gods had come surreptitiously to Kodagu, like the Haleri Rajas. Before the Rajas came, the Kodavas were strong and self-willed and they had no need for gods. They worshipped their ancestors, who constantly hovered over Kodagu and guarded them.

Nanji knew all this, but she was a religious woman and wanted to please the gods in any case. When the gods failed her, she grew desperate and worked on her son with every sort of food, medication and device that came her way. She buried him waist deep in paddy and left him to work his way out; she had him lie down with bags of bran tied to his ankles and goaded him to lift the weight. As a special gesture, she let him suckle till he was five, until one day she realized he did it for pleasure. Alarmed that she might be harming her son, she stopped suckling him. Subbu reacted with rabid tantrums, crushing a lamp with his hands, hurling a plate across the room and banging his head on the four-poster bed. Nanji stayed firm.

Subbu was stronger than any of his brothers. When the oldest boy ran home one day shouting, 'Crab in my shirt!' Subbu pulled the crab out, prised its pincers apart and gave it to Nanji, saying, 'I'd like it fried.' Once Nanji went about her work with unexplained giddiness—two days later while combing her hair, she found a leech the size of a lemon on her scalp, ballooned purple-red with her blood. It was Subbu who squeezed it till it popped explosively and splattered his face, proving that leeches could be killed without being set on fire. Subbu knew his strength and couldn't understand why the skill of walking was denied him. He stood at the window, holding the fat iron bars, envying everything that moved: children, parents, Yeravas, dogs, pigs, even the cotton catkins and chicken feathers that floated weightlessly in the air. He played alone; he flicked marble against marble, spun tops for two minutes non-stop on his palm, played with shells and cowries. He listened to the shouts of his brothers as they jumped and ran, played football and seven-tiles; he watched them and worked out the moves of each game until he was confident of being an ace sportsman if only his godforsaken legs would move.

Nanji carried him on her hip when she went to the estate and Subbu saw more of the world than did most children of his age. She took him to the edge of the stream where she haggled with the Maplas who came over the hills from Thalacheri and Kozhikode to barter their sardines for bananas. The Maplas carried baskets of sardines on their heads and

tramped through the scrub forests, entering Kodagu at
Makutta where the Kurubas tried to buy the sardines in
exchange for partridge and wild rabbit. The Maplas were a
squeamish lot and they did not relish stringy wild meat, so
they kept walking.

'*Mathi meenu . . .O Mathi meenu . . .!*'

Thin Maplas with burning eyes and skeletal grins walked
through Virajpet and Gonicoppa to Athur where they could
exchange fish for an endless variety of bananas. They traded
with Nanji who was a shrewd, fair businesswoman. She sold
the best bananas. Years back, when the coffee was afflicted
with *koleroga*—the dreaded black rot which ate away the
leaves—Nanji had had one-and-a-half acres cleared of dying
plants and started a banana grove. In two years, she had eight
varieties. The powdery, fragrant *rasa* and the chewy rich
chonda bale were reserved for guests, the rest she sold and gave
away to neighbours and workers. Beggars were never sent
away without a dozen freckled *mara bale* or the comma-shaped
poobale.

The Maplas came regularly; they squatted on the opposite
side of the stream and asked some worker or wandering
Yerava to tell Nanji. She arrived with Subbu on her hip, and a
Yerava in tow.

'Fresh fish, Amma.'

'How fresh?'

'Came in the haul this morning. I started out straight
away.' He scooped up a handful of slithering sardines, and a
few still-live fish writhed, glinting silver and gold. Nanji
judged the freshness of fish by the smell that wafted across the
stream.

'Two bunches of *rasa* or three of *poobale* for a basket of fish.'

'I'll take both, Amma. But please, some consideration . . . .'

The Mapla squatted a few feet away from Nanji and they
talked.

'Where will you sell the fruit?'

'*Rasa* must sell today, at Kannoor. *Poobale* will last till Kozhikode.'

'What will you do with the money?'

'I'm saving for a set of earrings for my oldest daughter.' A skeletal grin lit his face and he looked at her shyly. 'I hope to get a son-in-law before the year ends.'

Nanji sent a Yerava woman to bring the bananas and watched with hawk eyes as the Mapla emptied the sardines into baskets that Nanji's Yeravas carried straight to the kitchen to clean, and cook half into curry and half as a dry-fry. Subbu amused himself by watching the slow death-writhe of the sardines, he could see their little mouths and their little eyes move at the actual moment of death. At night when he crunched their curried heads, he became thoughtful and morose, because the fate of the beautiful fish saddened him.

It was Nanji's friendly, inquisitive nature that led her to the discovery that the climate in Kodagu was ideal for growing pepper. By questioning the Mapla she found that what pepper needed was a long spell of monsoon, fairly warm temperature for a few months and a good amount of shade. Like many of her neighbours, she had already experimented with a few vines that she planted around the mango trees near the house and they produced just enough pepper to use with fried pork. No one in Kodagu had thought of cultivating pepper in a big way until Nanji thought that it was worth trying. The Mapla who brought her fish also brought the first cuttings of pepper from neighbouring Malabar. She had them planted near every tree in a five-acre patch of robusta. Within a few months, the vines with their shiny green leaves had begun to climb the trunk; within a year the trees were festooned with the frilly apparel of pepper vines. Two years later, the vines began to yield the yellowish red berries which when dried became black pepper corns. These Nanji sold by the seer and what remained found many uses. As carminative, digestive and, when mixed with honey, to soothe sore throats that were common among the young ones during the monsoons. After Subbu's birth, she always carried a handful tied to the edge of her sari; you could never tell when a similar crisis might arise.

Uncle Boju and Bolle's husband Boluka were the only persons who had time for Kunta. Boju was a lazy youth who lived a carefree, indolent life in the middle path of least resistance; he saw in his nephew a restlessness which promised a flowering that he himself could only dream about. He carried Subbu on his shoulders and wandered along mud tracks shadowed by hospitable trees; he told him vibrant tales of rakshasas, devatas and apsaras with iron spikes for nipples. He gave Subbu his empty cigarette tins, round tins embellished with the figure of a galleon on green seas, with which Subbu built the fortresses of his dreams and then wrecked them with his hands. They spent hours by the water's edge and while Boju smoked, Subbu sat with his feet, in the stream. His useless, burdensome feet fascinated him. They were strong and compact, the bones prominent, the toes gleaming and slightly magnified by the liquid interface. So calm and stoic were his useless feet stagnating there while little tadpoles and stick insects darted mockingly over them. Subbu flexed his toes. Bunching them together, he grabbed little pebbles in the water; he extended his toes and let the pebbles fall and the tendinous ridges stood up like white ropes; blood-filled veins arched beneath his skin. Subbu was angry that his feet, which were almost, he thought, like any one else's feet, refused to move, but he liked looking at them.

In the evenings, he watched Boluka hunt for crabs beneath the rocks and chase after the juicy, big king crabs which hid in soft crevices of earth on the bank of the stream. If the crabs were few, Boluka got mushrooms or bamboo shoots or *koile meenu* from the water-logged paddy fields and they took them home for Bolle to cook. They went to the forest near Kundathbottu to see the Jenu Kurubas gather honey from the giant hives on the *athi* trees. The Kurubas let Kunta sit in the leaf-lined basket meant for collecting honey and pulled him up with ropes, right next to the hive. When they torched the hive and drove the bees out, they gave him chunks of dripping honeycomb which he ate, avoiding the few perplexed bees that slithered on it. In their mud hut, Bolle fed him *kanji* with *koile meenu* and Subbu ate with the five flat-nosed, curly-haired brats and watched Boluka roast jackfruit seeds in the fire till they popped, and went home with his pockets full of roasted seeds.

Subbu's strong carnivorous appetite made him eat more than he needed. He ate bending low over his plate and scooped food into his mouth in quick large handfuls, eating meat in big chunks, working it off the bone, sucking marrow and chewing cartilage with an expert's relish. He never paused to look at what went into his mouth. The staggering variety of meat and *puttoos,* the massaging with oil and peacock fat and the bribes to various gods spurred his legs to grow in length, girth and anatomic perfection but there was not a flicker of movement. Nanji dressed him in nothing but loose shirts till he was seven, this being her way with all her boys. It was quick and easy for half-naked roisterers to pee into the bushes and carry on playing instead of wasting delightful moments of play to open buttoned shorts, and Nanji understood this.

It was during his half-naked days that Subbu observed his manhood with wonder and curiosity. He observed its shape, size, the hooded tip and tiny lipless slit, its colour, personality, its softness and hardness. Sometimes he felt his heartbeat there and wondered if his soul wasn't enshrined in that friendly organ. Once, riding horseback with Baliyanna, halfway between Athur and Gonicoppa, he saw an elephant deluging the road. Subbu watched the quick, rain-like burst form a pool and flow away in a stream. But what fascinated him was not the pipe from which the rain came but the elephant's trunk. He was positive that it was the elephant's equivalent of his friendly organ. That evening when Nanji bathed him, he asked, 'Baliyakka, isn't mine like an elephant's trunk?'

'It'll grow just as big if you don't stop playing with it,' Nanji snapped. Subbu liked the idea.

He got his first pair of shorts when he started school, navy blue drills from an older brother. When he was chosen to be the raja in a play, Nanji sewed him a close-necked coat from her gold-dotted, red silk, wedding sari. Everyone said how royal the boy looked but Subbu did not want to look like a king; he wanted to be king, but how could he when his wretched legs refused to move?

He prayed. He stood with Nanji in the puja room which was a curtained alcove next to the bedroom. Nanji began her prayers early in the morning in a loud and crazy whispering that went on for an hour. Subbu joined her. He dragged himself on his hip, stood leaning against the wall with folded hands and closed eyes. Nanji spoke of her son's devotion with pride, unaware of Subbu's raging arguments with the gods.

'I'm not afraid of you. Others may cringe and prostrate themselves like criminals but I never will. I'm not even sure you exist. If you do, why don't you speak?' He accused the gods of giving him legs that did not move, he mouthed abuses, he threatened the gods with dire consequences if they didn't hurry up and rectify their mistake. In the evenings, Nanji herded the children into the puja room and they sang: 'Swami Deva, protector of the Universe, we pray to you, we pray to you.' Subbu sang: 'Swami Deva, you lout, I shall hit you, kick you, bite you, if you don't make me walk.' He never missed his prayers even once. He was confident that, sooner or later, the gods would heed his warning.

When Subbu was eight years and nine months old, a Kuruba woman came selling an ointment made of tiger's milk. She showed Nanji the ointment, the colour of baby stool, in little glass bottles. 'I milked the tigress myself and boiled the milk in an earthenware pot without a drop of water until it thickened and stuck to my fingers,' she said. It was guaranteed to make Kunta walk. 'Ever seen a crippled tiger?' she asked in reply to doubting questions. Nanji paid her four silver coins and bought all the ointment.

A month after the tiger-milk ointment was used on Subbu's legs, he fell ill with a raging fever. Dr Seshagiri came daily to prescribe yet another medicine but Subbu seemed to be slipping away. His face turned the colour of monsoon skies, his eyes swivelled, he sweated till the sheets and mattresses were soaked, puddles formed on the cowdung floor of the bedroom and the rising vapours made it smell like a cattle shed. He thrashed his arms, frothed at the mouth and muttered incoherent nonsense. And then when exhausted, he lay very still, Nanji was seized with the fear that he would stop breathing. She untied the knot on her sari, crushed some corns of pepper between her palms and rubbed the powder into his nose. This was at the height of his fever and Dr Seshagiri had said that there was no hope. But Subbu began to kick his legs.

Ten days later, the fever left him and he got up and walked like everyone else.

Chapter Four

'Kunta walks!'

Nanji did not stop to help Subbu across the swaying ramp. She saw him laugh at his reflection in the stream and she did not snub his confidence by making him wade through the shallow waters downstream as the old and decrepit did. The ramp was a single tree trunk sawn sagittally, laid with its flat surface up and held by ropes. Nanji walked with Subbu behind her and never once looked back.

They climbed the stile into the estate. The ground was soft and giving after the rain, the leaves plump and wet with water; creamy white buds of coffee blossom oozed fragrance onto Subbu's skin. He walked fast, calf muscles quivering in haste to lift his feet off the ground. The dripping branches brushed his forehead, dark wet leaves combed his hair, trickled water into his ears, got inside his mouth; leeches stuck to his toes, thorns pierced his unused baby feet. Subbu laughed and picked away the leeches and thorns, relishing the newness of his pain.

'Kunta walks!'

They reached the far edge of the stream where water flowed in a lazy swoop over fat, moist rocks. Further down, Boluka and his son Mutha stood thigh-deep in water, two brown bodies perpendicular against the sun, and hunted for the petrified crabs that hid beneath the stones:

'Can I get some oranges?' Subbu asked his mother.

The orange grove was across the stream and to reach it you had to walk along the bank to where the stream flowed beneath a wild mango tree before it plunged through the

Jammada fields towards Gonicoppa. The stream changed its personality here, it became a boisterous, wild thing and looped away from light to darkness. It was shallow enough but the moss-covered stones in the water were slippery and smooth; it wasn't an easy crossing.

'Yes,' Nanji said.

Subbu walked to the mango tree and stopped, with a sudden, momentary flutter of nervousness. He looked back at Nanji and smiled. Squatting, he grabbed the thick, rough bark of the tree to balance himself on the steep slope, then moved on his haunches until his feet touched the water; now he stood, and gripping the stones with his toes, began to cross, his ears filling with the sound of the water that tumbled and roared below him. Boluka straightened his angled body and looked anxiously at Nanji: should he go further down and be ready to help the boy? No, Nanji did not want that, so he stayed where he was. Nanji watched her son and wondered, was it fear or was it courage that made him do what he was doing? Perhaps it was both. He had to experience fear first, to know fearlessness. Nanji was a religious woman but she did not think about God or pray, it was wrong to supplicate at moments such as this when the risk itself was a blessing you were grateful for.

Subbu returned with the oranges and sat next to Nanji. He picked out the biggest fruit, dug his thumb into the skin and it burst with a hiss, spraying mist in his nostrils. Splitting the fruit in two, he freed the flesh from one half of the peel and shoved it in his mouth; his teeth sank into the flesh and the juice spurted out. He ate the other half and peeled another fruit as he ate, eating four or six, while Nanji ate two. She spat the seeds into the peel and watched Subbu swallow the oranges, seeds and all. 'Trees will grow from your navel if you do that,' she warned. Subbu laughed soundlessly.

There were many thirsts to quench and the thought of wasting time in classrooms seemed pointless to Subbu. Learning could wait till old age when the only thing worthwhile in one's body was the mind. Now life was made for dizzy excitement. Subbu led the team in kabaddi and hockey and was the best football player in Athur. Girls in modest long skirts and arms weighted with books lingered under trees on their way home from school, to watch the nine-year-old knock down boys twice his size.

By the time he was ten, he had licked every boy in hand-to-hand combat and was tired of tame games. So one Saturday when Boju Uncle asked, 'Want to see a cockfight?' Subbu gave the kabaddi match a miss and went with his uncle to the field behind the Civil Hospital to watch birds with vile, saffron eyes tussle in a maze of blood, dust and feathers. Subbu crouched beside the cockfight addicts and cheered the red-and black rooster that Boju had bet on. Boju won five rupees but it flowed away or toddy within the hour. On their way home, Boju stopped to show his nephew the art of rolling beedis. The Saturday sessions became frequent. Subbu developed a passion for cockfights and a preference for hand-rolled beedis, not the cigarettes in green tins that Boju bought when he had the money. But there was no straying beyond the limits imposed by his uncle:

'No opium, or toddy, and the best way to mask the beedi smell is to chew betel.'

When Subbu went home, he helped himself to a mouthful of betelnut that Nanji kept in a brass plate in the front room and there was never any problem. Though she was shrewd and wise, Nanji did not realize that her son had left boyhood behind without asking her permission.

Subbu was bored with boys his age and preferred to follow the pubescent youths who stalked the village in search of excitement. They joined festival processions, rocked before garish tableaux of gods and climbed hills to visit temples; they wore flowers behind their ears and danced at weddings, blocking the bride's path for hours, until the girl's brothers begged them to stop or the bride would faint from exhaustion,

Kavery Nambisan

and they stopped to glut on the wedding feast of pork, *palav* and *payasam*.

Baliyanna still called him Kunta, which was a matter of prestige for Subbu. Baliyanna hadn't the time to focus clearly on his children but the family kept growing, given his ardour and Nanji's fertility. After Subbu came two girls and five boys, the last being born when Subbu was thirteen. In spite of the straight fall of the Kodava sari, you could not guess Nanji's condition till her pregnancy was advanced. She had no need for confinement and she never pampered herself through that soft, middle stage of pregnancy when a woman looks her most beautiful. She controlled her womb with natural resilience, tightening the muscles of her back and resisting the downward pull of the foetus that tugs the belly down, arches the spine and causes insufferable backache and the duck waddle of pregnant women. Nanji walked straight. There were times when even Baliyanna never guessed her condition until the sixth month. She was too busy to rest until after the birth, when he came home to see the new addition scrubbed and gleaming by her side. Baliyanna learned to accommodate these births as unavoidable inconveniences. He referred to his children in the plural and treated them with objective, remote affection. Nanji suckled eleven offspring for twenty months each, and Subbu for five years, which meant she was often nursing two at a time. When the thirteenth child was weaned, she tucked her benumbed breasts into her vest as non-essential appendages and set about caring for her brood.

It was by no means easy. Bolle, who was both companion and servant, was her single greatest aide. She usually had children around the same time as Nanji. The two women reversed roles as midwives and all went well until Bolle's fourteenth turned out to be a hydrocephalic foetus with so much water in the brain that it was delivered dead at thirty weeks, causing a permanent downward slide of Bolle's womb. It decreased her efficiency and hardiness, but Nanji was too fond of the Yerava woman to send her away. Bolle stayed, doing as much or as little as her body allowed.

They fed the children at the black table next to the kitchen. Except for Nanji's second son who ate once a day, the rest were robust eaters, in need of endless rounds of nourishment. Nanji believed that the secret desires which lurk in young minds can be worked off by healthy acts of gluttony.

She worried a little about her growing sons. When Rao Bahadur Madaiah had bought the bungalow and property from Ramanna Sowcara, he had moved out of the Family House where the Kaleyanda clan lived in a maze of closely-packed rooms built around a central square with a courtyard for the men to sit in. The multitude of daughters-in-law trying to win favours from the mother-in-law led to complexities that kept the women busy. The men never managed a private moment with their wives except at night after dinner when the couples retired to their rooms. A story went round Kodagu that it was natural and not infrequent for eager husbands to enter the wrong room, and once the door was bolted and padlocked with the wooden crossbeam, it was less embarrassing to stay the night there. It led to intriguing, pleasant possibilities. It was only a story but it sometimes worried Nanji; if her sons had to adjust to joint families in the future, she hoped they would display the restraint and dignity expected of Kaleyanda men. Nanji sensed the mediocrity of her other children, but when she looked at Subbu she knew with a sure, sharp twist of hope that this cripple-turned-champion son would amount to something.

Sundays after lunch, when Baliyanna went to the *santhe*, it was always Kunta who offered to carry the bag and trail after him. Subbu liked the market, the odour and filth, the fragrance of jasmine mingling with the smell of meat and blood, the sight of butchers chopping meat with great big axes and the sound of bones and cartilage snapping on bloodied chopping blocks. Baliyanna bought mutton—a leg or a shoulder or chops—and the butcher rolled it in a sheet of fat which was a bonus, wrapped it again in a plantain leaf and gave it to Subbu who put it in the bag along with the onions, incense sticks, matches and jaggery. When the marketing was done, they headed for Kuttanda Thammi's toddy shop. Known as the Country Club, this was a shack made of bamboo poles, straw and gunny, which collapsed every monsoon and was rebuilt in two days. This and other shacks like it were the Kodavas' answer to the Bamboo Club in Pollibetta and the European Club in Mercara where the British planters met—clubs with walls panelled in rosewood, gleaming floors, Victorian sofas and curtained windows that guarded their exclusiveness.

Baliyanna's friends waited for him. Baliyanna never ventured in; he sat on the bench outside and sent his umbrella or cap or walking stick with one of his mates, who then wandered into the shack waving it like a promissory note in Thammi's face.

'Kaliyanda Baliyanna.'

It was the signal for Thammi to serve everyone. Subbu sat with his father, revelling in his longing for toddy, the taste of which he savoured in his imagination. He knew from the vinegary smell in his nostrils and the fumes burning his palate that it tasted something like a mixture of burnt pork, fermented sugarcane and chicken shit. Nevertheless he abstained for fifty years, not out of self-righteousness but because he wanted to please his mother with at least one virtue.

Among the regulars at the Club was Cachera Machiah, a second cousin and friend of Baliyanna. Machiah had retired from the army as a Subehdar-Major and was the only Kodava brave enough to sport a *galle meese* without ever having killed a tiger. His fine knowledge of English and self-important swagger earned him the title of General. He was sixty-five when Subbu first saw him but he had the audacious twinkling eyes of youth and silver hair sprouting from shapely ears, which he cleaned with a little silver scoop that dangled from the chain of his pocket-watch. He had a unique whistling breath with variations in pitch and tone. It was said that he had accidentally swallowed a policeman's whistle when young and since he didn't die of choking or blocked air passages, his parents had decided to leave it alone.

He had been married for twenty unhappy years to a saintly woman who prayed five hours a day and believed that to have children was proof of carnal indulgence. Like sex, food was a dirty word. You ate in shame, in privacy, and only when necessary. A vegetarian, she drank no milk because it was sinful to deprive the calf of nourishment, and she refused to cook meat. Machaiah's appetite had been nurtured on the meat of wild boar when young and on a vigorous diet of quality meat in the army; it folded up in dismay at the sight of rice and vegetables. He began to cook for himself, roasting liver or pork over the fire after his wife had cooked and got out of the way. As the years passed, the General's wife was so embarrassed about eating that she ate with her chair pulled to the wall, her back to him.

His wife's saintly frigidity forced the General to a complex life of arid austerity alternating with frenzied adultery. One phenomenal claim that could neither be proved nor disproved until his death was that the General had three testicles. None of the countless women whom he stupefied with his ardour could tell for sure if there were two or three. Subbu was convinced that this mysterious anatomical aberration was in some way responsible for the General's invincible charm.

The General had little interest in the mundane business of farming, so he undertook the writing of important missives as an alternative way of earning some money. He wrote job applications, wedding invitations, fervent love letters and marriage proposals in best-quality English and lyrical prose. He composed at the Country Club, with Subbu as his willing listener and critic.

The vet and the General were the only two from Athur who had ventured out of Kodagu and their vision of the world triggered the best debates at the Club. The General, being the more idealistic of the two, was also the more argumentative. Most of the time, the others merely listened, Subbu along with them. The General became so passionately zealous that he began to reprove the King—through letters—for ignoring Coorg, which he said had fallen into the hands of lackadaisical white men. 'Your Majesty may kindly institute measures to tighten discipline,' he wrote, 'and lead Coorg back to the days of plenty when housewives gave bottles of ghee and honey to beggars'. When the General was not at the Club, he was at the post office waiting for the King's reply.

Of all the men Subbu knew, the General with his youthful eyes, the *galle meese* and three testicles was the greatest. He always took Subbu along when he visited the two hotels in Gonicoppa as a self-appointed health inspector. They would go to the Mapla tea shop or the Brahmin Vegetarian Lunch Home and before he sat down, the General would skim the window ledge with an investigating finger, peer beneath the tables at cobwebs festooning the legs, walk into the kitchen and examine the filthy water in which vegetables were washed. 'I'm taking the bus to Madikeri right now to inform the Health Department,' he would tell the proprietor.

'Saab! Show mercy! Another week and this hotel will be a palace, I swear by the chastity of my wife and saintliness of my mother.' The General and his assistant would be plied with mutton fry, or *bondas* or *jalebis* and refused a bill. Everyone was in awe of the General.

Chapter Five

'Who's for work?' asked the vet.

The older boys slunk off, pretending not to hear, and the young ones were too small; so Subbu helped his father pack the instruments, and went with him. Baliyanna taught Subbu how to poultice carbuncles, clean gaping ulcers left by rotting horns, splint broken bones with bamboo and ease animals through difficult deliveries. He taught Subbu the knack of giving a ball of food to a sick horse by prising its mouth open with thumb and index finger, cautiously depositing the ball with the other hand and letting it roll to the back of the mouth. Subbu learned fast; when he was eleven, he delivered twin calves locked inside their mother with the cord looped in a double figure-of-eight round their necks. Baliyanna observed the deft grace with which the short, thick, sanguine hands of his son moved and thought he would make a good vet. But Subbu had bigger plans.

Baliyanna was the best horse doctor between Coorg and Mysore. During Mercara Week, when the Resident of Mysore who was also the Chief Commissioner of Coorg came with his retinue and stayed for the races, Baliyanna was in high demand. He treated crushed limbs, gashed hooves, lacerated wounds and raging stomachs and was called so many times in the week that he kept his bag permanently packed and his horse saddled. It was at the end of one such week that he received an urgent summons from Belquarren, the hundred-acre coffee estate and farm that belonged to the Foxes.

Belquarren, like Meachlands, Windsor Estates, Solyglen

and Grasmere had raised the social life of the British in Coorg to a high level of sophistication. Twenty-eight British families and thirty-two bachelors were ensconced in the hospitable where they felt neither hated nor intimidated. The First War of Independence of '57 did not touch the salubrious retreat barricaded by hills and forests. The British in Coorg decided that only a handful of the natives were worthy of social intercourse. Those chosen Kodavas regarded all things British as superior, and worthy of imitation. They absorbed everything, except the white man's religion for which instinct told them they had no use. They borrowed names, food habits, attire and etiquette with sincerity and it formed a flaky crust over their timeless culture.

That year, at the party in Belquarren following Mercara Week, there was enough evidence of the Anglicization of the Kodavas. Among the guests were Daisy and Babs Karumbaiah from Kodanad Estate (changed by brother Gary to Glenview), Tim and Joe Boy from Thenupare (which became Windermere) and Maletire Ammi—she moves like a duchess, the British said—from Kurudarahalli Estate (now Balmoral). These Coorgs laughed, talked and moved with the same precise confidence as the white men and women; they painted themselves, shrieked and flirted. That night after dinner, women in glittering dresses and men in tails and bow-ties busied themselves trying to impress each other; dark-skinned bearers moved unobtrusively among guests, offered drinks and sweated with fortitude inside the red-and-gold tunics that covered their scrawny bodies like carapaces. The only unhappy person at the party was the hostess.

Clara watched the merriment and wished she could make the whole stupid, frivolous lot of them disappear. After two years in Coorg, the monotony of her existence was choking her. She was sick of hearing about the price of coffee, the laziness of natives and the new brocade dress worn by the CC's daughter at the closing-day ball in Mercara. Clara detached herself from the guests and stood by the alcove in the passageway. She had come to Coorg in search of excitement and had received boredom in return. It wasn't just marriage but life itself that trapped her. She wished she could be like her guests and yet she did not envy their easy contentment. Such a state of unfeeling bliss was not something she could understand. Why was she who cared about life fated to waste the rest of it until she became a ripe old fifty or something equally dreadful, to then mince away towards death and be buried in the cemetery not half a mile away, with a wooden cross on her bosom? What had happened to her restless Irish blood, her eagerness for adventure? Clara was absorbed in her reflections when a syce hurried up to convey the news that Sir Arnold was choking on half a coconut that an inebriated guest had filled with champagne and shoved down the horse's throat. Sir Arnold was a prize horse, fathered by Neptune and foaled by Myrrha—the thoroughbred pair that had produced the largest number of Bangalore Derby winners ever.

Baliyanna was summoned. The vet grabbed his bag, shouted for Subbu and hurried to get his horse. Father and son set out along the road from Athur to Pollibetta with the bag of instruments jammed between them. The lantern that hung from Subbu's arm spread pools of light on the mud road and although his arms ached, the sound of hooves drummed in his ears the urgency of their mission.

'Sir Arnold is a horse fit for the Derby,' Baliyanna said.

'What's a Derby?'

Subbu listened to his father tell him about the most famous of all races, where men lost and won fortunes in seconds. Half an hour later, they were at the gates of Belquarren. Subbu had a brief glimpse of the party in progress, of brightly-painted laughing women and smart, foolish-looking men and then it was to the stable, with the syce holding a lantern over Sir Arnold. The horse was nearly gone; it lay on its back, legs kicking over its pale, distended stomach; it breathed in hard gulps in hysteria and panic and swallowed so much air that its belly was a taut drum, ready to burst.

49

Baliyanna opened his bag, stood astride the horse and stuck a wide-bore needle in its stomach. Air escaped with a hiss.

'Subbu,' he said.

The boy knew what to do. He knelt behind the supine animal and with a steady pressure of the thumb and index fingers of both hands, prised its mouth open. Baliyanna put his hand in, pushed the tongue to one side and retrieved the half-coconut, now brimming with frothing horse spittle. The red, gyrating eyes of the horse turned soft and limpid with gratitude.

The vet came out to wash his hands; Rupert Fox and his wife were waiting there. Rupert thanked him, instructed his writer to pay the fee and was about to go back to the party when Clara asked the vet: 'Will you join us for a drink?'

Rupert pursed his lips in displeasure. He had trouble controlling his wife who was over-friendly with the natives. Fortunately the vet declined. 'It's a long ride home in the dark,' he explained.

'Then come on Sunday for breakfast,' Clara said, 'both of you.' She smiled at Subbu and walked back to the house.

Subbu was delighted. Baliyanna pretended it wasn't a big deal, but it was. On Sunday, he wore his grey serge trousers and flannel coat and forced his calloused, bunion-covered farmer's feet into the stiff leather shoes that he hadn't worn since his Presidency College days; he used nine yards of gold-lined muslin to fashion his turban the way the Rao Bahadur had worn it when he went to Delhi with the ten-member delegation of Kodavas to meet the Viceroy.

Rupert Fox was a haughty Englishman who condescended to interact with natives only when necessary. He found them a confused, emotional, puzzling, variegated lot and he lacked the patience to try and understand them. He did not trust the natives, he was sure that even when they salaamed and called him 'Sir', they thought him a little stupid. Now his wife had gone and invited the vet to breakfast and he had to try and be civil. Really, it was most abominable but then there was no reasoning with Clara. She did exactly what she wanted.

Rupert hoped they wouldn't come but they did. He put on a facade of formal courtesy sprinkled with witticisms that failed miserably and there followed long gaps of embarrassed silence until the bearer announced breakfast.

Rupert attempted staccato bursts of conversation; Baliyanna ate runny eggs and hard toast, chewed bacon and speared the sausages with his fork. The sausages and bacon reminded him too much of the sheep and pigs they came from. Subbu had no such qualms; he was distracted by the bright white arms of the English woman and the stone-encrusted cross that hung on a chain above the smocked edging of her blue dress. He wanted to ask her about the cross and Christianity so as to justify the audacity of his gaze, but all he knew was that the cross was a dull brown piece of wood perched on British graves in the graveyard between Athur and Pollibetta. One moonless night, he had gone there with friends and they had plucked a cross out of a grave to see if the dead white men could be agitated. They brandished the cross and challenged ghosts of Englishmen to appear but none came and when Subbu went home, his father whipped him for being late. He knew that Christians went to the church in Pollibetta or Madikeri; he had listened to the priest speak from somewhere below his navel about the flesh and blood of Christ, which he then gave them to eat and drink.

But Clara looked nothing like a cannibal, although that husband with his close-mouth snarl might well have been one. Clara watched Subbu eat his sausages with jam, and spread mustard on his bread, and when he was about to sprinkle pepper in his tea she touched his arm and pointed to the sugar bowl. For Subbu, the enchanted breakfast was soon over. He said, 'Thank you, Sir' to Rupert Fox but couldn't muster up the courage to look at Clara. He was terrified of losing control over his eyes and other disobedient organs.

Clara intruded upon the innocence of Subbu's dreams, but he was man enough to suffer in secret. One afternoon, while hastily shinning down a guava tree, his pockets bulging with stolen fruit, Subbu saw Clara ride towards him. He landed heavily on the ground, she slowed her horse and stopped. He saw her ankle-length boots, beige trousers and shirt and wanted to tell her that she looked better in a frock. Instead he offered her a guava and fled, his ears flaming like red hibiscus. Subbu thought he had offended her, but the following week she astonished him by visiting their home. Subbu came from school to see her in the front room eating banana fritters with Nanji.

Rupert was appalled that Clara was visiting a native and reminded her of the horrors of the Mutiny barely fifty years ago; how incitable was the mind of a native, how vengeful when stirred to anger. The simple instance of cartridges greased in beef and pig fat had led the soldiers in Meerut to go on a rampage that spread like forest fire to Agra, Delhi, Kanpur and Lucknow; in Lucknow his own granduncle had died of starvation during the two-month siege.

'The Coorgs were wild heathens before the British took over,' Rupert explained. 'They consorted with devils, worshipped animals and ancestors, they even got married to dead tigers. They still do it! Barring a few, they're unpredictable and untrustworthy, like natives everywhere.'

Clara befriended Nanji in spite of Rupert's displeasure. Nanji was different from the likes of Daisy and Babs, she was neither awed by nor enamoured of the white people. She welcomed Clara because she liked her.

Subbu thought that Clara came because of him. He shouted and whistled in the front yard, swung from the branches of the mango tree and bullied other kids in the hope that she was watching.

The real reason for Clara's visits wasn't Subbu or Nanji, it was the grey-eyed vet who had plucked the half-coconut from Sir Arnold's throat and saved the horse from choking.

Against all convention, she visited his home on the pretext of meeting his wife, fording the stream on horseback. Later, she went in the horse-trap, which she left at the bank, crossing the treacherous ramp to reach the house. She dressed carefully for these visits in cool ankle-length dresses and braved her way through Nanji's high teas until one day the vet barged in while she ate sticky-sweet *thambuttoo*.

'How do you do?' she said coolly, praying the blood would not rush to her cheeks, but it did. The vet had the restlessness of a man uneasy with women. She had to think fast, before he abandoned her to the company of his wife.

'Our cows aren't yielding enough these days,' she said. 'Could you stop by one day and look them over?'

'Cows are temperamental this time of year. Their yield usually picks up on its own. But certainly, I'll come.'

When Baliyanna went that Friday to see the Belquarren cows, they had stopped sulking and the milk yield had returned to normal. Clara apologized for wasting his time and added, 'I thought we could be friends.'

Her abruptness was a relief. Baliyanna didn't like the sort of fussy white people who displayed excessive warmth only to clearly demarcate the difference between them and the native. Clara gave no further explanations and thus began their friendship.

It was a very susceptible season for the animals in Belquarren, who seemed to fall sick all the time. If it wasn't the cows, it was a dog or a pig or a hen. Baliyanna went in the afternoons and Rupert indicated his hostility by not talking to the vet for more than a few seconds. Sometimes Baliyanna came with his son who never talked; he ate everything that was offered to him at tea and stared at Clara with total absorption. Clara wasn't going to let his mildly annoying presence distract her but she was happier when the vet came alone.

They talked. Baliyanna told her about Coorg before the Rajas came. His mother's father had been a Diwan of the last

Raja till '34, when, along with most others, he shifted his loyalty to the British and helped the bloodless, unheroic transfer of power along. 'My grandfather was not proud of his role in history,' he said. 'He wept when the Raja was exiled to Benares, he was certain that what little remained of our culture would be ground to dust.'

Clara knew without him having to say it that he was hostile to British rule. Once she asked, 'Why do you hate us?'

'Matter of taste,' he said. 'Is our culture so thin that it can be forgotten easily?'

It was their private world, and they excluded his wife and her husband from it without guilt. Rupert showed his resentment with supercilious politeness and leathery smiles. He punished Clara with his silence; in any case he was busy with the estate. The recent telegram from the broker in Mincing Lane said, 'Suggest you accept twenty-five rupees per hundredweight,' which was quite a blow. Coffee prices had never been that low and it meant another year of loans from the brokers; it meant less money to spend on luxuries and no holiday in England—the round-trip-ticket, economy class, was fifty-six pounds. Clara was aware of Rupert's fury over her disregard for what the planters called a 'crisis'. She didn't care.

Chapter Six

Clara Ernestine Kearns was the youngest child of Desmond Kearns who had come from Dublin to Yorkshire as a stable boy and stayed on to become a horse-breeder. He paired anatomically perfect stallions with physiologically perfect dams and discovered that the size and stride of the English horse combined with the strength and elegance of the Arab stallion produced the best result. When three of his horses won three classics in one season, Desmond became known as the genius of equine matrimony.

Desmond Kearns, his wife and three daughters lived in York in a beautiful home with three Dalmatians and six servants; his wife visited charity balls and orphanages and was photographed with the nobility. Alexandrina, the eldest daughter, married the son of a newspaper baron and the second daughter, Patience, began seeing a nice young man in the Navy.

But Clara Ernestine, the youngest, was different. She was a restless girl who learnt fast and was bored easily. Clara needed a challenge every time. When she first rode a pony it was without a saddle, and she went on to be an excellent rider, equally at ease with hunters, ponies, cobs and Galloways. She could water and feed a horse and treat cuts, corns, cracked heels, thrush or fever in the feet like an expert.

Clara was fifteen when she first went to the Derby. The smooth elegance of wealth that her sisters and her mother loved did nothing for Clara; she began to tire of horses. At nineteen, she gave it all up and joined the nursing school at Guys Hospital. The rigorous routine, the detached caring for strangers and the contact with men of varied personalities convinced Clara that she should never marry for love but for convenience, if at all. Her parents tried to coerce their wilful daughter but she resolved never to set herself up for a match.

Clara worked her way up and became night superintendent in charge of the geriatric wards. Every evening, she got into her starched uniform and the tent-like cap, black stockings and shoes, and went on duty. Geriatric patients were easy to handle. They were timid, obedient and grateful, they said thank you even if you smiled a mechanical smile at them. Barring some nights when a seriously ill patient needed constant care, the wards were quiet at midnight. The only sounds one heard were intestinal gurgles, decrepit snores and the creak and snap of arthritic joints moving painfully in sleep.

After three years as staff nurse, Clara was bored. She took temperatures, checked blood pressure, dressed wounds, wiped bottoms, inserted tubes and charted the fate of unknown lives with dots, crosses and graphs for the doctors to see, she monitored the uphill or downhill course of sickness that was attached to a name, she dealt with life at its most fragile. Geriatric patients were like little injured birds fluttering in her hands. They either healed and went to a convalescent home from where they sent thank-you letters, or they died. Three years, and Clara was bored. She had nothing to complain about in her social life but parties bored her; garrulous young men who tried to impress her bored her. Heavens! What was life coming to if she was bored at twenty-five? Then she met Lady Feodora, with the injured hip.

Lady Feodora was vain and attractive even at ninety-two. When she was wheeled into the casualty department at Guys, she was more concerned about the satin ribbon in her hair that had come askew than she was about her hip. She showed her independence by refusing surgery ('I shall not be hacked!') and refusing traction ('leashed to the bed—never!'). Doctors smiled politely. Later in their tea room they prophesied she would never leave the hospital. If bronchopneumonia didn't get her in a week, then kidney failure, lung congestion or coma would by the second week. Lady Feodora defied medical prophesy and after forty-two days, began to move about in a wheelchair.

She slept between six and eleven at night, and insisted on a bath, Ovaltine and a hot water bottle when she jerked awake. She set her hair in curlers and by five in the morning combed it into a provocative mass of grey curls held on top of her head with a satin ribbon, the colour of which she agonized over each day.

It was the night before Easter. A coronary in the medical ward and a haemorrhaging ulcer in the surgical wing took away most of Clara's nurses and she was left to wheel Feodora to the bath. That was when she noticed the greenish-yellow pendant which reclined on the bony contours of the lady's neck.

'Pretty pendant.'

'Coorg. Bet you haven't heard of the place.'

'Oh, is it a place?' Clara said, helping her out of the wheelchair.

'What did you think it was, a brand of beer?' Lady Feodora was the offensive type, and therefore that much more interesting than the other old dears, who crumbled with gratitude at everything you did for them. 'It's a valley in the Western Ghats in India, don't you forget, even if you don't have the good fortune to visit the paradise.'

The pendant was made of a tiger's claw set in twenty-two carat filigreed gold, a gift from her husband Alistair when she had her first child. Alistair shot eight tigers in Coorg—and if Feodora was not so unfortunate as to be crippled with an injured hip, she would have taken Clara home where she had three tiger-skins attached to their stuffed heads, with all their teeth intact, and the eyes replaced by marbles. Those works of craftsmanship were by her son Bernard who was inspired into taxidermy by his mother's tiger-claw pendant which his hands had first grasped and used as a teething ring.

Lady Feodora told Clara about her fifty-one years in the forested valley that the British had annexed in '34. Lady Feodora had a meticulous memory and a way of romanticizing everything that had touched her life. All she needed to shape her narrative was time,and she had that in abundance. She wanted to tell it all.

A year after Alistair Fox marred Feodora in '55, they sailed from Ceylon where he had worked at a coffee plantation, to Travancore on the south-west coast of India. They took with them eighteen wooden chests filled with their belongings, but the most precious item was half a pound of coffee beans that Alistair stuffed into a black silk stocking and carried in the inside pocket of his tweed coat. He had picked the ripe red berries himself, off the healthiest bush, taking only the perfectly rounded ones from the middle branches, avoiding those at the crown which were overexposed to the sun and the ones at the bottom that got too little sunshine. Alistair didn't take the tweed coat off until they had reached Travancore and travelled in a cart for eight days, crossed the hills of Malabar and reached the thick forests of Coorg, where the air was like satin and the murmur of bees on the giant fig trees made maddening music you never forgot.

Alistair wasn't the first Englishman in Coorg. Some years earlier, when the plantations of Ceylon began to succumb to the borer insect, astute planters began to look for an alternative. Coffee grew best in dark moist soil, about three thousand feet above sea level, with plenty of trees for shade. Coorg, they found, was ideal. By the time Alistair came, coffee had been planted along the slopes between Mercara and Sunticoppa. The Bamboo Club in Pollibetta and the European Club in Mercara had been established; Rs 2,876 had been collected for building the first church, and Moegling, the intrepid American missionary, had begun his frantic attempts to convert the heathens.

Alistair had purchased sixty acres of land in Tenth Mile.

He appointed an overseer, and with the help of four Yerava workers cleared the wooded slopes. Seeds were planted, grooved face down, in raised beds covered with straw and planks of wood. Two months later, the seedlings were transplanted to the nursery and after four months, the sturdy young plants were moved to the two acres cleared by the Yeravas. From the three hundred and eighty seeds of coffee he had brought from Ceylon in a silk stocking, Alistair got his first eighty plants. With Feodora, he lived in a two-room cottage in Tenth Mile, brought all sixty acres under cultivation in seven years and employed forty workers. Rooms were added on to the cottage until it became a bungalow with eighteen rooms and was named Solyglen.

Feodora told Clara about the bamboo forests and mist-covered hills, the orange trees bowed with fruit and the sweetness of water from the streams. Her only unpleasant memories revolved around the toilet, which was a pit amidst the bushes during their first months in Coorg. 'It's better, my dear, to die of constipation than to use the pit. I feared that I would fall in and be devoured by those gross wasps teeming inside. My daily prayer was that if I fell, I should die falling. Alistair had a wooden commode designed by the local carpenter and then it was all right.' The blue-rimmed, ice-cold, enamel chamber pots had come later.

'My regret is that I didn't get to know the locals well enough. They're cleaner than we are and they know it. You'll never find natives washing their faces in basins of water or bathing in tubs. It's always running water for them. They kept their distance lest we polluted them but we should have tried harder to be friends. A pity.'

Lady Feodora died in her sleep the day after she got a letter from her grandson in Coorg. The letter said he was on his way to England for a holiday. She showed the letter to Clara, and a photograph of twenty-nine-year-old Rupert Fox. When he came to the hospital it was Clara who met him, and before he left, she invited him to her sister's birthday party.

Rupert was nice enough, lean and athletic with curly brown hair and humourless blue eyes. For Clara, who was dissatisfied with the routine of nursing, his most attractive feature was that he lived in Coorg. Once she had made the decision to go there, it was easy enough to engineer events that led to Rupert proposing to her. The following spring, she sailed to India and married Rupert at St. Mark's Cathedral in Bangalore. When the wedding ring was slipped on to her finger, Clara felt a brief twinge of distress at the thought of marrying a Fox but the feeling passed. Two days later, she set out with her husband on his Royal Enfield (she in the side-car) to the paradise called Coorg. They travelled all day and just as they entered the bamboo forests, had a puncture. They went the rest of the way in a hay-filled bullock cart and reached Belquarren at midnight.

It was all very exciting, but it hadn't stayed that way.

Rupert had no romantic notions about his work. Coffee prices had dwindled due to competition from plantations in South America. In Coorg, large tracts of the crop had been blighted by borer and leaf-rot; the sale of coffee was wretched business, dealt with entirely by the coastal agents in Malabar and Mangalore. The planters were dependent on them for yearly loans in return for which they had to hypothecate their crops. The agents shipped the pulped, dried coffee beans to London, where the price was fixed at the broker's office in Mincing Lane.

Rupert had learnt the business of coffee-growing from his grandfather Alistair. He supplanted his father, who had developed a fascination for stuffing animals at the expense of coffee. Rupert was confident that when he took over the reins at Solyglen he would tighten up on the workers and increase the yield. His father was a compassionate man who built houses of mud and sun-dried bricks for his workers. On Saturday afternoons, he paid them the weekly wages—five annas for men, three-and-two for women and two for a child. Between the workers and himself were the intermediaries who saw to it that subordinates did their job. The workers were supervised by the carpenter, who was supervised by the field boss, who was answerable to the writer, whose work was overseen by the overseer, who reported to the assistant manager, who in turn submitted to the superintendent and he to the manager of the estate. But Rupert managed Belquarren himself, having dispensed with all but the workers, carpenter, field boss and the writer.

Clara listened to her husband explain it all during her first few weeks in Coorg. 'It's a jolly nice place and all that, we have a neat social life going between the two clubs, but one can never be too cautious. About the natives, I mean. Until the British came and sanitized their lives, they were simple-minded rustics whom the Rajas conquered and subjected to all sorts of cruelty. Coorgs, I might as well tell you, sacrifice animals, worship guns, spears and ancestors. Missionaries are trying to bring them the message of God but results are slow.'

Rupert's father was a gentle, non-interfering soul, but his mother was a redoubtable woman, and she took Clara's social life into her hands, even though she lived twenty miles away. She called her Ernestine and made sure that she attended every tennis party, 'at-home', club session and ball. At the Bamboo Club, the ladies were expected to sit in a separate suite and occupy themselves with potato wafers, tomato sauce and gossip. The men played whist or billiards and drank for very long hours until one of the wives sent a message to her husband: 'Memsahib sends her salaams,' which meant that he had better call it a day and take her home. But for Easter, Christmas and the New Year, the billiard and whist tables were moved away and the club readied for the ball at which the women were allowed to enter the club, like exotic birds. What upset Clara was not just the attitude of the men but the uncomplaining placidity of the women.

Beside the clubs, there was Mercara Week (races, dances and gossip) and the Bangalore Fortnight (more races, dances and gossip). These events were attended with fervour and talked about for months afterwards. Clara never got to meet any of the locals except Daisy and Babs, Tim and Joe Boy and Ammi the Duchess, who were in any case clones of the British and therefore not interesting. If she went to the estate, the Yerava workers stared with dumb hostility, the carpenter, the field boss and the overseer said 'Good Morning, Madam,' servants, gardeners and the syce conducted themselves with efficiency but never spoke. In six months, she began to feel the suffocation. She rode alone, much to the consternation of her husband who warned that snakes, scorpions and dangerous natives lurked everywhere. She got to see much of Coorg but when she passed the locals, they averted their eyes.

Clara was bitter. Was Coorg to become the graveyard of her youthful dreams? She was lonely—more lonely when her husband was home than when he was away on those brief stints in the Voluntary Army. Rupert more than anyone else symbolized the drudgery of her existence. In an effort to occupy herself, she visited the library at Mercara Fort and borrowed books on Coorg. Reading history reassured her that life must progress, she too must move, however slowly, with it. Her life wasn't going to stagnate, even she would be a part of history.

In the unused shelves of the library, she discovered a yellowed manuscript, *The Rajendranama*, a biography-cum-historical record of Doddaveera Raja, the Haleri king who ruled Kodagu from 1788 to 1809. The veracity of the manuscript was questioned by British scholars but the book gave a poignant description of Kodagu during the reign of this ill-fated Raja, his suspicions about traitors scheming to overthrow him, his retaliation with reckless massacres. Once, he ordered that his two brothers Lingaraja and Appaji be beheaded. When he came to his senses, he realized his folly and asked that his command be repealed. Lingaraja was fortunate but Appaji had already fallen to the sword of the executioner. Several families had been wiped out in this way

and almost every time, the Raja repented when it was too late.
He suffered from frequent bouts of mania and died leaving his
oldest daughter Devammaji as his heir. Lingaraja usurped the
throne and ruled Coorg for thirteen years; when he died, his
son Chikkaveeraraja became the last king of Kodagu.

Clara read everything; she wondered what the Coorgs
thought about the British. Were they only being tolerated until
nationalist fervour gained momentum and drove them out?
She longed to find out. Then she met Baliyanna.

Chapter Seven ————————————————

Clara did not feel the need to pat her hair or smooth down her dress when the vet was around. Oh, she was a little disappointed that he didn't look at her the way she would have liked—he probably admired her as one admires a neat bed of roses in a garden. The bearer served angel cakes with the tea and left; it did not matter if the vet liked them or not, those things were easily dispensed with, and they got on with the talking.

Sometimes he read to her, and those were the best moments. He leaning forward in his chair, green veins ridging his hands, the tension of his wrists fading into long brown forearms and deceptively soft-looking biceps, beneath the half-sleeved shirt. She, listening, concentrating on different parts of him, wanting to remember everything.

When she didn't see him for some weeks, she wrote and asked questions:

'What's the best time to castrate cats?'

'Can a chicken get dropsy?'

'What is the treatment for cows with red eyes?'

He replied with precise advice. She never asked about the horses, because she knew everything about them, and when they fell ill she treated them herself. Only once, when she was desperate to have him stay longer, she asked him to see a horse with cracked heels. He snipped away the hairs, rinsed the sores in warm water, dried them with serge and rubbed in glycerine. 'Never allow the feet to be wet before riding,' he said. 'Dirt clings and makes them worse.'

'Yes, I know.' She told him about her father's stables

where she had cared for horses, fed and watered them.

He was puzzled. 'Why have you neglected your own stables?'

She had no answer.

They once met on the road to Tenth Mile—the vet was riding to Siddapur and for that distance they rode together.

'You ride well,' he said. 'Like someone who's learnt the proper way.'

'I learnt young. My father taught me that a good rider holds the reins with just a little tension; the gentlest flexion of your finger conveys the tug at its lips and the horse turns left or right or gallops or eases to a trot.'

They reached Siddapur. 'You have hidden your talents well,' the vet said as he rode off along an uphill track towards Siddapur. Clara wondered if there was a hint of irony in his voice.

She loved his letters as much as his visits. She tore the envelope open with indecent haste and scanned the pages, her eyes tripping over the lines, not really reading, just touching the words with her eyes. Then she read the letter and reread it, hoping to find some hint of intimacy. She loved the way his hands fashioned the alphabets. The shafted 's', the squiggly 'g', the jaunty 'f' wearing a hat, 'w' waving its arms and shy introverted 'r' reclining on the line and the secretive 'c'. She couldn't tell from the letters how he felt, she could only breathe on the pages he had breathed on, see his veined hand, and the shadow of his fingers move across the page. She absorbed him through his letters, she possessed a part of his mind. There were times when she found it difficult to write, because she was concealing what she really wished to say. Her hand was unsteady, she had to support it on the table in order to write; her fingers frigid, self-conscious and stiff even when she sent the briefest note about a horse or a cow or a hen.

In the midst of the happiness of her friendship, Clara felt the pain of not knowing him. It was only a segment of himself that he shared with her. He admired the provocative sharpness of her mind and her willingness to listen to criticism about her people. But what else? Studying herself in the mirror, Clara was filled with a fierce longing, a desperate desire to preserve her youth and beauty for him. She could commit any sin for his sake, it was a ruthlessness that made her feel good. But the only compatibility between her and the vet was that of the mind. Once he told her of his brother who had married a 'half-caste'. It hurt when he said it, as if the British half was unclean.

She could never analyze the sadness of his eyes. Grey—with orange flecks—and black pupils dilating to edge out the grey or constricting into pinpricks. At times, those eyes flowed over her in a sweep of understanding, as if he fathomed the convolutions of her mind, and a blinding pain knifed through her breasts. She wished she could touch his eyes with her fingertips, eyes that held a world she could not enter. She saw in them the pain of tragedies past; his ancestors had burdened him with the memory of their actions and lack of action. Who were they?

How little she knew.

She could never physically seduce him, he didn't deserve such shoddy treatment and he didn't seem the sort to be unfaithful to his wife. Clara herself was not particular about fidelity. In any case people had begun to say that while Rupert was a straitlaced stickler for morality, his wife was rather the other way. What use was it, her emotional fervour, it hadn't got her anywhere with the vet. Once he said to her: 'You British have no feelings.'

Oh, what was the use?

She liked and disliked the vet's wife: her schoolgirl thinness, her fleshless face, her sunburned skin and hardened limbs, oiled hair combed tight on her scalp; her wide, generous grin, her confidence in herself and her firm resistance to Western values. Such a frail-looking creature and she had borne thirteen children, her skinny body was the site of so much achievement. Clara did not know why she herself hadn't conceived. Dr Clatterbridge had said something vague to the effect that too much horse-riding had affected her pelvic organs.

Rupert never talked about it, and in any case she didn't want a hard, mean son like him. Of late, Rupert had become more contemptuous about the Indians. The other day, when a servant told them about cowdung being used to light fires, he had said, 'Well then, you need to build a temple to Sterculius, the god of dung, what?' and laughed at his own joke and repeated it at the club. Clara loathed his jokes, she couldn't laugh at them like the others.

She knew it wouldn't be long before the whispering started in the clubs about her and the vet. The whispering, in fact, had already started. Poor Rupert, they said: a deep one, that Clara, not gregarious or outgoing, quite cold, really, and now she's making a fool of herself over a native. And this before they knew about the hunting trip and the climb up the hill.

Chapter Eight _____

The showdown was inevitable. Rupert accused her of being a harlot. If she must throw herself at someone, couldn't she have picked one of their own kind? A hunting trip with the natives, that was all they needed to complete the humiliation she had brought on the Foxes.

Ah, the famous Fox reputation that she was never allowed to forget. Perhaps Rupert would disown her; but that was wishful thinking, he would never do anything so thoughtful. She wasn't going to explain that there would be at least twenty other people besides the vet, that it was only a short foray into the jungles of Kundathbottu, and that it would be over before dusk. She wasn't going to say anything. She hated quarrels, she didn't want to kill him with words. But she had to protect her emotional territory and prevent Rupert from charging in like a bull. So she let his tirade wash over her, not listening as he verbally ripped her to shreds.

She spent an insomniac night of delirious excitement. Would anything happen? No, nothing would happen. This was just kindness on the part of the vet, he knew she wanted to see how the Coorgs hunted. She decided to dress simply: light brown riding breeches and a white blouse beneath her jacket. She would take her riding cap and gun and that was it. Why then did she add perfume to her bath water, and set her hair in soft curls and then brush it all off, worrying that she looked fussy? Why the uncertainty over rouge, the deliberation over the shade of lipstick?

By morning she had exhausted her stock of indecision. The vet came early and they left without a confrontation with

Rupert who was inside somewhere, sulking. As they rode out of the gates of Belquarren, the syce, the driver, the gardener and the cook watched in curious, reverential silence. What were they thinking? On the road between Pollibetta and Athur, she saw the Tweedies going to church and further down, Mark Sprockett of Jambourie Estate riding to the club for golf, his syce walking ahead with the lunch and the boy who served it bringing up the rear. Clara did not miss the look of disdain on Mrs Tweedie's face or the pained expression on Mark Sprockett's countenance. Her reputation would be mud before she returned from the excursion, but she felt cheerful. She didn't want anyone, anything to come between them that day. She was ready for whatever was to happen or not happen, no one was going to ruin it. Nervousness left her, there was no foolish fluttering of her heart, only the exultation of riding with a good fellow rider.

It is the month of Tula, the vet explained, and a time to rejoice. In a few days the Kodavas would celebrate Sankramana, when at Talakaveri on the top of Brahmagiri hill the river springs out of the earth and flows to her people. The Kodavas go to the hilltop to bathe in the sacred waters. Coconuts dressed in red, jewelled and garlanded, are floated upon the river. It is the time of promise.

Sankramana would also signal the end of the monsoons. A light breeze played in the upper branches of the trees and the sky was covered with weighty clouds deliberating their moves. The vet rode as well as she did and they reached Kunda in an hour. The hunters were gathered there, waiting: mostly Coorgs, she could tell, by the graceful, tough shoulders and the lack of awkwardness when they moved. Baliyanna supervised the positioning of the dog-minders and their animals in a circle around the jungle. He pointed out a young man to Clara—younger than the rest, he looked barely eighteen. Like the others, he was in riding breeches, with a checked kerchief tied round his head. 'That's Nachappa, the best shot in Athur,' the vet said, 'he won't disappoint you.'

The signal was given—a sharp cry and the triple beat of a drum—and the dogs disappeared into the jungle with their minders following; the helpers sat on their haunches, the hunters waited, listening to the dogs bark as they sprang through the undergrowth. Baliyanna did not hunt that day; he stayed back to explain the events to Clara. The dogs were special breeds, he said, brought from the Nilgiris by the Voddas who travelled all the way to Coorg to find buyers. Rajapalayam, Kumbai, Chippiparai and Kanni were the best breeds for hunting, Kanni being the most favoured. They were well-muscled and lean, with powerful deep chests and sturdy legs for springing through the undergrowth, with button-ears or short straight ears folded at the tip, and without the pathetic tail-wagging of most dogs. They never threw themselves at humans for appreciation. 'Alsatians and Labradors are fashionable as pets among upper-class Kodavas,' the vet said wryly. 'But they're useless for hunting. We try to retain the purity of our hunter breeds.'

There was a crash in the undergrowth not far from where they sat, and then they saw the boar. A flash and a shot, a skid in the dust as the boar fell. Nachappa's kill. It was swiftly followed by two deer and several rabbits; by noon, the men were happy enough to call it a day. It was time to eat. Clara watched the operations from a distance. A mud pot appeared, and a sack of rice, salt, turmeric and chilli. The fire was lit and a just-killed deer was readied for the meal. The head and the right thigh were apportioned to the hunter to take home and the rest of the meat cooked. The dogs got their share of meat and bones; a bitch that was carrying got double.

'Would you like to climb the hill?' Baliyanna asked Clara. 'The food will not be ready till late afternoon; we can be back by then.'

They rode to the foot of the hill, tied their horses to a tree and began the climb. The hill was thickly wooded, steep, ridged by gigantic roots that clenched great mounds of earth between them. Overhead, the branches formed a screen of thick, wet, whispering foliage. Brown frogs the size of postage stamps with black stripes on their backs hopped in clusters, snails reclined on leaf beds, green scorpions hid in the moss, grass snakes flashed in the scrub and jungle fowl sauntered around, their blue plumes trailing. Baliyanna stopped to pluck wild fruit, which were found in many hues and flavours. Purple, orange, opalescent green, blood red, shiny black, speckled brown; juicy, acrid, honey-sweet, glutinous—Clara tasted them all until her hands and mouth were stained and sticky and the tang of the compound wild elixir permeated her senses.

They reached the top. A stone temple stood in the midst of a clearing, with a clump of banana trees to one side, a vast rock face on the other, ending in a vertical drop to the paddy fields below. The woods—dark, green, secretive—fell away from the summit. From where they stood they could see all of Coorg, the hills of Malabar and a grey strip of ocean.

He showed her a solitary oblong stone about two feet by one, balanced at the edge of the rock face. 'Pregnant women who come to pray at the temple stand on it and turn thrice, praying for the baby in the womb,' he said. Clara backed away, vertiginous at the thought of such foolhardy penance. 'Are there any accidents?' 'Of course not.' There was a mild contempt in his voice and she felt foolish at the shallowness of her belief.

It seemed that they stood on some strange promontory of earth, at the end of an epoch. Baliyanna pointed to the slopes along which they had climbed. 'Those forests were part of Kolebana—the forest of death. If a man killed another, he was brought here and left to the mercy of the tigers. The next day, the villagers collected his remains. Back in the village, they performed his last rites and addressed his spirit: "We did not kill you, we killed the cruelty in you. We want you to be born again in this nad," and they named the next newborn child after him. Every calving season, a calf, well-fed and healthy, was left in the forest to ensure that the tigers did not stray into the villages to prey on cattle and humans.'

He turned to look at her. 'Your government pays a handsome bounty to men who kill the tigers. We too have started shooting them in Coorg. When a man kills a tiger, he's married to it in a mock wedding. The skin is preserved and the women wear its nails as ornaments . . .' his voice was sad. 'One day the tiger will disappear.'

He talked about Kodagu before the days of the Haleri Rajas. Each *nad*, or group of villages, was ruled by a chieftain. They resolved feuds with a highly evolved code of honour: 'Outside each *nad* was a segregated area called *pulipale*—the place for the unclean. Criminals, thieves and perverts were banished there. Even traders from unknown places were forbidden to enter the villages. Pollibetta and Madikeri—the favourite places in Kodagu for the British—were originally *pulipales.*'

Suddenly, he got to his feet. 'I'll show you where the tiger lived on this hill.'

He led her down the slope where the rock face dipped into the undergrowth and where the rock formation folded backward on itself, forming a roofed, narrow enclosure. She followed. Dark and cool it was, with the sound of water dripping. In the darkness, she couldn't see him. 'Even now, they say you can smell the tiger. Can you?'

'No.'

Clara wanted to get out before he sensed her terror; she walked back towards daylight as he followed. She scrambled up the slope in haste and looking ahead, froze.

At the spot where they had sat on the rocks not a moment ago were two snakes. Cobra-di-capello, erect, silhouetted against the sky, entwined in an embrace. Clara was quick to react. She grabbed her gun and aimed. As she pulled the trigger, she felt it jerked away from her hand. The muzzle struck her jaw, she missed, lost her balance, and fell backward.

The vet stood next to her. There was only one snake now, its head raised above the half-coiled body, hood dilated, cloven tongue quivering; the hood was marked black like inverted spectacles, the frame white and the space of the imaginary glasses black. Beneath it, the fiendish eyes. They waited. The snake slithered away, a five-foot long shining whip.

Tears of terror and shame filled Clara's eyes. She was furious. So was he. She waited for him to speak; when he didn't she said, 'They're cobras. They're dangerous.'

'Not when they're making love.'

'Is that what—'

'You never kill mating animals. Or pregnant ones. Or those feeding the young. Or the young. That-is-the-law-of-hunting.'

She couldn't speak. She wasn't going to apologize, it wasn't anything criminal she had done. He sat next to her, silent. Her jaw hurt, and so did the inside of her mouth where her teeth had abraded it; his rudeness, and the humiliation hurt too, but he offered no apology. Instead, he spoke to her about snakes.

'A cobra has two poison fangs, one on each side of the upper jaw, curved inwards, sharp as a needle and hollow, with the root in direct link with the venom glands. When it bites, the fangs rise and compress the glands, and the poison flows into the wound. Cobras are vicious if rankled. That one—I'm surprised it let you off.'

Here she was, smarting for an apology and he was busy explaining things. 'People keep cobras to guard private treasures, many worship them. There used to be a man in Athur who handled snakes. He caught cobras, removed the poison glands and sold them to snake charmers. It was said that he embittered his blood by drinking an infusion of herbs that was an antidote to snakebite. After many years he sustained a bite that was fatal. The family prepared for the cremation, piled wood on the body and his oldest son lit the pyre. When he was half consumed by flames, violent movements were seen beneath the logs. The man was struggling to free himself. The shocked villagers came to the quick decision that since he was badly burnt, he was better dead than alive, so they piled more logs on him and ensured a sure demise.' Clara listened, nursing the abrasion in her mouth with her tongue.

'I want to tell you about my ancestor, from whom I got my name,' he said.

'During the reign of Doddaveera Raja, the granduncle of the last king, a faction of the Kodavas planned to attack the king's fort and overthrow him. But the king had received news of the uprising and when the rebels entered the fort, they were gunned down in the courtyard of the palace, several hundred of them. The Raja suspected that along with others, the Kaleyanda clan had schemed against him and he ordered that every one of them be beheaded. His executioners cut down all the Kaleyanda men and threw the bodies in the river. The Kaveri flowed red.

'Only one young man named Baliyanna, who had gone to Talakaveri to pray, was spared. Later, when the Raja realized his mistake, he tried to make peace by sending a pearl-encrusted *peeche-kathi* made of one hundred gold sovereigns to the youth and invited him to take a position in his court. Baliyanna sent the gift back with the curse that the dynasty of the Haleri Rajas would end before his own death. He lived to father many children who ensured the survival of the Kaleyanda clan and was an old man when the last Raja made his final journey out of Kodagu. Kaleyanda Baliyanna's curse came true. He was a massive man, seven feet tall, his *kupya* has been preserved by the family but there has been no one since big enough to wear it. We worship Baliyanna but for whom our clan would be extinct. His spirit lives, he speaks to us in our dreams, he guides our actions.'

The vet smiled a sad smile. 'You see, Clara, the importance of procreation.'

Listening to him had helped Clara simmer down. It was chilly and yet she could feel beads of sweat on her brow; across the valley, huge grey clouds that hugged the hills of Malabar were dragging themselves across the sky. 'It will rain,' Baliyanna said.

They took shelter beneath the overhanging roof of the temple. He picked a handful of leaves, some wild fruit and a few creamy-white flowers with elongated petals that grew on a tree next to the temple; he collected water from a puddle in his cupped hands and poured it over the lingam; he placed the flowers, fruit and leaves on it, and prayed. Clara felt left out. She wished she could pray to his god, the symbol of procreation. He took a flower from the lingam and held it out to her. 'A flower favoured by the gods,' he said. 'You'll find a *savanthige* tree near every temple.' He tucked it behind her ear, scooped cold water into her cupped hands. 'Drink it.' The water was so cold, it hurt her teeth and tingled on her gums.

It began to pour, a heavy, end-of-monsoon rain without thunder or lighting. They watched the water sailing off the giant banana leaves in a white stream, leaves bouncing with the weight of water.

'Wait here, I'll get some food.'

'Good, I'm starving. But from where—'

He was already walking down the slope.

She sat on the cold stone floor of the temple and waited. She waited until the sun came out and dried the rocks where it had formed puddles; she walked around, stood beneath the banana tree and listened to the sound of water pouring from the roof of the temple, looked at the conch-shaped maroon flowers and the bunch of green, tightly curled bunches of banana and wished they were ripe enough to eat.

Why had he left her there for so long? I won't be angry or hurt, she told herself. I'll pretend it's the most natural thing in the world to be left up here alone. She watched a column of flat beetles that looked like strips of black-and-white ribbon crawling with pitiful slowness on busy little legs. She touched one lightly with a twig and it curled into a shy round ball and lay still. She prodded the rest and had a circle of black-and-white spheres lying about her like vanquished soldiers.

She listened to the distinct, sharp sounds of the jungle: water dripped from leaf to leaf, branches rubbed against each other, insects warbled high-pitched cries of excitement. She heard an animal grazing near enough, cropping the grass with its teeth. The sound made her hungry. Was it a cow or goat or deer or—a wild buffalo? Not that, not a buffalo. 'Watch out for leeches, locusts and buffaloes,' Feodora had said. 'They hate white people.' It must be a buffalo. No tame creature could eat so much grass. What if it attacked her? 'Wife of British planter gored by wild buffalo and flung to her death': a juicy news item that would make readers shudder with distasteful pity and read on more avidly. The sound of grass being masticated went on as if the beast intended to eat all the grass and leave the jungle bare. The sound tore tiny shreds within her. What did the vet really think of her? Surely, a friendship that excluded everyone else must mean something to him. Did it, or didn't it? She had made up her mind just a moment ago to be unafraid. At any cost. She felt very conscious of herself, of her body. A woman's body was worth more than a man's, she could buy home, security, even a husband with it. But she could not buy love. She could never buy love. Suddenly the fear left her just as easily. She was calm and it seemed that the hilltop was a friendly place where animal sounds, bird sounds, insect sounds and the sounds of the trees wrapped themselves round her until she felt her life beat and flow with it.

He came bearing a leaf-wrapped package, with not a word of explanation for the delay. 'The hunting party had eaten everything so I asked the brahmin in the temple below to cook some food,' he said. He broke off a rain-soaked banana leaf, slit it in two, shook off the droplets and spread them on rocks. 'Come, eat.'

She ate greedily, stuffing her fingers in her mouth, shoving in rice and vegetables, luxuriating in the warmth of food in the stomach. She felt relaxed, happy.

'The leeches have probably got you by now,' he said when they had eaten, and he made her remove her boots. Yes, they had been at her and she hadn't even felt them bite. He took the leeches off her feet, put them in a little heap on the rocks and lit a match; the leeches had drunk so much blood that their greenish-red bodies burst in the heat. 'They're good phlebotomists,' he grinned. 'They smear the skin with saliva which has a deadening effect, and then sink their jaws in and draw blood painlessly. Don't look so horrified. They're clean creatures. A bit of gentian violet will heal the wounds. I forgot, but next time, you must wrap salt in a kerchief and tie it round your ankles. It keeps the leeches away.'

When they rode back, the sun was beginning to set, puddles of water on the road showed the clear sky and the trees as if through a window. The whole world seemed to have fallen away from her for the space of that day and now it was coming back, there was no escaping it.

That night, back in her room, she lay awake listening to the whistling breath of her husband. She stood at the window and looked at glow-worms lighting up shrubs and bushes like a thousand fairy lamps—females shining quietly, waiting for the males to alight. She stood there for a long time, understanding many things she had not understood before.

Chapter Nine

For sixteen weeks after Sankramana, Coorg was at its best: jewelled mornings, short sharp bursts of rain, fruity fragrances that replaced the fusty smells of monsoon, and moonlit nights when you could read better outside than under the lamp. Nothing had changed for Clara and yet everything was different.

She felt more at home in Coorg. At first when she came, she had been frightened by the gong-like voices of the natives, the curries had ravaged her stomach, ghee and honey overwhelmed her taste buds. The smell of fungus and rotting leaves, the heavy scents of lantana, lemon and mango mingling with those of dung and hay had been too much. Now she had grown used to these things and accepted them, and that was what her own people didn't like about her. She knew that they talked of her as the barren young wife of Rupert Fox who was throwing herself at the native vet. They were scandalized by her views about the injustice of British rule. None of it bothered Clara. She had even become bold enough to avoid the annual billiards tournament; she began to give the 'at-homes' a miss, she couldn't see the point in getting together to talk about shopping at Murthza Baig's or worrying over the price of tinned salmon, cheese and chocolates at Spencer's in Mercara. Clara couldn't help being different; she never did things she didn't like.

That year, she went back to nursing. Her patients were the Yeravas—the crinkly-haired, thick-lipped, flat-nosed labourers who were lazy and without ambition, but with a fierce capacity for work when they needed the money. They loved to work in the monsoons with the rain pouring on them, but in the dry months of March and April they worked only for one or two days a week. In their one-roomed, windowless huts they ate, slept, quarrelled, drank and sang. They never complained of illness but on enquiring, Clara found that their feet were covered with sores, their crinkly hair teemed with lice and they suffered from poor vision at night. She cleaned their sores with gentian violet and was amazed how quickly they healed. Great suppurating ulcers and fungifying wounds responded to simple remedies and now when she walked past their houses, the children ran out to greet her and the mothers watched from the doorway. They had ceased to be hostile and it made Clara glad.

'If you get so close to our people, you'll find it hard to leave,' Baliyanna said when she told him.

'Will you miss me?'

When they met again the following week, he answered. 'You and I—we treat sick animals and people, save lives. We don't know which lives are more precious, and that's a blessing. We try to save them all. Sometimes, you see it—a special appeal—in the eyes of a sheep or horse or cow or a human. Then it hits you. I—I will miss you when you go.'

The vet did not visit her as often as in the past. It did not matter, she had grown strong about most things. Even Rupert's unexpected, yet inevitable dalliance with Belinda Sprockett had caused just a sharp, brief burst of pain and now it was a dull ache that she folded and put away neatly in an inaccessible corner of her brain. It was easy to forgive when you didn't love. Rupert, in spite of having abandoned his scruples, had been judicious and discreet. He managed to guard his reputation, while hers plummeted.

Rupert barricaded himself from the natives with his superiority and distrust. He had an irrational fear of snakes, spiders, scorpions and insects of any kind and organized regular forays around the house to kill everything that crawled. He never ventured out without his boots and cautioned Clara about going out in sandals. His fear induced Rupert to buy a second-hand Austin from Alfred Weatherall. Weatherall, the manager of the Chrome Leather Company in Madras, came to Coorg in his Austin for Mercara Week and returned minus the car and plus six hundred rupees in his pocket. For Rupert, the car was a blessing; he liked the power behind the wheel, the thrill of villagers gawking, and the ease and style with which he could visit Belinda.

It was summer. Clara had written to Baliyanna some weeks earlier, and not getting a reply, wrote again. That Sunday, Subbu came to tell her about the mishap. A fortnight earlier, while preparing an extract from the livers of twelve sheep, his father had accidentally tipped the copper pot over himself. The boiling red fluid had burnt his arms, neck and chest; he was still in bed and not able to write.

She went with Subbu in her horse-trap. When they reached the house, Nanji came out, wiping her hands on her sari. Her eyes were bright but she looked tired. 'I was hoping you would come,' she said and led Clara to the bedroom.

His chest was raw and red; thick black eschar was piled high along the margins of the burnt area and over the neck and hands the hypertrophied scar threatened to form contractures. 'Tell him he must move the joints, he'll listen to you,' Nanji said.

Clara went regularly, to talk and read to the vet. Nanji cleaned his wounds twice a day. She smeared warm coconut oil on his wounds and in a strident, almost harsh voice, bullied him to move his joints; yet her fingers were gentle as an angel's. When the wounds hurt intolerably and he shouted with pain, she smeared egg-white mixed in marigold juice over them to ease him; she fed him broth made from a goat's head simmered in healing herbs. Slowly, miraculously, Baliyanna began to heal.

One day, Nanji took Clara to the attic and showed her the books lined along the rear wall where the sloping roof met the wooden floor. Wrapped in cobwebs and crawling with termites, the books were relics of Baliyanna's Presidency College days. Gray's *Anatomy*, the *Manual of Veterinary Practice*, *The Works of Shakespeare*, Thoreau, Ruskin, the *Puranas*. Clara opened *Walden*: a family of white termites crawled out and the pages crumbled in her hands like the powdery wings of a moth.

They got the servants to carry the books down. Nanji supervised from the top of the stairs and Clara stood below, fussing over the books as she would have over patients with broken limbs. When they had laid them on the round table in the front room, Clara cleared the dust and termites from the spines, gummed loose pages, and using bits of cardboard, bound the books. Nanji had six shelves made from seasoned teak and these were lined along one wall of the front room. The rejuvenated books, in spite of their age, filled the house with a newness that pleased Nanji.

It was while restoring the books that Clara found a volume of hand-written pages held with twine, titled 'Notes on Coffee' by Alistair Fox. She deciphered the long-limbed, tight scrawl of her husband's grandfather, who had presented the copy to Rao Bahadur Madaiah in 1872. It was an exciting find and when she showed it to the vet, he asked if she would read aloud to him.

'Coffee was first known to grow wild in a place called Caffea in Abyssinia. A brew made from the beans was drunk by the locals as a stimulant. It was a vital ingredient of "blood-brother" ceremonies where the blood of two pledging parties was mixed and put between twin seeds of a coffee bean and the whole swallowed. In the mid-fifteenth century, a sheikh who came to Caffea took a handful of beans with him when he returned and thus introduced coffee to Arabia. Religious groups looked upon the stimulant effects of coffee as harmful; but proclamations and warnings about inebriation from the evil drink did nothing to stem its popularity.

'The Arabs had a kind of veneration for coffee, and only men were allowed to prepare it. After roasting it in a special pan it was ground fine with a mortar and pestle; an exact measure of powdered coffee was put into an exact quantity of boiling water; this caused the boiling to stop, and as soon as the mixture started to boil again it was taken away from the fire. When it cooled slightly, it was put back; this was repeated until it had boiled three times. The result was a perfect drink with a slight froth on top, appetizing to view, rich in aroma, full of flavour and strong. It was poured into cups that had been pre-rinsed with hot coffee, and the rinsed liquid dripped on the ground as a libation to the coffee saint, Sheikh esh Shadhilly. Cups were only-half filled. To present a full cup or much less than half was an insult. Never more than two cups were offered, unless it was to an enemy. "The first cup for the guest, the second for enjoyment, the third for the sword", went the Arab saying.

'Coffee reached Europe a century later when beans were brought to Amsterdam from the port of Mocha off the coast of Yemen. The Dutch introduced coffee to Ceylon, Surinam, Brazil, Jamaica, Java and Cuba. In 1713, the Dutch sent a coffee tree as a royal gift to King Louis XIV of France. After a day of feasting his eyes on the exotic gift, the Sun King put the tree in the hands of Professor Antoine de Jussieu and ordered that every effort be made to cajole this royal gift to grow well. The first glasshouse in France was built for the tree at the Jardin des Plantes in Paris. It was from a study of Jussieu's and from direct descendants of this tree that Linnaeus named the genus Arabica, which, even now, is the superior variety of coffee.

'The first coffee house in England was started in 1657 by a Greek named Pasqua Rosee on St. Michael's Alley in Cornhill. The original handbill advertising the coffee house read:

> "*The virtue of the Coffee Drink, first made and publicly sold in England by Pasqua Rosee.*
> "The berry called coffee groweth upon little trees in deserts of Arabia ... it is a simple innocent thing, made into a drink after being dried in an oven, ground to powder and boiled with spring water. And about half a pint of it to be drunk an hour before food . . . to be taken as hot as possibly can be endured which will not

fetch the skin off the mouth or raise any blisters by reasons of that . . .

"It so encloseth the orifice of the stomach and fortifies the heart within, that it is very good to help digestion, therefore of great use if taken about three or four o'clock in the afternoon as well as in the morning. It much quietens the spirit and makes the heart lightsome. It suppresseth fumes exceedingly and therefore is good against headache and will stop any defluxion of rheums that distil from the head upon the stomach, and so prevent consumption and cough. It can cure gout, dropsy, and scurvy and is excellent remedy against the spleen, hypochondriac winds, and the like. It will prevent drowsiness and make one fit for business. Therefore you must not drink it after supper unless you have occasion to be watchful . . .

"It is neither a laxative nor an astringent. In Turkey where coffee is generally drunk, they are neither troubled with the stone, gout, dropsy or scurvy. Their skin is exceedingly clean and bright."

'Armed with these handbills, Pasqua Rosee opened his coffee house, thus popularized coffee and made it a greater favourite than tea or cocoa. When coffee houses flourished and became the centres for arguments and discussion, King Charles II heard black stories about the seditious nature of these places. Coffee was denounced as a hell drink and a heavy tax imposed on it but coffee houses multiplied. The popular coffee houses of London were The Grecian, Old Man's, Lion's Head, The Folly, Turk's Head and The Rainbow, but the most famous of all was The Cheshire Cheese.

'In France, the first coffee house came up in Marseilles in 1671 and in the next few years the number of coffee houses which were called cafes, rose to over a hundred. They occupied enclosed gardens, sidewalks and dark recesses where sailors with their girls as well as the better classes could meet; it seemed that old Paris centred around one vast coffee house that never slept. The most noted of all was the Procope at 13 Rue de L'Ancienne Comedie, the gathering place for the dreamers, thinkers and doers of

France: Voltaire, Rousseau, Hugo, Zola, Robespierre, Balzac, Napoleon, Verlaine, Bernhardt and Clemenceau frequented the Procope at various times. It was the scene of fiery debates and seething excitement during the Revolution.

'Coffee came to India in 1600 when a Muslim named Baba Budan went to Mecca on pilgrimage and drank a local brew called quahwah. When he returned to India he brought seven seeds of coffee tied round his waist. He planted the seeds on the hillside near Chikmagalur and from here the cultivation spread to Mysore, Coorg, Coimbatore and Goa, down to Travancore and the hills west of Tuticorin.'

Alistair's text concluded with sound advice for the British planters. 'It is wise to remember that but for coffee, the British would never have settled in the beautiful valley of Coorg; and the natives, in spite of all their ignorance, are wise when it comes to cultivation. It is unwise for us to regard with contempt all idea of instruction coming from them. Were the coffee plant, like ourselves, a product of North Europe, the prejudice might be intelligible but it is strictly a tropical plant; the European should be eager to learn something of its habits and requirements from native experience and follow native methods as closely as possible.

'The natives always plant under shade. Their gardens are nearly always warm, low lying, protected by fine old jacks and other wide-spreading trees. In their hands, coffee stays vigorous and outlives generations of proprietors while plantations of Europeans, where far greater solicitude and labour have been expended, but which were left fully exposed to the sun, have long since passed into decay and been abandoned. Coffee under shade yields a smaller crop but the plants are better preserved and the seeds sell at seventeen shillings and six pence per hundredweight.'

The text gave detailed instructions on how to start a plantation and make it viable. As Clara read, Nanji brought them coffee, filter coffee that no one made as well as her, a bit too sweet but still the best. Clara savoured the bitterness on her tongue before the jaggery sweetness flooded over and coated the gums but even then the bitter taste lingered. She could never make coffee like Nanji. Even when she gave instructions to her servants, they came up with something that was bland and tasteless.

When Baliyanna was fit enough to go out, he resumed his veterinary practice, his visits to the *santhe* and the Club, but he did not visit Belquarren as often as in the past. During the period of his physical incapacity, he had been building up a hostility towards the British. He talked about it to Clara when they met. Indians wanted freedom; it would be greatness itself for the British to hand over the government and leave. Clara understood; she also knew that her going was as inevitable as a free India.

Most Kodavas were busy aping the British and they had no time to worry about freedom. British culture was a flaky upper crust which could not be scraped away without leaving pits and scars in the younger generation. At the Country Club, after his fourth toddy, Baliyanna held forth about the shamelessness of his people who were naming their children Robin, Peter, Kitty and Pat; hundreds were already branded by the ridiculousness of their names. Baliyanna was depressed by the futility of an existence that had to see the shameful spectacle of Kodavas preening themselves on an alien culture.

Rupert was cool and hostile towards the vet. He had as little to do with him as possible, until an epidemic of fever affected several horses on more then a dozen English estates and the vet's help had to be sought. A week later, Baliyanna was summoned to the Collector's office, where Rupert and two other Englishmen sat with the Collector. They questioned the vet about the disease.

'It's venereal,' Baliyanna said, and seeing their perplexed faces, added: 'sexually transmitted'.

'How did so many horses get affected?' the Collector wanted to know.

'One stallion is enough to contaminate an entire stable,' Baliyanna said. 'Given the Western promiscuity, it's hardly surprising.'

He didn't mean to sound contemptuous but he was angry that none of them had had the courtesy to offer him a chair. It wasn't an oversight that he might have forgiven but a subtle gesture to humiliate, the type the British used all the time with an air of virtuous self-assurance that stunned the victim into inaction and, quite often, servitude. To show consideration to a native was a weakness and each of the four men felt it beneath him to do it. Baliyanna answered their questions, explained the use of arsenium and mercury, wondering all the while how he would answer their discourtesy. When the Collector thanked him and said he could go and that they would see to his fees, he lifted the empty chair over the table at which they sat and cracked its arms and legs as if it were an opponent in a fight. 'Looks like there's no need for this chair,' he said and walked out.

There were murmurs among the British about suing the impertinent vet but the episode fizzled out and died because the Collector did not wish for the added ridicule of more publicity.

One outcome of it was that the vet was forbidden to visit Belquarren. Rupert left instructions at the gate that he was not to be allowed in. Baliyanna acknowledged the insult and wrote his last letter to Clara.

Why did it have to end this way, was hostility between their countries reason enough to end their friendship? Clara hadn't looked for hurt but hurt had come to her. She treasured the friendship between them, even those moments of silence when thoughts like tenuous filaments stretched between their minds. Clara wanted to go back to clean, cold, sterile England where she could live an interior life, without a thousand eyes watching her. It was the right thing to do, only she was trapped inside a marriage and she didn't know how to free herself. She was conscious of her life being pulled like rubber over years of void when it could all be lived in a moment. Why did it have to be like this? Her father, who was a great one for pep talks, always said that if you really wanted something and strove for it, it would be yours. One of those over-simplified, idealistic flippancies. There was nothing more she could have done to get what she wanted. Where was the justice? Of course, one could say she had been saved from sin; her sadness was Nanji's joy. Yes, it was fair when you looked at it eye-to-eye.

It was one of those nights when she woke around two and lay awake and there was nothing to do but listen to the sounds of the night. Insects wound themselves like coils of a spring and then unwound, producing high-pitched shrieking noises; listless breezes chased a tin in the drying yard; trees talked in their sleep. She heard the forlorn mooing of a cow—was it pining for its calf?—the sound was both tragic and monotonous. There was nothing unique about pain, hers or the cow's or anyone else's. There wasn't any need to hold it close as if it were some precious jewel. But thoughts filled her mind and hurt like gravel abrading a mouth. A light pain moved over the left side of her chest which she would have enjoyed if it did not remind her of her heart. She went to the window and looked out. Beyond the drying yard, the coffee bushes gleamed in the cold light of the moon; and by the edge of the yard stood a jackal, its eyes glinting. Perhaps it had come in search of a secret, domesticated mate—a supercilious Dane, a stupid Alsatian, a flirtatious Pomeranian or a spaniel. How absurd!

She heard the sound of a horn cleave the night like a baby crying and it brought tears to her sleepless eyes. She heard the horn again, now from another direction; someone was foolhardy enough to drive at that time of night but it wasn't Rupert, surely, he was far too cautious. The vehicle was somewhere near Tenth Mile, she guessed, it was climbing the winding road that wrapped itself round the hill. She wanted to sleep, but the persistent sound of the horn kept her awake. It was nearer now, she could hear the faint sound of the engine.

Then she fell asleep, until she was wakened by the sound of the horn at the gates of Belquarren.

It was Dr Clatterbridge. Clara saw on his face a queer mixture of sympathy, lack of sleep and embarrassment. She showed him into the drawing room and he got it out quickly. Rupert had been visiting the Sprocketts and had left his wellies on the porch. When he put them on later, he was bitten by a Russell's viper that had taken shelter in one of his boots.

Rupert had been right in his anticipation, his superstitious horror of crawling things.

He was buried in the cemetery in Pollibetta. All the British families in Coorg were represented at the funeral but Clara felt alone and the only thought that filled her mind was the ridiculousness of symbols: she in black, mourning the death of a husband she had never loved, feeling an emptiness that had nothing to do with him. Rupert's mother held on to Clara's arm, Belinda Sprockett wiped her own tearful face with a lace handkerchief. Clara looked at the wooden crosses that dotted the graveyard and felt a twinge of envy of the dead.

Chapter Ten

Released from the death-sentence, Clara put the frivolity of 'at-homes', clubs and tennis-parties behind her. She grew used to the silent antagonism of her people and the unrelenting loneliness, just as she had got used to the monotony of monsoons, the heavy smells of fruit and fungus and the ice-cold enamel chamber pots that, like Feodora, she abhorred, but had learnt to accept. It was easier now to decide what she must do.

Rupert had managed the estate well, considering that in addition to the workers he employed only a carpenter, a field boss and a writer. Clara had thought that everything about Rupert was dull and boring but even dull people deserved the credit due to them. In an effort to make up for her apathy, she read, sought the advice of experienced planters like Edward Rice, Maurice Webb and Craig Jones. She learnt fast. In February, she supervised the laying of seed beds for the new clearing. The beds were laid forty inches across with eighteen-inch walks between them. Rocks, roots and weeds were removed, the beds dug deep, a few inches of top soil from the walks scooped off and worked into the beds. Then all of it was dug up, worked over, and smoothed with a rake; seeds were planted in rows three inches apart, grooved side down, and covered over with wooden planks and straw. Then the waiting, until the seed absorbed moisture, the endosperm swelled and burst through the seed coat and the stem arched upward, holding the seed at its tip; when the arch straightened, you had the 'little soldiers' in neat rows, with the seed like a cap on top. The straw and wooden planks were

removed and the seedlings allowed to grow in the shade of
thatched bamboo. In two months, the cotyledons opened and
arranged themselves in a cup around the central bud, like a
butterfly, ready to be transferred to the nursery.

There the seedlings were shaded with palm leaves to
decrease the drying effects of wind and sun. They grew into
sturdy little plants and in six months they were ready to be
shifted. The plants were dug up with a chunk of adhering earth
to form the ball-root, wrapped in banana leaves, tied with its
fibre and carried from the nursery to the permanent clearing
where the pits for each plant had been dug and the ground
was covered with mulch made from wet straw, grass and
leaves to retain moisture. Clara had to concede that Rupert,
like his grandfather, knew coffee. She had only half-listened
to him when he spoke about pruning and shaping coffee trees
to increase the yield, and when he explained to her about leaf
rust, borer, black rot, and mealy bugs.

After Rupert's death, she had grown closer to her
father-in-law but Rupert's mother never forgave her for being
a loner. Emily Fox was stiff and formal and it suited Clara.
Hostility was easier to handle than forced affection.

Bernard Fox was always happy to see her. That day, when
she set out to meet him, she knew she would learn a lot about
taxidermy and nothing about coffee. It was all right, she liked
the old man. There was a softness in him, a passion for his work
of stuffing animals that she envied, never mind that Solyglen
was slowly going to seed.

'You couldn't have picked a better day, my dear,' he said,
taking both her hands in his. 'A splendid kite brought down
by Tweedie the other day and now I'm almost halfway
through.' He led her into the long room next to the granary
where he worked. The bird was mounted on a wooden frame.
She had listened to him explain this a dozen times before, now
she listened again. 'I make a cut from the breastbone to the tail
and remove flesh, bones and internal organs. Got to be careful
not to damage the feathers while doing this. And I'll give you

a useful tip, I dust the inside with powdered borax to prevent rotting. I note the anatomical dimensions of the bird and make a replica from balsa wood. It's light, see? The neck is made of fine cotton wrapped on a wire which I pass through the body into the skull to hold the head. I use cotton to replace the muscles, put the replica inside the skin, wire the legs and wings in place and sew up the opening I first made.' He positioned the bird on its perch and fastened it with wires attached to the feet. 'He's more becoming with the wings outspread and head turned to the side, what? How's that? The only thing left now is to glue in the glass eyes.' He went back a few paces and looked appreciatively at his work.

He led her next to a larger work-table where he was working on a panther. 'Shot in Sunticoppa, this one, the hunter has done all the right things before sending it. He has measured the parts of the body before making a cut underneath and up the inner side of each leg. He's scraped the flesh off, salted the skin, cut away the muscles from the skeleton and cleaned the bones. He sent the skin and skeleton together with the measurements. Couldn't have done it better.

'Now this work, Clara, is quite different from doing birds. The skin's got to be tanned to stop it from cracking and the hair from falling out. This I do by soaking it in dilute tannic acid. Then I set the skeleton up and hold it with a wooden core and iron rods, then I cover the skeleton with wet modelling clay in the exact shape of the living animal. When it's dry, I'll make a plaster-of-Paris mould of the clay model. When that sets, I remove the sections and line the inside of each with papier-mache. I join the sections together and put the whole thing in water to soak until the plaster-of-Paris is soft enough to be broken away. This model, the manikin, is an exact copy of the clay-covered skeleton. I fit the tanned skin over the manikin with paste, glue in the glass eyes, brush and comb the hair. Then I paint the faded parts of the skin around eyes, nostrils and lips. I hope I didn't bore you, my dear,' he added, as they walked back to the house. 'Emily must be waiting with the tea.'

On her way back to Belquarren, Clara stopped the horse-trap near the cemetery. She walked to the low hedge skirting it and looked at the wooden crosses, the sad testimony of her people. A strange thing was religion. Even if you never thought about it in the waking moments of your life it somehow managed to pursue you to your death, when you went with a crucifix on your breast. It wasn't anger she felt but an impatience to be away from faked symbolisms. And faked happiness. There was no one else to blame; she had played with the basic rules of marriage, knocked herself and got hurt.

Five years. She would give herself five years to build Belquarren into a worthwhile estate and then she would be off. She did not know what she would do back in England but there was no doubt in her mind that in five years she would be well and truly done with Coorg.

Part Two

Chapter Eleven

Having delivered thirteen—including the unlucky first—Nanji decided that she had done her bit for the Kaliyanda clan and set about changing the personality of the house. She got the Yeravas to clear the weeds which invaded the porch and threatened to grow through the windows and walks. In the garden, she refused to imitate neighbours who were busy following the British. The disciplined, neatly bedded flowers in front of English bungalows impressed the Kodavas and they lost no time in getting their workers to hoe their gardens into measured plots. They planted poppies, phlox, asters, violets, snapdragons and nasturtium with meticulous precision, trimmed their hedges into monotonous greenness and began a chain reaction of unvaried copying. They felled the flowering shrubs of hibiscus, pulled down the honeysuckle and snipped the creepers of bougainvillaea that preened on the roofs.

The sight of well-groomed flowers smiling from their geometric beds saddened Nanji. She would not do anything so crazy. She tossed sunflower seeds in a corner near the granary and they filled the gloomy space with cheeky brightness; thick-petaled hydrangea that changed colour from pink to purple to blue and indigo were left to tend themselves near the mango trees, hollyhocks poked their lanky stalks over the well, golden canna with red flecks like drops of blood lit the slopes, the royal *rajakirita* nodded with indolence, the inverted bottlebrush swung its woolly strands; the sweet-scented lantana with its cluster of little stars that children sucked and then strung into chains formed a hedge all the way to the stream, and poinsettia flashed fiery tongues from their midst. Marigold, jasmine and dahlia jostled with kaleidoscopic crotons and frothy white lilies; *sampige*, *savanthige* and *kanakambara* grew wild and unfussy, ensuring fragrant flowers for the puja room and for the girls who wore them in their hair.

In the house, when Nanji let things slide during Baliyanna's illness, animals, birds and insects mistook negligence for hospitality and strayed in. No one thought of getting rid of them, so they stayed. Rats multiplied in the attic and on the roof, shooting about the rafters and shaking the house like an unruly army; pigeons roosted in the eaves and all kinds of birds built nests on the roof and the breeze brought in their feathers to form soft mounds in every room; termites and bugs proliferated along the wooden beams. The most persistent and invincible of the invaders was the army of beetles that appeared as if from nowhere. Harmless, soundless, clean and black, the size of rice grains, they crawled inside coffee cups, pillow cases, shoes, pockets, nostrils and chamber pots, marching like soldiers, and multiplying so fast you could see the battalions grow before your eyes.

And the flies: dark noisy swarms that buzzed crazily and got inside the mouth. Even if one was clever enough to clench the teeth in a barricade and open the mouth a mere slit to eat, they got in. Nanji devised a double strategy. She placed a skinned jackfruit glistening with sticky wax on the dining table; hours later, when the jackfruit looked like it was covered in currants, she had it thrown to the pigs and a freshly skinned jackfruit brought in. The other graveyard for flies was a basin of soapy water into which children flung the flies they caught and had competitions to see who caught the most.

One day, a column of red ants appeared in the store and next day a scorpion carrying creamy-white babies on its back was spotted behind the coffee pitcher. It was all-out war now, and it lasted two months. Tiles were taken down and dusted with borax, beams smeared in turpentine and the attic fumigated with gunpowder; a mixture of twelve pungent herbs was put over a tin of hot coals and carried from room to room, until the house was freed of all intruders except for a lame pigeon on the roof and a blind bandicoot in the attic.

The beastly invasion ceased, but the house was often densely populated with relatives. Kaliyanda was a large and prosperous clan scattered as far as Madikeri, Somwarpet and Sunticoppa. When relatives visited, they came in carts, through jungles and across streams, and stayed for days, or weeks. One summer, six families arrived the same day carrying boxes, infants, legs of meat and jars of dried pork. The assortment of children amounted to thirty-three, assuming Nanji's counting was accurate. Sometimes it became thirty-seven but she never bothered to find out which was right because counting children could be as difficult as counting sardines slithering in a basket. Nanji fed them four times a day and after three weeks, when the last family left, carrying a jar of Nanji's bamboo pickle, she wiped her face with the edge of her sari and said, 'Now I know I can feed an army.'

This overabundance of relatives upset Baliyanna. Even when they were gone he felt the house was overpopulated, although it was only his family and the servants. He sat in the porch all day, gazing at the swaying areca palms, while the outrageous revelry of his children passed by him like gusts of wind. He was quiet and morose and when he sighed, it sounded like the bursting of a paper bag filled with air. For Nanji, saying her evening prayers in the puja room, the mystery of his tortured preoccupation had already been solved. She knew he missed the Englishwoman but she did not feel threatened by Clara. Baliyanna was attracted by her mind, that was all and Nanji was too generous-hearted to worry about it. Her husband was devoted to her and after watching her give birth to Subbu, he had become her admirer for life. But she was aware of a restlessness stirring in him and she also knew she was powerless against it. He loved her, she was his beautiful, bone-thin, ever-fertile wife. He never spoke a harsh word or raised a hand even when full of toddy on Sunday nights, but Nanji could not fulfil the longing of his thick fingers; her tired breasts failed to respond to his restless groping. He longed for a softness she did not have and she did not resent it because it was not wrong to long for softness. Nanji pitied her husband and knew that sooner or later it would happen. In the gentle sadness of his grey eyes she saw the inevitability of adultery-to-come. She prepared herself, and built the graveyard of their love in her heart, long before it happened. At night, she felt the desperate thumping heartbeat of his desire and she calmed him with her bony fingers. In an effort to end his torture, she began to nag him without reason, so he would be driven quickly and guiltlessly to his sin. Exhausted by lust, Baliyanna wandered.

He went to the Country Club every evening, wearing the black cap to ward off the chill and with the umbrella crouching like a big black bird on the back of his coat. Nanji watched the sad wide swoop of his shoulders as he walked out of the gate and prayed that his restlessness be quelled. He went along the rutted path that wound between paddy fields where lived gypsy families which had come from no one knew where. The dark, sensual women with shiny faces and earlobes brushing their shoulders squatted by the path, and when they read the sadness in his eyes they welcomed him to their homes. They fed him steamed tapioca and foot-long bananas, and when their men were away, lay down on the cowdung floors of their huts with him. Baliyanna would come home from these women, scowling with displeasure, and Nanji, pitying, would forgive him with her gentle, bony fingers.

Nanji was happy that of late, the General who was her husband's most constant friend had more time for him. The General's luck had turned when his wife left him and joined an ashram where along with other women she was said to vomit pearls of devotion which were strung into garlands for Sri Krishna. Once released from his matrimonial dungeon, the

General fornicated with an innocence that was devoid of hypocrisy. When the wife departed, the General had decided to care for himself. Since he hated the shoddiness of servants and abhorred the tedious frustrations of cooking, he nourished himself at wedding feasts: *puttoo* with pork, rice with chicken, mutton *palav*, *payasam*, ten bananas, six or twelve laddus and a kettle of coffee did him nicely. Like a seasoned pilgrim he went from village to village in pursuit of weddings; he walked, hitchhiked on bicycles, cars, motorbikes, and bullock carts; he sat in the rear seat of an Austin or amidst chickens in a cart with equal detachment and grace. His gentlemanly demeanour moved the owner of the vehicle he travelled into to thank him for the honour.

The General was a regular at Thammi's Country Club but one Sunday, when he defaulted, Baliyanna and Subbu went to his home. The door was open, so they walked in, through the squalid front room and passageway to the smoke-filled kitchen. The General squatted by the fireplace, trying to revive the dying coals by blowing through an iron pipe. He puffed away at the cinders but the coal was congealed in fine ash and refused to light. He gave up and rose wearily. 'I always insist that a visiting card be handed in at the door,' he said. 'Well, for once I shall bypass protocol. I never send my guests away without tea but the environment today is unfriendly. Shall we socialize in the garden?'

Subbu carried three chairs from the front room and set them near the hedge at the back of the house where the General's clothes hung, drying. 'My laundry man—whose clientele includes Edward Rice, the Foxes and the Tippets—is rather overworked, so I've laundered my own apparel.' He looked sorrowfully at his clothes on the hedge. 'Just the other day, I washed all my ties and put them out to dry on the hibiscus bush. They have gone, every one of them.'

Baliyanna pulled thoughtfully at his whiskers, observed the declining standards of the General's lifestyle and said,

'How about living with us for a while? Nanji will be happy to have you stay.'

'You expect me to take advantage of her hospitality?' shouted the General. 'I'm an army man with a—a—standing in society.'

'I understand,' said Baliyanna.

Subbu didn't. Why did the General refuse his father's invitation to live with them? He continued to live in his miserable home; nothing changed; but the General was never the same without his ties.

When he visited Baliyanna, Nanji was so glad that she begged him to stay all day and batten on her hospitality. The two men sat in the porch and held long, philosophical discussions. Machaiah cleaned his ears with the silver scoop, filed his finger nails, and talked about the National Movement, the high-handedness of the British and the future of the country. The vet, who believed that nothing in life amounted to anything, also knew that only the toddy and his friendship with the General were constant. Neither made demands, so they were not tainted by false feelings of virtue, obligation and guilt. They drank toddy till four and then Baliyanna coaxed Nanji to serve fried meat or fish to go with the brandy that he brought from the wooden cabinet, which had sixteen compartments for his bottles. When the children returned from school, swinging their tiffin carriers, and when their hunger was appeased with Nanji's snacks, they burst upon the front yard like just-hatched chicks. In summer, mangoes ripened and fell and they raced the pigs for the fruit which Baliyanna sliced for them with his penknife. In the month of Chinyar, when the red-tinged leaves of *madh thoppu* were cooked with rice and eaten with honey, he ate greedily like everyone else and joined the boys when they lined against the coffee bushes to pee and to show off their scarlet arcs. If a child had a loose tooth, he sat the brat on his lap, shooed away the others, and while the General offered verbal ministrations, he circled the offending tooth with strands of thread and eased it

out of its socket. Then he put the tooth inside a pellet of dung
and got one of the older boys to throw it on the roof, to
guarantee a strong new successor to the evicted tooth.

Baliyanna never once talked about Clara. The fact that
their companionship led nowhere had dawned on him and he
knew it was only kind to both that he stop seeing her. But he
often thought about Clara, he dreamed of laying his head on
her cool concave belly and feeling his blood pulsing with hers.
She was so unlike the fat, flatulent gypsy whores he went to
now out of habit and boredom. Sometimes his longing was
acute and sometimes it was a dull ache and always it was
toddy that kept him alive. Toddy and the gentle
companionship of the General gave him the contentment of
the partly-living and he tried not to fight it. You cannot
manipulate every event in your life.

Chapter Twelve

When the foreign-returned, just-married Barrister had walked away with the smell of coconut gravy and ghee-fried bananas on his hands and the words, 'Don't come back as long as I live!' in his ears, he had decided that he would never go back to Kodagu. Appachu knew when he married Marjorie Hicks that he had defied Kodava tradition but it was surely not such a terrible sin that he should be shunned by his family. He became bitter and reinforced his fervour for his wife's religion. It was fervour not faith but Appachu wasn't aware of the difference till afterwards.

Kodavas who visited Bangalore returned with the news that Appachu had set up practice on South Parade, a hundred yards from the imposing statue of Queen Victoria holding the orb and sceptre, and that he had rented a bungalow near Fraser Town. They heard about the elegant wife, the gracious home, the green house and the garden chairs, the buttered scones and Eccles cakes that were served to the guests on Wedgewood and Royal Doulton tableware. The Barrister was seen driving around Bangalore in a two-horse chaise with his wife and children. Some years on, this outward appearance of harmony and plenitude crumbled; Appachu Basil Pinto's wife left him, with the household effects, two daughters, the harmony and the plenitude. The Barrister sold his chaise, gave up the bungalow and began to live in a single room on South Parade with his son and youngest daughter. The landlord, worried that the Barrister would bring him ill luck, asked him to vacate. Appachu refused. When repeated threats failed, the landlord had the doors, windows and the tiles removed. Appachu worked at his table in the roofless room and slept there with his children, a tarpaulin canopy protecting them from the elements. Although his clients dwindled, the practice was still viable because Appachu was one of the best lawyers in Bangalore.

When Nanji heard all this, she wrote him in her laborious crow's-feet scrawl that the money from Appachu's property, which she kept in a green casket, was there for him. 'Name a reliable courier I can send it with,' she wrote. Appachu was still too young and proud to be wise. Nanji's letter was never answered. The green casket stayed in the trunk beneath her bed, and it filled with coins of gold and silver.

In the same casket, Nanji kept the money earned from Boju's property. The youngest son of the Rao Bahadur was of perfect physique and an incorruptible innocence that finally landed him in trouble. He was a practical, religious survivor who did not believe in wasting energy until called. He mingled with friends of similar disposition and wandered, sporting a red hibiscus behind his ear and, if he had been to a temple that day, with a cream-coloured streak of sandalwood paste on his forehead. He sat by the stream eating mangoes or wandered along the village paths, not harming anyone, never squandering any money but his own (which was replenished when he visited Chambavva at Crystal Palace), not indulging in malice and never coveting other men's property, wives or daughters. Baliyanna did not try to draw his brother out of the chrysalis of prolonged youth and Boju showed his gratitude by not doing anything disgraceful. Nanji knew that sooner or later this handsome rake of a brother-in-law would settle down, and then he would need his money.

The week after coffee-picking, Nanji decided to visit her father. He was unwell with a skin disease that had turned one half of his body as dark as a Kuruba's and the other as fair as an Englishman's. Hair, nails, skin and tongue gained or lost melanin and scared his second wife and the children. When Nanji heard of his illness, she got ready to go in her boxcart with sugarcane, steamed *puttoo* wrapped in banana leaves, two jars of chutney made from wild tomatoes, a jar of pork-and-bamboo pickle and a pot of salted venison. Just as the cart was being loaded came the news that one of Boluka's daughters was vomiting worms, so he could not drive the boxcart to Tenth Mile.

Twenty-four-year-old Boju, living in peaceful harmony with life, had just risen and was sitting beneath the mango tree, brushing his teeth. 'Baliyakka, let me drive you to Tenth Mile,' he said. Nanji gratefully accepted and Boju convinced her that he had really better take Subbu along, to help unload the snacks and carry them up the slope to her father's house.

Just before dusk, they reached the foot of the hill and saw the house, a white smudge on the darkening slope. Boju and Subbu unloaded the sacks from the cart while Nanji set off, her lean body angled forward with the eagerness. How often she had climbed this slope with her grandmother, weary-limbed from a day in the fields; how joyfully she had washed her feet by the well and entered the kitchen where her mother waited with a meal. It had been a happy home, a modest one, and Nanji learnt very young that as a woman you could be as strong or weak as you wished. 'A Kodavathi is born tough,' her grandmother said, and proved it. She learnt to shoot, using the heaviest rifle in the house because she did not expect to have a second escape from a tiger. Once, walking home from Madikeri with her six-year-old son, she had seen a tiger asleep not ten yards away, down the slope. They had hidden in a wild mango tree until next morning the tiger left; when they came home, Neelakki asked her husband to teach her to load a gun and shoot. She never shot any tigers but brought down a wild pig and a rabid jackal that lurked near their drying yard. The men in the family joked that she should have been a man; Neelakki said she was happy enough to be a woman because a woman could be as strong as a man but a man could never acquire a woman's strength. The men laughed without understanding the truth of what she said.

All this Nanji remembered as she walked.

Nanji's stepmother appeared at the door and surveyed the gifts Nanji had brought. She smiled and welcomed the guests and balanced in her mind the equation of feeding three persons for three days. Behind her stood Chinni, Nanji's youngest stepsister. She held a lamp that lit her face briefly before she placed it on the corner stand and went in to call her father. The old man came, feet scuffing the floor as he walked. My father is withdrawing from life, Nanji thought, as she bent to touch his feet. For three days she stayed, soothing her father with trivial news of her family, and recalling the happy days of her childhood. It was different now. Her brother Nanu was cheerfully drinking his way to oblivion and Anni went on hunting sprees from which he returned with a deer, rabbit or a string of partridges. Disillusioned by his sons and dominated by his second wife, Nanji's father had lost interest in life. The mysterious ailment that had claimed him was an expression of a sorrow that had no cure.

When Boju saw Chinni, standing behind her mother with the lamp, he bit his tongue and could not speak till the morning. No one noticed. In the next three days, he got fleeting glimpses of Chinni's face, a flash of her fair ankles and swirling skirt, or of the end of her long, plaited hair. He roamed the house and garden in a maddening search for her and all he got was to listen to her laughter. Once he stumbled into the kitchen, following the sound of her laughter and was blinded by the dazzle of her smile before she disappeared behind the large, unfriendly back of her mother. On the last night of their stay in Tenth Mile, Boju confided in Subbu. 'I'm jumping into the well tonight, and please don't stop me,' he said. 'At least in death I may be noticed.' Alarmed, Subbu ran to tell Nanji. 'Put wet towels on his head and don't let him leave the bed till morning,' Nanji said. 'I'll sort this out tomorrow.'

Boju survived the night. At breakfast, Nanji asked her father, 'Can I take Chinni home with me? I need help with the younger ones.' 'Of course, why not?' her father said, hoping that his pretty young daughter would secure a handsome match just as Nanji had done.

Boju sang all the way as they rode back home and he was too full of joy to notice that his fourteen-year old nephew was stricken by the same malady as he.

Boju enlisted Subbu's help to try and find Chinni alone so he could declare his love. 'She's in the garden,' Subbu would tell his uncle; they would go there only to find that she had climbed the guava tree near the well. When they hurried to the tree, she was gone, her footprints heading for the stream. They would go there and find her on the other side, in earnest conversation with the neighbour's wife.

Chinni ate with the children at the long black table and Boju missed countless possibilities of engaging her attention during a meal. Subbu was fortunate: he sat opposite her and watched her eat the *akki otti*, holding it in her right hand with the left hand beneath the *otti* to catch the dripping butter and banana jam; he fought with his brothers to get the *otti* hot and crisp and offer it to her. She accepted the *otti* and ignored Subbu. When Chinni helped Nanji to pour warm oil into the ears of younger children with earache, Subbu developed an unbearable pain that needed oil twice a day. Boju saw him lay his head on Chinni's lap while she ministered to his imaginary pain, and that evening, he took Subbu behind a coffee bush and thrashed him. 'Next time you fake earache and go troubling her I'll shoot your ears straight off your head ,' he said. Subbu was too elated to realize that his uncle meant what he said.

Boju sat in her favourite guava tree, sure that she would come for the guavas she loved. He wrote her name on fruit that hung ripe from the tree, and waited, wrapped in the fragrance of bruised guavas that wafted into the house and across the compound to the stream from where he could hear laughter. But she never came.

In the evenings, he watched her clean the lamps. She lined them upon the long table, trimmed the wicks, wiped the glass shades and poured oil; then she lit the lamps and carried them to each room where they hung on racks like angels and cast winged shadows on the walls. Boju watched his angel move between light and shadow as she worked and he decided to dramatize his agony by offering her a cupful of his tears, or better still, a cupful of his blood, to pour into the lamps. 'Tears and blood don't light lamps,' Subbu said, wisely. 'She'll think you're dim.'

Chinni ignored Boju but she acknowledged Subbu's existence by teasing him. Subbu had once told her of his dream about the woman wearing nothing but a *vastra* draped over her hair and shoulders. It was a dream that he dreamed often and shared only with Chinni but when she told everyone, he felt cheated. But she said it was a blue *vastra* when actually it was white. Subbu kept that knowledge to himself as a consolation that he could keep some secrets from her.

Puthari was drawing near. Weeks before full moon, the fattest pig was slaughtered, the pork fried, topped with six inches of fat and stored in jars; a sack of jaggery was boiled with powdered rice and grated coconut, flavoured with cardamom and the sticky mixture made into laddus; bunches of bananas hung above the fireplace in the kitchen to ripen just in time for *thambuttoo* on Puthari day; the best quality *jeerige-sanna* rice was cleaned by three Yerava women. Their hair thick with dust from the rice and their mouths red with betel juice, they spanked and shouted at the children who scampered over the mounds of rice; the women laughed and joked as they worked because the best time of the year was only weeks away. As soon as Puthari was over and the paddy sold, coffee-picking would begin and that was the only time when the women took home twice as much as their husbands. Even when burdened with an infant straddled on a hip, the nimble-fingered women picked five or six barrels of coffee a day. At one anna per barrel, it was good money to take home.

For Boju, lovesick and fretting, the festivities seemed trite and unnecessary. Why worry over food, clothes and crackers, when his heart was at stake? 'I have a strategy that cannot fail,' he said to Subbu the day before Puthari. He explained it to his nephew and having won his approval, stood outside Nanji's bedroom and looked through the window. Chinni, with Subbu's sisters Chondakki and Kanike, was seated on a mat, rolling wicks for the lamps. Nanji sat on the bed and cut strips of cloth for the wicks. Boju muttered a short prayer and went round to the door.

'Baliyakka—I'm dancing the *kolata* at the *mandh* on Saturday.' He held the cluster of thin red canes in front of Chinni but spoke only to Nanji. 'Will you decorate the *kolu* for me?'

'Of course,' Nanji said, kindly. 'Go practise your footwork, and get your *kupya-chale* ready. I'll get it done.'

'The *Pariakali*,' Boju said, his voice now hoarse with frustration. 'I'm in it. I'm fighting Baletira Mandappa—'

'Mandu? No one's beaten Baletira Mandu at *Pariakali*!'

'I'll beat him.'

'Be careful, Boju.'

On Puthari night, when the first sheaves of paddy were cut to the cries of 'Poli, Poli Poli Deva . . .!' Boju's voice was the loudest. He looked at Chinni who carried the lamp with her hand cupping the flame, and he prayed that the most beautiful girl in Coorg would soon be his. When the sheaves were tied to doors and bed-posts, food and drink offered to the ancestors and crackers burst in the front yard, the men quenched their thirst with toddy. Boju drank in moderation and waited patiently for his heroic moment that was some twelve hours away.

In the village *mandh* in the morning, Boju in black-and-red *kupya-chale*, danced the *kolata*, matching his intricate footwork with the other dancers; in ever-decreasing circles, he moved, to the beat of drums, striking his cane-cluster with its tiny bells that had been strung with ribbons by Chinni. This music, layered on the music of the *kombu*, *kottu* and *dudi*, was to him like her saying, 'Kaliyanda Boju is the best!'

It was time for the *Pariakali*, in which the opponents strike each other with canes, but never above the waist. The sport at times is used to settle feuds between villages, and if the game gets fiercely bloody, sensible elders pull the opponents apart. The Takka, officiating, was watchful as the star performers, Boju and Mandu, embraced each other, moved back three paces, and began to stalk in slow circles as the *dudi* sounded its feathery beats. The beats became faster and the wind sang sharply through the canes as they aimed their swipes. They held their shields of woven bamboo before them, leapt in the air, and circled on their haunches, canes shrieking, shins dripping blood. Boju was precise, vicious and unstoppable. In the end, Mandu the Invincible lowered his shield and embraced Boju, acknowledging defeat. Boju did not hear the cheering that rose from the spectators. But when he looked over his opponent's shoulder, he saw Chinni hide her smile with her hands.

A few days after Puthari, Boju found Chinni alone near the stream and he said something to her about the music of the stream and fragrance of the pink-fleshed guavas she ate, but the breeze carried away his words and Chinni never heard him. Boju suffered; he felt like an old man who couldn't take another breath without it hurting. At Nanji's insistence, Chinni had begun to eat with the adults and the sight of her so close to him drove him to the limits of his sickness. So when Nanji said one day that it was time for Chinni to return home, Boju spoke out loud and clear: 'I will take her back to Tenth Mile.' Chinni smiled but when he added, 'I wish to speak to her father,' she burst into tears and refused to go.

Nanji intervened. She sent Chinni home with Boluka along with a letter for her father. Three weeks later came the reply that her father was willing to give his youngest daughter in marriage to Bojanna, the son of Rao Bahadur Madaiah.

Chapter Thirteen

Baliyanna was an arrogant vet with the belief that his work was superior to the money earned. Money was the by-product of his excellence and could not buy him prestige, which he already had. His clients were friends, neighbours, relatives or relatives of relatives; if and when they paid, it was in oranges, coffee or pepper for which Baliyanna had no use, he had enough of his own. Only the British paid promptly, but with less than fifty British planters in Coorg, the best vet led a life of genteel poverty.

If it hadn't been for Nanji's instinct to work and save, they would have become a family of paupers. She believed that if you wanted wealth, you had to put money and effort into the land. She put in the effort, but where was the money, the right amount at the right time? Fertilisers, sprays and manure had to be paid for in rupees which one did not have until the coffee from the previous year had been sold. Each year, one hoped that the blossom showers would come at the right time and that the monsoons would be adequate to soften the fields for ploughing. The ancestors did their best but sometimes it wasn't enough.

Baliyanna's generosity was laudable but it did not help to feed the family. He was incapable of returning from the Country Club without spending the last anna in his pocket. His friends accepted his hospitality with the cruelty of friends who never stop to think that the most generous of men will one day be penniless if he spends more than he earns.

Twelve children and an honourable husband amounted to heavy expenditure. Coffee prices were dismal and half the paddy produced was used for the family, workers, guests and beggars. Nanji struggled; she cared for the children, handled them in herds, spanked and loved them in a unit. She patched their clothes, reworked seams, shared out everything, wasted nothing; she taught her children to make do with essentials, which excluded luxuries like shoes, slippers and ornaments. Such things could wait until the boys went to college and the girls to their husbands' homes.

Lack of money was not such a terrible thing but Nanji was vexed by lack of purpose: 'There must be something better in life than hunting, and getting drunk at the Club,' she would tell her husband and he would only smile and try to comfort her with embraces. Nanji worried about the children. Her two girls would quietly fall into place when their time came but she wasn't sure about the boys. Most men were dreamers, with great dreams, but not the strength to make them come true. Nanji wanted to educate her boys so that they could go to Madras, maybe Calcutta; the one who showed promise would be sent across the seas to bring the fame that had been snatched away from the family when Machu drowned in the sea at Torquay and Appachu married a Christian.

Nanji longed to share her dreams with Baliyanna but she saw in the stoop of his shoulders and the haze in his grey eyes, the inevitable signs of depression. She knew it the day she saw him drag himself up the front steps when he returned from the Club via the huts of the gypsy whores. She watched him through the window—for it is easier to observe when you are not seen—and recognised in the reluctance of his movements the first signs of the pain of existence. Baliyanna indulged in long sessions of loneliness. He stared at the crazily swaying areca palms and let forth those heart-rending sighs that sounded like the bursting of air-filled paper bags. Nanji longed to comfort him, but knew that neither she nor the gods, the Country Club, the gypsy whores nor the English woman could do anything.

Nanji did not give up. From her grandmother she had

111

learnt that women were stronger than men. She remembered every line and shadow on her grandmother's face, the fissures on her work-worthy hands as she pounded rice, cleaned crabs or boiled hibiscus with coconut to make an oily concoction for the hair. When, exhausted after a day's work in the fields, they rested beneath the *athi* tree, she had pointed to the clouds wrapped around the hills of Thadiyandamolu.

'There live your forefathers.'

Nine-year-old Nanji did not pause to think if her grandmother was weaving a story or telling the truth. She watched the clouds that trailed like fugitives, unfurled as banners, became angels, warriors, weapons, rakshasas and gods. When Nanji was sad or afraid, she looked at the sky and even a few powdery, chopped-up clouds pulverised against a summer sky infused her with confidence. Neelakki said that the only honourable way to live was to rely on yourself and that was what Nanji did. She became a woman when still a child, faced widowhood after a luckless marriage and returned home to work like a servant until she was rescued by Baliyanna, a princely man with princely ideals. She saw her first-born die after three gasps, her father-in-law rot away from life and her father recede into the darkness of no return. Baliyanna's affliction would have made any woman bitter but Nanji barricaded her feelings with her iron strength and showed him only the warm, morning side of life.

Boju's marriage rescued Baliyanna temporarily from the onslaught of depression. 'It will be the grandest Kaliyanda wedding in two hundred years,' he announced at the Club. He had a shamiana built in the front yard of the house, a *mantap* for the *muhurtam* and a bamboo outhouse at the back for cooking; he bought floats and baubles from Mysore, five hundred bottles of soda and fifty of whisky. Nanji consoled herself that it was unavoidable expense and God willing, she would refill the casket in good time.

In his enthusiasm to put up the shamiana, Baliyanna cut down two of the best mango trees. Nanji saw the sacrilege when workers began to hack the massive trunks and she swallowed her dismay without berating her husband. He would regret it and his sadness would be punishment enough. But the felling affected Subbu. Mango trees were his favourite and he liked shinning up their rough trunks more than climbing easy trees with smooth effeminate branches. He had spent hours sitting beneath the trees in companionable silence with Boju. When the trees were felled and the branches dragged away like carcasses, the smell of crushed wood and leaves set off in Subbu an attack of wheezing. Nanji gave him a mixture of honey and pepper, made him inhale steam from an infusion of eucalyptus and dribbled milk boiled in turmeric up his nose. Then she wrapped him in five blankets, and kept him in bed for three days until the affliction left him.

Chambavva came from the House of Widows and she pleaded with Baliyanna to send for Appachu. 'This is the last family wedding, his only chance to eat proper pork, *kadambuttoo, palav* and mango chutney,' she said. She knew that her second son loved good food. She remembered his letters from England about the boiled meat with boiled cabbage, carrots and potatoes. At noon, you can smell cabbage up and down the length of England, he used to write. His stomach craved for chicken drowning in coconut gravy, for fish curry, aromatic *palav* and fried pork. Chambavva wondered how her son managed now, when his home was less than two days away and when he knew better than anyone that whatever the Kodavas did or did not do, they ate like kings, always.

'No, he cannot come,' Baliyanna said; the wedding proceeded without Appachu. At the *muhurtam*, Boju bent to touch the feet of his elders who had come to bless him. It was a ritual that left the bridegroom with a strained back but for Boju it hardly mattered. The heady fusion of floral fragrance that filled the *mantap* mingled with the elixir of love and made him immune to anything so insignificant as pain.

Subbu, standing behind the bridegroom to brush away

the rice grains that the guests sprinkled, could not share Boju's excitement. He had stopped talking to his uncle but that wasn't noticed by Boju or anyone else. Subbu knew that if he had been even three years older, if he had had the slightest downy growth on his chin and chest, and a voice not like a broken pin grating on stone, he would have staked his claim and challenged his uncle whom he now loathed. He nursed his grudge and schemed to defame him by less than honourable means. He longed to grab the *peeche-kathi* from his uncle's waist and to drive it through him, but not having the courage, fed him senna in his coffee—a potent, veterinary dose usually reserved for constipated horses, then waited with criminal glee for it to take effect.

It was a splendid wedding. Women flitted about, offering drinks and snacks; the village beauties preened in silk saris and puff-sleeved jackets, with the half-moon *kokkethathi* of ruby and pearl reclining on their bosoms, chains of beaded gold and serpent-hooded pendants hugging their lovely necks; tiger-claw brooches, peacock earrings and bangles of diamonds suggested the solidity of the girl's background. The most bashful men shed their shyness and danced and even as they danced, looked at the preening beauties. The Kodava girls were not so shy that they could not look into the eyes of men, read messages and send messages.

Clara would have turned down the invitation to the wedding but when she saw her name written on the envelope in the vet's hand, she knew she must see him. She wore a blue suit with hat and gloves but in the midst of all the colour and gold, her dress looked too plain and the hat, ludicrous. Baliyanna left her in the company of the women who plied her with food, smiles and hospitality. It was the General who saved her. 'I've come to keep you company,' he said, drawing up a chair, and then it wasn't too bad. He spoke charmingly even while expressing his displeasure about the British rule. 'It's time they made a graceful exit, don't you think, Madam?' At lunch, he wanted her to taste everything. Clara ate bravely but when he offered her soda in a bottle with a marble stopper, the pink colour turned her stomach and she refused it, and would not change her mind even when he exchanged it for yellow and then green soda.

In the afternoon, the wedding party set off for the bride's home in Tenth Mile. The women went in carts, the men rode horses or walked. A short while after they had crossed the stream and got on the road in a long column of carts, horses, men and children, their progress was hampered by the bridegroom having to visit the bushes. He had to repeat the visit soon after, and then again—in all, no less than fifteen times. The elders became worried enough to consider a postponement of the wedding, but Boju was confident of his constitution. He believed that the frequent evacuation of his bowels was a manifestation of overexcited love. Good fortune prevailed and all was well by the time they reached Tenth Mile. It was past midnight and at the bride's home the wedding feast had been heated and reheated. Subbu prepared to execute one last effort in defence of his love by making a speech, but even as he tried to summon courage, he saw Boju garland Chinni and make her his wife. 'I will not covet my uncle's wife,' he promised himself virtuously and sobbed softly through the ceremony until early next morning, when the wedding party returned to Athur.

Boju's wedding marked Chambavva's last visit home. It also established the final statement of Nanji's celibacy. She changed from the green and gold star-spangled sari that she wore for the wedding into a white handloom with a dull brown border, and from then on she never wore anything but white with borders of blue, green and black that were no less dismal than the first.

Nanji suggested that the newlyweds stay on in the house. 'It's big enough for all of us,' she said. Boju liked the effortlessness of such an arrangement and Chinni was pleased that she could stay with her sister. The marriage itself was idyllic, given Chinni's innocence and Boju's ardour. Only

Subbu suffered his martyrdom in silence. Gone were the days of aimless wanderings, cockfights and surreptitious smoking. He steered away from his brothers and playmates, avoided Chinni and when he had to speak, he was serious and dignified. He had a strange fear that she might visit his dreams and discover that he often dreamt about her; and at night, he tormented himself with an overworked imagination about his uncle making love to his aunt.

In a big house with many children, the listlessness of one is likely to go unnoticed. But Nanji saw it, and knew that her son needed sorting out. Subbu was in the process of struggling into manhood, a stage when boys became unhappy for silly reasons. Nanji herself had no time to brood over disappointments but she cared a lot for this son of hers. She pondered as she went about her work and one day suggested to her husband that perhaps Subbu could stay at Crystal Palace with Chambavva for a while. 'Your mother will be happy to have someone do her marketing,' she said. 'And Subbu can go to the school in Kunda.' Baliyanna knew that Nanji must have a good enough reason for sending Subbu away and he agreed readily; Subbu did not care one way or the other.

When Chambavva saw her grandson, with his unnaturally long arms, pendulous earlobes and sadness dripping from his eyes, her anile heart was overcome and she decided to set things right for him. Chambavva had aged: her soft, round baby face was an overripe fruit held together by thin skin. Over the years, she had developed an intimate friendship with the bottle and in that large-hearted household of widows, she could drink freely. She carried the bottle like most women carry their purse or umbrella. The inmates of the house knew what it was like to be shackled to husband, home and society, and that past experience made them extremely sympathetic to each other's minor vices and addictions. People said the widows were crazy but the truth was that they were women who had learnt to be unafraid.

Chambavva's awakened maternal instinct told her that

what Subbu urgently needed was discipline. She saw to it that he attended school with unfailing regularity and after school, studied for two hours. Then she had him help her cook dinner and when darkness fell, sent him to the arrack shop to refill her bottle. Subbu was obedient and trouble-free, only once he tried gentle treachery by pocketing three pice from the two annas she gave him. Chambavva squinted at the money and caught his ear in a vicelike grip until he relinquished the three-pice coin in his pocket. Nights, he slept on a narrow cot opposite her four-poster bed. She tucked herself in and said, 'Uhn.' Subbu began to read. It was the same routine every night, strictly a chapter a day from the thick, cloth-bound volume of the *Ramayana*. Lulled by his own voice, the dim light of the lamp and his grandmother's crepitous breathing, Subbu would be weighed down with drowsiness. At times he tried to skip pages but Chambavva couldn't be fooled. She poked him with the stick that she kept by her bed. 'Low-caste bum! Turn the page back to where Sugreeva challenges Vali to battle!'

She fed him well and the widows fussed over him. Subbu grew taller, his neck elongated, arms dangled through shirt sleeves, and thighs showed brown below the edge of his shorts. When he went home after six months, he had grown three inches and had to look down at Chinni. He spent a week at home and then went back to Crystal Palace, just three days before the tragedy.

It was Sunday. Bolle brought an offering of mushrooms tied in her sari—the first pick after the thunder showers—wide, thick, fleshy mushrooms that were a lustrous black on top and a delicate, lambent white underneath. Mushrooms were Boju's favourite: Chinni washed and fried them with onions and tomato and stirred in a paste of garlic, ginger and turmeric. She spooned some into her palm, licked the gravy and ate the mushroom. 'Perfect,' she said, happily, covered the vessel and left it by the fire so it would stay hot for lunch. Then she went to her favourite guava tree to hide in the topmost leafy branch until Boju returned from the *santhe* as always, with crisp *jalebis* and a leaf-cup of jasmine. She saw him turn in at the gate. Laughing, she began to climb down and her foot missed a branch; as she fell, a sharp piece of wood spiked her left eye, and went all the way in, six inches.

Chapter Fourteen

Boju wandered aimlessly, conjuring up visions of Chinni. He saw her toe pebbles in the water, her ankles blinding him as she waded the stream; he saw her lean over the well and let the pitcher down, and he wept because he wasn't sure if it was the gurgle of water, or Chinni laughing; he saw her on the guava tree, her limbs smooth like the branches, he listened to her sigh when he sighed, heard her breathe when he breathed; on Sundays, he brought crisp orange *jalebis* and a string of jasmine from the *santhe* and left them on Chinni's dressing table where they stayed until the flies had feasted on the *jalebis* and the flowers turned brown. The servants threw them away when Boju wasn't around.

Subbu had come from the House of Widows to be his uncle's companion, dog and shadow. Boju longed to die but he knew that Chinni had had a revulsion for suicide which was common in Coorg. Two weeks after Chinni's death, Kambiranda Bollakka jumped into the well; the following week, Ballachanda Kalappa shot himself and Adengada Gappu excused himself in the middle of his daughter's wedding, went to his room, untied the red-and-gold sash round his waist and hanged himself with it. Motiveless suicides, with no letters of indictment or farewell. With death in the air, and a series of funerals in the neighbourhood, Boju was tempted. He begged Subbu to remove sharp objects, guns, knives and ropes from his reach, so he would not succumb to his weakness and anger Chinni. Baliyanna worried that the sorrow which was above tears or weeping would drive his brother mad. When Nanji said, 'Why not send Boju to sell the coffee in Mangalore?' Baliyanna was relieved. He had grown used to the fact that Nanji, with her sharp intellect and reasoning mind, usually came up with the best solution.

Every year after Puthari, when the week-long feasting and the village sports were over, Kodavas got down to the serious business of selling coffee at the auction markets of Mangalore. A month before the event, the ripe red coffee beans were plucked, dried in the sun till they turned black, packed into sacks and stacked in bullock-carts. The carts then set off on the three hundred-mile-long journey through the hills, with armed guards to protect them from tigers, wolves and dacoits.

'I'll go if I can take Subbu with me,' Boju said.

As soon as they left home, Boju handed over the responsibility to his nephew and retreated into his sorrow. Subbu hadn't any choice but to take it like a man. He fed the bullocks, rested them and replaced the sick ones; in the hot, dry afternoons, he huddled against the sacks of coffee in the cart and slept; at night he watched the eyes of the bullocks that shone like scattered stars and listened to the music of the bells round their necks mingling with the songs of the riders trying to stay awake, and he was sure that he heard the tigers and wolves not far away. Danger pursued the travellers until they left the hills and reached the plains of Tulunad. When the bullocks smelt the sea breeze, they slowed their pace and the men knew that they were close to the plains, and out of danger.

The hardships of the journey passed Boju by like a dream. The coffee was sold at the auction in Mangalore and like the others, he received money in silver coins; he stuffed them into a bag that Nanji had given him and they started the journey back.

On the last night, when the carts grated along the road between Madikeri and Athur, Boju said, 'I'm sure there is life after death. Chinni lives. I must talk to her.'

Subbu tried to reason with his uncle. When a person died, the body disintegrated beneath the ground or was charred by flames. Chinni had died, properly. It wasn't one of her jokes, she wasn't playing some vanishing game just to tease them. But his uncle was unconvinced. 'I'll talk to Chinni,' he said.

At dawn, when Nanji heard the carts approaching the stream, she lit the lamp in the puja room and came out to welcome them. Boju washed his feet, sprinkled rice into the copper pitcher and handed the bag to Nanji. 'Here's the money, Baliyakka.'

'How much?'

'I'm not sure . . . will you count?' With an apologetic look, he went in to the house.

'Arrange the coins in stacks of ten,' Nanji told Subbu. They counted the coins and tested them for counterfeits by striking each coin on the floor; then Nanji put them in the green casket in the chest beneath her bed.

Boju meanwhile searched the bookshelves in the front room till he found the title: *Occult Practices and the Dead. Part 1.* Clara had rescued the book but many pages had been ruined by termites and what remained were words on a paper filigree of pages. Boju shut himself in his room and struggled to comprehend the half-destroyed words. When it became dark, he cried to the servants to light him a lamp and when none came he seized the lamp, filled it with kerosene, lit the wick and read all night; when the moon was out, he wandered out to read in the blue brightness that was better than the lamp's. A few weeks later, he wrote to his brother in Bangalore and asked him to get *Occult Practices and the Dead. Part 2, Self Hypnosis, Death and Afterlife* and *Conversation with the Dead.* 'I'll pay you for everything,' he wrote.

From the urgent, desperate scrawl, Appachu understood that the tragedy of his brother's love was worthy of help. The Barrister himself had not been lucky. He had married because of an illusory longing which he mistook for love, and got deeply enmeshed before he realized that he had been momentarily blinded by the glow of Marjorie's pink arms. That shrewd daughter of an undertaker in Tooting Bec had lured him into her solid arms that later looked to Appachu like great big cuts of meat. He had struggled helplessly and then lain quiet and married for eleven years. He had become a Catholic to please his wife, changed his name to Basil Pinto and gone to church where the padre proclaimed that suffering was good for the soul. Appachu could never believe that suffering was good for him. May, June, Patrick and Emerald were born and then a longing for his past began to surface. He longed to go back to Athur and be a Kodava again but how could he when his own brother had denounced him? One Sunday, he sat in his pew next to his wife and four children and contemplated his plight. The sermon ended and the congregation said 'Amen.' Through that devout sound reverberating from the chapel walls was heard another— 'Om . . . It came from the depth of Appachu's penitent soul. The padre was convulsed with anger, the pious crossed themselves, Marjorie, May and June burst into tears; five-year old Patrick who was clean fed up with the dreary sermon, giggled and Emerald, only two, clapped her hands. Appachu never went to church again and the battles began at home. He fantasized about running away, he even packed a bag in readiness for flight. He had read or heard somewhere that if you wished for something with all your heart you could make it come true. Appachu wished fervently that he would lose his wife and not be able to find her. His prayers were answered sooner than he had hoped. Even the loss of silverware, money and two daughters did not hurt. He was free, and he had his son and Emerald, the youngest. Appachu never found out why Marjorie did not take the sniffling son and podgy daughter with her. He suspected it was because Patrick had giggled in church and Emerald had clapped her hands.

When Boju asked for the books, Appachu wrote to a bookshop in Bloomsbury and three months later, the books arrived. They cost him two pounds, ten shillings and sixpence, which was a lot of money for a Barrister living in a roofless room but he never asked Boju to pay him.

Boju allowed Subbu to read with him, knowing that the

boy understood only about a tenth of what he read. They were both like children learning. They filled in the gaps by arguing with each other or they supplied facts from their imaginations.

A month later, Boju decided to try his experiment. Nanji was in the fields and Baliyanna was attending a sick calf in Ammathi. Boju locked himself in the bedroom with Subbu, darkened the windows with black paper and sat himself on the bed. 'When I have excluded every thought from my mind and achieved a complete blank,' Boju explained, 'the luminous light of the other world will appear before me. Don't disturb me till I speak.' He closed his eyes. Subbu waited; after a very long while, Boju rose unsteadily to his feet.

'Notepad and pen! Quick!'

Subbu opened the window just a slit so he could see, and gave his uncle the writing pad and pen. Boju sat with the pen poised over the blank page. The pen shivered and flew across the page, leaving behind a line and a half of indecipherable squiggles and words. Chinni had proved her existence.

Boju stopped his restless wandering; he would not eat, drink or speak to anyone but Subbu in whom he confided that he would bring Chinni back, or go over to the other side.

One evening, Subbu saw his uncle readying the boxcart for a journey.

'Uncle, where are you going?'

'To see her.'

'Can I come?'

They pushed the cart through the shallow water downstream, hitched the horses and began their journey through the chill haze of an October morning. Halfway through the journey, Boju said, 'Last night, she told me she will meet me in Tenth Mile, at the foot of the slope that leads to her father's house.' Late in the afternoon, they reached the bridge across the Kaveri river at Siddapur and they stopped to rest the horses and eat. As the sun moved west Boju became restless. He whipped the horses, and when Subbu said that the horses were doing their best, he shouted at him.

The long journey tired Subbu and he closed his eyes. When he opened them, the hills stood black against a sky shot with twilight gold. He nodded off, and on waking saw a purple sky turn violet and then black—trees, hills, sky and earth merged in darkness; he couldn't see a thing and he wasn't sure if his eyes were open or shut. The lantern dangling from the side of the box cart went out and Boju goaded the horses to go faster on that narrow road where one false step meant a fall down the slope. A half moon rose in the sky; when they were a few furlongs from Tenth Mile, Boju stopped the cart.

'Get out.'

'Please uncle. Let me come.'

'I promised Chinni I'd meet her alone,' Boju said and pushed him out. 'I'll be back in the morning.' He whipped the horses to a start, then he looked over his shoulder. 'Get off,' he shouted again.

'Uncle, that's your shadow.'

'I can feel the son-of-a-whore's spittle on my neck.' He wiped the collar of his shirt, and kicked the vacant seat. 'Did he get off?'

'Yes, uncle.'

Boju drove off, leaving Subbu stranded in the darkness.

When the cart was gone, Subbu moved to the side of the road and groped along a hedge till he found the stile to enter the estate. He climbed in and lay shivering on the soft mud beneath a coffee bush. He wasn't sure if he slept or if he became unconscious from fear and more than once he heard Chinni's laughter carried by the wind. In the last deep hour of sleep, he dreamt that he had become lame again. His legs had withered into useless twigs, he had to be carried around. When he woke, the dream was vivid in his mind and he didn't dare to try his legs. If God had been foolhardy enough to make him a Kunta a second time in one life, he would pay dearly for it.

Fortunately for God, Subbu's legs were normal. He wiped the mud off his clothes and set off towards Tenth Mile. Daylight made him bolder, more curious. His uncle had spent all that time with Chinni, so he wouldn't mind Subbu seeing her now. He reached the foot of the slope and saw the cart by the edge of the road, screened by the branches of an *athi* tree. His uncle wasn't there, nor was Chinni.

He ran up the slope, all the way, until he reached the house of his grandfather. A few days later, he was taken home to Athur and in a month, he returned to the House of Widows.

Chapter Fifteen

'The House of Widows is not for mourning,' Chambavva said.

Subbu did everything with a donkey-like devotion; he washed clothes, went to the market, chased intruders from the compound and looked after the five fatherless infants. On Sunday afternoons, when the widows rested, Subbu patted the babies to sleep and roamed the house, trying to weave a link between the tragedy of the widows and his own. He refused to be conquered by the mystery of death or the futility of love and pondered over the injustice of his uncle's disappearance. One Sunday Chambavva found Subbu lost in his reverie while the babies kicked and cried in their cradles. She had to slap him six times before he came round.

Chambavva had the clear vision of the elderly. 'Subbu needs the company of boys his age,' she wrote to her son. 'For eight rupees a month, he can be a boarder at the Madikeri Convent School.'

Baliyanna told Nanji, who arranged a hasty sale of pepper in order to get the thirty-two-rupee deposit for the school. They were sliding deeper into poverty which, though honourable, was no less difficult. After sending the two older sons to college in Mangalore, Nanji knew that for the rest, Matriculation would have to do. Subbu, who did not know of it at that time, had decided he was going to be someone but did not know who and he could never concentrate on his desires long enough to decide.

The Convent School in Madikeri had been designed by Irish nuns dedicated to discipline. Classrooms were built like barracks; windows distracted young minds and were therefore dispensed with in favour of a skylight in the tiled roof and one small hole near the blackboard, so the teacher could look out and escape the dullness; walls were painted black three-quarters of the way up and then a dirty white to avoid brightness that might distract. The thirteen nuns of the convent wore black habits and starched white wimples that projected four inches beyond the face, and a wooden cross on their bosoms. They prayed six times a day and caned the children. Rich Kodavas could send their children to schools in Ooty, Coonoor or Bangalore but the middle class made do with the Convent School. When all was said and done it was run by white Christian nuns and reputed to be better than the Municipal School. If one had asked the children, they would have said that if it wasn't for the kind-hearted Neema Rose in the dining room, Sister Brigitte in the office, and Nursie, it would have been unbearable.

Sister Brigitte was a kind woman whose harshest punishment was to make the students kneel in her office and say a hundred Hail Marys. Sister Neema Rose, with her wrestler's build and golden hair on her masculine arms, sneaked in extra rations like bananas and oranges for the boarders, although Mother Superior made it clear that basic food did not include luxuries. And Nursie, who was soon to be a nun, looked after the children's ailments with considerable kindness. The boys constantly fell sick so they could go to her room and watch her adipose body swimming inside her dress as she moved.

Boarders were divided into three classes as distinct as castes. Parlour Boarders ate in a dainty curtained room next to the chapel, got chicken on Sundays, honey with their bread, and had their sheets washed once a fortnight. Their parents paid twelve rupees a month to maintain their children in this state of luxury. Ordinary Boarders ate in a barrack-style dining room, washed their own plates and bathed once a week. And Third Class Boarders slept on the floor and no one knew what they ate. They had big, hungry eyes and skinny bodies and they fared badly in school. It was said that they were orphans and illegitimate, unwanted children baptized in the chapel and raised by the nuns to wash, sweep, cook and maintain the dignity and neatness for which the convent was famous. Subbu was an Ordinary Boarder. The drudgery of learning, the gnawing hunger, the meanness of nuns, teachers, bullies and sneaks occupied all of Subbu's thoughts and left no place for sorrow.

The nuns employed twelve teachers; of them only two were not stupid, slovenly, greedy or mean. Kodira Chengappa, the English master, started class at nine hundred hours with *'God Save The King'*. He wore a brown hat that had faded with the years into a dusty buff, a tie that had turned from blue to grey, and shoes that were resoled and stitched with twine every two years. Chengu Master was in love with the English language and his mission in life was to teach it. Subbu was better at English than the others and Chengu Master liked to show him off before the class. He would hold a bunch of keys or a box of matches and ask: 'What is this?'

'Key bunch!'

'Match box!'

'Subbaiah?'

'A bunch of keys, Sir. A box of matches, Sir.'

Chengu Master's fascination for the English culture was not based on any petty ambition to please, it did not rise out of the complex that led many to ape the rulers. Chengappa's love was pure. When he married, he changed the name of his wife from Muthamma to Pearlie, encouraged her to sew frilly, valentine cushions with figures of English maids in crinolines, and photographed her in printed frocks and high heels along with their children Shirley, Sally and Prince.

Chengappa had been at school with Barrister Appachu. When he heard that Appachu's unfortunate marriage had ended, he journeyed to Bangalore to see his friend. He met the lawyer in his roofless room, half of which was partitioned off with a tarpaulin and served as living quarters for the Barrister and his two children. Seated behind a ramshackle table weighted with papers and a typewriter, Appachu displayed a graceful serenity that puzzled Chengu.

'Appachu, my friend—I sympathize,' he began.

'Chengu, don't waste your sentiments. The marriage was a mistake. Now I wake every morning in this humble home and thank God for the release. I'm a happy man, Chengu.'

'Are you—still a Christian?'

'When my wife was kind enough to leave me, I dropped her religion. I'm a Kodava again.'

'We need a good lawyer in Madikeri.'

'My brother threatened me with a gun, my mother showed me the door, only Baliyakka was kind. No, my friend. I will stay here. Times are precarious and clients shy away from an advocate who cannot afford a roof over his head. But I have confidence and talent. Only, I wish better for my children. Can you help?'

Chengu returned to Kodagu with Patrick and Emerald. Appachu would have liked to give them a head start as Parlour Boarders but the fee of twelve rupees a month was not affordable, so they joined as Ordinary Boarders and Chengu Master was their guardian.

Patrick was tall and scruffily handsome, with his mother's big, popping eyes, retractile eyelids, and long limbs. His knees knocked, his large flat flipper feet got in his way; his khaki school shorts ended way up the middle of his thighs and he had the self-conscious stoop of frenzied anabolism. He injured himself constantly so Nursie gave him a bottle of tincture of iodine and cotton to carry in his pocket for emergencies.

Patrick, who was several years older than the others, turned out to be one of the cleverest boys in the school and once the teachers realised it, they left him alone and concentrated their cruelty on others. Subbu admired Patrick for the sharpness of his mind and wicked irreverence. Appachu hoped his son would join a prestigious medical or engineering college, but Patrick looked beyond such limits, his popping eyes were fixed on a future infinitely greater than that his father wished for him. He indulged in schoolboy mischief but never forgot for a moment that he must snap out of the mediocrity of his environment. The only thing that interested him was his own future. Patrick's behaviour was not always exemplary but he made it a point to attend chapel every morning. His father had told him that the best religion in the world could stuff itself up its arse but Patrick was worldly enough to keep his gods until he could decide if he needed them or not.

Like Chengu Master, the Maths teacher was an exception. Satyanarayana was a *shendi*-sprouting brahmin with gold ear-studs, *janiwara* and a streak of white ash on his forehead signifying his Saraswat caste. He lived with his family in the two rooms behind the Omkareshwara temple. In the mornings, he performed the *abhisheka* and *mangalarathi*, hitched a clean white dhoti between his hairy legs, put on a coarse brown coat to protect him from the morning chill and set off for the Convent School, with his seven children trailing behind. His children ranged from five to fifteen and all but Govinda were girls in *lehenga* and blouse with orange *kanakambara* braided into their plaits. There were teachers who maligned and hated Satyu for his scrupulous, near-fanatic integrity but it was impossible to deny the first position to any of his children.

Watching Satyu Sir in class as he explained the intricacies of algebra, Subbu was aware of the grandeur of austerity. The same austerity attracted him to puny, ever-smiling Govinda with the beaked upper lip and small black eyes. Govinda had one set of clothes that was washed every night and worn next morning. He was the only student besides Patrick whom the teachers never scolded or whipped or asked to frog-jump. The nuns wished he was a Catholic so they could display him as an example of good behaviour. On Sundays, Subbu followed him to his home behind the temple where his mother served coffee in small brass cups, and *upittoo* or *vadas* with coconut chutney.

Subbu's other friend was Sunny Boy, the son of a poor Kodava widow who agreed to have her only son baptized in exchange for free board, lodging and education. As a bonus, she was allowed to sweep the dormitories and make the Parlour Boarders' beds. The teachers, nuns and students said Sunny Boy was mentally slow; but beneath his vacant smiles, rambling conversation and rare, explosive temper, there was wisdom and gentleness in Sunny. He was the friend of stray dogs, cats, lame pigeons and the decrepit cows that wandered near the school. He stole food to feed his animal friends and if he caught any boy stoning dogs or harassing a cow or cat, he would knock him down with a leg twist and a punch in the belly. He had an infantile honesty the awkwardness of which showed, and it set him apart. Subbu liked Sunny. A week after he joined the Convent School, he gave him his brown half-sleeved coat with eight pockets that had belonged to Boju uncle and was too loose for him. Sunny was strongly built, much bigger than boys his age and on his broad shoulders, it looked good.

Sunny had an infected leg wound that Nursie and the local doctors had given up on. The day Subbu gave him the brown coat, Sunny expressed his gratefulness by showing him the ulcer. A sickening sweet odour rose from the wound as Sunny peeled off the bandage made of sleeves ripped from the castaway shirts of Parlour Boarders. The inner layers were yellowed and adhered to the dusky, serpiginous margins of the ulcer, the centre of which was pink and heaped over with glistening, cream-coloured maggots.

'If I show it to Nursie she'll pour turpentine on the wound and that will choke the maggots,' he said. 'They nibble my flesh painlessly, where's the harm? Only thing is they multiply so fast. Once a week, I pick them out, like this, with my fingers, put them in this leaf cup tacked together with twigs and leave them in the bushes.' When he had found a refuge for the maggots in the moist, hospitable soil, he rewrapped the bandage over the wound. 'Sometimes the smell gets too much and then I put toothpaste on it to make it smell better,' he said. 'Discarded tubes thrown in the dustbin by the nuns and by Father Leece. Give the tube a good squeeze, and there's usually enough paste to last a week. Lovely stuff.'

With Patrick, Subbu renewed his habit of smoking and from him absorbed an elaborate knowledge of sex. Once, he visited Chambavva at the House of Widows with Sunny and Patrick. They were fed tasty snacks but the youngest widow complained to Chambavva about the salacious look in Patrick's protuberant eyes and the unbearable sweet odour that emanated from the leg wound of the imbecile. So their first visit was their last.

Six months after Subbu joined the Convent School, Baliyanna came to visit. Subbu saw in him the first signs of slovenliness. His shirt was crumpled, the buttons loose, his shoulders soft and doughy, the assertive paunch flaccid, the front seam of his trousers gaping. He came with a packet of puffed rice mixed with round pink sweets that he had bought in a Mapla shop in Gonicoppa.

As Subbu ate, Baliyanna explained the sad state of their fortunes. They had only picked half a *candy* of coffee that year; Subbu's two older brothers in Mangalore were a perpetual drain on the finances. They did not clear the exams, spent heavily, borrowed, and wrote letters with reasons concocted to wheedle money from Nanji. After five years in college, neither had cleared Intermediate and when they came home in the holidays, they behaved like strangers. 'I'll try and see you through high school but I cannot promise,' Baliyanna told his son. 'Then you'll come home and help your mother.'

When Subbu told his friends, they were stunned. 'There's the scholarship money of five rupees a month,' Govinda said. 'You can get it, if you work hard.'

'Get baptized by Mother Catherine Joseph, she'll let you stay,' was Sunny's advice. 'You don't have to be an orphan or anything, but you have to be Christian.'

Christianity was the dullest religion in the world, but becoming a Christian was a small price to pay if it would enable him to finish school. He began to visit the chapel every evening, to kneel and cross himself and dip his fingers in holy water. He looked at the sweet bland porcelain figures of Jesus, Mary and Joseph and couldn't connect them with God. His own gods were exciting, ferocious, heroic and full of tricks. Patrick was dead against Subbu's scheme of conversion. 'Don't offend your gods,' he said. 'Stay with what you got at birth. Look what happened to my father. Spat upon by the Christians, kicked in the arse by the family. Don't be a fool. You can't stop after high school. You've got to be a double graduate. Or an LMP, or a Barrister.'

Subbu felt that Sunny Boy's advice was the best. Sister Catherine Joseph who minded the chapel was delighted with Subbu's transformation. Standing on the stone steps to the chapel she held forth about the purity of Christ and the sinful indulgences of the Hindu gods. Subbu, listening, felt like a traitor.

A month before the exams, the Mother Superior summoned Subbu to her office. With elaborate kindness she told him that they were forced to send him home. 'Your father hasn't paid you fees for six months. We cannot keep your on charity forever.' The humiliation went deep. For six months, he had lived on the generosity of the nuns, it was impossible to consider staying even a day longer; and he was too proud to ask about being baptized.

Subbu left without telling his friends. He walked all the way from Madikeri to Athur, stopping a night in Tenth Mile where his grandfather was in the terminal stages of his illness.

Nanji was at the stream, bartering with a Mapla. Sardines and bananas changed hands, the Mapla took the bananas and the three pice that Nanji gave for tea, and crossed the ramp; the Yerava woman lifted a basket of sardines on to her head and Subbu helped heave two more baskets to put on top of the

133

first. Then he told Nanji.

'A few months. I'll scratch up the money to send you back to school,' Nanji said. They walked home, following the Yerava woman and the smell of sardines.

Chapter Sixteen

There were more calamities to come: The two sons of Nanji and Baliyanna who were studying at Mangalore contracted typhoid and died within eight days of each other, the funeral for Gappanna coinciding with the seventh-day ceremony for Kaverappa. The deaths became the catalyst to the causeless depression of Baliyanna who now felt guiltless enough to begin drinking before breakfast. While Nanji groped in the shadow of death, her ninth son began to vomit worms. The six-inch-long, pink things began to come out of his mouth, ears, eyes and navel and they formed a fist-sized ball that blocked his guts. The British surgeon in Madikeri cut him open and scooped out a whole basin of worms which wriggled on the floor of the operating theatre long after the belly of the dead boy had been neatly sutured.

That was three dead, in eight weeks; Nanji bore the shock as if it were a physical battering and was grateful for the never-ending rituals of mourning which left no time to brood. 'I've nine living,' she said to neighbours who came to mourn with her, and offered them coffee and *thaliya puttoo* with tomato jam.

Nanji wasn't callous, just truthful. She cared for her children. The son who suffered from constipation had been cured when he ate a whole jackfruit, purged fourteen times in an hour and from then on began to frequent the pit amidst the coffee bushes like the rest; the boy with a musical cry had got over his weeping tantrums and become a sober lad with good manners. Of her two daughters, Chondakki was the plump, red-faced, giggly type whose stupid gaiety annoyed Nanji. She would have no trouble hooking a husband. Kanike was tall and bony, with bat ears that Nanji had tried to massage into shape when she was a baby, lustreless grey eyes and long hair that fell in a frigid plait behind her. She tried to compromise with her height by walking with her bosom in and knees flexed but it made her even less attractive.

Nanji wasn't in any way proud of her children. They were all normal, and mediocre. It saddened her. She wished she could do something to stimulate their feeble brains but can you make great men that way? And Subbu, who she knew was destined for greatness, was back at the Gonicoppa school, showing his lack of interest by wandering with his friends. With them he poached, stole, and when bored, frequented the hospital with a pretended cough to wheedle the sweet, marigold-coloured, peppermint-smelling cough mixture from Dr Seshagiri, until the doctor realised the truth and added quinine to the mixture.

At forty-six, Nanji accepted the status of old age with grace. She wore no jewels except for two black bangles on her bony wrists, gold studs high on her earlobes and a nose ring which had worked its way into her flesh and would not come off. She had gifted away all her tiger-claw brooches but three which she kept for her daughters-in-law. She spurned fashion even before the days of nationalistic fervour, when it became fashionable to be unfashionable and women rejected colour, silks and ornaments in favour of handspun khadi. But Nanji had always held beauty in contempt. She never looked at herself until after Subbu was born, when Baliyanna bought her a hand-sized mirror framed in blue-painted wood. In it, Nanji could see three-quarters of her face and she used it every morning to check that her hair was parted in the middle. She never gave herself a chance to worry about the craggy lines that had formed around her eyes, the varicose veins that stood out green and tortuous on her legs, or the outward tilt of her right hip, from carrying Subbu till he was eight. Nanji had faith in her robust constitution and good appetite. She ate meat, ghee, rice, and puris fried in pork fat without gaining an ounce of weight, she never suffered from indigestion or colic. When Baliyanna doubled his intake of toddy, Nanji began taking snuff. The cylindrical, thumb-sized tin in its saffron wrapper which she added to the *santhe* list each week was her only luxury. Twice a day, she took the tin from beneath her mattress where she kept it with her keys, prayed briefly to the figure of the Trimurthi on the saffron-coloured wrapper, pressed a pinch of the pungent powder to her nostrils and wiped away the excess with the free edge of her sari. Snuff was the only comfort she allowed herself while she weathered tragedies. Then came the calamity at the stream.

Kanike was seventeen and engaged to marry the son of Kolimada Karumabaiah in two months. Nanji's days were full: jars of mango, lime, and bamboo pickle lined the attic, spices and jaggery were bought in sacks and three pigs reared for slaughter; she made two forays out of Coorg to buy Mysore silk saris and leather slippers for the bride; she summoned the goldsmith from Thalacheri to the Kaliyanda house to weigh her sovereigns and made him promise to have the earrings, *pathak, kokkethathi* and pearl necklace ready in a month.

Kanike understood the misfortune of being too tall and too plain. Her complex about her looks gave her a haughtiness around the mouth and eyes and it put people off, although she regularly complained to Nanji about amorous-eyed men who followed her if she went to the stream or the fields. She preferred the company of the Gowda girl from the house across the stream because she was as plain-looking as herself. That day, she went to the stream with clothes to wash but the clothes were an excuse to gossip with her friend. Two strapping lads were busy at work in the Jammada orange grove near the stream and their presence provoked the girls into a fit of giggles. The boys peeped through the hedge and it triggered Kanike's excitement to such an extent that she lost her balance and slipped off the rock she stood on. Her friend screamed, the two lads leaped over the stile and rushed to the rescue. While they argued as to which of them should have the privilege of a chivalrous act, Boluka, who saw the mishap, jumped in and grabbed Kanike by the hair.

Kanike was furious that the Yerava had messed up her chance of a dramatic rescue. 'Don't touch me!' she cried and hit him. Her fist landed in Boluka's face and broke four of his already loose, rotting teeth; he fell back in the water with a momentary dizziness. Children on their way back from school gawked, the Gowda girl wailed and the two lads argued, while Kanike was carried off downstream. Two days later, she was washed ashore near the orange grove—garlanded in weeds, her skirt around her neck and the washing soap dented with the print of her petrified fingers.

Baliyanna never recovered from the tragedy. Nanji encouraged him to go hunting in the hope that the hardships and real dangers of hunting would help slough off the illness that clung to him like dirt. Baliyanna agreed because he wanted to please his wife. He went with his team of two Kodavas, six Yeravas and six dogs. At times he took Subbu with him because the boy was both helpful and unobtrusive. Once, in the hot dry month of Minyar, before the monsoons, they wandered for four days without luck. The supply of rice ran out but the men were loath to go back empty-handed. They pushed deeper into the jungles of Kuthnad, surviving on wild fruit and berries, until Subbu thought he would die of hunger and exhaustion. On the fourth day, in the cold grey light of morning, when he spotted a deer grazing not ten yards from where they slept, he seized his father's double-barrelled gun and aimed. He missed and the deer escaped, leaving a trail of blood.

'The usual punishment,' Baliyanna said, refusing to listen to the other men who felt that the boy should be forgiven.

Bravely, Subbu leaped over the boughs of bramble held by two men who raised them as he jumped. The cuts on his thighs which bled freely were not as hurtful as the humiliation of the punishment. 'Hands steady, eyes sharp, reflexes quick,'

Baliyanna said, in consolation. Three days later, one of the men shot a bison that stood six feet high and measured twelve feet from nose to tail. The done thing was to roast the meat on a slow fire, sprinkle it with salt, dry it in the sun and then carry it home. But the men were famished. They cut the rump and thighs into chunks which they beat against the rocks that were still hot with the sun's heat, and ate the meat. The grainy richness of raw meat minced and part-roasted by being dashed upon hot rocks stayed in Subbu's taste buds forever.

The hunters stopped at Ponnampet to soak themselves in toddy. And they began to sing:

'Come, oh wild boar,
Here I stand.
Today I will surely,
surely take you home.
Oh fattened wild boar,
I'll quickly melt your fat.
Here look, here look,
My knife is sharp for you.
Your thighs are for me,
Your breast for my mates.
A cut for the Yeravas,
Your head for the dogs.
Come oh wild boar,
Here I stand.
Today I will surely,
Surely take you home.'

When they reached home it was midnight. Baliyanna woke Nanji. 'Fry the meat and get the children up! They must eat now, when it is fresh!' Rubbing their eyes, the children ate the meat and went back to sleep.

Baliyanna's disintegration was gradual and no one noticed it but Nanji. The serial deaths of his children lessened the guilt about his determination to end his life. But he had to clear the minor complications of existence, tie up loose ends, so Nanji would not suffer more than necessary. He wrote his will, cooed endearments in Nanji's ears until he annoyed her and waited for the moment when his death would go unnoticed. He sat in the porch and drank steadily, in spite of Nanji's warnings that his liver would rot like that of her long-ago first husband. When she was in the fields, he cajoled servants for fried pork or salted liver to go with his drink. He read the paper and discussed national events with the General, but he no longer cared about the future; 'I won't be around to see men in khadi bush shirts and Gandhi caps rule the country,' he said emphatically. He dealt with the obstacles which might have hampered his resolve and wept in secret pity for himself.

He was still in demand as a vet and after treating the General once, he became a people's vet.

It was Saturday evening. The weekly advance had been paid, the granary opened and paddy measured out for the Yerava workers; the women collected the paddy in sacks with children helping, while the men sat on their haunches, smoked and planned their toddy-drinking sprees. The women heaved their sacks, chewed betel and looked over their shoulders in sad fury and schemed how to guard the coins from their husbands till next morning when they could go to the *santhe* and buy jaggery, oil and sweets for the children. Baliyanna sat in the porch digging between his teeth with a pocket knife. Nanji was in the drying yard, talking to the carpenter and writer. The General walked in through the gate to the porch.

'Sit down Machu, have a toddy.'

'Can't sit. You'd better take a look.'

In the bedroom, Machaiah lowered his trousers. 'Rectal abscess, needs draining,' Baliyanna said. 'Better see the Civil Surgeon.'

'Why don't you do it?'

Baliyanna protested that he was only a vet. 'So what? If the thing's ripe, cut it open.'

Baliyanna heated the scalpel and forceps, Subbu brought hot towels and spirit, and positioned the lantern so the squeamish yellow light illuminated the operating field. The General bent from the waist, holding the four-poster bed for support and Baliyanna stuck the sharp point of his veterinary scalpel into the burning flesh. The General mouthed British obscenities but kept still until the abscess was lanced and a bowl of creamy green pus evacuated. His backside healed in a week and Baliyanna's reputation as a surgeon was made.

Baliyanna applied himself to human patients with the same diligence with which he treated animals. He got a white, blue-bordered enamel tray and red rubber tubing for enemas, a thermometer, syringes, needles, bandages, gauze, pills, ointments and lotions and set up his clinic in his father's study. Subbu helped; he boiled syringes in a clean saucepan in the kitchen, cut gauze, rolled bandages and helped his father in minor surgery.

Subbu longed to go back to the Convent School in Madikeri. He longed to pass his Matriculation and enter college but he bore the beheading of his ambition with grace. Besides hunting expeditions and medical forays with his father, he helped Nanji in the fields. Unlike most Kodava planters who wore bowler hats to shade themselves from the sun and supervised the writers who supervised the workers, Subbu worked with them. Like Nanji, he toiled in the fields, sweat flowing, hunger hoofing his belly, and he did not realize that these were the best days of his life. He would think of it later, remember the stickiness of bubbling, rain-soaked mud, the smell of rotting leaves from the sprawling jackfruit and *athi* trees, the itching from sweat that cooled on his back. He was committed to nothing, to no cause, to no one, he carried no burden, only the soft, sweet fragrance of his love for Chinni.

Nanji knew that Subbu was restless, he yearned to be back at the Convent School. The inanities of coffee, paddy, pepper and orange bored him—the endless cycle of pruning, manuring, digging and waiting for the gods or ancestors to feel sympathetic enough to send rain; the waiting for blossom showers, back-up showers and the deluge of the monsoons. He didn't like to suck up to God, or grease the palms of his ancestors and keep them smiling. It was too much of a strain. Subbu wondered it wasn't better for him to get baptized so he could be back at the convent. He broached the subject with his mother. Nanji promptly sent a five-sovereign chain with a serpent-headed pendant to the goldsmith in Thalacheri, trusting the Mapla with the skull-faced grin to bring back money. He came after a week, with sixty rupees. And Subbu went back to the Convent School.

Chapter Seventeen

This time, Nanji went with Subbu to readmit him at the Convent School. She listened to the Mother Superior talk in sweet, gentle tones about the losses incurred by the nuns, and the kind hand of Jesus that helped them along; with Subbu, she followed the Mother to the classroom, where Chengu Master was in the middle of an English lesson. When the children saw the Mother Superior, they rose to their feet, and continued to stand until she signalled with her wimpled head that they could sit. Nanji, watching, envied the children.

Rows of young faces, and feet huddled beneath the desks; keenness and glow on some faces, on others, restlessness. Knowledge attracted Nanji. She admired people who knew things, like her learned husband and his Barrister brother. But even as she prayed for her son to be wise and full of knowledge, she wondered if it really had anything to do with the practicalities of living. As a little girl, she had attended the village school in Tenth Mile for two years and after that, nature was her classroom. If she had been fed the intricacies of knowledge that books, schools and teachers offered, would she have led a wiser life? What about Bolle, the Yerava woman who never went to school? And Boluka her husband, who was older than Baliyanna by a decade and agile enough to make daily forays into the jungles for mushrooms, bamboo and wild fruit so his thirteen children never went hungry? They were wise and good in spite of no schooling. But still, Nanji wanted the best for her son.

Chengu Master pointed to a seat in the fourth row and Subbu sat there next to Sunny. It was time for Nanji to go. She blessed Subbu silently and walked out of the school to the gate where Boluka waited with the box-cart.

That night she stayed at the House of Widows in Kunda, with her mother-in-law. Theirs was a lasting relationship, preserved because each was sensible enough to leave the other alone. Nanji admired and respected the widows who had been set free by circumstance. They had matured into a hardy bunch; it was fallacy to believe that women needed men to complete their lives but Nanji did not wish for their type of freedom. She would let her husband and family feed on her as long as God willed.

For Subbu, it was a smooth, unembarrassing return to school. Sunny followed him as before, his ulcerous leg emanating the odour of slowly dying flesh. Govinda and Patrick had changed somewhat, they talked like adults, about the Satyagraha Movement. Their interest had been triggered by their proximity to the two teachers who had clear sharp minds but different views. Chengu Master believed in the supremacy of the white rulers. Satyu Sir hated the British but did not like confrontation; and having lived in poverty all his life, he was unable to believe that Gandhi's doctrines would lead to freedom. The boys read newspapers, listened to the adults and in time developed their own views.

Patrick was anti-Satyagraha. 'This three-anna Freedom Struggle's not for me. An anti-*ahimsa* agitation is what we need. Would lead it myself if they'd let me.'

'Gandhiji teaches us to be self-reliant.'

'Spin cloth and clean latrines, he says. Work is virtue, he says. It's virtue only if you get someone else to do it. Any other type of work is vice.'

Subbu wasn't sure if non-violence was a good or bad thing, but when he listened to Patrick, with that manly ring to his voice, he felt heroic and mature; and it thrilled him to hear Patrick talk about his own future: 'I've planned everything. Intermediate, then Honours in Economics which will lead me straight to the ICS—the creamiest, dreamiest letters to nestle beside a name. Up there, in Delhi. I won't let any grave-digging politicians transfer me to a rotting countryside like Kodagu. Delhi is the Land of Gods, from there I'll make destinies. When I scratch my pen on a document, the nalushtion will laugh or cry, groan or writhe. I'll be a household name.'

Patrick wasn't bragging, his confidence was real and he was angry with Subbu for giving up. 'If your mother could sell a chain and produce sixty rupees, she must have more to sell. Bits of gold dangling from ears and arms and necks can be put to better use. Want me to talk to her?'

No, Subbu said. He had heard about Barrister Appachu's only visit to the house and he did not wish such humiliation for his cousin. The Barrister was facing hard times. After a year, Emerald had had to join the Third Class Boarders in the convent. Subbu liked Emerald whose exophthalmic eyes looked as if they might fall out if she moved them too much. He was attracted by her dark legs, her sullenly straight hair and her lack of shyness; he liked her in the hand-me-down dresses from Shirley and Sally, which she wore because there was no one to tell her that the dresses were too short and too thin. The nuns chose to ignore the shortness and thinness of Emerald's dresses, because a remedy would prove expensive. For the nuns, to do anything more than the minimum for the Third Class Boarders was a strain and they never failed to mention it in their annual letters to the parents. The girls in the free boarding category became kitchen maids, ayahs, cooks and occasionally nuns. The ambition of every free boarder was to be a nun or a priest, because they knew that these men and women were the most secure people in the world.

Patrick, Emerald and Sunny Boy went twice daily to the chapel which was only ten feet away from the nuns' refectory. They prayed, with the smell of fried eggs or baked fish smothering their senses and hunger mauling their stomachs. Once a week they confessed to Father Leece, the tall, blue-eyed Irish priest with slim hips, a poetic face and gold-brown hair that was like chopped coir. He wore a flowing brown cassock fastened with a wide belt that accentuated his waist; his legs moved within the multitude of folds with a helplessness that intrigued the boys. When nervous or intimidated, he plunged his hand into the deep pocket of his cassock, withdrew his gold-rimmed spectacles and put them on, in defence against the world. The nuns pampered Father Leece with frothy politeness and excellent food, for which he had a weakness. Sunny who habitually peeped into the nuns' refectory gave amazing reports of the gluttonous feasts devoured by Father Leece. The boarders grudged him his Epicurean delights but only Patrick was bold enough to retaliate. He did this by relating his made-up vices in intricate detail to Father Leece during confession. The priest fidgeted, breathed hard and listened in awe to the fifteen-year-old talk of his imaginary sexual escapades. When he heard of the homosexual tendency of the boarders in school, he exhorted Patrick to say a hundred Hail Marys every night and he stalked the boys' dormitory with a torch around midnight. His voyeurism was never satisfied. Years later, back in Ireland, Father Leece would relate the horrors of sinful indulgences in Coorg but no one in his country cared.

To Govinda, destiny beckoned: his father saw his only son sweep the temple floors and learn the austerities required of a *pujari* and wished that he should rise above such wretchedness. When Govinda was in the sixth form and topping the class, Satyu Sir approached Bill Fulton, the Anglo-Indian manager of Windsor Manor and Estates and asked for a writer's job for his son. The estate belonged to Edward Rice. As a dockworker in Liverpool, Rice had heard about Coorg from a businessman who supervised the shipping of coffee from there to England. Rice had listened carefully, got together his savings of one hundred pounds, left the docks and sailed to India. He bought twenty acres near Madikeri which he gradually increased to three hundred and devised a system of employing a retinue of subordinates to run the estate, so he could relax in kingly comfort. Rice went back to Liverpool once in three or five years, saw the 'Fish'n' Chips' he used to eat at and the pubs like the Wild Boar and Old Swan where drinking a pint of bitter on Sunday was the high point of the week, and congratulated himself on having moved to Coorg. When Bill Fulton, his manager, recommended Govinda for a junior writer's post, Rice merely worked his lips around the cigar in his mouth and said, 'Okey doke.' Little did he realize that the brahmin boy would start a chain of events that would lead to Rice abdicating his kingdom.

The Satyagraha Movement did not spare Kodagu but few Kodavas were swept off their feet by it. They were busy copying an alien culture and too simple to try and conceal this copying. Their unquestioning, genetic loyalty touched the pragmatic hearts of the English who mingled with these chosen Kodavas for golf, bridge and tennis; they invited the likes of Kitty, Babs and Ammi the Duchess to 'at-homes', and even visited them. The Kodavas in their innocence believed that the British were doing them a favour. Baliyanna's open dissent before the Collector had earned him the admiration of some Kodavas but most found it honourable to serve, and Kodagu continued in this state of tranquillity until Mallappa came on the scene.

It was a month before the Matriculation exams. The classrooms reverberated with the soulless echolalia of students who swotted with the hope of retaining a fraction of what they read; even the most boisterous became dull and morose. The tyranny of exams was inescapable. At such a time came the confrontation between Mallappa the potter and Jane Peacock, the wife of the Chief Commissioner of Coorg.

Mallappa lived in a hovel on the lowland in front of the fort. He made mud pots, perfectly round pitchers, shallow vessels and cups, baked them at his kiln and sold them at the market on Fridays; he supplemented this meagre earning by supplying coal to the two Mapla and one pure brahmin hotel on the main street of Madikeri. An hour before daybreak he set off with his hand-cart, the creak of its wheels rupturing the

night's silence long before the cocks crowed and the birds
trilled themselves out of sleep. It was a depressing sound. The
people of Madikeri heard it in their sleep, absorbed it in their
dreams and it never bothered them. The British were not so
tolerant, and they grumbled about the damnable nuisance,
although, for most of them residing some distance from the
town, the sound was muffled. The person most riled by it was
the Chief Commissioner's wife. The Commissioner, who was
also the Resident at Mysore, came to Coorg for short intervals
on official work and more importantly to grace social
occasions like Mercara Week. His wife Jane—a chronic
insomniac of delicate, irritable constitution—always fell
asleep just before dawn and rose at noon to display her fusty
bad temper to the staff. The insufferable grate and creak of
Mallappa's cartwheels was like a cart wheeling its way to hell,
she told her husband. It had to stop. She kept on about it, so
the Chief Commissioner spoke to his deputy who spoke to the
traffic inspector, who went to the mud hovel where Mallappa
lived and ordered him to take an alternative route, along the
stone-strewn mud path winding its way behind the Fort.

Three days later, soot-stained, sweat-drenched and
exhausted, Mallappa paused at the top of the slope and met
Govinda who was on his way to school. 'Where's Shiva?'
Govinda asked about Mallappa's son who studied in the
Municipal School and walked down the slope every day with
him.

'There will be no more school for Shiva,' said Mallappa.
'He has to join me at the kiln and earn some money, now that
I must stop carrying coal.' He told Govinda about the orders.
'It takes two hours to reach the main street, and that's too late
for the hotels.'

Govinda told his friends. 'Mallappa has no one to speak
for him, let's do it,' he said.

They responded in earnest. They wrote to *The Kodagu*,
questioning the justice of the order imposed on Mallappa.
Chengu Master's English lessons had not been in vain. 'The

honest means of livelihood for a poor man have been curtailed in order to satisfy the lazy habits of the Commissioner's wife,' the boys wrote. 'It will be far more simple, humane and just for the lady to plug her ears with cotton.' The boys wrote their letter on two pages of lined notepaper and, with youthful haste, took it to the printing press of *The Kodagu* so as to save on postage. The editor tracked down the boys to establish the truth of their statement and moved by the purity of their audacity, published the letter the following Sunday. It was read by the locals with some interest but it turned British faces purple with rage. Discussions were held at the North Coorg Club where every member felt that such blatant disrespect should be firmly dealt with. The Commissioner exchanged telegraphic messages with Mysore and Madras, orders were despatched, retracted and reissued about the best course of action. A week after the letter appeared in the paper, the court issued a warrant for the arrest of the four boys and the editor of *The Kodagu*.

The Kodavas were offended by the court order and the boys became heroes overnight; people protested before the Commissioner's residence and Jane Peacock, watching from her bedroom window, fainted. She feared the worst. 'Let's get out of this country of mad people,' she implored her husband. But the Chief Commissioner's prestige was at stake. After another round of frantic calls to Mysore and Madras, he gave orders for a court hearing.

The hearing was fixed for an early date so the accused would not have time to hire a good lawyer. But news of the 'harassed coal-carrier' had spread to Bangalore and Barrister Appachu sent a telegraphic message indicating his desire to fight their case. The following day he arrived in Madikeri and the drama began to unfold.

First he went to the House of Widows to make peace with Chambavva and receive her blessings. He stayed with Chengu and got down to the task of preparing for the case. He met Mallappa, the boys and the editor of *The Kodagu* and read the letter which the British claimed was seditious; he gauged the mood of the Kodava mind and the depth of its discontent, which had for the first time been revealed in the letter written by the schoolboys; he did it all in three crowded days before the hearing.

In court, Mallappa spoke hesitantly about the loss of earnings that would follow as a result of the order. 'I hoped my son at least would learn to read and write but his fate is the same as mine,' he said.

Appachu defended the letter as a sincere act of service for a fellow-sufferer. The boys had meant no disrespect: 'Mallappa hasn't the means to fight for himself,' he said. 'If the order is instituted, his children will never go to school again.'

The accused were acquitted. Mallappa was allowed to resume his previous route on the condition that he oiled the wheels of his cart regularly. He continued to carry coal along the usual path for the next twenty-two years and then he was replaced by a lorry service.

The episode turned Jane Peacock into a complete insomniac. She withstood the humiliation for eight months and when her husband's tenure was over, they returned to Maidenhead where they entertained friends and enthralled them with stories about their glorious stay in Coorg but the true story of Mallappa the potter lay buried forever in their past.

Chapter Eighteen

Satyanarayana ate just one helping of rice with *bendekai sambar*; he rolled up his leaf with the half-eaten meal in it and watched Govinda finish his second helping with *rasam* and a third with buttermilk. How could the boy eat like that, after having done what he had done? Oh, the pig-headed arrogance of youth! The stupidity of ignorant courage! He looked sadly at his son. Govinda's appearance was disappointing; he was short, with beaked lips, large ears, small eyes and a habit of stroking the *shendi* at the back of his head—for confidence—as other men stroke their moustache. When he had scooped the last traces of buttermilk from his leaf and sucked the piece of bitter-lime pickle, his father said:

'Beg pardon from the CC's wife. Go fall at her feet, or you'll lose the job at Windsor Estate.'

I can see better, Satyanarayana wanted to tell his son, my eyes are not clouded with youthful idealism. Do not go against the British. What better, more bitter lesson than the First War of Independence, when in Lucknow, Kanpur and Delhi they hanged men on trees as figure-of-eight corpses? 'Go now before it's too late and beg pardon,' he said.

Govinda refused to sully his motive. 'I'm not guilty.' He said it with humility, as he rolled his banana leaf. Govinda was neither stupid nor ignorant; he had confidence in his ability to think, he had a brahminical tenacity and persistence that belied his age. Just because his family was dignified and poor, it was not wrong or sinful to aspire to be dignified and rich but one had to go about it quietly, with precision. The incident which involved the Commissioner's wife and the potter was his first act of disobedience, but he had meant no disrespect. He knew he had hurt his father and tried to atone for it by studying twice as hard. Outside school, the Satyagraha Movement continued to make noises but for Govinda the extra effort of studying for the Matriculation was more important. He liked the monotony of discipline, which brought results. He wasn't superintelligent like Patrick and had to rely on hard work. He rose at three instead of four, read till five, swept and washed the stone floors of the temple, prayed to Omkareshwara, smeared sandalwood paste on his forehead, ate his breakfast of *avalakki* and went to school, following his father and six sisters across the paddy fields of Neravanda Karumbaiah.

On the last day of school, when the exams were over, the boys lingered, saying goodbyes. Until the results were announced, the future was uncertain and Govinda, like his friends, knew that the school would no longer be a binding force. Patrick was restless, impatient to be off. 'I'll write, I'll write,' he said but Govinda knew he was just saying it. Patrick had already detached himself from dull, beautiful Kodagu, his future was elsewhere. Patrick was so unlike him and yet they were more akin to each other than to Subbu or Sunny Boy. Govinda stacked his books in a neat pile, filled his bag and stepped out of school, confident that his own future was secure in his hands.

The results were announced after a month. Patrick was on top and won a scholarship to study at Madras University. Govinda got a First and Subbu scraped through. Sunny Boy failed.

Govinda wore his only pair of trousers and a starched shirt and went to meet Edward Rice. Rice was astute enough not to reveal his prejudice against the boy who had defied the Commissioner's wife, and employed him. Govinda proved so efficient that in six months he got an increment of two rupees a month. A year later, he was promoted to the senior category of writers. The workers—most of them twice his age—called him 'Govindanna'. On Sundays, Govinda visited his home behind the Omkareshwara Temple, and was pleased to see that his father was proud of his success.

The last months of school had proved exciting for Patrick and Subbu. They went to Chengu Master's house in the evenings to read the papers but the real reason was the hope of striking a friendship with Shirley or Sally.

Shirley, who just missed being pretty, accentuated her buck-toothed smile with red lipstick, set her hair in curlers, squeezed her feet into shiny high heels, carried bright-coloured plastic handbags and wore bras that embarrassed those who looked at her. She had no time for gangly, stooping Patrick or for Subbu. On her nineteenth birthday, Shirley ran away with a businessman who promised to make her an actress at the Bombay Talkies. Six months later, she came back with weals on her back and twins in her womb. Chengu Master felt obliged to maintain the dignity of the Kodavas, so he got her a typist's job in Bangalore. Shirley raised the twins on her salary and became another grim example of woman's folly.

The boys tried to befriend Sally but the girl had her dancing brown eyes set on none other than the Assistant Commissioner's son, who returned the compliment. It was said—in hushed tones of shock and envy—that the English boy would marry Sally. Chengu Master was torn by the predicament. He felt obliged to oppose the alliance although he felt a secret pride at the thought of his daughter marrying into a British family. In any case Sally was beyond redemption; she smoked cigarettes held in long slim holders, wore transparent stockings that came from London and believed that some celestial error had caused her to be born in Coorg and not England. A few months later, the problem solved itself and freed Chengu Master of the need to show his loyalty one way or the other: one night when Sally and her English boyfriend were driving back from a party in Sunticoppa, the car plunged two hundred feet down a slope and killed them both.

Thus the boys were freed of distractions before they left school. Patrick stayed with his father before going to Madras. The Barrister had spent what little money he earned on second-hand books which he prized above his law books. He quoted from these scriptures while they ate tragic meals in filthy hotels. Once, while they drank tea sitting with peons and menial workers in a tea shack that made Patrick cringe, Appachu said, 'Beware of another's dharma. I realized it too late.'

Patrick had no time to waste on philosophy, so he nodded and went on eating. The truth was that although the Barrister had changed his name back to K.M. Appachu, and had won the court case against the Commissioner's wife, the Kodavas had forgotten him. He never received a wedding invitation, no one called him home, no youngster bent to touch his feet and seek blessings. The Barrister hoped that Patrick, who had his brains and his mother's cunning, would redeem him. Patrick of course had no time to think of such responsibilities.

When the nuns at the Convent School realized that Sunny Boy had reached his level of competence, they helped him set up 'Sunny Stores' outside the school gate. Sunny sold six types of coloured sweets and jaggery toffee made in the convent kitchen by the free boarders and sold to the children for three pice apiece. Sunny was smarter than the nuns thought. He sold cigarettes and beedis without their knowledge and that earned him more than the sweets from the convent kitchen. His love for animals prompted him to offer his services to the butchers in the market. He went three times a week to do the job with tenderness and skill, stroking the animals and talking softly to the petrified goats and sheep that looked at him with gratitude and went quietly to their fate. Sometimes the butchers gave him a leg of mutton, a plump hen or a sheep's head in payment.

Subbu went home and joined his mother in the fields. I

was easy for Patrick to talk about Intermediate; but it would cost him two hundred rupees which they could not afford. One heard of lucky families who discovered pots of gold buried by their ancestors but such luck bypassed him.

It was six months since Subbu had left school. Coming home from the fields in the evening, he found his parents on the porch, arguing. A letter had arrived from Barrister Appachu with the news that he had suffered a stroke. His right hand and leg had become useless and he was bed-ridden. 'May I stay with you till I recover?' he asked in his letter to Baliyanna. Baliyanna was adamant in his refusal and Nanji had tried all day to reason with him. Next morning, she sent Subbu with a letter to Chambavva to see if she could intervene.

'If you fail to bring Appachu home, there's no need for you to do my last rites,' wrote Chambavva. She was past seventy, with elbows like knotted treetrunks and fingers like twisted tapioca root; she had chosen to live in the House of Widows in spite of her crippling arthritis because she was unwilling to forsake freedom, which was a rare and precious gift for a woman her age. She lived on a monotonous diet of minced meat and rice, nursed the bottle, spent hours getting in and out of bed and was happy. Baliyanna could not bear the humiliation of being denied the right to perform his mother's last rites and agreed to have his brother home.

Nanji gave Subbu ten rupees and sent him to Bangalore. Subbu remembered Appachu Uncle's jaunty defiance in the courtroom and had often been told by Nanji that he was the fairest and the most handsome of the brothers. Then he met him in his roofless room and realized how pitiful it is for a handsome face to be struck by deformity. The mouth was pulled to the left, the brow sagged, the paralysed eye showed itself between partly open lids. 'The landlord has won,' the Barrister said with what sounded like a laugh. He gripped Subbu's hand very tight and tried to walk but his useless foot scuffed the floor and in the end, Subbu carried him into the taxi.

Subbu couldn't really understand the bodily infirmities that made the Barrister drag his leg as he walked and use his left hand to lift his right hand. He had a faint recollection of the agony of his own handicap and felt a remote sympathy for his uncle.

Baliyanna banished his brother to the attic. Having lived in a roofless room with crows shitting on his typewriter, Appachu accepted his fate without fuss, ate and slept in the attic where books were his companions. Subbu bathed, clothed and fed him, and listened to his rambling which almost always nearly made sense.

'What do you think is wrong with me?' Appachu asked Subbu.

'You're paralysed. Mava—I think we should get the Civil Surgeon in Madikeri to see you. He may know of some injections—'

'I know what's wrong with me. It's a chemical mess-up in my brain that's caused a short-circuiting of the nerve centres that control my right half and a dysfunction of the pulleys and ropes and muscles that move my limbs. The chemical mess-up happened in the first place because of guilt and resentment, both negative emotions that sour body fluids and cause body parts to malfunction. How can some stupid injections save me? A black hen can lay a white egg but can a white hen lay a black egg? No! The crux of the problem is—*parodharma bhayavaha*— beware of another's dharma. You may think I'm mad, actually I'm slightly off. But rest assured, I have harmed none and no one can harm me.'

Incarcerated in the fusty attic, Appachu had auditory and visual hallucinations that turned him into a near-lunatic. Yet, living thus on the edge of madness, he was spared from the deadlier malady that had killed his father and struck his brother. Nanji gave him the green casket with one hundred and eighty silver rupee coins and eighteen gold sovereigns. Appachu kept the casket near the head of his bed, knowing he had money but not the strength to use it. Although his greed for good Kodava food was unabated, he could not chew, so he asked Nanji to buy him arrowroot biscuits, cheese and Ovaltine from Spencer's in Madikeri. Nanji cared for him as well as she could. He called her Baliyakka and said she was a goddess.

One thing that made Appachu happy was that he could now put Emerald with the Parlour Boarders. Thus Emerald became the only child to have been through all the categories at the convent. The sudden change in status disrupted her personality. In spite of eggs and milk, hot food, good thick frocks, and ayahs to comb out the lice from her hair, Emerald lost weight, became moody and sullen and in her protuberant eyes one saw the yearning for stability.

The year passed; Patrick came to see his father and stayed a week. The sprawling Kaliyanda home, the estate and the paddy fields amazed him and he wished with a momentary feeling of anger that his father had not hitched himself to someone so uninteresting as his mother. He made the best of his stay, siphoning great quantities of food into his lanky frame, filling Subbu with wondrous tales of city life, and avoiding at all times the attic where his father lived. Patrick knew with the selfish insensitivity of youth that his father had settled into a final course of decline. He put his father's illness out of his mind, and concentrated on Subbu.

'So much wealth and no money to send you to college? I can't believe it, Man.'

'Land may be wealth but it isn't money,' Subbu said. 'If my parents had the means, they would have sent me.'

Nanji disliked Patrick who she feared would corrupt her son. She knew the boys smoked and that Patrick filled Subbu's mind with unsavoury tales about city life. She watched the admiration for his cousin in Subbu's eyes and she prayed to Swami Igguthappa to rescue her son.

Igguthappa answered her prayers. Patrick went back to college and life at the Kaliyanda home returned to normal. It was the bustling marriage season when Nanji had at least two weddings to attend each week; she went with her daughter Chondakki in tow, distributing goodwill and tiger-claw brooches; it was at one such wedding that plump, giggly, red-faced Chondakki was spotted by an aunt of Chendanda Subbaiah's son and the match fixed.

Subbu attended weddings when his mother wanted him to go. A few days before the onset of Kakkada, when for thirty days it is inauspicious to hold weddings, he accompanied Nanji to a marriage in Pollibetta. At lunch, Subbu sat with the guests and ate *nooputtoo* with chicken curry, when he heard a voice say,

'Ghee rice?'

He saw the fair plump hand, the rounded wrist with bangles glinting, the fair fingers clasping the wooden spoon; fumes of cloves, cinnamon, cardamom and ghee smothered his senses and his eyes swam with tears. He nodded without looking up, his eyes riveted to the hand that served the rice. A pyramid of fragrant, yellow, ghee-glistening rice teetered on his leaf and he managed to say, 'Enough.' When he looked up, he saw her as she moved away with the self-consciousness of a girl wearing a sari for the first time. Subbu's eyes followed her through the throng and he quite forgot his mother who was waiting for him to take her home. The girl disappeared in a group of formidable women who ate betel leaf and gossiped. Subbu joined the men who danced in the front yard of the wedding house, young men who danced to show off, to digest their food, and warm up for the final dance when they would block the path of the bride as she entered her husband's home. Subbu danced, knowing that somewhere from the gaggle of women, the girl looked. But when Nanji pulled him away saying she didn't want to go home in the dark, Subbu realized that the girl was gone. He didn't even know her name.

Nanji knew that Subbu had caught the fever she hoped he would and told him casually that the girl was Mallige, daughter of Kademada Kalappa, from Kadanga. 'Send a marriage proposal,' Subbu begged his mother.

'You're almost twenty, you have no business sending a proposal to a thirteen-year-old girl,' Nanji said. 'You'll get a better match. Kokkale Kalappa has a mere thirty-five acres of coffee, a thousand *battis* of land and three sons.'

Chapter Nineteen

Having decided to claim Mallige for himself at a more suitable time, Subbu placed her in his mind's quiet corner. It was the month of Kanyar; warmed by the sun and caressed by October winds, the green shoots of paddy kept growing; the cardamom and pepper needed no attention and manuring was almost done. Subbu had little work to do, so he went with his father to the Country Club and listened to inebriated men talk passionately about the freedom struggle.

The British loyalists in Coorg had proclaimed their allegiance to the Crown; the Commissioner talked of it with pride to the Governor in Madras and to the Viceroy in Delhi, in the same way that a teacher talks about his best student to the headmaster. Coorg was hailed as a model state.

At the Country Club, it caused a stir.

'When we throw the British out, we'll send these eunuchs with them!' Baliyanna was on his fourth drink and visibly upset. 'It's shameful to be called a model state by the enemy. The Congress should speed up its action.'

The General was more anti-Congress than anti-British. 'With freedom will come pro-hi-bition! Bring Congress, and throw out the life-sustaining drink of the gods!' He withdrew the silver spatula from his pocket and cleaned his ear, an orifice of gratification, then wiped the spatula on a handkerchief. 'Bring the Congress in and close down Thammi's Country Club! Thammi, you heard me? First thing the Congress will do is put a big, fat lock on your door!' He rose, stroked the bamboo-and-straw thatched door of the Club and broke into manly sobs.

Thammi was a large, bull-shouldered, genial man and he served toddy at the Country Club with a dedication that was praiseworthy. He had his principles: no women, no credit for new customers, no brawls. By some tacit understanding, only Kodavas went to the Club. Others would buy a bottle to take home but they never came in to sit on the hospitable wooden benches inside. When the General embraced the door of the Club, Thammi produced a series of dry, ejaculatory coughs which was the signal that it was time to close. In twos and threes or as lonely singles, the men dragged themselves out, carrying with them their lanterns, umbrellas and confused dreams. 'What we need is a dozen or more fine, pork-eating Kodavas at the helm,' the General said, rising. 'India needs dis-ci-pline. I've said it all in my letter to the King . . .'

When the last of the men had lurched out, Thammi lowered the wick of his lantern, closed the bamboo door and walked home. Subbu held his father by the shoulder and they went along the mud-track to Athur. The discussions that he heard at the Country Club served to embellish and magnify his own dreams which were bigger than the others'. These men, including his father and the General, were of another generation; fettered by families, girded with responsibilities, maimed by age, the only thing they could do was talk. But he was young and fit and vigorous. He wanted to do things.

But what? Patrick was way ahead, Govinda had a job, and Sunny owned a shop. Only he was worth nothing.

One evening, while Subbu helped Appachu Mava into his trousers after a bath, the Barrister said, 'Why don't you join the army?'

'Mava?'

'A Kodava makes a good soldier. When he wears army green, laces his boots and lifts his gun, there is no fumbling, no clumsiness. You have the physique, fearlessness, and lack of cunning. You'll do well.'

And it hadn't even occurred to him! Subbu became excited. A soldier had chiselled goals, he knew his enemy, his battle was a pure one 'Mava, you're right,' he said, earnestly. 'I'll ask Alamenda Nanu. He's a Lance Naik now.'

The young men of Athur were envious of Alamenda Nanu—the quiet, lustreless young man who joined the army and came back with a magnificent chest, stiff-shouldered walk and a way of sitting with one foot over the other knee that did not go unnoticed by the pretty girls of the village.

'You've got to be an officer,' the Barrister said. 'And for that you need money and influence. I have influence, your mother has money. When I appeared for the Bar at the Middle Temple, I made friends. I can rely on them to help get you into Sandhurst.'

But there was no getting round Nanji. 'If it's the military you want, you must join like everyone else. We cannot afford privileges,' she said, firmly.

Subbu's ambition hung in suspended animation. Early one Sunday morning, while he supervised the measuring of paddy for the workers, he heard the creak and rattle of a bicycle. It was Govinda, in ungainly trousers held high around his waist with a black belt, and shiny brown shoes that made him walk in pigeon-toed discomfort.

They sat in the front room and talked: Nanji served coffee, thinking, 'They're only children but they talk like adults.' Govinda had done well at Windsor Estate. He earned twenty-seven rupees a month, of which he sent twenty home and saved the rest. 'But I haven't come to tell you that,' he said, pouring the coffee into the saucer and sucking it through his beaked lips. 'I've joined the Congress. There's a party meeting today in Madikeri. Do you want to come?'

Subbu became the youngest member of the Kodagu branch of the Indian National Congress. The following month, Govinda quit his job at Windsor Estates and started a printing press which he installed in his home behind the temple. Mukambika Printing Press became the centre of party work; it worked from within the temple walls where bells, bhajans and the chanting of prayers drowned the sound of typewriters that tapped to the rising fervour of nationalism. Satyu Sir was inconsolable. Govinda had thrown away a lucrative job to dabble in Satyagraha. He prayed to Omkareshwara that his son be cured of this new and terrible malady.

Subbu helped him write anti-British pamphlets and, every evening, he rode off on Govinda's rusty bicycle to distribute them. Pamphlets appeared in markets, shops, offices and homes, posters were pasted on doorways, anti-British slogans were splashed across walls. Subbu carried the burden of his idealism like a privilege. It did not matter anymore that he could not go to college or join the army. He worked with a joy that was near madness, slept late and woke early.

Nanji tried to reason with her son. 'Freedom will not improve our lot,' she said. 'Our fate depends on the benevolence of the gods.' Baliyanna was angry with Subbu but he could do little; for most of the time now, he was immersed in the bottle. His crooning in Nanji's ears as if she were yesterday's bride annoyed her and she shut him up curtly and went on with her work. Only Appachu understood her fears and consoled her.

'Idealism is a disease of youth, it gets washed away with time. Look at me, all the fire burnt out, my skin thick like a wild boar's. Subbu will come out of this, he'll be the son to make you proud.'

Subbu lived on the road, cycling for hours to take the pamphlets to village subcentres. One evening, while riding with a fresh stack of pamphlets to Murnad, he collided with a cyclist who, like him, was without lights. When they untangled themselves, Subbu realized that the cyclist was a policeman. His precious pamphlets were scattered on the road and flew about in all directions. This is it, Subbu thought, I'll now be marched off to jail.

'If you just stand there, your papers won't come back to you,' the policeman said gruffly. 'Come on, let's get them before it's too dark.'

They managed to get all the pamphlets but a few which had got under stones or were impaled on bushes. Just then a sleek black Austin came along the road; it was the Chief Commissioner's car. The policeman saluted smartly, Subbu followed; the Commissioner acknowledged them with a nod.

'Ride carefully, and don't have another accident,' the policeman said to Subbu as he rode off. 'Next time, you may not be so lucky.'

How the British discovered Mukambika Press remained a mystery. One morning at seven, Subbu was at the temple for *mangalarathi*, waiting for darshan before he slipped into the Press. The door of the inner sanctum opened and Satyanarayana came out with a lighted lamp; just then a troop of policemen appeared at the stone steps of the temple and marched round to the back. They found Govinda with the fresh stack of pamphlets printed that night and arrested him.

Satyanaraya blessed his son and smeared a streak of sandalwood paste on his forehead. 'A prison sentence will teach you it's better to follow the middle path of least resistance,' he said.

The closure of the Press was a blow. The Congress workers held secret meetings in the threshing yard behind Jammada Subbaiah's house in Athur. They sat in a circle in the wide open yard where paddy was threshed during the day, and, reclining on haystacks, discussed the future of the nation. Cyclostyled pamphlets continued to circulate; four young men besides Subbu kept them going. When police vigilance grew tight the young men worked from their homes. Subbu typed in the attic. He cleared away pickle jars, chutney bottles and earthenware pots of mango in brine to make place for his typewriter, sat cross-legged on the wooden floor and typed, with Appachu watching him from his bed. 'I don't know who reads these pamphlets,' Appachu said to Nanji, 'but he works with a purpose that lights his face and robs him of sleep. Let him do it, it's good for him.'

Just as Nanji feared, one day four policemen appeared at

the gate. She saw them from her window and whispered to Baliyanna who was in the porch, slicing a mango with his penknife. The police walked with quick, determined steps which did not hide their nervousness. This was the home of the late Rao Bahadur Madaiah, a British loyalist and friend of the government.

'We have information of anti-government activities,' the inspector said. 'We want to search.'

Baliyanna ate the mango, sucked the seed and rose from his chair. 'I hope none of your men have sensitive lungs,' he said, leading them in. 'My wife is making new mattresses.' In the three bedrooms, Yerava women cleaned great piles of cotton and stuffed them into pillows. Nanji was there in one of the rooms, her legs stretched out on a straw mat, sewing. Cotton fluff covered the policemen as they stoically went to every corner, crevice, cupboard and trunk, looked beneath beds, behind boxes and shelves and found nothing. 'Where is Subbaiah?' the inspector finally asked, through the air thick with cotton fluff.

'Reading. In the attic,' Nanji said. 'I'll call him.'

'We'll go up ourselves.'

They found Subbu reading a moth-eaten copy of *Fifty Famous Detective Stories* and Appachu with a belligerent scowl, rolling leaves of tobacco. The police searched the attic and found only pickled mangoes, gooseberry wine, jars of chutney, sacks of jaggery, dried coconut and huge copper vessels stacked away for festive cooking. 'I think we've seen everything,' the inspector said, defeated.

'There's the chicken coop, the cowshed, the pigsty, the bathing room and the well. I'll take you myself.' And Subbu led them into the chicken coop where they had to bend double, made them breathe the air of the pigsty, step over dung in the cattleshed, look in the well at their own reflections and peep into the bathroom where water steamed in a huge pot; then he insisted they should not leave without searching the latrine. 'Now you've seen everything,' he said when they stumbled

165

down the slope from the steaming, wasp-infested pits.

Livid with rage, covered in fluff, reeking of chicken and pig shit, the police left, determined to get him another time. When they had gone, Nanji rescued the typewriter from the ashes in the fireplace and Subbu went up to the attic to resume work.

He worked on for six months; one day at a meeting held in the compound of the Civil Hospital in Gonicoppa, while Subbu was hoisting the tricolour flag of Free India, the police came. Subbu was allowed home to pack his things and tell his parents. He touched their feet and pressed his palms against his forehead.

What sin have I committed that I should lose seven of my children and now lose Subbu, to this Swarajya madness, Nanji thought. What have I done to deserve this? But dry-eyed, she blessed him, 'May you live to be a hundred,' and in a soft whisper, added, 'Don't wait too long to claim a bride.'

Chapter Twenty

It was late evening when the prisoners reached Alimpur and Subbu was tired enough to sleep fitfully on the bare prison floor with a blanket beneath him. Govinda greeted him in the morning with warm cheerfulness. He was thinner, his owl face more lean and the smooth brahmin roundness of his shoulders more rugged; and in spite of his brush with modernism, the *janiwara* and *shendi* stayed.

It was nothing short of a privilege to be among great men in prison, he said. 'They share their knowledge with us, it's university education for free. I'm up at four in the morning, finish my yogasanas and read the *Gita* before the others wake.'

The political prisoners stayed in a long dormitory-type room adjoining the cells of thieves and criminals. Each newcomer got two coarse blankets and a piece of mud-coloured soap to wash clothes and keep himself clean. Twice a day they were served a *kanji* of rice and dal with long brown bugs floating in it. Subbu refused to eat and tried to survive by filling his belly with water, and coffee that tasted like water. On the third day, he contemplated his meal: cockroach legs, decapitated insect bodies, transparent wings and whole shiny bugs floating in tranquil death in a bowl of glutinous rice and dal. He picked out bits of fragmented insects and ate the *kanji*, fearing he would bring it all up. But his craving belly accepted it gratefully. Next day, he squeezed the insects between thumb and finger so as not to lose any nourishment, and ate. Govinda observed his unnecessary fastidiousness and said, 'It's protein and it's well-cooked.' Subbu began to eat his *kanji*—bugs, bug essence and all.

The senior Congressmen organized lectures, bhajans and religious discourses. Subbu read avidly, studied History, Economics, the essence of the *Vedas*, the *Koran* and the *Bible*; his uncluttered mind absorbed everything and the intellectual nourishment enhanced his health. When Nanji and Baliyanna visited him, Nanji was surprised to see that he looked so well. 'The only food I eat is rice, dal and bugs,' Subbu said. Nanji thought her son was exaggerating. She was angry that the outcome of her son's valour was to languish in prison but at least his body throve in spite of the meagre diet.

As the months passed, Subbu's restlessness began to surface. His body that had fed on the moist, cool air of Kodagu was stifled by the arid weather of Alimpur. Lectures and bhajans failed to sustain him, the lack of physical action made him ill. His thighs ached for movement, he paced the courtyard endlessly and hated the guards who had the freedom to move in and out of the prison gates. It was like being Kunta the cripple, when he had stood clutching the iron bars of the bedroom window and envied everything that moved. He drank water by the pitcherful and remained thirsty; his tongue burned and his skin turned scaly, a hot dryness scalded his eyes, his joints creaked, his ears itched, and his hair was like dry husk. He was alarmed when after drinking three pitchers of water a day, he passed a mere cupful of urine. He reported to S.V.N. Shree Shree, the octogenarian homeopath who had been jailed for two years and lived on one coconut a day. 'Your thirst is a reflection of hidden desires,' Shree Shree said. 'Great minds think of great things, little minds think of petty things like the weather, and comfort. The answer to all sorrow is to cancel desire from the mind.'

It was not possible, or necessary, to cancel desire from the mind. In an effort to overcome drudgery, young prisoners shared details of amorous loves, imaginary and real. Subbu satisfied himself with thoughts of food. It was less sinful than thoughts about sex, and once he started on that journey, there would be the agony of bridled desire. So he let his mind dwell on Nanji's cooking. He had a passionate love for food, he always ate more than his body needed. Now, starved by meagre rations, he dreamed of Nanji's puffed-up *akki otti* and banana jam, eleven varieties of steamed *putoos*, pork roasted over hot coals till crisp and oozing fat, mutton *palav* the smells of which flooded the house an hour before lunch, the bamboo shoot pickle and fat slippery mushrooms that burst in the mouth. Subbu recalled delicate flavours until he could make the watery jail coffee taste like Nanji's filter coffee, the *kanji* like *palav*, the floating bits of insects like crunchy roasted pork. He longed for bananas which he used to eat by the dozen. Oranges were laborious to peel, and he had little patience with squashy papaya, sticky mango or jackfruit. Bananas were his favourite and what Nanji grew were the best: thumb-sized *poo bale* that you ate in one gulp and felt the fibrous centre snap in your mouth, the meaty *verachi*, cardamom-scented *yelakki*, the red *chonda bale* which was best eaten with honey, the powdery *rasa bale*, tangy *mara bale* that his mother gave away by the sack and the royal *raja bale* were his favourites and Subbu longed for them now with a fresh ache that brought tears to his eyes.

Subbu resisted for six months, then slipped into the habit of buying beedis by bribing the guards. He smoked guiltily and in secret but Shree Shree caught him. 'Is a beedi more important than integrity?' he chided.

'Yes.' He hadn't meant to say it, it just slipped out. 'There are moments when a beedi is the most important thing,' he tried to explain. 'Just like first thing in the morning, the most important thing is to shit.'

The insistence on absolute morality was puzzling. How can you be good when dealing with bad people? The prison officials were mean, pathetic and evil as weak men in power usually are and the jail superintendent was the worst: Desmond Caring, with his hollow pink cheeks and high-stepping gait, inspected the prison on Mondays. He was a self-conscious man who believed that his lack of skin pigmentation compensated for every mindless act of stupidity. He was an underdog back home and here, a bully. Subbu hated Caring just as much as he hated the fat pedigree dog which followed him with a smugness that matched his master's and wagged its hips like a woman. One particularly unhappy Monday, when Subbu was overwhelmed by the wretchedness of his plight, the sight of the swaggering superintendent made his skin burn. When the inspection was over, Caring stepped into the quadrangle to talk to lesser men; his dog followed, with its stupid canine smile and wagged its hips at Subbu. Subbu was angry for all sorts of reasons and one was that the dog should be devoted to a man so pathetic as Desmond Caring. In a sudden unleashing of his anger, he dealt a vicious kick to the dog. It recoiled with a terrified whelp and hid behind its master. There was a spontaneous burst of cheers from the prisoners and Subbu would have killed the dog if the guards hadn't pulled him away. He was marched off to solitary confinement. Subbu stayed next to the cells of the criminals; he was made to stand eight hours a day with his hands up in irons. The pain distracted him from his misfortunes and he felt nearer to the real tragedies of men who faced death. He listened to their weeping and wondered which was better—to be executed for a real crime, or fester in jail with pretty dreams of a free India. To be shackled in prison while life rushed on outside was too big a price to pay. And now he was being punished for a stupid folly that he couldn't even be proud of. Every evening, when he was allowed to walk for ten minutes in the courtyard, he could feel the resentful eyes of his friends from their prison cells. He had shamed their belief in *ahimsa*. Subbu wished he could argue for his action. Attacking the dog hadn't been such a mindless act, he had kicked it with passion. That weak-minded, macho, meaty, rugged, stupid dog was hollow like the officer it wagged its tail for, it was just as hateworthy as he. The dog symbolized British snobbishness, the British form of justice, for which you had to supplicate and be grateful; but there was something greater to be resolved. Honour. He had listened to his father speak of it with the General during their heated debates in the Country Club. He was still vague as to what honour was. Would he recognize it or would it pass him by? He was desperate to do what was good and honourable but he wasn't clear in his mind what that was.

Separated from his mates, unable to listen to lectures, bhajans or advice, Subbu killed time by reliving his past. He probed memory until it yielded hidden, forgotten moments that lurked in the folds and speculations of his brain and remembered his school days; he stood next to his friends and saw himself play hockey and football; he shuddered with pleasure over his dreams of Chinni and Clara; he remembered the shared confidences with Boju uncle who won Chinni only to lose her; he recalled his crippled days and went right back to the first moment of awareness, the feel of his mother's bony contours and the warm sweet smell of her milk. He wandered carefree, up and down the bylanes of the past which was better than the present.

When exhausted by his efforts to recollect the past, he tried what was easier—to remember all that his mother had told him, or he had overheard when she talked to some neighbour or relative: how as a young bride she had peeped from the box-cart at the Kaleyanda house which was to be her new home; his grandfather who died vomiting blood over the chamberpot; Chambavva's panthers and their unfortunate end at the hands of the British Range Officer; his father at eighteen, shooting his first tiger; his famous forefather who fought Tipu Sultan on the hills of Malethirike, defended the temple and ousted the invaders from Kodagu; and the legend about the execution of the Kaleyanda men which was never proved but nevertheless believed: that only one man had survived slaughter by the Raja and lived on to perpetuate the clan.

Back in the main prison with the others, Subbu was sorry to lose the privilege of his loneliness. Only the blisters on his palms and pain in his wrists were there to remind him of its horrors. Even when he talked about Swarajya and non-violence, he was aware of his decreasing conviction.

To fuel his doubts came Patrick. He journeyed all the way to Alimpur to see his friends and berate them on their stupidity. He was leaner, more handsome, with a worldly self-assurance that Subbu envied; in every word he spoke was the emphasis of his self-assurance.

'Passivity is a crime,' he said. 'There's no use languishing on insect-ridden *kanji* and spinning cloth when you should be fighting the enemy.'

Govinda answered with patience. 'Don't be rankled by the enemy, my dear Patrick. However hard a nature may be, it will melt in the fire of love—'

'Tell that to your fat-arsed prison officials. Our men fight the bloody war, while the British lord it over them as officers. What does your Mahatma have in mind for the army? *Ahimsa* and a diet of milk and dal? Tilak, that grand old Maratha, was more aware of priorities. He devised a pan to train Indian officers for the army, tried to get help from America, France and Russia. Did you know that? But the British pressured them against us. Only recently, a handful of Indians were enlisted at the Military Academy for officer training.' He looked at Subbu. 'That's where you should be. Pledge your loyalty to the British, offer an apology and get your release. Fight like men.'

'We will win freedom without bloodshed,' said Govinda. 'And you, Patrick, will eat your words.'

'Listen to him, slipping on shit and mouthing obscene spiritual philosophy. We've got to move into the world of achievement, like the Americans. Every man for himself, each person a business unit. Every cell in every body is worth so many rupees, dollars, pounds—or—chickenshit. Money buys. There's nothing else.' He looked at Subbu. 'Yes, There is . . . one thing. What you need is—a woman.'

Subbu brightened. 'You know—I think you're right. There's this girl I want to marry—'

'Marriage? Who's talking of marriage? Man, never

burden your heart with attachments. Appease sexual hunger and be free for other things.'

Govinda rose stiffly, thanked his friend for the visit and left. Subbu, caught up in the immediacy of his desire for Mallige, paid no heed to Patrick. Two years and eight months later, with Govinda and fifteen others, he was released from prison. He returned to Kodagu, confident now that he could claim Mallige for himself.

Chapter Twenty-one

A gentle drizzle had softened the mud-track from Gonicoppa to Athur: Subbu's feet sank into the ground and water splashed the trousers that he had rolled to his knees. He was happy to be home. When he turned in at the gate, Nanji saw him through the bedroom window and hurried to welcome him. Subbu removed his chappals—rough, wide ones that looked as if they were made of snipped cycle tyres—washed his feet, sprinkled rice into the *chombu* of water and stooped to seek her blessings.

Baliyanna watched from the porch. It was the hour of dusk when, with three bottles of toddy inside him, he felt a pitying compassion for everything that lived. And here was his son in coarse khadi trousers, bush shirt and Gandhi cap, with the wooden charkha on top of his tin box, making out that life was worth living. Kunta was a man now. He was shorter than most Kaliyanda men but there was strength in his shoulders and in his long arms and hands that reached to his knees; he had dark eyes and soft pendulous ears like his mother, and a fearless audacity in his stride that had gladdened Baliyanna ever since he had first begun to walk. Kunta had the type of face that had no need of a moustache to give it strength.

The rigours of prison life hadn't chastened him, if anything he seemed more deeply enmeshed in Satyagraha. While Nanji went in to bring coffee, Subbu sat with his father and talked, like an equal. He was eager to show off.

'When every Indian wears khadi, we'll boycott the Lancashire silks and cottons. The charkha is the symbol of industriousness. The tricolour flag depicts renunciation, peace and productivity . . .'

'Feeble symbols,' Baliyanna said, in rage and disbelief. 'Why not a lion's paw, a tiger's eye, a cobra, an eagle or something beautiful . . . like the lotus?'

He watched his son set the charkha down opposite the proud shelves of books in the front room. When Subbu had filled himself with the best of Nanji's food, he sat down to spin. Yeravas and neighbours came to watch, fascinated by the speed with which the yarn was made. From the very first day of his son's return from prison, Baliyanna nursed an immediate and permanent grudge against the wheel which had invaded the house and threatened to overthrow their ancient traditions of valour. He hated Congressmen.

'Effeminate bastards! They talk of freedom without ever having held a gun. Adolescents posing as men in ludicrous Gandhi caps and bush shirts the colour of baby shit!' Maddened by the sound of the charkha, he countered it by buying a second-hand gramophone and tried to drown the noise of spinning with horrendous music from three scratched records. Baliyanna refused to wear khadi or allow Subbu to hang his hateful, emasculating cap on the wooden hat stand in the porch. The rosewood stand which had been a gift from Alistair Fox to the Rao Bahadur had held sleek hats, golf, peak and fez caps, turbans, police helmets and checked head scarves. The hateful white cloth cap that folded like some miserable kerchief was not fit to hang there. The friction between Subbu and Baliyanna was threatening to erupt but it kept Baliyanna's mind off the revolver that he hid beneath the pillow. Nanji was more open to the changes sweeping over them. She listened to her son explain the ideals of Gandhiji, about *ahimsa*, honesty, unselfishness and truth; she became an admirer of the bat-eared, bespectacled, dhoti-clad leader; but the one dictum of Gandhi's she abhorred and but for which she would have allowed his photograph to join the deities in her puja room, was Gandhi's crazy belief in equality.

She could not understand it. Nanji was proud of her heritage. Her ancestors had come from the hills of Thadiyandamolu, Malethirike, Kundathbottu and Pushpagiri: Kodavas who lived by their weapons and their honour, oblivious of the myths about their origin that excited scholars. The myths were many: Kodavas, it was said, were descendants of the troops of Alexander. The Macedonian soldiers, faced with the hazards of a perilous voyage back to Attica, deserted their chief and set out in search of a peaceful corner of India to settle in. They trudged south of the Vindhyas and after months of wandering through hostile lands, discovered the lush forests in the western Ghats where water was clear, sweet and abundant, the soil soft and fertile, where fruit and flowers grew without effort and the few fierce-looking tribals were a lazy, pleasant lot compared to the sly, sharp-eyed, conniving men they had battled with in other regions. The soldiers of Alexander inhabited this heavenly hill country and lived with local women. After two hundred years of prolific reproduction, the number of females increased enough to allow the practicality of marriage.

There were other myths: among the Kodavas were the nobility whose blood was said to stay red for six hours after death; and clans with the most beautiful women, so beautiful that in bygone days a bride was won when a man fought and vanquished nine suitors. Today's Kodava cut down nine banana trees at his wedding, and every Kodava wore a small curved dagger at his waist when he set out for an auspicious event. It was even said that there were clans that could be identified by the hair on the hidden parts of their body which always took the shape of Kodagu. Nanji did not believe every one of these myths and she did not know the truth herself but she was a firm believer in the goodwill of ancestors. She had heard it said that the spirits of the best among the Kodavas resided in the clouds that hovered over the forests and wooded slopes of Malethirike, Pushpagiri and Thadiyandamolku and blessed their land with plentiful rains. When the ancestors were happy with their progeny, the rain fell vertically and nourished the land; if the spirits were displeased, the rain slanted at an angle when it fell and a lot of water was wasted; if the ancestors were truly incensed—as when a Kodava married an outsider—the rain fell transverse, beating horizontal tracks of such fury that it cut through persons who dared go out, it slashed its way past fields, it broke doors and windowpanes, lifted entire rooftops and fell in shuddering waterfalls from the slopes of the hills.

Nanji did not know many things but she believed it was honourable to be born a Kodava. Now here was Gandhiji, a saint and seer who said that all were equal and actually encouraged the intermingling of castes. How could anyone else be equal to a Kodava or a Kodava be equal to anyone else? What would happen to their race, already sullied by the wicked Haleri Rajas? As if making such stupid statements was not enough, Gandhi called the *polayas* 'Harijans', ate and slept and lived with them. Nanji was shocked by such stupidity and even more alarmed when Subbu accepted it as gospel truth. 'You won't defile this house by bringing in *polayas*,' she warned but she saw the defiance in his eyes and knew that her son had slipped out of her control.

Subbu worked in the fields as before, and on Saturday afternoons went to Congress meetings held in the threshing yard behind the sprawling house of Jammada Bheemaiah, the seniormost Congressman in Kodagu, the only Kodava who had attended the 1924 All-India Session in Allahabad and met Gandhiji. He had started a Yerava colony on the ten acres of land donated by Baliyanna. Yeravas had lived in Kodagu as long as anyone could remember along with the Kurubas who roamed the hills and collected wild honey, and the Kudiyas who climbed the bearded palm trees and tapped toddy. The pug-nosed, curly-haired Yeravas were comfortable in their illiteracy which gave them confidence and detachment. They were happy in their destitution and could not understand why all of a sudden the Gandhi-inspired, khadi-clad Congressmen should take such pains to settle them. They built houses for the Yeravas, showed them how to grow tapioca, carrots and onions and sell them in the *santhe* and get money to spend on clothes, combs and soap so they could become clean and civilized like the Kodavas. The Yeravas listened with laughter in their eyes; about living they already knew and did not need to be taught. They also knew that it was wicked to work when there was no need for it. They did not argue but when the Congress workers left, the Yeravas sat on their haunches, ate betelnut and tobacco, drank toddy, picked nits off each other's heads, made love, and forgave the audacity of the intruding Congressmen.

Subbu came home from the Saturday meetings with his friends; Nanji served them coffee and when they showed no sign of leaving she fed them *akki otti* with chicken or fried *mathi* with rice. Nanji liked these friends of Subbu, rustic lads shining with clean open goodness, moving like shafts of light; theirs was an arrogant confidence that was also sincere and she prayed that their dreams should not be defiled.

Subbu spun khadi and talked of non-violence but he did not believe that India could win freedom that way. Doubts about his own conviction had begun to disturb him like an ingrown eyelash. It wasn't the austerity he feared: he could rough it out anywhere; he could sleep on gravel, mud or ash, sit on a sack of rice or a pumpkin or an armchair with velvet cushions. He could adjust to anything, but his conviction wasn't pure. He saw on the faces of his mates the soft, smug glow of faith which was only Gandhi's faith and not their own and it was gummed on their faces and souls; he realized that neither he nor his colleagues who now abhorred violence would ever be able to follow the grim path of non-violence to the end. He wished he could opt out, but did not have the courage to made a clean, quick break.

Govinda, who had no time to contemplate the ethics of his actions, became the clean, clever man of politics, and was now the vice-president of the District Board of the Congress. He was affable with Subbu, but the distance between them was a result of the diverging force of their beliefs.

In the midst of the bustle of Congress work that invaded the house, Baliyanna quietly schemed his release. Each morning he got out of bed with a supreme effort, drank toddy with his morning coffee and went on drinking till evening. Loyal Kudiya friends climbed palm trees with the bottle and knife slung round their necks and tapped the fresh toddy which he stored in a deep, wooden chest with sixteen compartments for standing the bottles upright. The wooden chest, which he had got made out of the best teak, was kept near the head of their bed, and the brass chamberpot at the foot. Subbu, who could not understand his father's decline, showed his displeasure by making lofty statements on the evils of drink. Nanji nagged but her nagging was gentle, without anger. Baliyanna was patient with them both. He was a kind-hearted man, and when drunk he was a courteous prince; he ignored the rest of his family, not for lack of love but because he understood perfectly the uselessness of his love. Life became monotonous, like the creak and groan of his gramophone records, there was neither joy nor comfort in toddy or fried meat or arguments at the Country Club or in sleeping with the gypsy women. He wanted to go without fuss, causing the least possible sorrow to Nanji, whom he loved and admired. But he had to wait for his ageing mother to die. It wouldn't be fair to deprive Chambavva of the honour of having the last rites performed by her son.

When Chambavva died, eighty years old and no longer pleasured even by toddy, he brought the body home and gave her a proper funeral; once he had lit the pyre, his mind was at peace. Now he could plan his own death. He wrote his will, shared the property between his sons and wife, cleared away any obstacle that might harass them after his death and hit upon the idea of slipping off on Puthari night.

That auspicious night of the full moon when the harvest was ripe, they would go to the fields to cut the first ripe sheaves of paddy and tie them to the doors and to bedposts; they would offer the best of food and toddy to the gods and ancestors, and then the fire-crackers would be taken out and lit by the young men and children in the midst of the excited, high-pitched warnings of the women. In the midst of all this merry-making and noise Baliyanna would go quietly to the bedroom; he would shut the door, lie on the four-poster bed on which Nanji had delivered twelve of their thirteen children and on which he had taken her a thousand times, and with the revolver that was ready and loaded, press the trigger at the pulse in his neck and go quietly. Baliyanna planned every detail, he even got a rubber sheet from Nanji's chest of drawers and put it beneath his pillow so he wouldn't mess up the mattress. He took such joy in his planning that it made his cheeks glow and eyes shine, and Nanji, while praying the night before Puthari, thanked Iguthappa for having cured her husband.

That night, Baliyanna died in his sleep.

Part Three

Part Three

Halfway through her prayers, Nanji sensed that her husband wasn't breathing. She calmly wiped the spittle from his lips, closed his eyes and his mouth and removed the revolver from beneath the pillow; uncoiling her hair, she rubbed off the red kumkum from her forehead and went to tell the family.

But the first person she met was Bolle, who was coming in to empty the brass chamberpot. The Yerava woman was younger than Nanji, but she was severely disabled by the downward slide of her tired womb between her thighs. It got in the way of swift movement and caused her to leak urine as she walked. Nanji could have opted for a younger, more capable substitute but she never once thought of doing such a thing. Now at the time of her greatest bereavement, it was Bolle who wiped away Nanji's tears with the edge of her filthy sari, knowing that a woman always needs another woman at a moment such as this.

The mourners filled the front yard and porch and the rooms overflowed with women in white. The General, followed by Thammi and a retinue of toddy drinkers from the County Club, was among the first to come and last to leave. They stood by in wordless grief. Nanji sat on a reed mat near the body and, even as she mourned, worked out details for the eleventh-day ceremony, when guests would be fed in honour of her dead husband. Looking across the room at Subbu, she knew the time had come for Kunta to prove himself.

Subbu tried bravely to hide his agitation. His older brothers had forsaken the family and moved away, Appachu Mava had defected from the religion, and so the burden fell squarely upon him. He stood at the door accepting words of sympathy, conversed with the village elders, and hoped that the one person he wanted to see would not disappoint him.

She came. Men stood aside to let her pass, and women led her to the front room where the body lay. She placed the wreath at the foot of the bed and knelt beside Nanji; Nanji's hand clung to hers in shared grief, her bony fingers wrapping themselves around Clara's wrist. Clara watched the mourners surging back and forth, their collective sympathy spreading like waves around Nanji. She marvelled at the strength of communal grief and the stoicism of the woman who sat by her husband's body. When she got up from Nanji's side, she was momentarily dizzied by the sea of white; leaning on a bookshelf that contained the books she and Nanji had rescued from the attic, she grieved. She wished she hadn't worn black; she looked incongruous, like a gawky crow among these people.

Clara could not bring herself to look at the vet. Sometimes you tried to cancel out one hurt with another. She could stand outside herself and experience the pain, look at it, and then it wasn't so bad. It was sharp and acute, her pain, unlike the bite of a leech that drained you painlessly. He had loved her, she knew, but he had never said it even once. No, she wouldn't look, she would walk to the door and go away, remembering only his smile, the rare smile that scalded her memory. Her heart was drenched in love but there was anger mingled with it. Her loss was final.

She felt a desperate urge to be alone and pick at her sorrow. The men looked at her the way natives do at white women—slyly, furtively—it pleased her somewhat, this attention. The curious-eyed son of the vet was near the door but she didn't wish to speak to him. He would know the depth of her grief.

Subbu was hurt that Clara hadn't spoken to him. The day after the cremation, he walked to Siddapur to scatter his father's ashes in the river. He had shaved his head, bathed, prayed for his father's soul and, even as he followed the rituals, tried to fight the sadness that had nothing to do with his father's death. When the eleventh-day ceremony was over, he resumed going to Congress meetings, spun khadi and sweated in the fields; he went tired to bed but never slept.

Nanji observed his restlessness, knew the cause and the remedy, but could not bear the thought of festivities in this house that had long got used to tragedy. She had hardened her mind against memories of her dead baby, of her typhoid sons, of Kanike who died clutching the washing soap, of Chinni, Boju and Baliyanna. There was time enough for grief but not for rejoicing, and as always there was work, work and more work.

It was the month after Puthari; the Kaliyanda family did not celebrate the festival that year. Coffee-picking had just begun. The Yerava women left early for work and returned late, not stopping for a midday meal or to give the breast to bawling infants who had to assuage their hunger with squashy bits of banana, a piece of jaggery or a sprinkling of puffed rice. The women squatted beneath coffee bushes that were heavy with fruit and plucked ripe clusters without dropping a single berry on the ground. Their tireless hands, scoured by black lines, with chipped grimy nails, worked unceasingly. The women were skilled, they had clear minds that translated work and the amount of coffee picked into money, and money into sustenance. They did not have the debauched habits of their men; the only vice they allowed themselves was a hard nut of areca to redden the lips and appease hunger.

It was one such morning. Subbu was talking to writer Machaiah when Mutha handed the day's newspaper to him over the hedge. Subbu opened the *Kodagu* and read the press report.

He ran all the way home and into the bedroom where Nanji sat on a mat rolling wicks for the oil lamps. 'Govinda has been arrested. He was taken to Vellore prison last night.'

Nanji ripped a strip of cloth and ripped it again into a

square and rolled it into a wick on her thigh. 'What foolish thing has he done or said?' she asked.

'He spoke at a meeting in Madikeri, favouring the Dandi March.' Subbu knelt before his mother. 'Baliyakka—I must go and see him.'

'When the coffee has been picked and the first round of weeding done in the new clearing,' she said. Even as she said it, her breath quickened at the thought of the grief that Govinda's parents must bear. Oh, the irresponsibility of youth that could never understand such grief!

When the three *candies* of coffee had been pulped and spread in the front yard to dry and the weeding was well under way, Subbu went to see Govinda. Nanji hoped that a deeper involvement in the freedom struggle would absolve him of personal sorrow.

Subbu travelled for two days. The straight, broad fall of the back of his head was more obvious now that his head was only covered with short stubble and his forehead glistened with sweat; his was the type of face that people stared at when they knew he wasn't looking. Half an hour beyond Bangalore, he began to feel as breathless as an old man and he wasn't sure if it was the heat or the restlessness that plagued him of late.

Just before he entered the gates of Vellore prison, he checked the items in his pocket. He showed the guard at the entrance the letter from Govinda's father introducing him as a relative who should kindly be allowed to see Govinda.

The guard did not look up. 'You're anti-government.'

'What?'

'You're anti-government. You cannot see him.'

Subbu reached into the pocket of his bush shirt and withdrew four cigarettes. He laid them on the table. 'Navy Cut.'

The guard grabbed the cigarettes and gazed pensively at them; he put them carefully in the pocket of his uniform trousers and shrugged.

Subbu held out a tin of snuff.

The guard took it, smiling. 'You're still anti-government.'

'I'm also anti sons-of-mother-eating prostitutes,' Subbu said. 'I wear khadi but I don't believe in *ahimsa*.'

'Go in,' the guard said.

Govinda looked well, a paunch was visible beneath his shirt; the muggy heat did not bother him. He had just led a fast protesting against the food. 'We run the kitchen now,' he said, proudly. 'Our efficiency has upset the British and they're wondering if it's worthwhile to keep us in prison.'

'It's a terrible thing Gandhiji has done,' Subbu argued, 'by asking the students to join, he's buried their future.'

'Young men make good workers.'

'When the British leave, we must build our factories, start industries and be self-sufficient. And here's Gandhiji telling the youth to throw away their careers.'

'You talk like Patrick, without faith.'

'I have faith but not like yours. I'm not blind to the blind spots of great men.'

'Gandhiji has no blind spots.'

They talked then about the one thing that occupied both their minds. 'My parents want me to marry as soon as I'm out of prison,' Govinda said, trying to hide his eagerness, anxious to imply that he merely wished to please his parents. 'She's a graduate in Political Science from Hubli.' He took a photograph out of his shirt pocket. 'Ahalya.'

Ahalya was round-faced with a pretty mouth and thick black hair parted in the middle; her prettiness was slightly marred by the seriousness of her expression. Govinda took the photograph back when he felt that Subbu had stared at it for an indecently long time.

Subbu told him about Mallige. 'Why waste your time, then? A wedding is just what a family needs when it does not know how to come out of mourning. It's your duty to get married.'

Subbu was grateful for the words he had so badly wanted to hear. Just before he left, Govinda told him about his plan to buy land. 'I'm finished with doing estate work for someone else,' he said. 'I have enough money in the bank now to buy one hundred acres from Biddanda Muddaiah in Palangala.'

'You're a capitalist in khadi clothes.'

'Subbu, my friend, I am a practical man and must look to my means of livelihood. Nothing buys respect like ownership of land, which you are fortunate to have inherited. It has made you complacent.'

When Subbu went home and told Nanji that he wished to marry Mallige, Nanji was surprised. 'Her father has only thirty-five acres of coffee and a thousand *battis* of land to share between his three sons,' she reasoned. 'And that too in Kadanga, where the monsoons are too heavy for paddy and coffee. The girl is pretty enough but will be married off with next to nothing. Apparanda Muthanna is waiting for us to send the proposal for his daughter. And Biddanda Ganapathy's wife has just been to Mangalore to get *kokkethathi*, *pathak* and *ponnumale* for their two very pretty girls.'

'I've decided, Baliyakka.'

Her favourite son was also the most stubborn. Nanji sat at the bedroom window and in her crow's-foot scrawl wrote to Kademada Kalappa. Kalappa deliberated for two weeks. He knew of Rao Bahadur Madaiah's bountiful estates and of Baliyanna the vet. The boy too had good credentials, the only black mark against him was that he dabbled in the freedom struggle. Kalappa looked carefully at the photograph of Subbu with his parents, observed the carved rosewood sofa on which the parents sat and was impressed. He sent a courteous reply to Nanji, inviting the prospective groom and relatives to lunch the following Sunday. 'If you can make it convenient to be here at eleven we will go to the Subramanya temple to match the horoscopes,' he wrote.

On Sunday, the Kademada family was ready and waiting. At twelve, the guests still hadn't come and Kalappa sent a servant as far as the road from Virajpet, to watch for them. When there was no sign of the guests at two, he ordered that the gates be closed and they have lunch. Just as they finished the mournful feast, the guests were seen at the gate. Kalappa sent a curt message: 'It's time for my afternoon nap and I will not be disturbed.'

Mallige wept. She did not have the courage to speak to her father and entreat him to be kind. Daughters never spoke that way. Subbu had stayed in her heart and she had declined other offers, knowing he would come one day.

Subbu had been delayed at a Congress meeting that had dragged on three hours longer than scheduled. Now he waited with his party at the gate, hoping to meet Mallige's father in due time. But Kalappa got up from his afternoon nap, drank his coffee and went through the back door and along the mud track to his estate. When he returned at dusk, the guests were still there, waiting. When daylight gave way to darkness and the lamps were lit inside the house, Kalappa relented and had the gate opened.

It was a precarious truce; Kalappa was still furious about the indignity of having had to wait for the boy's party and if he hadn't been the grandson of the Rai Bahadur, the gates of the house would not have been opened. Kalappa accepted Subbu's apologies with grudging grace. The temple formalities would have to wait till morning. The guests ate warmed-up leftovers and retired to their rooms.

Subbu did not see Mallige that night but he was ecstatic that he was staying under the same roof as she. In the morning, he sent two trusted friends to the temple to talk to the *pujari* and bring back his assurance that all would be well. After a leisurely breakfast of *kadambutoo* with pork, the party arrived at the temple. The horoscopes matched and when the *pujari* invoked the blessings of Subramanya Swamy, a single white flower fell from the hand of the god, a sure sign of his blessing on the couple. Subbu was forever grateful to the *pujari*, who for a mere silver rupee had persuaded God to toss the white flower of good omen.

Kalappa was satisfied but Mallige's brothers teased her.

'Our sister will marry a little Gandhi,' they said. 'Our poor sister will wear khadi and cycle-tyre chappals for the rest of her life.' Like all girls in love, Mallige was impervious to the opinion of her brothers—and she quite forgot a certain boy who had played with her in the paddy fields until not long ago and who was earnestly in love with her. So intense was his passion that he was tongue-tied in her presence and now the Kaliyanda boy had beaten him to it. In the months that followed, Mallige received missives from the unhappy lover, who also wrote to Subbu imploring him to call off the wedding. When Subbu ignored the letters, he wrote to Nanji that Mallige had half her left forefinger missing as a result of clumsily using the knife on a chicken.

Such trivial details failed to deter Subbu. Nanji came out of her mourning to prepare for the wedding and she was appalled by Subbu's insistence that no alcohol be served during the two-day ceremony. 'No alcohol and it ceases to be a Kodava wedding,' Nanji said.

'It's a matter of principle,' Subbu said. His diminishing faith in Congress ideals was still a private matter and he could not bring himself to contradict abstinence from alcohol openly.

'How can we deprive our relatives and the village elders? And we can't let the bride's party leave without a touch of it, even if it is fermented gooseberry wine.'

'No, Baliyakka. We will serve coffee, and the first-class soda that I'll order from Mysore.'

The news of Subbu's crazy decision to have a dry wedding spread through Athur; at the Country Club, they decided to boycott the ceremony. 'It's shameful that Kaliyanda Baliyanna's son should be miserly on the most significant day of his life,' the General said. 'I've known the boy for years, I've watched his transformation into a Congress worker. I'll try and din some sense into him.'

Nanji served the General fresh toddy and fried chicken liver while he waited for Subbu to return from the fields. The General talked to Subbu but it wasn't any use. Subbu had secretly longed for the stuff when he had sat at Thammi's Club with his father and inhaled fumes that lingered in his nostrils, and imagined with absolute clarity the taste of it. Now he believed he had cancelled the desire from his mind and refused to take the General's advice.

There was one invitation that Subbu had to deliver personally. He walked to Pollibetta and when he reached the gates of Belquarren, he remembered his first visit with his father to treat a choking horse, the breakfast with the Foxes, the subsequent visits, and the unforgettable sweetness of her voice.

A lorry waited near the porch. A multitude of servants and helpers packed wooden crates into it, while through the doorway he could see a large wardrobe being dragged out on one leg, like a dead monster; china was being wrapped in paper and straw and gently lowered into boxes; shelves now empty and desolate were being dusted, the rooms swept. 'She will be leaving in three days,' a servant told Subbu. 'She doesn't want to meet people.' Subbu scribbled his name on a piece of paper and asked the servant to give it to Clara.

Clara was resting with a scarf tied round her eyes. She had a headache, one of those rare, ominous headaches that made its presence felt by gently teasing nerve centres and setting them on edge. A feathery throb almost like a caress that soft-shoed between her temples and behind her eyes; she could hear every scratch and scuttle outside her door, she could hear her servants trying not to disturb her, their soft whisperings, footsteps and the gentle scuffle of the broom that seemed to be sweeping over her brain, and outside the window the twittering of birds. So it was the son who wished to see her. Should she refuse? She did not really wish to see him, he was unlike his father—short and compact with disproportionately long arms and searching eyes. But she couldn't be rude; she agreed to see him.

Subbu sat in awkward stiffness on one of the few chairs left in the drawing room. She sat opposite. 'I came to invite you to my wedding.' He handed her the invitation card.

'Kind of you. But as you see—I'm leaving in a few days.'

'Why do you leave? We will miss you. You have done so much for the workers.'

She knew he was sincere. It isn't feeling redundant, she wanted to tell him, but a desire to snap ties that hurt. She knew very well that she didn't belong in England. She wasn't leaving because she was unhappy, it was just the end of one phase of her life. It had ended with the death of the vet.

The servant brought tea and biscuits. 'My father admired you,' Subbu said. 'He always talked about your courage and your goodness.'

The blood rushed to Clara's face in a deluge of happiness. 'I'll write,' she said.

Chapter Twenty-three

The barber shaved Subbu using milk to soothe the skin, and was gifted money, rice and the mat on which Subbu sat. Subbu bathed and dressed in a white *kupya* that was fastened with the red and gold *chale* at his waist. Round it he wore a chain of silver from which hung the *peeche-kathi* and the heavy *odikathi*. The best man placed the gold-lined turban on Subbu's head and seconds before the *muhurtam*, led him from the Kaliyanda house to the wedding *mantap*, shielding him with a white umbrella.

In Kadanga, the bangle-seller took Mallige's fair wrists in his hands, slid six black bangles on each and received his gift of money, rice and the mat on which the bride sat. Mallige dressed in the red sari with silver dots that her mother had worn as a bride; on her neck she wore the *jomale*, *kokkethathi*, *pathak*, pearls and the necklace with the cobra-headed pendant; three earrings hung from each ear; her hair was parted in the middle, pinned back and adorned with gold clips and jasmine.

At the same auspicious moment as Subbu, she stepped out of her father's house, taking the first step with her right foot for luck. Her ankle chains with gold stirrups attached to her toe rings flashed in the sun as she walked on the white sheets that were laid along the path from the house to the *mantap*. Her aunt held the white umbrella over her head and two girls with brass lamps walked on either side.

The *muhurtam* began at the same time in both homes; guests pressed forward to bless the couple. Subbu saw Barrister Appachu carried into the *mantap* to bless him; he saw the tears on his cheeks and knew they were tears of regret for his own unhappy marriage. Among the guests was Govinda, who had married as soon as he was released from prison; he came with Ahalya but stood a little away from her as if it was indecent to stand too close to one's wife. Ahalya's broad face was haloed in jasmine and charming confidence. She glowed with the complete happiness of a newly married woman.

It was the first dry wedding in Kodagu. Nanji was aware of the communal resentment and did her best to keep up the festive air. Pretty girls served snacks, weaving strands of colour and gold between the groups of men in black *kupyas*. They stood in clumps with hands on their silver-sheathed daggers, accepted snacks and bottled pink soda with sullen-eyed disappointment, spat the soda and abuses on the ground and left without lunch. The Kaleyanda boy has crossed the limits of decency, they said. The village band played music with what fervour it could muster without being provided a few drops of the essential. Here and there stood friends of Subbu, conspicuous in khadi and unable to comprehend that they were outcastes. Many of them were crude dhoti-clad men who ate noisily, belched *palav* fumes, relieved themselves amidst the coffee bushes and looked with amorous eyes at the girls.

None of this affected Subbu, whose mind was full of Mallige. He had seen so little of her that he could only remember the fair plump hand that had served him ghee rice. The fumes of incense swirled around until he felt quite giddy and didn't know if it was the fragrance or the music or the intensity of his longing that made his head reel. After the *muhurtam*, he joined the young men in dance, and danced so merrily that people wondered what powers besides toddy could have inebriated him.

It was late afternoon when Nanji stood by the stream and saw the wedding party off, on their way to the bride's home. Watching her son on the ramp, Nanji remembered the day when he had first walked and proved his fearlessness. 'O

Iguthappa Swamy, may the girl my son has married be worthy of him,' she prayed. Turning, she went home to supervise the feeding of the guests who would come back with the bride from Kadanga.

In Kadanga, nine trees of banana had been planted in a row outside the bride's home. Subbu cut them with nine neat swipes of his *odikathi* and danced as if he had really annihilated nine suitors to win Mallige. He was quite unaware that one suitor who had sworn that the wedding would never take place was there in the crowd, impatiently waiting to do what he was determined to do. Inside the *mantap*, the bride sat with her head bowed beneath the veil, her soft, plump hands clasped in her lap. As the band set the tempo of music, Subbu took her by the hand, helped her to her feet, lifted the veil and held the garland over her head. A shot rang out sharply and Subbu fell at the feet of his bride.

In the uproar that followed, the young man who had shot Subbu confessed his crime and offered to atone for it by marrying Mallige. But Subbu was confident of his strength: 'I'm going through with the ceremony,' he said, as they carried him indoors.

There were many ready to interpret the attack on Subbu as an ill omen and they advised Mallige's father to call off the wedding. But when Kalappa saw his daughter weeping with her head on her mother's lap, he knew that she was as good as married to the Kaliyanda boy.

'Don't stop the music! Let the men dance!' he shouted. 'And call the doctor, quick!'

The bullet had lodged in Subbu's right leg. The doctor dug it out and washed the jagged wound with carbolic acid, while the band played and the men danced. An hour later, Subbu limped back to the *mantap* and married Mallige.

Nanji, waiting at home, wondered about the delay. The lamps were lit inside the house and a dozen lanterns hung in the shamiana where the guests would be fed. She had not yet resigned herself to sharing the house with a daughter-in-law.

Nanji wasn't given to thinking too much about herself but she was already battling with her jealousy for the shy, sweet girl who had captivated her favourite son.

At last they came. The bride broke a coconut near the well and carried a pitcher of water to the house and, like all Kodava brides before her, stood the trial of patience and stamina while young Kaliyanda men danced and blocked her path. They danced for two hours until Subbu pleaded with them. Mallige entered the house, sought the blessings of the elders and became a part of the Kaliyanda family.

In the night, along with Mallige, Subbu was filled with a terrible shyness. Everything he had wanted to say to his bride slipped away from him. Mallige sat before the dressing table and began to remove her jewels; Subbu stood at the door, watching.

'Can I help?'

Mallige half-turned to look at him and shook her head. Subbu leaned on the padlocked door, one hand on the *peeche-kathi* that hung from his hip. His injured leg throbbed but more unbearable was the terror and the excitement of being married. He watched Mallige remove the three pairs of earrings, the *jomale*, *kokkethathi*, *pathak*, pearls and the necklace with the ruby-encrusted cobra head, the bangles, bracelets, ankle chains, the gold stirrups and toe rings; he watched her undo the gold clips from her hair and the string of jasmine that was wound round her plait.

'Now you can help,' she said.

Chapter Twenty-four

Nanji welcomed her daughter-in-law with elaborate graciousness, hoping that the girl was intelligent enough to perceive the hostility beneath. It was a hopeless match, she knew, the girl did not deserve to be a Kaliyanda bride. When Nanji had married Baliyanna, she had used cunning, good humour and a strategic display of efficiency to establish herself in her husband's home. She had accepted the maddening household from the first day, determined to strengthen both house and family. Her toughness mingled with the mud with which the walls were built and the varnish that coated the beams; it was infused into the cowdung used to wash the floors, and spilled into the marshy fields of paddy and the soft soil of the coffee estate. You could taste her determination in the oranges and the sweetness of her hospitality in the flowers that grew wild around the house.

Nanji had nothing to fear from her fragile flower of a daughter-in-law. She was not afraid of losing her son's devotion, which showed itself in the tone of his voice when he called her 'Baliyakka', and in the way he sought her blessings, touching her work-worn feet with his palms and pressing them to his eyes. The other sons only made a gesture by bending at the waist and sweeping their hands over her feet, insulting her with their false show of respect. Subbu wasn't like that. He was the only one of her sons who sat with her on the low stone wall skirting the tulsi plant when she went there to light a lamp at dusk. If something worried him, he went to her in the morning before anyone else was up.

Nanji resented her son's marriage and Mallige's modest

background. Families with prestige gave gold and silver to their daughters, to be displayed on the night of the wedding. Mallige had come with two tin boxes—one filled with clothes and the other with an assortment of vessels not worth more than fifty rupees. Her bridal finery, which had astounded everyone, had been borrowed. Her jewels amounted to no more than a gold chain, *pathak* and silver toe-rings. Nanji had seen the contempt in the eyes of the guests who went away saying, 'The grandson of the Rao Bahadur could have done better.'

Subbu was a foolish young man in love with his wife. He would come home at absurd hours, sneak up to the kitchen and announce himself with a projectile cough. Mallige, who sat on a low three-legged wooden stool kneading rice and rice powder for the *akki otti* would rise without looking at him, wash her hands and follow him to their room. When they came out, Subbu disappeared and Mallige resumed kneading; it wasn't the blowing with the iron pipe that made her bosom heave, it wasn't the fire that made her face flush and it goaded Nanji into a burst of activity and ill humour.

Nanji had a great contempt for Mallige's natural daintiness and delicacy of manner; she hated the way Mallige broke the *otti* into small bits, scooped tiny helpings of honey and ghee to her beautiful lips and chewed with slow thoroughness. Mallige could never keep up with the rest of them, so she hardly ate anything. That also exasperated Nanji, who was a robust eater herself.

Every man in Athur was in love with Subbu's wife. She charmed them with her effortless grace, her simple attire, her shy smile and girlishness. Only Nanji saw her as an incompetent housewife who could not get the servants to work. The only thing she did well was to carry trays of coffee and snacks to the guests. Her smiles won them all, and Nanji, who had laboured over the preparation of the delicacies, looked on with anger.

Like most women, Mallige believed that an ideal home

had to be filled with decorative fluff. Mere weeks after her marriage, she was saying to Subbu: 'Get me two vases and I'll make this drab house beautiful.' The following Sunday when Subbu went to Madikeri he bought her two vases of coloured glass. Mallige arranged a cluster of *rajakirita* with green-and-yellow crotons in one and a bunch of pink *thavare* and white lilies in the other. Her artistry was admired and coloured vases began to proliferate in every room. 'Beauty without usefulness is criminal,' Nanji cried out in frustration, 'there's work, work, work waiting to be done!'

In response, Mallige took out her sewing basket and book of embroidery and made six heart-shaped, red-frilled cushions and embroidered on them the figures of English girls in flowing skirts, bonnets and ribbons, in a garden of violets and iris. She sewed 'Good Night' pillow cases and 'Good Morning' tablecloths, mirror-work bedcovers, cross-stitch tea-cosies, satin-stitched Duchess sets, runners and doilies; she crocheted a lace curtain for the front room and strung it with beads of coloured glass that made maddening music all day and drove Nanji crazy. It delighted visitors, though, who sent their daughters to borrow patterns or learn a new stitch from Mallige.

Nanji was angry that this butterfly could rob her of her kingdom. Her power was being snatched away by a scrap of a girl who scattered her beads and her useless embroidery around. And she had the nerve to be haughty when it was more in order for her to be humble, having married several notches up! Mallige, who had nothing, behaved as if she was a rose among dahlias. She stayed aloof and spoke only when spoken to, she never allowed intimacy of any sort. Honourable, honest, forthright Nanji fell into the age-old trap of jealousy and began to disparage her daughter-in-law. She told the neighbours about Mallige's miserable background, criticized her lack of knowledge, her ignorance in the kitchen, her delicate constitution. No one countered Nanji because it was the mother-in-law's right to belittle her son's wife. Nanji's animosity puzzled Subbu but he couldn't take sides. Women, he realized, had strange ways of getting angry with one another; their tempers simmered for unknown reasons.

With all the ardent attention from her husband, it did not take Mallige long to start getting sick in the mornings, and then the cravings for tamarind and raw oranges with chilli began. Subbu catered to her whims. When Mallige began to show the glow and swell of motherhood, and Subbu prepared to take her to her father's home, he received a letter from Kalappa. 'The monsoons have been particularly heavy here,' he wrote, 'and medical facilities are not as good as in Gonicoppa. . . .'

Mallige stayed in her husband's home. Nanji cared for her daughter-in-law, remembering her own motherless days, and although she had no belief in the *lehyam* and rich concoctions given to pregnant women, she submitted Mallige to all of it, lest someone should say that she was negligent. Nanji was confident of handling the delivery at home but a week before the crucial time, Mallige began to plead with Subbu that he take her to a doctor. When she got the first twinge, Subbu rushed her to the Civil Hospital in Gonicoppa, paying three rupees for the taxi. It was a difficult labour; three days later, Mallige delivered a snivelling boy, as delicate as herself. To Nanji's dying day this hospital delivery was a humiliation. 'I could have guaranteed a strong, handsome boy for you,' she said to Subbu, who was trying to hide his disappointment at the fragile disaster that was his son.

Ahalya delivered two weeks before Mallige. Govinda and Subbu each invited the other to the naming ceremony of his first-born, each proud of his virility in producing a son. At Govinda's, the rites were simple: a temple puja was performed by the grandfather (who had retired from the school but not the temple). The grandmother applied a large black dot of coal mixed in ghee on the baby's forehead and named him Vishnu, and served a lunch of rice, *sambar, palya* and *payasam* to the dozen guests who sat in the temple courtyard. The Kodava ritual was elaborate: Mallige insisted that every family they knew in Athur be invited and of course all the Kaliyanda and the Kademada clan. The guests admired the infant, thrust rupee coins into his hands and ate chicken *palav*, pork and *paputtoo*, mutton fry and egg curry, while the infant bawled continuously and ended up with fever that night.

Subbu's son decided that he did not like his father. When Subbu tried to hold him, the boy turned and reached for his mother with a panic-stricken cry and extended arms, the way babies do when strangers pick up them. The boy was small and sickly and demanded all of Mallige's time and attention. He was named Thimmaya and Mallige shortened it to Timmy; Subbu who did not like the Anglicisation called him Thimmu and Nanji referred to him as 'that boy'.

Timmy's arrival provided Mallige with renewed opportunities to show off her sewing skills. She filled a chest-of-drawers with bibs, bonnets, mittens, lace socks, coverlets, wraps, and pillow cases with scalloped edging, and 'Timmy' embroidered on them. It was little wonder that from a young age Timmy began to think of himself as a prince.

Mallige bathed Timmy in a basin, not the proper way by sitting him astride her feet with his arms round her legs. Bolle's daughter Kenchi was brought in to help but Mallige never let the girl touch him. Timmy caught chills and gripes, he coughed, cried and vomited. The more Mallige fussed, the more sickly her son became and he resisted all food except fried chicken liver, pickled mangoes and coffee. He was up every night with a cough or tummy ache or a bout of sulking and Mallige carried him up and down the front room, cooing her love. 'That boy will grow up to be a sissy and a bully,' Nanji warned. She watched with suppressed anger at the way Mallige coddled him. 'He'll end up with a snub nose if you don't massage it with warm peacock fat. There's never been a snub-nosed Kaliyanda child.'

Subbu became a helpless insomniac and suffered the neglect from his wife stoically. Family life left little time for party meetings; until he received a message from Govinda one day. Gandhiji was visiting Coorg; a meeting had to be organized for the southern zone and Gonicoppa was the most central place. Govinda asked Subbu if he would arrange for the Mahatma's stay.

Subbu got a thatched hut ready in the coolest part of the orange grove, overlooking the stream. The hut was swept and washed with cowdung, two goats heavy with milk were tied to the porch and the hut filled with fruit, vegetables and nuts. The Kodavas were perplexed when they learnt that they could not show proper hospitality to Bapu, that he would not eat their mutton *palav* or taste crisp fried pork. While the Kodavas fretted over the Mahatma's nutrition, the British officials worried about the impact of Gandhi's visit on the simple-minded Kodavas. A police force was sent to patrol the area near the Civil Hospital in Gonicoppa where Subbu had been arrested years ago, and where he now supervised the laying of school benches to make a platform for the meeting. Thirty-six benches were laid aside, covered with straw matting and white khadi sheets, and a microphone placed in front of pillows.

The Mahatma sat with his legs tucked beneath him, skinny knees to one side; he looked so small and helpless that the Kodavas felt renewed alarm about his diet and the British officials wondered why they had bothered to sabotage his speech by cutting the power supply to the microphone. It was ploughing time, and only a hundred or so had managed to attend the meeting. Many came from as far as Mendalenad by crossing streams, trudging through marshes or by hiring bullock carts. Nanji and Mallige walked by the short mud track past the huts of the gypsies; they came early so they could sit on the straw mats laid out before the platform. Appachu, who swore against Gandhi, decided at the last moment that he wanted to see the conniving bastard, so Boluka brought him in the bullock cart.

The microphone didn't work. Govinda cast a furious glance at Subbu and began his welcome speech, which did not suffer because his voice was loud enough. He welcomed the Mahatma and pledged the support of the local people to the cause of freedom. Then Bapu spoke. Subbu listened to the gentle, dry monotonous voice that was without passion or rhetoric, and he realized that he must leave the Congress because Congress had very little to do with what Bapu taught. That night he dreamt that Bapu had embraced him in farewell when he left Kodagu and Bapu's bones had hurt him when they embraced.

A week later, Patrick arrived. He was a double graduate with honours from Presidency College and all set to take the ICS. He was shocked to see Subbu quietly dying in his plantation. 'I'm worried about your future,' he observed with sympathy. 'You must get out of this rut or you're finished. Leave your coffee and pepper and the dunghill of village politics and join the army.'

'I'll give up politics,' said Subbu, grateful that at least Patrick understood. 'But I must stay on here and look after my land and family.'

'And tramp behind bullocks in marshy fields and soothe your children on your lap? Join the army and rise, man. Look at me. I won't be happy just doing the ICS. I'll go to Oxford for a while, study the British in their country, find out how the piddly little island conquered half the world. I'll come back and take the ICS. My only obligation, Subbu, is to the devil.'

'You're going to Oxford? When?'

'There's only one hitch. Money. Father's too much of a miser to part with what he has. But I have a plan that will look after you, me and the money that your mother has stacked away. Let's borrow it. Not steal. Borrow. Right now her money is dead, no use to anyone. It'll be enough for my passage to England and for my college fees. When I'm there, I'll speak to the British officers and see that you join the army the proper way, through the Sandhurst Military Academy.'

'Mother will never part with the money.'

'Don't ask. The old woman has nothing to worry about if

she doesn't know. Money with me is like money in the bank. I'll double and treble it and return it, and throw in your passage to the Military Academy.'

Subbu said he would think about it, but that was only politeness. 'Marriage has robbed you of courage,' Patrick grumbled. 'Marriage is for those who want to rub each other's backs and sit in armchairs and recount with bitter nostalgia the young, energetic life of their past.' Patrick said casually that he had a woman in Delhi. 'I love her just as much as you love your wife but I'm not bound hand-and-foot. But is it marriage, or is it Gandhi's influence that has addled your brains? Any man who believes that the prick's only for peeing should be in an asylum but he's leading our country to freedom instead. Marvellous. This morality crap—put it in your back pocket, man, and sit on it, like the Americans. They designed back-pockets for trousers so they can stuff their morality and forget it. That's why they're going places. The British with their gentlemanly virtues are trailing. Never believe in morality. Can you see it or feel it like power and success? The only truth, Subbu, is that two plus two is four. Mathematics. Give me mathematics, not morality. Look, I'm not forcing you. Don't do it if you don't want to. I just thought being a friend and cousin, I should help. Time's running out and what have you got to show for yourself? Govinda, that cunning brahmin, is way ahead of you, he's someone in the Congress. Even Sunny Boy, selling cigarettes and slaughtering sheep is better off than you.'

Patrick stayed a week and in the end he convinced Subbu that he was doing everyone a great favour by taking Nanji's money. That afternoon, while Nanji was at work, Subbu and Patrick went to her room. Subbu rolled the mattress down and found the stout iron key along with her snuff and the *Gita*. They padlocked the bedroom door, opened the casket and took four hundred silver coins and five gold sovereigns. Patrick left the same evening.

Nanji discovered the loss and guessed what had

happened. She never mentioned it to Subbu because she knew he was already regretting what he had done. Though Nanji was worried sick about the money, she diverted her mind by staying with the Yeravas from sunrise until dark.

A year later, Subbu got a letter from Patrick. England offered everything Patrick wanted, and more. He would finish in a couple of years and return to India. He mentioned casually that the value of money had dwindled and the four hundred silver coins and five gold sovereigns were worth only half that amount and that he was hard pressed to return it.

Chapter Twenty-five

Subbu had known it all along; but until the letter arrived, he had hoped with a small burning hope that Patrick would pull off a miracle and get him across to Sandhurst, and greatness. Now he was certain that no such luck awaited him; sadness marred his countenance.

Mallige noticed. She had grown used to the constancy of Subbu's ardour and the unchanging loyalty of his love. She knew, of course, that his love for her could never match his love for the nation. At first, she had hated his yearning for abstract freedom; she had hated the way it made him wear coarse khadi and ugly chappals, sit cross-legged on the floor and talk of Gandhi and Nehru and a free India. But there was never any cause to complain of lack of passion on his part. Now there was this new restlessness: he would let days and nights go by without a word of endearment. She resented the change in him but was too preoccupied with her maternal duties to dwell upon the cause or realize that even when they shared physical intimacy, they were never intimate in thought. Her love for Subbu was locked securely in her heart and she hid it from everyone, even Subbu. Mallige believed that her love was a weakness, when in fact it was her strength.

Nanji could see into Subbu's grief and she suffered with him. He loved the land just as much as she did and worked for it. The coffee yield had increased by two *candies* that year, the granary was full, pepper fetched four hundred rupees and cardamom two hundred. But Nanji saw the absence of joy in Subbu's eyes as he went about his work and knew that one day she would have to let him go. It was no use telling him that to work for the land was superior to any kind of valour. Nor was she going to suggest that he look for his fortunes outside Kodagu. He would do what he must do but she wasn't going to tell him to do it. The thought of losing him was too painful, she wouldn't make it happen.

The dependence on land stifled Subbu as much as the virtues of Congressmen. It was all right for his mother to believe that his ancestors were up there in the clouds, ready to minister to their needs. Subbu did not believe it. No matter how well you cared for your ancestors and the deities by offering the best of meat and liquor, they did as they pleased. The land made endless demands until it became a burden that drove the young men out of Kodagu. His two brothers had deserted without ever soiling their feet in the paddy fields, or straining behind a plough. But he had worked alongside his mother and never shirked. Now he was seized by an urge to prove himself and appear strong and astute before his wife. He was afraid that she was disappointed with him; at times he saw contempt and a coldness in her eyes and it hurt him.

That day when he told Mallige, she was standing before the mirror, braiding her thick, long hair in a plait. It was that brief moment in the morning when the children slept and he was alone with her. He looked at her and wondered how she would accept the swiftness of his decision.

'I've decided to join the army,' he said.

She went to him and touched her lips to his cheek. From Mallige who wore her coldness like an armour, such gestures of tenderness were rare. 'I have to join the ranks,' he said and seeing the surprise in her eyes, added quickly: 'It's better to be a sepoy than to rot here.'

'Appachu Mava has friends in England, he can help,' Mallige said. 'And your mother has the money.'

'Mava can't do anything. He thinks he can, but he can't. And how can I ask Baliyakka for money? The few coins in her casket are her security.'

Nanji welcomed Subbu's decision. At least he would

slough off the dreams of nationalism that weighed him down because he did not believe in them anymore. Better to take up arms than spin cloth and talk about *ahimsa* while you hated in your heart. The pain of separation she would keep to herself.

The Barrister was surprised by Subbu's quiet submission to fate. 'I've friends in the army. Maybe they can fix you up at Sandhurst,' he said.

'I'll work my way up, I'll be all right.'

'You should take lessons from my son,' the Barrister said, bitterly. 'He deserves to be shot for treachery. You deserve to be shot too, for being stupid and generous.'

Subbu managed to join the ranks. Hundreds were recruited daily, because the British needed soldiers to help them fight the forces of Hitler that battered them at every front. Officers were being brought from England to train the sepoys. It was a good time to join.

'Not a word about nationalism or your wonderful Congress,' the Barrister warned. 'Show off a bit, get noticed. That's what the white men understand. That rogue Patrick has a gift for it. But one thing—you must always seem less knowledgeable than the British. These men who run the army haven't read a book after they left school. Be humble, even while you show off.'

Subbu listened, not wanting to argue with his paralytic, dribbling, mottle-skinned uncle. It wasn't pity he felt but a remote sympathy. It was impossible to pity the trivial problems of age. How could a young man like him understand what it felt like to have saliva stick in the throat or to struggle to work one's eyes or move an arm or get a stupid dead leg to work itself off the ground? How could he identify with such problems? And his uncle could not understand his need to join up and prove himself. He couldn't tell him that he wasn't joining to please the British but to please his wife. He could not impress Nanji so easily as that but some day, that too would come.

Subbu received orders to report at the Training Centre in

Belgaum. But first he went to Madikeri to officially quit the Congress. Govinda was now an MLC, a powerful man in the district, and a planter with a hundred acres of coffee. His new house had white-washed concrete walls and a long front veranda where he received visitors. He was on his way to a meeting, swaddled in thick, close-buttoned khadi, and fenced by a dense thicket of political aspirants, supplicating favours. When he saw Subbu, he freed himself from the gaggle and greeted his friend.

'You're defecting at a time when we need you,' he said. The brightness had left Govinda's eyes and moved to his cheeks, which shone thanks to the good food Ahalya pampered him with and a general glow of success.

'I can serve the country better by joining the army.' Subbu was conscious of the meaninglessness of his words even as he spoke. He wished he did not have to justify his actions. It was demeaning, unnecessary. He wasn't going to let Govinda make him feel guilty.

Govinda was persistent. 'You can do more as a Congressman. We've made headway, we're governing in five states. I know there's talk of corruption and high-handedness. As if the British have no faults.'

'We cannot handle freedom now. We must first learn to govern.'

Ahalya came to greet Subbu, bringing with her the smells of *sambar*, *kootu* and some ghee-smothered sweet. She was fatter now, and moved like a large, colourful awning around her husband.

'I'm not troubled with estate work,' Govinda said, proudly. 'Ahalya supervises everything. She reads the newspapers, listens to the radio and tells me what's important.' Ahalya sat a little away from them in cherubic silence, nodding only to emphasize Govinda's words; Vishnu sat near Ahalya's feet and played with bright wooden toys. He was the same age as Thimmu but small, with Govinda's black eyes. The child looked at him boldly and carried on playing, unruffled by his presence, unlike Thimmu who would have run and hidden behind his mother to announce himself. Subbu felt a twinge of envy.

Subbu spent all his last day at home wiping away Mallige's tears and promising her that he would take her with him when he got his first posting. In the morning, he went to sit with Nanji on the low stone wall skirting the *tulsi* plant where she was stringing hibiscus into a garland. She didn't stop when Subbu went and sat with them, she didn't lose the concentration needed to twine thread round the flowers and knot it just right so that the thick red petals of hibiscus opened to one side. Stringing hibiscus was different from stringing jasmine that you strung as buds plumped with dew, and then kept wrapped in a banana leaf till they bloomed. If *kanakambara* was used with jasmine, it lasted only a very short time; rose and *tulsi* when strung together made the favourite garland of the gods; *sampige* and *savanthige* with their strong fragrances were never mixed with other flowers. They lasted barely half a day, then the edges turned a curly brown and went limp. Flowers were to be offered to God or worn in the hair but to put them in vases was to insult them.

When she had finished, Nanji spoke to her son. She told him that she had offered a gold-handled *peeche-kathi* to Igguthappa so he would make a true soldier of him. 'Kaleyanda men always come back heroes,' she said. 'They win, or they die fighting.'

Chapter Twenty-six

Nanji also gave her son a satin pouch with one gold sovereign and ten silver coins. 'May this multiply in your hands to one hundred gold and ten thousand silver coins,' she said. 'And God give you wisdom to use it in a way befitting the Kaliyanda clan.' Nanji, with her face scared and shadowed, propped her misshapen hip against the front door and held Neelu by the hand. Her sari was stained with chicken gravy and she reeked of the kitchen and of snuff. Subbu touched her knobbly feet with his palms and raised his palms to touch his eyes, seeing only the brilliant whiteness of her perfection.

Mallige stood with her hands on Timmy's shoulders. She would not look at Subbu. 'I'll go-and-come,' he said to her, not knowing what else to say. He held out his hand to his son but Thimmu clung to his mother and wrapped the free edge of her sari sullenly around him.

'Thimmu, look after your mother and grandmother,' he said. The boy looked back at him sullenly.

Subbu took the KP Roadways from Gonicoppa to Bangalore, and boarded the train for Belgaum. He mingled with the unknown, smelled the smells of different castes, religions, languages and customs; a man performed asanas in the passageway and tied his body in a knot, another knelt for the namaz. Subbu stepped over him to reach the toilet that had a door that did not bolt, so he looked the other way until a fat, distressed-looking woman came out with her sari hitched up to her knees. Inside, the mud-coloured sink was filled with vomit that had slivers of cucumber and banana dotted with floating, oily bits of puri. On that twenty-four-hour journey,

Subbu travelled farther than the train could take him. He journeyed within a journey, and felt the impatience of wanting to reach where he was supposed to reach and wondered how he could do all that he wanted to do without tripping, falling and failing.

The Military Training Centre at Belgaum was a mass of concrete barracks on vast open grounds cordoned off by trimmed hedges and black-and-white poles. Subbu was amazed that anyone could have dared to put up such ugly structures as those army barracks. But he was new to this world, and determined to get used to it.

In the gloomy barracks, the recruits in their uniforms all looked alike, like matches in a box, but they were a varied lot—high-caste Brahmins, hardy Sikhs, wily Marwaris, shrewd Keralites, gleaming Tamilians, lazy Kannadigas and athletic Kodavas. It was no better than the prison except that food was plentiful. Of the two British officers at the training camp, Major Apple was very red-lipped, religious, polite, and grateful to be ignored by the recruits. Actually, they avoided him because they thought that his politeness was a subtle form of insult. Major Fullbright of the Durham Light Infantry was fat, heavy-breasted and moustachioed, with a bull neck and mean eyes. He never lost an opportunity to harass his underlings. The men were disciplined because none could bear the humiliation of Fullbright's punishments. Subbu was in good physical shape, his bones, muscles and reflexes were made for action and he handled guns with easy grace. But the Major did not spare him.

'Darn it, Subbaiah—wipe that arrogance off your face. Who d'you think you are—the Army General?'

'Sir, I wasn't . . . .'

'Liar! Ten laps round the football pitch during the lunch hour!'

Or it was:

'Goddamn you, are you trying to have *relations* with the horse? I said get *on* it, not *into* it.'

'Sir . . . .'

'Don't argue. Fifteen laps round the hockey field *with* equipment after dinner!'

It was a new world of rifles, grenades and starched uniforms that hurt when you moved, a world where your mind tip-toed on metal, a world where your saliva turned bitter in your mouth like someone else's vomit and where you ran until blood vessels burst at the back of your throat and you kept swallowing the blood and bringing it back up and swallowing it again because you couldn't afford to have Fullbright catch you spitting, and your chest hurt so much but you ran on because it was less painful to drop down dead from your heart popping than it was to face Fullbright's meanness. Subbu wondered how he could achieve greatness this way, with Fullbright and Apple as superiors, but in the army you didn't ask questions.

Many didn't last. There was Khalid Rizvi, said to be from a princely family in Kutch, with luxuriant curly hair that he massaged with oil every night. He tried to smuggle his soft mattress of dove feathers into the barracks but was detected and made to sleep like the rest on the regulation bunk bed. In the afternoons, he dipped surreptitiously into a green tin that he kept under his bed. He took a pinch of powder, placed it under his tongue and fell into a trance, or sang ribald songs and regaled the others with stories of his father's harem. Sometimes he took out a penknife and swore he would slit Fullbright's throat, sometimes he danced on the bunk and wept: 'Allah, why this fate for me?'

One Sunday, when Khalid had gone to the town, his friends stole the green tin, helped themselves to the mixture and lay down to experience ecstasy. Khalid, when confronted by the empty tin that had contained his year's supply, wept pitifully and divulged that it was made of nineteen secret ingredients including seven ground jewels, and it was guaranteed to make a man of him. But Subbu and the three others had grossly overdosed themselves and ended up with

213

nothing more exotic than violent purging that lasted four days.

There was Mohinder, a tall, fair Sikh whose mission in life was to write poetry that ranged from torrid love lyrics to fiery patriotic songs. He composed all the time, and read them to the others at night. But he fared badly in physical training and was punished every day.

Khalid lasted four months and Mohinder eight. Khalid wept copious tears and distributed laddus when he left. Mohinder went missing: the recruits woke up one morning to find that both he and their shoes were gone. The shoes were finally traced to the terrace above the recreation room where thirty pairs of shoes were strung, laced together, each pair containing a poem. They were late for PT and punished but it was a touching farewell.

After ten months of training at Belgaum, Sepoy Subbaiah received his first posting as orderly to Brigadier Parsons in Siliguri. The rest of his battalion boarded the steamer and sailed to Turkey to reinforce the Allied Army.

Part Four

Chapter Twenty-seven

Brigadier Parsons was florid and rusty-whiskered. He held to the firm belief that to be too courageous was also very stupid because if you got shot or blown to bits by a grenade, your courage went with you; it died and became pointless. He arranged to be posted to a peace station and then dedicated himself to the unheroic job of overseeing the mess for the soldiers. It took him not more than two hours a day after which he sat back to smoke his pipe, drink tea and contemplate the tragedy of war—he was certain it would inspire him to write a book someday.

He liked to observe the sepoys at work.

Parsons' impression of the natives was based on generalization. He defended himself from their obsequiousness, timidity and their sudden bursts of emotional fervour with a cavalier attitude that earned him the reputation of being difficult. He was happy they thought of him that way; with the natives it was easier to be difficult than anything else. Familiarity, even with his own people, was something he hated. But his new orderly, Subbu, was interesting. He spoke English and had a sound knowledge of the world. His gentle nature belied the fearlessness in his eyes; he was never awed by his superiors, he was not shifty-eyed, nervous, servile or surly and he went about his work with a stubborn determination.

Subbu polished the Brigadier's buttons, shoes and epaulettes, ironed his uniform, heated water for his bath, made tea and cursed God for having given him an unfair deal. He felt like a castrated dog, a eunuch, not a soldier. What was he to write to his wife and mother, how would he face Sunny Boy without the war medals, what about the fierce tales of battle he was going to tell his children? Igguthappa accepted the gold-handled *peeche-kathi* from his mother and forgot to return the favour. If only he was there at the front, if not in combat then at least as a signalman, a truck-driver or a stretcher-bearer. Anything was better than polishing buttons and brewing tea for an unheroic Brigadier.

He wrote passionate letters to Mallige and respectful ones to Nanji. Mallige replied in her rounded, childish hand, conveying the unvarying news of visitors, the weather and Thimmu's health. When Subbu left home, she had given him his barely read copy of the *Gita*, which she covered in pink satin with his name embroidered in red. Subbu took it out of his box every day only because he liked to feel the satin softness. It was like Mallige's transparent, marble-cold skin that warmed with his passion; he remembered the exact length of her bones, her small shapely ears, plump fingers deft with thread and needle, her curly hair that refused to grow, her small breasts and youthful ankles. He imagined his fingers moving over the knobs of her spine until they disappeared into her unending softness. He thought about his wife with longing and passion but when he wrote, his letters were as dull as hers.

Nanji wrote in a big-lettered scrawl that was like crows' feet dragged over ink. She filled pages with details of field work, coffee-picking, the sickness of workers and the health of cardamom bushes. Subbu could sense in her letters the eagerness to communicate her ambition. She always ended with: 'May Igguthappa bring you greatness.' Subbu wondered how that was possible, doing what he was doing. Just because he wore uniform and shoes that echoed against the floor like wood and because he dealt with guns and had learnt to talk rough, he wasn't going to become great. In the army they were taught that every duty, however insignificant, was important but Subbu didn't buy that line.

He suffered his job for six months and then one day he

pleaded with the Brigadier to recommend him for front-line soldiering.

The Brigadier looked closely at his orderly. 'No guarantee you'll come back.'

'I know that, sir.'

'Married?'

'Yes, sir. I have a son.

'Well—don't you like working for me?'

'Sorry, sir—I don't.'

The Brigadier took the pipe out of his mouth. 'Live for an ideal, don't die for it!' he shouted. 'No ideal is worth dying for. It's a simple bit of advice but it may see you alive at the end of a war. Got it?'

It wasn't like that. Subbu was not burdened by an ideal but by a restless urge to impress, a pure urge, like wanting to be the best shot at Kailpodh.

'I'll see what I can do,' the Brigadier said and promptly made arrangements to ensure that Subbu would continue as his orderly till the next posting. A soldier with Subbu's type of courage risked being killed, he was the foolish type who would disregard safety for valour. The Brigadier believed that even if the orderly hated him for doing it, he would be saving him for his wife and son.

Subbu did not avail of his leave when the year was up. He could not bear the humiliation of facing his family until he had completed this dreadful sentence of working as housekeeper.

'This talk about Independence,' the Brigadier asked Subbu once. 'What do you think?'

Subbu was silent.

'If the British leave, who will run the government?' the Brigadier continued, speaking of 'the British' as if he was talking of an alien race that had nothing to do with him. 'Not Gandhi and his ridiculous bunch of squabbling Congressmen, some of whom I gather cannot even speak English.'

'That has little to do with running the country, Sir.'

Parsons had the natural composure of his countrymen

and he did not reveal either his amazement or his annoyance. A year later, Subbu was moved to the mess and then to the Brigadier's office; Subbu suffered with fortitude, worked in silence. At the end of his term, the Brigadier sent a confidential report to headquarters, which said: 'Definite officer material.'

Officers were in demand and Subbu's luck was good. After a year's training at the Cadet Training Corps and eighteen months at the Military Academy in Dehradun, Second Lieutenant Subbaiah went home on leave before his new posting to Agra.

At home, in his absence, the two women had spent a most harrowing time together. While Nanji tended the fields, shouted at errant workers and wrangled over the sale of bananas and oranges, her mind was on Subbu, who was her only hope and only reason to carry on breaking her back over the estate. Mallige thought incessantly of Subbu, whom she loved madly, and drove herself crazy trying to hide the fact from everyone. Subbu was the only real event in her life and she couldn't bear the separation. She fussed over Timmy, crocheted lace tablecloths that could never be used; she sewed and knitted constantly to fill the long days of uselessness.

Mallige's sweetness and serenity were a constant irritant to Nanji. She would sit in the kitchen grinding rice into powder and through the window see Mallige in the front room embroidering cushions or knitting some useless fluff, the needles clicking, tapping and scissoring in a bewildering maze, and a miracle forming beneath her fingers. 'People waste time making things that will never be used,' Nanji would fume. 'I am an unfortunate woman who has Yeravas working in the house in spite of having a daughter-in-law.'

Mallige's needles clicked faster and the scarf or sweater grew with alarming speed. It was as if she was knitting her bitterness into her work so it would be preserved for ever. When she had exhausted the wool and made enough sweaters for Thimmu, a cap for Appachu Mava and a scarf for Nanji that she would never wear, she ripped the sweaters apart and did them again. Purl, plain, twist, turn, cross over and back again, clicking needles into intricate patterns and weeping for the fate that had forced her to live with Nanji. At times, the ball of wool tucked beneath her arm fell to the ground and trailed. Mallige picked it up, undid the plexus of woollen strands, rewound the ball and started again. She made lace curtains for the windows, a canopy for the bed, frilled pillow-cases, cross-stitched bedcovers with red-beaked parrots sitting on brown branches; she made table covers, runners and beaded lampshades.

Nanji showed her scorn by using Mallige's cushion covers when she needed a bag for coffee, rice or jaggery and wiping her snuff-stained fingers on the lace curtains until they were brown with grime and had to go. Mallige watched with helpless rage as the symbols of her talent vanished. Nanji fumed in the next room, wishing Mallige would react to her in some way but she didn't. Mallige's ignorance about coffee and paddy, and her timidity with the servants, were to Nanji's advantage. Mallige's feeble attempts at cooking went unnoticed, her suggestions were ignored by servants who bypassed her and did what they felt like or waited for instructions from Nanji. The air thickened with the tension between the two women. The Barrister, Thimmu and the servants were unable to help. It was at such a moment that Subbu returned.

The monsoon had lasted longer than usual and rain fell in sporadic, violent bursts; the earth was water-logged, the trees green, the air moist and sweet with rain. Subbu took the proper road from Gonicoppa to Athur because the mud track was flooded. He held his tin trunk high above the puddles in his left hand so the water wouldn't damage the precious gifts inside: a cream silk blouse for Mallige, halwa for his mother, balloons and wooden toys for Thimmu. As he walked past the huts of the gypsy women, they greeted him with friendly smiles. Subbu did not understand the tacit welcome in their eyes but he slowed his pace and savoured the warmth of their greeting.

When he saw the family he realized how far he had journeyed from them. He was a military man with the knowledge of war inside him, a war where nations fought and men died in thousands for their country, while here his mother and wife fought for no reason at all. Mallige's sweet face was etched with lines of bitterness but she smiled her shy smile when he gave her the blouse piece and told her about his new posting. She listened to him speak of military training and white officers and the war to which he had never been. She had many questions to ask but didn't know how to ask them. His son seemed alien, like someone else's son. Thimmu watched his father with a sidelong glance, grabbed his balloons and ran.

Time had been merciless with Nanji. Her stoop was marked, the tilt of her hip more pronounced, her toes splayed, her eyes screened by wrinkled lids. Her legs were a lattice of tired blue, green and purple veins; they made her legs ache but she ignored the pain and continued to slog in the fields as before. After the age of fifty-five, she stopped counting her years, not out of vanity but because by doing so she could live in a state of ageless grace and carry on doing what she did. She knew that during his four years as a soldier, Subbu had been unable to fulfil either her dreams or his. It was not his fault, though, and she prepared to welcome him with an abundance of love and good food. Subbu had planned to tell a few well-chosen lies about his heroism but seeing his mother and feeling her bony fingers on his shoulder when he touched her feet, he decided it would be foolish and unnecessary. His mother was strong enough to take the disappointment. And now that he was an officer, he had the chance to prove himself.

With Subbu's homecoming, the house that had been brooding in sorrow woke and shook itself out of gloom. Two of Subbu's brothers—one was a bank manager in Hubli and the other worked on a tea estate in Wynaad—made polite appearances and vanished. They came only because they were too apathetic to break the habit of visiting home every year. They were delicate men, content to prostitute themselves for fixed hours of work; the Kaliyanda streak of honour had been gouged out of them. They came and left with an abruptness that did not hurt Nanji; she had lost them years ago. Subbu's sister Chondakki came with her brood of five, exhausted everyone with her unbelievable capacity for gossip and left after three days, unable to comprehend the silent, determined hostility of Subbu's wife, who resented all women.

Two months after Subbu returned, Mallige was pregnant. Nanji was determined to nurse Mallige during her second pregnancy. She had resolved to handle everything and ensure a healthy baby this time. She observed the flat bottom of her daughter-in-law and said, 'It will be a girl.' She disregarded custom and did not bother with the *lehyams* and oils that filled a house with the smell of pregnancy. Instead she put Mallige on a diet of pork, *puttoos*, honey and bananas, and insisted she walk once a day past the fields of ripening paddy to get her into a tranquil frame of mind. The night before the full moon, Mallige went into labour and an hour later, a triumphant Nanji presented a lusty long-limbed girl to Subbu.

Subbu's daughter was dusky like her father, with long ears and limbs, completely unruffled by the excitement her coming had caused. She lay quiet and aloof in her cradle with her long arms crossed over her chest and thin legs folded up on her tummy. 'Like God's Insect,' Nanji observed, thinking of the praying mantis that sat next to the photographs of ancestors and figures of Kali, Ishwara and Igguthappa in the puja room. The girl was named Neelamma and called Neelu, but Nanji called her God's Insect.

Neelu was easy to handle—no tantrums, screaming fits, colic or sniffles and at her happiest when Nanji cuddled and cradled her. She slept and ate without fuss and hardly needed looking after, while Timmy grew into a cocky boy who was always showing off. If a guest entered their home, or someone stopped by the gate to talk to Nanji or Subbu, he sang and whistled and made sure he was heard and appreciated. He couldn't jump very high, climb trees or turn somersaults so he thrashed his sister to assert his importance. He stayed close to his mother and kept away from Subbu and Nanji. He was soft, pink-cheeked and delicate, and gave Mallige enough reason to pamper him.

Chapter Twenty-eight

Mallige packed their belongings into large tin trunks and argued that it would be foolish to take Nanji with them. Nanji solved the problem by deciding that she did not wish to leave home and go to an unknown place. Besides, the Barrister needed looking after.

Several times a day, Subbu would climb the stairs and sit with the Barrister. Incarcerated in one corner of the attic and subject to hallucinations, Appachu lived on the edge of a madness so real that the other illness which took his brother and his father spared him. His conjunctiva slid down like nictitating membranes and he refused to see what he did not wish to see.

And he rambled: 'Listen, boy. Marriage is tricky business, you know that now. It would have been trickier if you had changed your dharma for it. Or for any other stupid reason. What happened to Dronacharya in the *Mahabharata*? He gave up his brahminical ways and adopted a kshatriya lifestyle to get even with Drupada. He ate meat, acquired a kingdom, fought wars and sullied forever the sacredness of his birth. The Kauravas who revered him as their teacher never absorbed him into their fold as one of them and he died fighting for a cause that was not his. I was born into a dharma but I didn't stick with it. Look what happened.'

Subbu listened patiently, not knowing what else to do.

Nanji sent them off to Agra with coffee, pepper, rice, salted pork, pickled mangoes and a jar of stringy banana jam that was Subbu's favourite. But it was Neelu she would miss more than her son. The little girl stayed all day with her as she worked and in the evenings listened most attentively to her stories: tales about the orphaned twins who lived on tiger's milk and about the prince who changed himself into a parrot so he could visit the girl he loved and about the nine-foot crocodile found in Beppunad with a woman's silver anklet and toe ring in its belly. At night she liked to sleep with Nanji in spite of the smell of snuff, the noisy breathing and the soft trickle into the chamberpot at night. Nanji would miss her more than anyone else. She took the little girl in her arms, ran her fingers over her ribs and said, 'One day, when I'm longing to see my God's Insect, I'll get in the bus to Bangalore and then the train and come there . . . and let's see . . . . I'll bring a jar of pickled pork, bamboo, dried *mathi*, four bottles of honey, a sack of jaggery, *raja bale*, salted mangoes and the biggest jar of banana jam you ever saw.'

Life at the Agra Cantonment had all the attributes of a peace station and an air of slothfulness that was attractive because it was compulsory; the empty hours had to be filled with precision and exactitude and in the army, one was paid to live in style. The valour they had to show in the battlefield had to be repaid in comfort and ease during the years of peace. The army made the point that men were not meant to be valorous—it was a high demand on them to be heroic. So just the way pregnant women in Kodagu were battened on *lehyams*, the armed forces throve on a meticulous and fastidious type of laziness that had its own decorum. Officers dressed in tight trousers, spurs and epaulettes that made even the most mediocre shine with an impressive, non-specific smartness. The wives fell in line and most of them blended into the downy softness of conventional army life, which had separate rules for the women. They exchanged sweater patterns, learnt pudding recipes and made perfect cakes shaped like boats, rockets, Mickey Mouse and Donald Duck for their children's birthdays. Women from diverse backgrounds met at the army confluence and devoted their lives uncomplainingly to such sophistication, and turned out super-smart children equal in every way to the best products of elite public and convent schools.

Mallige bloomed as an army wife. Her home was impeccable and filled with evidence of her sewing prowess; she wrote devoted letters to her mother-in-law each week and savoured every day the freedom of not having her around. It was the single greatest victory of her life. It gave her the determination she had never had and she used this new-found strength to consolidate herself amidst the fluff and flutter of army wives.

Her only adversary was Karan Singh, Subbu's orderly. The swift-footed intense young man was devoted to 'Saab' and he treated Mallige like an impediment, an unnecessary appurtenance that Saab had no need of. He ironed Subbu's clothes, polished his shoes and epaulettes, took care of his every need. Subbu, who was still new to his officer role, was more at peace with this coarse young man of the hills than with the officers and he could not understand the power struggle between Karan Singh and Mallige. He submitted himself to his wife and orderly without realizing that he had forsaken his independence within the house. Mallige and Karan Singh fell over each other to bring him food and drink. When he woke in the morning, Karan Singh was ready with coffee; in the evenings, Mallige beat the orderly to it with the *nimbu paani*. Karan Singh kept two buckets of hot water for Subbu and only half a bucket of lukewarm water for Mallige; fresh hot chappatis went on Subbu's plate and if he did not want them, to the children but never to Mallige.

Thimmu went to the Jesus and Mary Convent School in a rickshaw along with nine other children from the Cantonment. Thimmu admired Hitler and cycled around the Cantonment sporting a flag made of a cushion cover with a swastika painted on it. Mallige believed it to be a sign of her son's superior intellect; Subbu ignored his precocious son. Neelu was quiet and did not give trouble but she really missed her grandmother.

Subbu climbed the army ladder without hitches and became a captain, but he was a misfit in the army. He did not drink, out of a sort of loyalty to the Mahatma and as an unspoken promise to his mother. He looked uncomfortable in his uniform, as if it hurt him somewhere. There were times when he felt that he had been better off as a Congressman. Army life meant having your mind riveted to your body with steel, saluting seniors and addressing them as 'Sir' even when you hated them. Army morality would have pleased Patrick—it was purely mathematical.

Sometimes he dreamed of Chinni. Her voice spoke in his ears like a pleasurable ache that he tried to ignore but couldn't. She was unhappy and bored with death, she said. The feeling of uselessness in life was reversible, death wasn't. Boju had been a fool to believe in life after death. There was only death after death. 'I tried to tell him that but he was too eager to be with me. Now he is in the middle, knocking on both doors, belonging nowhere. No matter how wretched you feel, never opt out of life,' Chinni said.

The urge to impress had gone out of him and he resigned himself to the fate of achieving nothing. The only way to live out one's existence was not to think about it. That was how he survived, until one day the city magistrate asked the army for help to curb a protest march by women Congress workers who had threatened to *gherao* the officials in the Secretariat. Subbu was wary of the idea of confronting women with anti-government ideas when he himself did not know where his loyalties were. The last thing he wanted was to open fire on the women or use any kind of force, so he instructed the sepoys to empty their rifles of cartridges. Thus unarmed but appearing to be armed, the sepoys approached the women. There were hundreds of them of all ages, bold, angry and in no mood to listen. They shouted slogans and jeered at the army for siding with the British. The sepoys became so demoralized that they wanted to retreat. Helpless, Subbu approached the five women who led the protesters.

'Please disperse,' he said in his most polite voice. 'Or we'll be forced to shoot.'

'Go on, shoot.'

'Indian soldiers shooting their own women. What courage.'

'You may even get promoted, Captain.'

'What do you plan to do?' Subbu asked the women.

'We're *gheraoing* the officials. We'll wait here till they come out and listen to us.'

The women gathered around the gate and waited. Subbu instructed the sepoys to stand a few yards away and not get ruffled by what the women said. It was difficult: the sepoys were restless and it was obvious that they sympathized with the women. When it got dark and chilly, the women drew their saris tightly around themselves and shivered. Subbu sent for blankets from the messes and distributed them among the women. He wondered if they would refuse his gesture of goodwill but they accepted gratefully. When it was totally dark, the women dispersed quietly without the soldiers having to fire a single shot. Subbu ordered the sepoys back to the barracks and climbed into his jeep when he felt someone touch his elbow. It was one of the women who had led the protesters. She was short and dark and dressed in white khadi.

'Could you spare the time to meet me sometime, Captain?' she said. 'My name is Devaki. I live at 24 Reading Road.' She turned and walked into the crowd, leaving behind the smell of coconut oil.

Subbu got into his jeep and forgot her.

Chapter Twenty-nine

It was some weeks after his confrontation with the Congresswomen that Subbu received a short, terse note from Devaki. He placed her immediately and called at her home on Reading Road.

'Ah, the army man. Come in,' she said. The drawing room was small, with a table, chairs and two seats made of boxes covered with coarse bedspreads; the table was cluttered with books and a dusty radio, a shawl trailed from the chair on to a pair of chappals on the floor.

'I don't know your name, Captain.'

It was hot and humid; sweat poured along his forearms into the hollows of his elbows and dripped to the floor. 'Subbaiah. You asked me to meet you, but I hadn't the time . . . '

'You're a sheep in wolf's clothing, Captain. The uniform doesn't suit you.' Her tone wasn't hostile or rude, but he was hurt because she spoke the truth.

'You called me here to tell me that?'

She smiled. 'Yes. And to be friends.' She had thick hair, grey woven into black, and tied in a careless knot at the base of her neck. She was too young for all that grey hair. Her sari was a cream-coloured khadi with a green tear-drop design along the hem and she wore it carelessly, with the free edge flung in a crumpled heap over her shoulder. The blouse was high-necked and tucked into her sari at the waist.

She rose and switched on the fan. It started with a sullen creak and blew muggy air at them; Devaki went to the kitchen, and returned with *nimbu paani* flavoured with *tulsi* leaves. The sweat dripping from Subbu's face and neck cooled and relaxed him. 'I did not mean to offend your group that day,' he said. 'I had to do my duty.'

'You offended us all right, and please don't talk about duty,' she snapped. 'Does it not shame you to ape the British? Why don't you ask to be deported to England, so you can serve better? We have enough problems without having to fight our army.'

'Is that why you dislike me?'

She laughed, and her teeth sparkled like a young girl's. 'If I dislike someone, I'll be very sweet.' She was serious again. 'I've worked for the Congress since I was fourteen, with my father. I don't trust all Congressmen, they show off too much with their austerity, I trust only my ideology—of freedom.'

Subbu told her of his involvement in politics, of his days in prison, his disillusionment. He tried to justify his commitment to the army: 'If the Indian officers and soldiers rebel now, the British will leave without imparting any know-how, and we'll be helpless to defend our borders. Gandhiji is way off the mark when he talks of non-violence.'

'You favour violence, Captain?'

'I hate violence. But a strong army is the protective instinct of a nation at work. We must be ready—the British are not the only people with imperialist ambitions, look what happened in the war. The Japanese nearly won Burma.'

'We disagree about most things, Captain. But come again. I live here most of the time, doing party work. My husband's a scientist in Patiala.'

Subbu visited her again out of politeness, and later as a friend. She was always disarrayed, alone and in khadi. In the few months preceding Independence, she was away often on party work, and he waited eagerly for her return so that they could sit in her cramped drawing room and talk. She was like a young girl then; Subbu envied the purity of her idealism and wished he could feel that way again. Devaki never talked about her family. Once he took Neelu with him. For nearly two

Kavery Nambisan

hours he and Devaki argued about the state of the country and the girl sat quietly, listening. And from then on they went together. Once when he went without her, Devaki asked, 'Where's Neelu?' and seeing the surprise on Subbu's face, added: 'We're friends, don't you see? The army life hasn't touched her. It usually gets the children.'

That's when Subbu asked her if she had children of her own.

'What gave you the idea I'm married?'

'You said your husband's a scientist in Patiala.'

'Sorry, that's my fictional husband. Life's much easier for a woman if she says she's married. Sorry.'

Once India won freedom, there was more prestige in being an army officer. Subbu loathed army life and stayed only because Mallige wanted it. He knew he was not a good husband, but he tried. He still loved the girl who had served him ghee rice at a wedding. He went home every year to see his mother and each time he asked her to come, she said not now, perhaps next year. Mallige was relieved. The cold war she fought with Karan Singh supplied just enough conflict to comfortably occupy her mind; with Nanji around, it would be a battle on two fronts and she didn't want that. But a fate worse than having Nanji at home awaited her.

Soon after Independence, Subbu was posted to Uri, a non-family station at the Indo-Pakistan border. Mallige begged Subbu to get his posting changed, to ask Patrick who was an ICS officer in Delhi to use his influence. Subbu refused. Mallige wept as she packed their things into eight trunks and set out on the three-day journey home.

Nanji had been living in peace with the Barrister and when Mallige arrived with the children, she was grateful for the intrusion of noise. She cooked great feasts, lurching on her splayed feet; she sat in the kitchen on a three-legged stool and while Neelu dipped her hands in rice flour, Nanji disembowelled sardines, rubbed in a mixture of coriander, chilli and salt and dropped them into sizzling pork fat. She plucked the feathers off a just-killed chicken and cut it into twenty-one identifiable chunks for the curry and told the Insect about the chicken that had carried a gold sovereign in its gut. Mallige made brave attempts at pretended harmony with her mother-in-law but Nanji wasn't really interested in wasteful sentiments.

Uri did not alleviate Subbu's apathy. The weightlessness of his existence frightened him. He shackled his body and mind to military operations, to training and vigilance; like a lapidary, the army rules chiselled and shaped his thoughts until they fell in vertical channels and arrayed themselves in soldierly formation, intractable and precise. But when he gave in to real thinking, he could not see the greatness in maniacal firing, bayoneting and flinging grenades to snuff out lives. He had once thought that a soldier's life was simple, a mere matter of loyalty, obedience and doing one's duty. Now he knew that the simplest was also the most difficult and his love for his country was not so fervent that he could carry with grace the burden of taking human lives the way Sunny Boy slaughtered sheep for the butchers in Madikeri. As a soldier, it was too easy to kill, it was the ease that frightened him. Subbu had not gone to war and he did not long for it anymore.

He knew that the army, like him, suffered from a severe malaise. The army chief had been sidelined by the Defence Minister and frustrated by the casual attitude of the government. The Congress pandered to the people and campaigned for the next election, firm in the belief that it was hardly the time to worry about imaginary dangers from neighbouring nations. The army chief cautioned that neighbours could not be relied upon to remain passive, in spite of the reassuring scene of Prime Ministers releasing doves of peace into the sky.

Subbu was due for his promotion when he decided to quit. He met Patrick in Delhi when he went to submit his resignation. Patrick had studied at Oxford and then at Harvard before taking the ICS; he was comfortable with the different factions in the government and indispensable as a bureaucrat. He had married his girl, Rosie D'Cruz and they had two sons. 'Some things in life are inevitable,' Patrick said, glumly. 'I don't love Rosie but by God, I admire her. I need her aggressive charm to help me along here. She wins half my battles.'

Rosie was modelling towels when they met and Patrick knew straightaway that she was meant for more important things. 'How would you like to marry an ICS officer?' he had asked her. 'It would be a damn sight better than draping towels round myself to make a living,' she said. 'But I'm not marrying a smooth-talking guy who aims to be an ICS officer. Be one, then we'll see.' Patrick knew then she was hard-headed enough for him. She was with him at all important occasions: 'One, because she's white-skinned and stylish, men notice her. Two, she knows what to say when and to whom, which in the Land of Gods is important. Our leaders like nothing better than being flattered by a beautiful woman.'

Patrick took time off his busy schedule to persuade Subbu not to leave the army. 'You're doing well, there's nothing to stop you from rising to the top. You may even end up as a General and they will put your statue up in Gonicoppa.'

'A statue for crows to shit on.'

'Even Sunny Boy has more brains than you. There's only one life to live, man. Can't you see? Once you're lowered into the grave and the mud's evened out over you, or you're sat on a perch of wood and set fire to, you think you can have second thoughts then, you think you can come back and try to claim your missed opportunity to do this, this, this? To hell with dharma and karma and afterlife. The only way to immortality is to do something now when you're alive.'

Patrick put Rosie on to convince Subbu. 'Patrick has influence here,' she said. 'He can arrange to have you transferred to a city.'

Subbu resigned from the army and went home. But first he took the train to Agra. It was late evening when he reached Reading Road; Devaki was in blouse-and-petticoat, her hair drenched in coconut oil, her skin reeking of it. He sat in the front room while she went in for her bath and he tried to guess her mood by listening to her bathe. She scooped water and poured it in quick splashes that made him sense that she was cross with him for arriving that late. She came out with her hair glistening wet, a towel flung over her shoulders to catch the dripping water. The fragrance of her just-washed body distracted Subbu as he spoke.

Devaki was not puzzled by his decision to quit the army. 'I knew it. You were not comfortable, the awkwardness showed. About upsetting family and friends, forget it. The choice is yours. Look at me. I opted out of the Congress last week. I'm delighted with the independence of being independent. I'll speak my thoughts. I'll win or lose by my worth, not just the party's. My father is furious but he loves me too much to stay angry for long.'

'You need the skin and sensitivity of a reptile to succeed in politics. You should get out.'

They ate chapatis and dal at the kitchen table. Sitting across from her, Subbu remembered Patrick asking, 'What's she like? Army wives are usually attractive.' Devaki isn't an army wife, he had replied, she's in politics, she's only a friend. Even better. Women in politics are sexy. I should know. For a woman to get on in politics, she's got to be sexy.'

Subbu told her he was worried that Mallige would take it badly. 'When you love a woman,' Devaki said, 'and the woman loves you, she gives more than love. There will be no problem. Mallige will protect you from harm. So will your mother and the Insect.'

'And you.'

'And me.'

He asked her to visit Coorg the next time her work brought her south. 'I'll come anyway,' she said.

Chapter Thirty

When Subbu reached home, the first person he saw was Nanji; she was seated behind the fat iron bars of the window where he had stood as Kunta and wished he could rip the bars apart and run out. He knew his mother would take the news of his quitting the army as calmly as she took everything else; it was Mallige he worried about. He couldn't see her but as he walked from the gate towards the house, he sensed her presence and his heart beat fast, like a lover's heart. He would hide the news from her for the moment, delay having to see the hurt in her eyes.

In the year that Subbu had been away, the children had grown. The Insect thrived on the sweet moist air of Kodagu and filled the house with girlish, bubbly happiness. She was shy at first with her father, and spoke only when spoken to; she liked to spend her time with Nanji, the Barrister, Boluka or the General. Boluka, who was older than Nanji and now blind, spent most of his time walking to keep his body warm and agile. Twice a day, he came to rest beneath the stone wall that skirted the tulsi plant. He never asked to be fed, he did not even ask for half a coconut shell of jaggery coffee but when he sensed Neelu's presence he would call out and say, 'Ask your grandmother if she wants crabs. I'm going to catch some today.' Nanji, who knew that he was past catching crabs, would say that crabs were welcome but he must eat some *thaliya puttoo* or rice with salted *mathi* before going down to the stream. When Boluka returned in the evening, it was with the promise of bamboo or mushrooms or *koile meenu* the following day. Neelu sat with him while he ate a plateful of rice with pork and told him about school; the crabs were never mentioned.

The General's visits were rare now, and when he came he stayed all day. He sat on the porch in Baliyanna's armchair, and talked to Nanji. 'I've stopped going to weddings,' he told her, sadly. 'Because when I sit down to eat, children gather around and make fun of me. Do they think I'm a derelict, a homeless nobody in need of free food?' He had been hurt by the ill manners of young people but he was always courteous and polite; in spite of his painful arthritic knees he stood up when Mallige came out with a plate of fried meat or chicken liver to go with his toddy. Neelu would sit on the steps and listen to him tell her grandmother about his letters to Nehru in which he proposed that the best way to govern the country was to put a pork-eating Kodava at the top.

Thimmu was unhappy in Kodagu. He preferred Agra where he could ride his bicycle with the swastika flag and pretend he was a Nazi. He befriended three Jammada boys and swore them into the secret society of Indian Nazis that preached the supremacy of the strongest and planned to annihilate the black, short, pug-nosed Yeravas. As part of their training, the boys killed twenty chicks from Nanji's chicken coop by twisting their necks and when this became tiresome, by crushing them swiftly beneath the rice pounder. The massacre wasn't discovered until the stench from the granary led searchers to the foul, rotting bodies of crushed chicks that lay buried in the paddy.

It was two days before Kailpodh. Sunny Boy came with a leg of mutton wrapped in banana leaves and handed it over to Nanji in the kitchen.

'Get me the red cock with the black plumes,' she said to him by way of invitation to lunch.

Sunny aimed with his catapult and hit the bird on the leg. He carried it to the stone near the well and with the fingers of his right hand pulled upwards on the head while with the left he pressed the winged breast down, thus elongating its neck;

237

gently, he squeezed with the right hand, turning clockwise; the wings flapped with a faint rustle, legs twitched, the eyes stared. When he brought it to the kitchen, Nanji had steaming water ready to dowse the bird and soften it so the feathers could be plucked easily. 'If I go back to school and finish Matriculation, can I be a soldier?' Sunny asked her.

'Who will bring me good cuts of mutton, then?' Nanji asked. 'It will be hard to manage without you.' Sunny Boy was placated. He hitched up his trousers and showed her the ulcer that had spread like a big, black mushroom across his shin to his knee. 'See, it's doing nicely.'

Neighbours came for the Kailpodh lunch; they were proud to belong to the same village as Rao Bahadur Madaiah, they had had high regard for the vet; they also knew that the Kunta showed promise in spite of having quit the army.

Nanji had reared a big, black sow for the occasion. The day before the festival, Subbu shot the sow neatly in the middle of the forehead. Three Yeravas managed to squeeze her corpulent body through the gate of the pigsty and carried her to the roasting pit that had already been dug and lined with straw; the sow was lowered into the pit and the straw lit. The roasting went on all day until the hairs were charred; the hide turned to granite and gave off the smell of half-cooked pork. Sunny Boy, with Neelu on his shoulders, supervised the roasting. 'It's done! I can smell it!' he shouted to Nanji who waited in the kitchen with a huge pan of sizzling fat.

The evening before Kailpodh, Subbu got the guns from the gun rack and cleaned them, and while he cleaned he talked to Neelu about the hunting trips of his childhood, about tiger weddings and about eating raw meat beaten on hot rocks. Thimmu peeping through the window was unable to control his curiosity. 'Show me how to shoot,' he asked. Subbu taught him to load a gun, wondering even as he did why he was never comfortable with his son.

In the morning, the guns were crowned with *rajakirita* and lined up next to the photographs of ancestors and the icons of the gods. The puja was brief, like all pujas without a brahmin to do the honours: Subbu prayed that the family and village should be blessed with prosperity. Food was offered to the deities and to the guests who sat on straw mats in the front room. The workers ate outside.

Gun sport followed lunch. This was the moment when young men showed off their shooting skills by aiming at a coconut balanced on a pole. The strongest among them lifted a boulder as heavy as the heaviest man, raised it over his shoulder and flung it. The old folk gathered on one side and watched. Many were really old, with bowed legs, bunioned feet and wispy white hair blowing over their faces; their ropy fingers clutched walking sticks, their toothless gums worked on betel nut that was too hard to eat and too good to spit out. Only a few among them were strong and straight and proud.

Nanji realized that she too belonged with the old, who had formed their own horizon, standing there to one side like a palisade beneath the row of areca palms, while the vigorous, cocky, hot-blooded youths fired and whistled, hooted and sang their invincibility. Nanji looked at the old people and spotted without doubt the figure of her husband among them, with his black cap and his umbrella crouching like a big black bird on the back of his coat. She saw the Rao Bahadur in *kupya-chale* and turban with silver whiskers that joined his sidelocks, one hand on the *peeche-kathi* at his waist, posing for posterity; she saw her father, not in the throes of his last illness but as he had been before that; she saw her soft-skinned, baby-faced mother-in-law with the panther cubs and tiger-claw ornaments; and she saw her grandmother Neelakki, proud and strong, with the shoulder cloth knotted over her bosom. Nanji thanked God for having sent them along to bless her son.

People said Subbu was her favourite. It was true. What could you do when something bigger than yourself pulled you to one child over the rest and you hung on to him with teeth that were stronger than a tiger's teeth, until you knew you had to let go because otherwise he would struggle free and your teeth would maul him? That wasn't what she wanted for her son. Her only disappointment was that her son had married a weak wisp, a petal of a girl. Such folly could neither be mended nor revoked, so Nanji prayed: how much longer did she have to wait before she was banished as a black-and-white photograph to a corner of the puja room? Without a strong wife, Subbu needed her even if he didn't know it, and most men didn't. They never saw the role women played in their lives. Looking at her ancestors Nanji was aware of a strength that linked her to her grandmother, and to her son who she had no doubt would pass it on to that long-limbed daughter of his. Such thoughts concentrated in Nanji's mind until they formed a cicatrice in a corner of her brain, so clear and good and solid that she could put her bony fingers around it. The Kaliyanda clan was not doomed to oblivion. Subbu's brothers would come and go like shadows, they would achieve nothing; her only daughter Chondakki had slid uncomplaining into motherhood. But Subbu would make up for all of them.

'Baliyakka—what are you smiling at?'

It was Neelu, tugging her sari. Nanji bent down and lifted the girl on her hip. 'My little one, I'm smiling because just now I saw your grandfather, great-grandfathers, great-grandmother and great-great-grandmother whom you remind me of. They had come down from the skies and were standing here a moment ago watching the gun sport. Isn't that nice?'

'I'm glad they could come,' the girl said.

Nanji needed her son now more than ever. She did her best to cope but her body could not keep up with the physical demands of the land. She had guessed that her son was unhappy in the army; but she hadn't asked him to join, and now she wasn't going to ask him to leave.

Some weeks after Subbu's return, Patrick arrived on a visit. The Barrister shook his fist and swore at his son, but the words were incoherent and lost in the tobacco-stained spittle that bubbled on his lips. His body had crumbled with the years and he was confined to the attic, except when he was carried down every evening to be bathed. He stopped eating at the table when he realized it was too much work for the servants to carry him, and no matter how much Nanji pleaded, he refused to occupy one of the bedrooms. Nanji became his nurse, companion and angel, she fed him, talked to him and listened to his chatter that only she understood; she knew that his was a weakness of the tongue and not the mind, Appachu Lawyer's mind was clear and sharp. She remembered him as a handsome young man, just returned from England, she remembered his confidence and the appetite with which he had eaten her chicken curry, *paputtoo* and the red, ghee-fried bananas. The lash of Baliyanna's rebuke had left an open wound in Appachu and she tried to make up for the unkindness of her otherwise gentle husband. It was perhaps because of this that she forgave Patrick and did not ask for her money. Appachu's daughter Emerald, who was headmistress of a school in Bangalore, sent her father a quarterly present of arrowroot biscuits and Ovaltine. Once she came and tried to communicate with her father in the shadows of the attic, then reverted to the ritual of sending him gifts of biscuits and Ovaltine.

Patrick kept well away from the attic after his initial attempt, but his father's anger and rejection did nothing to dilute the conceit with which he spoke about himself. Patrick's face had begun to take on the same pattern as the healthy side of his father's face. The lines on both their faces fell in formation; transverse on the forehead, pouched under the eyes, curved brackets around the mouth, wavy folds on the neck. Though the stroke had flattened the lines on one side of the Barrister's face, father and son resembled each other to a remarkable extent. The only difference was that Patrick had inherited his mother's big, protuberant eyes while the Barrister had the shapely long-lashed eyes of the Kaleyanda clan; on the paralysed side, the lower lid drooped and the eye watered.

While Nanji was busy with the coming and going of guests, Neelu took over the task of feeding the Barrister. The faint smell of incontinence did not bother her as much as the watering eye and she frequently wiped it with her hand. While she fed him, he told her meaningless jokes interspersed with flashes from the past. Neelu stunned Nanji one day by asking, 'Tell me about your sister who married Thatha's brother.' Nanji, who had never talked to her about Chinni and Boju, stopped in the middle of pickling bamboo with pork and told her about them. When the Barrister rested, Neelu read his books; he observed her in the skein of light that filtered through the skylight, and said: 'One thing you never, ever forget is that it is dangerous to change one's dharma. You understand?' The Insect looked at the dishevelled, old man and nodded, wondering.

One evening when the family was at supper, Neelu came stamping down from the attic and tugged at Nanji's jacket.

'What's it, Insect?' Nanji asked.

'Appachu Thatha.' Nanji grabbed a glass of water and ran up the attic steps; the others followed. The Barrister was hunched over on his bed, the paralytic eye dribbling profusely onto his cheek. Nanji gave the glass of water to Patrick.

'Give him *thirtha*,' she said.

Chapter Thirty-one

Subbu fired two shots with the gun that Boju had used years ago to announce the death of the Rao Bahadur. The body was brought down from the attic, bathed and dressed; Nanji made garlands of hibiscus, *kanakambara, sampige* and rose petals, lit *agarbathis* and the lamps, and began the vigil. From her seat on the reed mat near the body, she issued orders to the Yerava servants to brew jaggery coffee in the largest copper vessel and to steam *kadambuttoo* in readiness for the mourners who would begin to arrive.

But no mourners came. At midday, an emissary arrived from the villagers. 'It is unwise to burn the body of an outcaste in the family *smashana,*' he said. 'Better send it away to Bangalore for a Christian burial.'

'Appachu Bava has been punished enough for his one youthful mistake,' Nanji said. 'Can we not make amends now that he is dead?'

The emissary went away and the family continued its vigil. A few of the village folk approached the gate with a rupee coin each for the funeral expenses but none came in. Patrick looked at the wasted body sat up on the chair and felt a hostility towards his father who had embarrassed him in life and more now, in death. The Kodava rituals irritated Patrick, he couldn't see the point in wasting time on flesh that would soon rot and putrefy; it was all right to pay tribute to the living, but not to the dead body of a person who had achieved nothing. It was certainly more sensible to take the body to Bangalore. 'The padres will oblige me even if they don't want to,' he said.

Subbu, like his mother, had the confidence of his convictions. 'The pyre will be lit in our *smashana*,' he answered.

'What's the use, it'll annoy your ancestors,' Patrick said, only to contribute in some way to the stressful situation. He did not care for the sentiments of the dead but he hated to have to be around at his father's funeral.

The fumes of putrefaction began to permeate the incense, tulsi and sandalwood aromas. 'We must cremate him before the sun goes down,' Nanji said. She sometimes saw people as being of two types, those who liked going to a funeral as a social occasion and those who went because it was an essential ritual. For Nanji, it was the culmination, the final full stop to a life; you could bypass a wedding or a naming ceremony, but to miss a funeral was unthinkable. Why then had these good, noble Kodavas hardened themselves against sorrow? Appachu had regretted his mistake a million times, he had advised others against changing one's dharma, and yet he paid dearly for having violated the code once. It wasn't fair.

Subbu, Patrick and two Yeravas carried the body in a bamboo chair strung with rope. Patrick lit the pyre; the Barrister was cremated like his parents and brothers, in the family *smashana*. Subbu gathered the ashes in a brass pot and Nanji sent up a prayer to the ancestors.

It was a mourning to mourn about. Never in the history of the Kodavas had a death not been grieved for by neighbours. Mourners always came to stay with the family until the cremation. Till the eleventh-day ceremony, there was never any need to cook, because the neighbours brought food. Relatives, even those who lived as far as Sunticoppa, would come to share the burden of grief. Inevitably, there was the uncle or aunt or fourth cousin who took advantage of death and sponged on a grieving family. When the stay went well beyond the limits of mourning and hospitality, the sponging relative was gently ordered out. But when Appachu Lawyer died, the only mourner besides the family was Chengu Master, his friend and classmate. He missed the funeral by a few hours but stayed till the eleventh day. He wore the scuffed grey coat, white shirt with collar studs and shoes that had been resoled every year for seventeen years, but the hat that he always raised for a lady, and the red tie, were missing. He sat in the front room with his cheek resting on his walking stick and talked to Nanji about Appachu who had got a bad deal in spite of his superior intelligence and looks.

Emerald came the day after the funeral and stayed two weeks until they went to Talakaveri to scatter the ashes. She understood nothing of the rituals but liked going to the top of Brahmagiri to pray for her father's soul. With a schoolteacher's eyes, she saw that besides Nanji, the one most stricken by grief was the Insect and she comforted the girl with her strong, reassuring schoolteacher arms.

Emerald was a large woman with big shining eyes, straight bobbed hair and the habit of wearing thin blouses that maddened men. She was a serious woman who found men more interesting than women; she talked earnestly about the future of the education system, while the men listened and tried not to think about the thinness of her blouse. Mallige was annoyed by Emerald's presence and showed it by staying in her room for most of the time that Emerald was with them.

When Chengu Master and Emerald left, Nanji resumed work in the fields. Sometimes the Insect went with her and on their way back, she begged Nanji to take her to the *smashana*. The gnarled old woman and the girl climbed the stile at the far end, walked past the mango, tamarind and *athi* trees and entered the clearing where each long-dead pyre was marked by a *tulsi* plant, surrounded by a profusion of marigolds and cockscombs which were hardy enough to thrive without care. Neelu crouched near the spot where the pyre had been lit for Appachu Thatha with her legs folded beneath her skinny thighs, her arms embracing her knees, and her skirt often riding up her legs. Nanji bent from her waist, grabbed the weeds with ropy fingers and when she was done with weeding, gathered the just-fallen figs and waited for the Insect.

She knew she should really tell the girl to pull her skirt down but modesty was not important at times like this, so she left her alone.

The Insect was one of a kind. She would pull away and take off over craggy rocks and jungle and if you were a good parent or grandparent, the only thing to do was to let her go. Individuality, like talent, could never be suppressed but it was not easy to find it even when it shone like gold or silver before your eyes. You needed something yourself to see it in others. She waited for the girl to rise and they ate the figs as they walked home. Neelu thought of her ancestors lying peacefully beneath the earth. She knew that except for Boju and Chinni and five of Nanji's children who died young, the others had been cremated but in her mind she saw every one of them lying there in peace beneath the cockscomb and marigold.

The villagers continued to ignore the family. The women who visited Nanji, the men who stopped at the gate to talk, and those who came for Subbu's help to get their sons into the army, now turned away or averted their eyes. Subbu was hurt but Nanji knew that it was an expression of faith in a tradition. 'They admire us for what we did but they are honour-bound not to show it,' she said. 'It is as it should be.'

The month of Minyar passed and there was not a drop of rain nor any sign of clouds; the sky remained blue and naked, the paddy fields were hard and crusted, the coffee shrivelled. The villagers were convinced that the stupid disregard of a custom by the Kaleyanda family had cost them their livelihood again. It was the curse of the ancestors. A delegation of villagers approached Nanji and exhorted her to perform Satyanarayana puja and Ganapathi *homa* to absolve the family of its crime, and insisted that she offer a gold crown to Igguthappa as penance. Nanji refused; she had done her duty by her brother-in-law and she trusted her ancestors. Every morning, and again in the evening, she prayed. She never pleaded or asked favours; she prayed that justice be meted out.

It was many weeks before Adare clouds began to gather

overhead. Pot-bellied, tantalizing, mocking, sullen clouds—grey, hunch-backed, sinister monsters that sulked above Athur and lolled in the sky and took on the colour of a crow's neck. Thunder rolled, lightning gashed the sky, the wind shook the trees and the rain fell in lovely glistening sheets. It fell straight down to the earth and proved that the ancestors had forgiven the Barrister and the Kaleyanda family. Athur had its best monsoon in forty years.

Amidst the immediacy of grief, Subbu decided to tell Mallige. He sat by her side while she sewed, and tried to tell her but when he saw the tranquillity, the dreams for their future in her eyes, he put it off only to spare himself the pain of seeing her sadness. Even though he loved her, he had made her cry so often and he suffered more when she cried. In the end, when he told her, he was heartlessly abrupt. 'I'm quitting the army,' he said. 'I filed the papers in Delhi before I came.' The light faded from Mallige's face; she looked at him for a long while, then she bent down and went on sewing. She didn't cry or make a scene. It was really very easy.

Two weeks after the Barrister's death, Patrick received a typed letter of condolence from Govinda who was the Minister of Education in the Mysore Government; it ended with an invitation to visit him in Bangalore.

Patrick, with Subbu and Sunny, announced himself at the ministerial wing of the Vidhana Soudha; they were ushered in through the carved sandalwood doors of the office. 'You're having lunch with me,' Govinda said and sent his PA to phone Ahalya. 'You know about the public function this evening on RSV Grounds? I'm chief guest. We'll go together.'

They drove to his bungalow in his flagged black Vanguard. After lunch, they moved to the drawing room; Patrick and Govinda talked of political matters while Ahalya plied them with *kesari baath*. She looked permanently parturient, permanently happy. Govinda talked incessantly, even more than Patrick. He believed his views were important, and while he waited for the others to finish, he drummed his fingers on the sofa, shook a leg or ran a finger over his upper lip with turgid impatience. Patrick was more attentive, he cared about what the others said although he rarely agreed. They talked of different things. Govinda turned to Subbu and said:

'If you hadn't left the party, you would have been here with me.'

Subbu was silent. Of what use was it to speak of his sadness to Govinda, a Minister with a bungalow shaded by *gulmohur* and jacaranda, a garden and a pond with goldfish, what use was it to talk to him of snuffed-out ideals?

'From a poor, agricultural nation, we have stepped into the modern world,' Govinda said. 'We're industrialised. When the British ruled, we imported safety pins, biscuits and blades. Now what is it we don't make here? I have the statistics. Thousands of villages have electricity, every village has a school, a hospital, a bank and post office. We work for the masses. In ten years, every Indian will be above the poverty line.'

'And every politician will be above the prosperity line.'

Govinda was hurt. 'None of this belongs to me, Subbu—not the car, the bungalow, servants, peons. I believe in truth and austerity. Ask Patrick. Ministers in Delhi have a Dodge or Studebaker or Mercedes, I make do with a Vanguard, I'm not greedy.'

Subbu walked in the garden with Sunny while Patrick and Govinda talked inside. 'I have a petition to show him,' Sunny kept saying. 'It's about dogs.'

'Yes, yes, show it before we leave,' Subbu said. He couldn't overcome his sadness. How easy and smooth was Govinda's climb to the top, how unwholesome his pride in his success. Of what use was achievement if there was no purity in the heart of man?

'The dogs . . .' Sunny reminded him; they went in and he gave the petition to Govinda. 'The municipality in Madikeri sends a van to round up the dogs,' he said. 'They take them behind the prison and shoot them. I made this petition protesting against the cruelty.'

Govinda scanned the petition. 'We have more important matters to worry about, Sunny.' He meant to say it kindly but his smile was distorted by his annoyance that so slight and stupid a matter was taking up his VIP minutes. He handed the paper back.

'What's more important than dogs being killed for no fault of theirs?'

'These dogs carry diseases that can spread to humans,' Govinda explained. 'The municipality is doing a service by getting rid of them.'

'They don't get rid of people who carry diseases.' Sunny was appalled by the stupidity of it. 'I've been carrying this leg for years, but no one's got rid of me.'

'Sunny, the municipality is doing its job.'

'You were a better chap when you were in school,' Sunny said, angrily. 'I'm going.'

To cheer up Sunny, Subbu took him to a film starring Raj Kapoor and Nargis. Sunny got the tragedy of the lovers mixed up with the tragedy of the stray dogs and cried through the film. In the afternoon, they drove to the RSV Grounds; Govinda was ushered on to the dais, Patrick sat right in front; Subbu and Sunny occupied seats in the eighth row.

Govinda sat on the floor with party workers; a large tricolour badge on his coat, more obscene than opulent, announced his patriotism. When he rose to make his speech, his movements were slow and deliberate. He paused to adjust his breathing pattern to an easy rhythm, his stomach muscles were neither tight nor flaccid, and a tiny contraction of the muscles around his eyes lent a brief gleam of compassion and hid the coldness. His hands were clasped behind him to avoid the nervous twitching that could start involuntarily even though he was not nervous; his head projected forward showing his concern and enthusiasm but inwardly he held himself with a steel hardness that was untouched by adulation.

It was an inane speech like all political speeches but without too much emotion, which was currently out of fashion with the leaders. Subbu listened with a part of his mind. How confidently Govinda spoke of truth and austerity, how perfectly rounded the words, the tone, the pauses. What was this truth Govinda spoke of? If you shook it in people's faces, would they recognize it? Did it have a hardness, a softness, a voice, a smell, a temperature that you could measure and say, 'Ah. Truth'? How could you tell real truth from half truth, pseudo truth, hypocritical truth, inflated truth, deflated truth, cavernous truth, malicious truth and apocryphal truth? The open wickedness of Patrick was nobler than the unrelenting hypocrisy of Govinda.

The speech ended and the applause came like a massive, collective reflex; garlands were heaped until they buried Govinda's head and weighed on his neck. For a moment, Subbu saw Govinda's eyes bulge, his skin suffuse into an ugly red as if he would strangulate, then he hastily took off the garlands and smiled an uncompromising smile that made Subbu wish that the garlands had strangled him.

When they went back to their hotel room, Sunny was sadder than ever. 'What's the use of having a friend who's a big-shot minister if he won't help?' 'Ministers can't be obliging their friends all the time, they have important matters to attend to,' Subbu explained. Sunny shot up in bed, fished out the petition and flung it at Subbu. 'He didn't even read this.' Of the three signatures on the petition, one was the signature of Satyu Sir.

Sunny took a long while to get over his anger. When he returned to Madikeri, he sulked for weeks, keeping his shop open but serving only the customers he wanted to and chasing the others away. He went back to slaughtering sheep after making a deal with the butchers—he could feed as many stray dogs as he wished with the entrails left after the meat for the market had been set aside.

Chapter Thirty-two

Nanji droned her prayers and looked through the window at Subbu as he came out of the house, broke a mango twig and two soft, wet leaves to clean his teeth. Chewing, he walked out of the gate and crossed the ramp; Nanji continued the soft whispering of her prayers, cleared away dead flowers and *agarbathi* ash and with a part of her mind followed Subbu. The stream, now full with rainwater, would gurgle friendly greetings at him as he walked past the Jammada threshing yard to Kaleyanda land. He would sit on the rocky bank and watch daylight pour out of the darkness and light up the far end of the stream as it flowed away into the Maneyapanda paddy fields. He would spit out the chewed leaves, wash his mouth with the cool water and know that here in Kodagu was where he wished to be. He belonged here, to this one place that breathed peace and did not suffocate him. Subbu was in love with his land and Nanji knew it.

He would stay till there was light enough to see the row of mud huts that Nanji had built for the Yeravas and until Maneyapanda Uthappa's tile-roofed house with blue windows announced itself on the opposite slope, flashing between the areca palms. He would then walk home, past Somaiah writer's house, where the tall bony wife of the writer would be stooping over a basket of dung with which she swabbed the just-swept front yard of her house. Somaiah's wife would straighten herself in greeting and stoop again for more dung.

There Subbu was now, walking in through the gate as the workers began to arrive in clusters; the women wore their saris at mid-calf with long-sleeved jackets, they covered their hair with bits of cloth and carried baskets for the manure. Men in muddied shorts were ready with scythes, axes and hoes to clear two acres for the planting of Arabica. When the men and women had fallen into separate lines, Somaiah writer began the roll-call.

On Nanji's bed, the Insect still slept, with her knees tucked against her belly. Just as Nanji finished her puja, she heard Subbu start the tractor. Nanji loathed the red-and-yellow monster that carried a cloud of smoke on its back and polluted the sweet air of the morning, but it was she who had goaded Subbu into buying it. It was quicker than the bullock cart for carrying coffee seedlings from the nursery to the new clearing, and for transporting paddy, coffee, hay and manure. Later, when the rains became erratic, she convinced her son that it was worth taking a loan to buy an artificial irrigation system. The ancestors had given up on the super-smart, English-speaking, sophisticated mediocrity that was now the Kodava race; the clouds could no longer be relied upon to bring rain, so it was practical to supplement rainwater by artificial means. When Edward Rice, the best of British planters, decided to go back to drizzly, cold Liverpool and sold Windsor Manor, the two-hundred acre estate, his new model Austin, his BSA motorbike, the furniture and estate machinery, Nanji told Subbu to try his luck.

Windsor Manor and the estate were bought for thirty-five thousand by Chendanda Joe Boy. (The house had undergone a total renovation in recent times: the coloured glass panes disappeared, the walls, doors and windows were painted white and it was renamed The White House.) Subbu met Rice just before he moved out, and negotiated the purchase of the irrigation system.

Edward Rice was the same as Subbu remembered when years ago he had seen him during a veterinary errand with his father—straight and lean, with precise, economical movements. Only his voice was softer, his movements slow.

They sat at an oblong rosewood table in the massive dining room from which most of the furniture had been removed and lined up outside to be packed and dumped into lorries; the house was suffused with the smell of the past.

'What will you do when you go back?' Subbu asked, unable to imagine what life would be like for Rice in his country. His status in Coorg seemed to suit him so well, it was a pity that he had to leave.

'It'll take me a while to get used to Liverpool,' Rice said, sounding neither enthusiastic nor unhappy about the displacement. 'It's as it should be. I haven't any regrets. My wife and children left last month, I'll be taking the steamer next week.' He paused, letting his gaze sweep across the garden that was already showing signs of neglect, to the coffee plantation beyond. Rice was proud of his estate. He had been sensible enough to learn from the natives while making the best of the knowledge the British planters had to offer. He could stay on but it would be a fossilized existence, a clinging to the past when everywhere around him life turned unpredictable corners. 'You remember Clara Fox?' he asked Subbu. 'I had a letter from her. She tells me there's an Association of Coorg Planters in London—I must become a member. Clara plans to visit Coorg, next year.'

'It may be better for her not to come.' Subbu said abruptly. 'You see—there aren't many people around who know her.' The actual reason was that he did not want to see Clara as an old woman, it would be uncomplimentary to her past. She was the kind of woman whose beauty would fade with the years. She was unlike Nanji who cast off beauty and carried on because it never mattered to her; or Devaki who would age happily because she wasn't beautiful: or Mallige, who would stay beautiful, like a pressed flower, in old age.

When Subbu proved that the yield of coffee and paddy could be increased a hundred per cent, his neighbours became eager to modernize. They pooled their money, got loans and bought tractors and irrigation sets that could be shared by half-a-dozen estates. It was happening all over Kodagu: crops increased, co-operatives fixed fair prices, the Coffee Board was established and the Kodavas found themselves with money in the bank. Electricity and pumped water entered homes, western toilets replaced the bogs in the bushes (future generations would scarce imagine what their forebears had gone through to complete the daily ritual of evacuating their bowels). The telephone came and then the fridge, cars replaced bullock carts. The Kodavas were now a rich race—but they had always behaved like the rich. Even in the days when they had lived on wild meat, bamboo, crabs and mushrooms and had no money for a bus journey to Bangalore, no one thought the Kodavas were poor. They had the air of wealth about them. Now it became reality.

Subbu scorned the systematic sophistication that came with wealth. By the time the British left, the Kodavas had already been snared. What started as adoration of a new culture, masked and nearly obliterated the old. To succeed in life it was logical and right to emulate your superiors and who could be more superior than the snooty, patronizing British? The Kodavas, with their natural grace and charm, did it better than others. Subbu did not like these clones of white men and he shunned them with the same ferocious coldness with which he had shunned Majors, Colonels, Brigadiers and other cardboard cut-outs. They named their children Dicky, Willie, Robin and Joe Boy, Tiny, Kitty and Birdie. They convinced themselves and others of their exclusiveness and were content to drink at elite clubs like the Bamboo Club in Pollibetta and the North Coorg Club in Mercara. Kodava women bobbed their hair and wore slacks, served tea with cream cakes and sandwiches and kept beautiful gardens to assuage the guilt of their men who felled and sold trees to get rich. The men drank Scotch and beer, served sherry for the women and maintained rich stocks at home even when they could not afford other things. They sent their children to exclusive boarding schools in Bangalore and Ooty where they learnt to eat with knife and fork; the boys returned with polished accents and the belief that social refinement was the key to success, while the girls turned into efficient, glamorous hostesses. The Anglicization which Baliyanna had sniffed out and abhorred became their way of life.

Subbu knew that for all their sophistication, the Kodavas now were no different from their ancestors. Sophistication was a shell. You were what you were, children of Thadiyandamolu, Malethirike and Brahmagiri, with a kernel of honour and fearlessness, born to care for the land made sacred by the goddess and protector of Kodagu. That was the goddess who, when she left her home to punish her unfaithful husband Agastya, flowed away as a river but promised the people that she would go gently and with serenity, so wherever she flowed the water would seep deep and nourish the earth. Subbu was sure that one day the errant men, like himself, would see the truth of their destiny and return to it.

Subbu was alone in his belief and strong in his aloneness. When he left the army, people said he had done so out of cowardice, he had thrown away his chance of greatness and in doing so denied them glory. The Country Club that was now a brick-and-whitewash building frequented by the not-so-rich Kodavas, did not welcome the son of Baliyanna the vet. On Sundays, he went to the marketplace and bought the best cut of meat or a goat's head from butchers in blood-splattered vests; and then he walked past the Country Club and went home. Misunderstood by his people, ridiculed by his friends, despised by his son and resented by his wife, he wrapped himself in his isolation. Nanji and Neelu were his only companions.

Mallige had argued that their son deserved a better education than the coarse village teachers offered in Gonicoppa. Subbu agreed because he wanted to see his wife happy. He rented a house for them in Bangalore and mother and son went happily to their new-found freedom. Mallige wasn't weak-minded as Nanji thought; she was determined to give her son the best and prevent him from being a coarse villager like his father. In Bangalore, away from Nanji's carping, Mallige blossomed again and tried to rebuild her dreams around her son.

Neelu stayed back to study at the Gonicoppa Municipal School where her father had studied before he went to Madikeri. With Mallige away and no orderly, Subbu sewed on his buttons and patched frayed collars, liking the monotony of such work. When he left the army he donned khadi again—not as a statement of belief but as an austerity that comforted him.

There was happiness in their isolation. Subbu went to the fields three times a day, alone in the morning, with Somaiah writer at noon and in the evening with Nanji and Neelu. Neelu's return from school was usually announced by the rattle of the tiffin box inside her bag. When she had washed, eaten fried bananas or *kadambuttoo* with honey, or *kajaya*, they set out, walking slowly to keep pace with Nanji who stopped at the huts of the Yeravas and talked. They went to the far end of the estate where the stream flowed into the Maneyapanda fields, sat on the rocks and watched the sun sink behind the areca palms. Neelu picked smooth pebbles from the stream and pestered Nanji to play an old game—you had to throw a pebble in the air, pick up the rest from the ground and catch the pebble in the air before it fell. Nanji who had played it as a girl had taught it to Neelu who now played better than her.

Subbu watched Neelu, who was skinny but strong with a mobility and grace that matched Chinni's. Subbu was reminded of his long-forgotten desire for Chinni and he feared the violence of passion in the minds of other men who might look at his daughter. He worried constantly about finding the right boy for her; he couldn't bear to have her out of his sight. If she was a few minutes late from school, he set off down the mud path and met her on the way where she would have stopped with her friends to taste a just-fallen mango or jackfruit.

When Neelu tired of the game, she got up and walked

along the curving bank to the wild mango tree where the stream flowed away from light to darkness. She walked over the slippery stones to the opposite side. They could hear her laughing and chatting with the Yeravas and then she walked back, holding the oranges with both her arms against her chest.

'What are you smiling at, Baliyakka?' the Insect asked, placing an orange in Nanji's lap. Nanji dug her snuff-stained thumb into the orange and shook her head. 'You smile and you never tell me why you're smiling. What is it? What is it?' But she couldn't get an answer out of her grandmother.

Nanji talked less and less; she languished in age, but she had lived her life as best as she could. Her dreams for her son were behind her now and she lived in an inner world that was very peaceful; she could let her thoughts flow gently like the stream. The one greatest blessing was that she was allowed to stay in her home and was not hauled away to Bangalore or other strange places.

Nanji had shrunk in size and concentrated her being into that small parcel of shrivelled skin and twisted bones. Her thinking was sharp, her eyes clear but the ageing body had grown weak and she was deaf in both ears. She sat by the window and when neighbours passed by the gate, they came to pay their respects, to stand by her window and talk; Nanji curved her hunched back forward, nodding, understanding most of what was said without having heard anything. The young boys and girls who went to the newly built college in Gonicoppa came in through the gate when they passed that way. They came because they liked to see the old Kaleyanda woman the way one likes to see a monument. Nanji's friends were few. Bolle had succumbed to an infection that permeated her blood through the over-expanded birth passage, and the General had died a tragic death the previous year. An uncharitable husband, infuriated by the knowledge that the General's youthful twinkling eyes had charmed his wife, finally resorted to violence. He mutilated the General's manhood and flung him into the river at Siddapur to bleed to death. The body was found next day and a sad truth became apparent: the General, like all men, had just two not three.

Besides Subbu and the Insect, there was Boluka, who seemed to have shunned death altogether. After Bolle's death, he gave up work and spent all his time squatting beside a radio that his son Mutha brought from Mysore with the money Subbu gave when Bolle died. He listened all the time, turning the knobs endlessly, until the radio ceased to work. This led to a bitter quarrel between father and son, as a result of which Boluka was thrown out. But his short affair with the radio had changed him into a young man with music in his blood. He sang and hummed continuously; his hair turned fine and dark, his skin smooth and he actually walked with a straight back. For a few weeks, he was seen wearing a pair of army shoes that Subbu had given him but the shoes caused such insufferable pain that he politely returned them to Subbu and continued to walk on his calloused feet. His hearing seemed to have improved, and he stood by Nanji's window, listening to the visitors talk to her, or simply stood by while she filled a notebook with *Sri Rama Jaya Rama Jaya Jaya Rama*.

Nanji wrote with a squeaky nib, dipping it in a bottle of ink that Subbu replenished when it ran dry. The books she filled she put away in a long wooden trunk that looked like a coffin. She informed her son that when she died she didn't care what they did to her body; she wanted the books to be sent to Kashi where a new temple was being built so that her books would go into the mortar for the temple. Religion for Nanji had become a habit that could not be cast off, she prayed and followed her rituals, even though the gods had neglected to grant her any special favours.

She did not understand the swamping of Kodagu with money, so she allowed her mind to roam in the bylanes of nostalgia and think about her girlhood, her princely husband, her daughter who died in the stream and her typhoid-susceptible sons. There were numerous others who had died before she could imprint them on her memory and she had nothing but a vague remembrance of their scratchy voices. She nourished her mind on the past; it was better than thinking of the present because it now angered her to think that her son had joined up with a ridiculously stupid woman for life. A wife's duty, Nanji believed, was to have faith in her husband's imagination, to make him realize that he had the power to achieve whatever he wanted to achieve. Subbu needed such a wife but he had married Mallige who only served to desiccate his dreams. Even when Mallige was away and out of sight, Nanji could not help disparaging her. Subbu and Neelu had to think of ways to divert her from it.

Two months after moving to Bangalore with Thimmu, Mallige wrote asking Subbu and Neelu to visit them. It was not so much to see them as to replenish the supplies Nanji had sent with them. Subbu and Neelu went with rice, coffee, jam and pickles. When they had sat down in the drawing room and Mallige had served them tea and biscuits, she asked, 'How long are you staying? I must order extra milk.'

'A few days. Baliyakka is alone.'

Thimmu was like a stranger; he sat in the dainty drawing room with his hands clasped in front of him, answering only when spoken to and then excusing himself because he had homework to do. Neelu disliked Bangalore. She tried to help in the kitchen but it was not like helping Nanji; she was aware that her presence irritated her mother. She was happy when her father said, 'We will go to the market and bring some meat,' and Mallige gave him a list of things to buy. Neelu went with her father, with a shoulder bag and a basket and they bargained with the women in the market who spoke with harsh, raucous voices but were actually quite friendly.

In Bangalore, Subbu woke early but there was no desire to get up. He listened to the sounds of washing, scratching, swishing of vessels, grating of vegetable carts, the snort and fart of vehicles, of humans waking to live out another small chunk of their desperate lives. Later in the day, the shrill temple music would mingle with the muezzin's call from a

mosque and along with all the street noises would be flung
like offal in his ears.

When they left for Kodagu, he went with some sorrow, a
final acknowledgement that he could never win the affection
of his wife.

Chapter Thirty-three

'Look who's come! Baliyakka, look!'

Nanji knew. There was only one person whose coming could excite the Insect so much. Devaki was attending a rally in Bangalore, and from there it was only a day's journey to Kodagu. Nanji sent a Yerava to catch the black-and-orange rooster, another to get king crabs from the stream, a third for the jar of salted fish from the attic and someone to call Subbu from the coffee estate; and while she supervised the cooking, she grieved at her son's misfortune in not having met this woman earlier.

Devaki went to the fields with Subbu, sat with him on the rocks by the stream, and watched the Yeravas wade through the water in search of crabs. She had nothing to ask of Subbu and nothing to give but her understanding. The first time she met Subbu, she had seen the burden of his belonging here. It showed as an awkwardness, a deformity that screamed out of his concrete uniform. He couldn't sell himself to the military, couldn't become a statue of a handsome officer with nothing but emptiness at the end of his life when he had *this*. She was momentarily angry that he had gone away and wounded himself.

Subbu knew it. Something stronger than the ambition to be a Brigadier or a General had brought him back; voices whispered in his ears and they whispered so low that he never caught the words, only the wisdom.

Devaki was to contest the elections from Agra as an independent candidate. 'You're wasting your life, fighting vulpine Congressmen,' Subbu said. 'Why, Devaki? You must be one of the few left who actually believed in the Mahatma.'

'He wasn't a Mahatma or anything so trivial. He was a practical man who wanted to clean up India. He was obsessed with hygiene and purity, neither of which is important to us. When Gandhiji talked of cleanliness, we could not understand because we don't understand practical things, so we made him into a Mahatma and forgot his principles. He became a symbol. I can't get over the tragedy of his existence. I fight elections not to win but to make a point about our hypocrisy. Better to reject Gandhi, crush the statues, smash the photographs, forget the speeches, books and lessons about him. That will be more respectful.'

She stayed five days and then went back to her work. The next day, when Mallige came with Thimmu and stayed a week, Nanji talked about Devaki and when she saw that Mallige was hurt, she kept it up, quite exaggerating the former's virtues. Mallige retaliated with excessive sweetness to her mother-in-law and her husband but at night, Subbu could sense her coldness, the tension in her limbs, the accusation in her breath and her eyes. He was powerless to do anything.

Neelu was to go to college that year and Subbu, knowing that she would be unhappy with her mother, decided to send her to Mysore. Nanji worried. 'Just because you're going to a big town don't lose your head,' she said at breakfast. 'Don't become a city slut with red lips like a blood-spurting corpse, like those types who wear blouses without sleeves as if their husbands cannot afford to clothe them, the types who push their bosoms out like prostitutes. Don't be like those sluts.' She would repeat it at lunch and then at dinner until Subbu said, 'That's enough, Baliyakka. You've said it.' But Nanji would say it again at night when Neelu went to give her the digestive tonic laced with a teaspoon of brandy.

It was some days before Neelu was to go to Mysore. Nanji liked to milk the cows in the evening and she did it outside the shed, squatting. The sweet smell of milk, the warmth and the sound of the filling bucket were part of what still made existence worth cherishing. The bucket was half full when Neelu came to sit with her. She watched the thin jet of milk escaping from beneath Nanji's bony fingers, and the froth rising in the bucket. She looked up at the stark blue sky and let her eyes sweep the horizon in search of clouds. From Nanji she had learnt to revere and love them. Long after she stopped believing that her ancestors lived in them, she continued to think of clouds as her friends. Now as her eyes scanned the sky, a single white fugitive cloud, fat and friendly, came skimming across as if to please her. It was followed by several small, frothy clouds that swam and frolicked around it and the sky didn't look so bare and naked anymore. As she watched, the clouds moved about mopping up smaller ones, but the solid, stationary, rotund fellow did not move.

For a long while Neelu looked at the buttery clouds that formed soft white peaks in the sky and then she spoke to her grandmother. 'Baliyakka—why are you always angry with Amma?'

Nanji was hurt and angry, for she cared what the Insect thought about her. Anything to do with Mallige annoyed her so she waited for her anger to cool while she thought about the morning's chores; *paputtoo* to be steamed for breakfast, butter to be churned, the servants to be fed. But the Insect's question hung between them.

'Your mother's a strong woman. I want her to know it.'

'She cries alone in her room.'

'Everyone gets hurt. We're all delicate and strong. If your mother wishes to drown herself in weakness, is it my fault? Look—men can be clay in our hands and every woman knows it, but we must never misuse our power. Or exist only for them. You understand?' The Insect frowned, filing Nanji's words away in her mind to chew on at some other time. She looked up at the sky and saw that the rotund cloud was nowhere to be seen.

The bucket was full with milk and Mutha came to carry it to the kitchen. 'It's time to steam the *paputtoo*,' Nanji said, and began to walk towards the house. Neelu followed, wondering where the cloud had gone.

Just before Mallige and Thimmu were to go back, a letter came from Patrick saying that his family and Govinda's would be in Bangalore for a week. 'Ask them over to dinner,' Mallige said, happily. 'They're your proper friends. I'm sure one of them can help Timmy go abroad.'

Mallige went back with her son and Subbu followed a few days later, with Sunny. Sunny's ulcerous leg had been freed of maggots after a three-month stay in the Civil Hospital in Madikeri; the nuns took him there because the sweet odour of his ulcer drove everyone away from the shop. The nurses poured turpentine on the wound and killed the maggots. Sunny wept bitterly for the harmless maggots that had never troubled him. When a reputed surgeon from Bangalore came on his twice-yearly visit, he examined Sunny's leg and said it had to come off. He was a keen, clever doctor, full of concern and he sat by the side of Sunny's bed and explained to him the dangers of blood poisoning from a dead limb. Sunny smiled and stayed quiet out of politeness but when the surgeon left, he jumped out of the window and went home. The maggots never came back but at least he got to keep his unique leg. Sunny was given to bouts of sullen ill humour and contemplation but on the whole he had achieved the tranquil status of a happy man.

Patrick's constant association with politicians had made him irritable; his handsome face was drawn into pouches and shadowed with patches, his hair was grey, his stoop pronounced. He looked decades older than Rosie, whose pampered skin, poise and pleasing manners endowed her with an ageless glamour. She wore her artificiality with such amazing grace that even those who could see the falsehood were enamoured of her.

Rosie delighted in her closeness to wealth and power. She turned out to be smarter than Patrick imagined: she penetrated diplomatic society with even greater ease than Patrick and they spent their evenings being entertained at various embassies. Their two sons were in the US, studying, and judging from their letters it was obvious that neither wished to return. 'Fools,' Patrick said. 'They'll make money but they'll never have power. Here they could have had both. Money without power is nothing. Might as well be poor.'

Patrick opted for an early retirement just to spite his wife whom he now hated. She now controlled his body and decided what went into it and what didn't: less sugar, less salt, less fat, less of everything except vegetables that gave him nausea and salads that turned to water in his mouth. He was determined not to let her control his mind and took to writing a regular column called 'Focus' for a leading weekly that specialized in Economics. Through it, Patrick said, he managed to keep the intellectuals of the nation slightly out of focus 'because if anyone is truly focussed, they'll know what shit this country is in and millions will hang themselves or take Tik 20. So instead I give them this crap about unified pyramidal national substructure, cohesive interstate panlinguistic dynamism, mirror-imaging or success-oriented, multicultural symbiotic, non-synergistic pressure groups and more exotic garbage and images of unreality. With that I've become the highest paid columnist in the country. I only read the Sunday papers—seven of them—and ten magazines, eight of which are international, and I type out my column in ten minutes flat. Haven't read a book in twenty-three years. Where's the time?'

Govinda, with his dyed hair and meticulously tailored khadi, looked younger than his friends. He was so used to the unrelenting pressure of work that it no longer affected his equanimity. He had ceased to talk of self-denial and austerity. He had a Mercedes and a family Fiat, and he had sent Vishnu to the US.

Ahalya nodded agreement to everything her husband said, and drew her Conjeevaram firmly around her fat shoulders to indicate exclusiveness. She was haloed in jasmine, gold and diamonds cluttered her bosom, and her

tumescent, glowing face was a picture of happiness. Rosie and
Ahalya had a tacit understanding in their superiority and they
demonstrated it with the cruelty of women who relish the
chance to isolate another in order to humiliate. They ignored
Mallige. She tried valiantly to please her guests with the dinner
that she had planned for a week; she impressed upon them
that Timmy was bright, and eager to take the advice of the
brilliant IAS man and the Minister. Patrick did not listen.
Govinda pretended to but when he left he forgot all about
Subbu's son.

Chapter Thirty-four

With the Insect away in Mysore, Nanji and Subbu lived in a
tight and whorled companionship, only possible between the
mother who had stopped counting her years and the son who
enjoyed the privileges of growing old with his mother. Nanji's
varicose veins, which had grown worse with each of her
thirteen pregnancies and which she had stoically ignored till
now, began to bother her. The veins formed bulging rivulets,
the overlying skin became scaly and eczematous, the ankles
swelled; the blood pooled into the veins, draining away from
the rest of her body, and she became increasingly breathless.
One day at lunch she was overcome by a vigorous bout of
itching which hampered her always robust appetite and
worried Subbu. He sent a Yerava to get cooling leaves of
doddapatra and while Nanji went in for her afternoon nap, he
had the leaves crushed into paste, wrapped the paste in muslin
and went to her room to apply it on her ankles.

'Baliyakka . . .'

Blood dripped steadily from Nanji's bed into the
chamberpot while she lay there, haemorrhaging. Subbu
wrapped a snuff-stained sheet around the bleeding leg,
shouted for the servants to lift the foot of the bed, and wished
that his father, the vet who was a better doctor than most
doctors, was there to save Nanji. This was the most
undignified way for her to die and he wasn't going to let it
happen. He put his hand on her chest, felt the crackling
vibration of her breath and knew she lived. In spite of his wild
panic, Subbu did what his father would have done and he
saved Nanji.

Before the doctor from the Civil Hospital arrived, he managed to give her two teaspoons of brandy and a whiff of asafoetida with crushed pepper that brought her back to consciousness. Alarmed by the sight of the soaked sheets and the chamberpot filled with just-clotting blood, the doctor ordered bed rest for ten days. The wound, caused by Nanji's uncut nails, healed and when she finally hobbled out of bed, it was Subbu who was more shaken, by the shock of nearly losing his mother.

He had lost too many brothers, an aunt whom he loved, a sister, father, uncle. He was not in a hurry to cremate his mother. Subbu wanted to preserve Nanji at least as long as he lived; he followed her like a shadow, helped her out of bed and into it. He led her to the toilet—a room adjacent to her own and possessing a wooden commode; this was the closest Nanji would come to the modern system of having a toilet in the house. She had protested violently for years before giving in. (The day Neelu attained maturity, Mallige had managed to convince Subbu that they should live like decent people and have a proper toilet.)

Subbu also bathed his mother; he did not trust the Yerava women any more. The cheeky, bold daughters of Bolle and Boluka had tasted money; now they spent their wages on hairpins, ribbons and plastic chappals; they worked not with the unhurried loyalty of their parents but with greed for prosperity in their eyes. It diminished them. Only Boluka who came every day to sit in the backyard was sincere in his intentions when he said that he would go in search of crabs or bamboo or mushrooms.

Subbu fed his mother at the table, breaking bits of *akki otti*, scooping up the gravy with chunks of meat and putting them in her mouth. With fried *mathi*, he was very careful, freeing the white flesh from the feathery bones and retaining the slivers of skin that Nanji loved. She ate great quantities of meat: it was a must three times a day. Her guts craved for wild meat—though it was a need and not a luxury, it was now hard to come by. Occasionally, some intrepid men of the village defied the law and hunted in the fast-disappearing woods. If they shot rabbits or boar or some of those brilliantly-hued fowl with plumes of blue velvet, they brought a share of the meat for Nanji.

Every night, when Subbu poured her the bright green digestive tonic and mixed it with two teaspoons of brandy, Nanji asked if he would have some brandy with her. Subbu broke his life-long abstinence to please his mother. He only drank at night—never more than two fingers in the glass, but the story went round Athur that mother and son had become secret alcoholics. Subbu did not feel the need to guard his reputation; reputations mattered only to men like Govinda who bought and sold with their souls. He enjoyed this hour of peace; it had become a companionable ritual. He talked about the day's work and Nanji listened and understood without hearing because when it was anything to do with the land, their thoughts flowed in one unending stream.

Around this time Subbu discovered in himself the signs of a malady that had affected his father and grandfather—the insidious, unrelenting consciousness of the futility of existence. Subbu did not fight it because he could not fight what was in his blood. But he wished he could get to the kernel of the matter; then he would give in with grace. He began to carry his grandfather's revolver with him, the same revolver that the Rao Bahadur had rejected in favour of his diamond ring, the one that Baliyanna had kept beneath his pillow when death came unawares and denied him the luxury of choice.

Subbu carried the revolver as an ally, a comforting aide. It was there in his trouser pocket, massaging his thigh as he walked, and beneath his pillow at night, assuring him of the greatest choice. It was comforting to know that he could die exactly when it pleased him. It gave him the determination to live until then. Unlike his father and grandfather before him, Subbu did not suffer from indecision and failed attempts at taking his life.

He was physically fit, except for a strange, undetectable itch that troubled him at the most awkward moments and seemed to be the outer manifestation of his discontent. It started in the depths of his right ear where his finger could not reach and then it moved away and he could not tell where he itched. He scratched his armpits, shins, chest, nose and navel, he shut himself in the bathroom and scratched his private parts; he studied his anatomy in the mirror and examined himself with a magnifying glass to try and find the cause of his torment. He noticed with disappointment that his shrivelled cheroot hadn't, after all, grown anywhere as large as an elephant's trunk. It had atrophied, like his dreams.

While mother and son lived their gentle, unhurried existence, life elsewhere gathered momentum and rushed at a frenetic pace. Subbu sat in the porch and Nanji at her window and they watched the dizzy, turbulent, forward crashing of life. They resisted intrusion and made a pact against the insidious temptation of the radio that could have brought the world inside. Subbu read the newspaper and sometimes he called out important news to Nanji, knowing that she neither understood nor cared.

He read the headlines and the editorial, then the sports page, foreign news, matrimonial column, obituaries, ads, cinema guide, the weather and finally the dull, in-between news. He imagined the faces behind the matrimonial columns, looked at the obituaries and wondered why the photographs of people looked different when they were dead. A dull listlessness glazed their eyes; it was like looking at the calendar of a year that had already passed. Which one of them among the four friends would go first, he wondered. When you reached a certain age, what else was there to do but die? He hoped that when he really made up his mind, he would not need the revolver or a rope or any aid to death but be able to will himself to stop breathing until dead. But it wasn't that simple. The process of dying started during life; death cackled from dark corners, it lunged at you unawares, but always, it chose its moment. Until then you were tethered.

When Thimmu finished college, Mallige realised that her son needed her less and less each day, so she moved back to Kodagu and took over the management of the house. She undid everything Nanji had established and created a kingdom of her own in which even Subbu felt an intruder. She chased away the Yeravas and brought in a Tamil couple who had worked at the Bamboo Club and learnt the fine art of culinary etiquette from the British. Mallige sewed with renewed energy and made new curtains, cushions, table covers; she even invaded Nanji's room with her extravagances. If Nanji messed up a bedcover or pillow case with her spit and snuff, Mallige had another ironed and ready to take its place. Nanji was trapped in her own house. The new servants refused to clean her commode, so she had to humiliate herself by using the flush-toilet like everyone else; she managed to hang on to her chamberpot, which Subbu emptied down the flush each morning.

When Kailpodh came, Subbu cleaned the guns and decorated them; he watched the young men shoot and hung on to his revolver for comfort. Mallige had ceased to need his affection and she rejected his endearments with total indifference. But she was sure in her mind that she did not want to live as a widow, and she looked after him so that he would not die before her. She worried about his diet, decreased the salt, sugar and fat in his food until he was so starved that he would creep down to the larder when she went for her bath and eat a cold cutlet or bread with ghee.

Thimmu joined a bank and resigned after two desultory months. Like many young men, he wanted more than anything to go abroad and he believed that his father could help him. Even when he needed his father's help, he asked with the contemptuous tone of a son who believed that his father was incapable of achievement. 'You have two influential friends,' he said. 'They can get me there with a letter or phone call.'

'My friends are my friends,' Subbu said, stubbornly. 'I don't ask them for favours.'

Thimmu went on his own to see Patrick, who he felt was less intimidating than Govinda. Patrick offered to help, not because he thought the boy deserved it but because of his affection for Subbu and the long-forgotten debt that he could now repay. But after his retirement, Patrick was not as influential as he had been and his health was too precarious to permit him to exercise any of his previous dynamism to help the boy. Thimmu's dream of going abroad remained a dream.

Six months earlier, Patrick had contracted a fever which doctors failed to cure; he stubbornly refused his sons' entreaties that he go to the US for treatment but allowed his blood to be sent across in eighteen sealed tubes for tests. The American physicians failed to arrive at a diagnosis but they prescribed newer and stronger antibiotics, which his sons sent at exorbitant cost. The fever stayed. Patrick sat all day with his feet in cold water and an ice-pack on his head and begged the doctors to finish him off, or tell him how to get a heart attack or something that killed in five seconds. If they would tell him what to do or not do, he would pay them well, in dollars. It was indecent to live when you had an illness even the best doctors could not diagnose. He couldn't bear Rosie's accusing eyes on him and the tone of his sons' voices on the phone saying: 'Are you all right?' Rosie, who was tired of her cantankerous, fever-ridden husband, organised a rota for the servants to look after him in their Bangalore house, and went back to pursue her interests in Delhi.

Govinda meanwhile had fared worse. He had suffered from a weak stream for years; he struggled to prevent it from spraying the toilet and woke six or seven times at night to empty his bladder. It made him an insomniac and he resented Ahalya for the first time since their marriage because she slept undisturbed. The urologists told him he had the old-age curse, an enlarged prostate and advised surgery to avoid a total block. Govinda wanted to think it over; two months later, while on a tour of Mysore, his urine blocked off. With a bladder riding above his navel, he took the Air-India flight to New York, having denied a previously booked passenger his seat. Govinda reckoned that nothing less than Sloan-Kettering was destined to remove his prostate. The Indian press went to town about the waste of national funds on an old political fogy. A rattled Govinda issued a statement just before anaesthesia that his prostate was worth a lot since he was responsible for the well-being of millions in his constituency.

Four reputed urologists, who devoted all their time to VIP prostates, took his out. But the collective resentment of the Indian people, the disparaged Indian urologists and his enemies followed him to the US and forty-eight hours after the surgery his bladder filled up with blood clots and he was taken back for a second look. Two more urologists were called in to reinforce the team. The second operation took four times as long the first. Govinda was in hospital for twenty-one days and when he left, he could not control his water for more than a miserable half-hour. The constant, embarrassing incontinence, the smell of urine and the need to dash to the toilet disfigured the personality of the meticulous, body-pure brahmin. He became irritable and unconfident; he walked with a shuffling gait, with his knees together. A year later, he consulted the surgeons in Delhi and opted for a permanent catheter with the bag strapped to his thigh. When the next elections came, his party advised him not to contest. So, Ahalya in tow, he moved to a new locality in Bangalore where ministers, film producers and influential men like Patrick bought houses.

Subbu visited his friends. In their infirmity, he saw his future like a mirage. When you passed a certain age and were ill, you were ignored. You might as well be a ghost for all anyone cared. Subbu fingered the revolver in his pocket, feeling its hardness, dents, projections and the smooth lines of the barrel; he ran his fingers over every angle and depression and tried to familiarize himself with the object that gave him the choice to stay or leave when it pleased him. He had no desire to lead a beggared, sickly existence, accompanied by a trailing catheter or a fever raging through the blood. Govinda maintained an outward dignity but the surgery had traumatized him in many ways. His mind was blunted perceptibly, his sharp brahmin reasoning left him. Patrick's tall frame, now emaciated by fever, was like a slowly crumbling pillar.

Subbu stayed in Bangalore for some months, and spent the evenings with his friends. At four, he would take a bus to Govinda's house. While he drank coffee and ate the snacks that Ahalya brought, Govinda made elaborate preparations for the walk. He wore a khadi bush shirt and loose khadi trousers so that the urine bag strapped to his leg would not show and he went with Subbu, refusing the walking stick that Ahalya offered. They made their way to Patrick's house. Halfway along the street Patrick would be waiting in readiness, swaddled in sweaters, scarves and a woollen cap. They walked round the block, stopping when a vehicle went past because infirmity had robbed them of the confidence to keep walking when a car or truck or a super-speeding Bullet came from behind like a predator, mocking their lethargy. At one end of the block was a patch of green where they sat on a bench of concrete and listened to the piercing shrieks of children at play. Patrick talked. Subbu listened, Govinda was silent and remote; Subbu watched the children and wondered who would go first. When Patrick died, Rosie was sure to remarry; for Govinda, the flag would fly at half-mast, there would be a government holiday in Mysore, mournful music on AIR, pretended sympathy, letters to wife and children, a state funeral. But how many real mourners would he have?

Sunny came to visit his friends and went with them on their evening walks but he was puzzled by the aimlessness of walking and after a few days, went back to his butchering and selling of sweets and cigarettes.

When Thimmu realized that he could not go abroad, he

came home to live out his frustration. Kodagu bored him, his mother's ministrations annoyed him, his grandmother's decrepitude disgusted him; he hated the long empty evenings and the constant presence of his father in the porch. With friends of similar disposition, he went to the Bamboo Club when he had the money, to the Country Club when he didn't. There he heard about the possibility of easy wealth from the sale of timber. Kodagu had an abundance of trees and their estate had plenty. Felling trees and selling the timber would bring money without effort.

Subbu refused to allow it. He remembered the mango trees girdled with pepper vines being cut down before Boju Uncle's wedding. Each tree had gone without fuss, just the scrape and crunch and the enormous crash that had started his wheezing attacks. In the end he gave in to Thimmu's pressure because if he didn't give in the trees would be felled anyway. It wasn't just the trees he grieved for but a greater loss that he couldn't explain. A son who was hostile, a daughter away from home, an ageing wife, a dying mother, felled trees. Life's decline was terrible, unyielding, devoid of joy. He hated the way each of them had begun to live a separate existence in private territories of pain.

Like his mother, he had started spending more time in bed. In the afternoons he rested with Mallige and listened to the sound of trees being split into logs—the smell of bleeding wood. People talked of loving trees but cut them down without regret, as if the money they got in exchange could replace the loss. As the trees were chopped down and flung in a mounting heap, Subbu punished himself by watching their dismembered carcasses from the bedroom window. When he took his short midday nap, he dreamt that each log of wood got up and walked to him, stood at his window and with newly sprung leafy arms encircled his throat. You let us be killed, you let us be killed, we'll show you how it feels. The leaves tickled him mercilessly, the branches suffocated him and he woke weeping.

He wished the Insect would come home. He missed her acutely all the time, and worried about her. Would he ever find a man good enough for his daughter? She would soon be twenty-one and over-smart, foolish-looking young men were sure to make advances and then one could never say what might happen. No, he must warn her against all men. He wouldn't talk about it when she came home, it would be impossible to sit and tell her what he felt but he would write her a long letter.

That night he woke and lay there listening to dew fall on the leaves, lizards rustling in the dry grass, beams snapping overhead, the turbulence of his half-digested meal inside him. And then the smell. What was that smell? His olfactory senses, usually calm at night, were roused. Was it the sweet warm smell of Nanji's milk permeating from his infantile memories, was it Chinni and the bruised, pink-fleshed guavas, was it Mallige's ghee rice or Clara's perfume or Devaki's coconut oil? A burning in the nostrils—was it dried fish, rancid oil, camphorated clothes, or the scent of pepper—damn it, was it something dying, something being born? Or the vapours of his heavy evening meal— he must watch out and not get too greedy—a bloated stomach disturbed sleep. He rolled over on his soft belly and ignored the smell but it wouldn't leave him, it hung over him like an illness. What was it? Then suddenly, he knew.

The haystacks were on fire.

Subbu groped for the switch: as the light came on his pyjamas fell in loose folds around his ankles. He hitched them up, fastened the string with slow-moving, clumsy fingers and went to the steps at the back of the house from where, beyond the well, the haystacks were visible. Gold and orange flames burst in the sky, lighting up the moonless night. There was a wild stampede all around him; Thimmu was in charge.

An old man was useless in an emergency. He went into the house and paused at Nanji's door, listened to the reassuring sound of her open-mouthed breathing. He went to his room and lay down to worry about the Insect who was coming home for two days.

He waited all morning. At breakfast, he picked at the *paputtoo* and carped at everyone. Did the Insect not realize that he needed her and Nanji needed her? She could have taken the eight o'clock bus and been home by now.

Did she not care?

Then he heard the knock. He looked through the window over the corpses of trees and saw her lugging her box through the gate. Thimmu went to open the door. Subbu rose. Yes, it was she. But before he greeted her he had to go to the toilet to scratch himself, properly. Then he would meet her.

READ MORE IN PENGUIN

In every corner of the world, on every subject under the sun, Penguin represents quality and variety—the very best in publishing today.

For complete information about books available from Penguin—including Puffins, Penguin Classics and Arkana—and how to order them, write to us at the appropriate address below. Please note that for copyright reasons the selection of books varies from country to country.

In India: Please write to *Penguin Books India Pvt. Ltd. 11 Community Centre, Panchsheel Park, New Delhi 110017*

In the United Kingdom: Please write to *Dept JC, Penguin Books Ltd. Bath Road, Harmondsworth, West Drayton, Middlesex, UB7 ODA. UK*

In the United States: Please write to *Penguin Putnam Inc., 375 Hudson Street, New York, NY 10014*

In Canada: Please write to *Penguin Books Canada Ltd. 10 Alcorn Avenue, Suite 300, Toronto, Ontario M4V 3B2*

In Australia: Please write to *Penguin Books Australia Ltd. 487, Maroondah Highway, Ring Wood, Victoria 3134*

In New Zealand: Please write to *Penguin Books (NZ) Ltd. Private Bag, Takapuna, Auckland 9*

In the Netherlands: Please write to *Penguin Books Netherlands B.V., Keizersgracht 231 NL-1016 DV Amsterdam*

In Germany : Please write to *Penguin Books Deutschland GmbH, Metzlerstrasse 26, 60595 Frankfurt am Main, Germany*

In Spain: Please write to *Penguin Books S.A., Bravo Murillo, 19-1'B, E-28015 Madrid, Spain*

In Italy: Please write to *Penguin Italia s.r.l., Via Felice Casati 20, I-20104 Milano*

In France: Please write to *Penguin France S.A., 17 rue Lejeune, F-31000 Toulouse*

In Japan: Please write to *Penguin Books Japan. Ishikiribashi Building, 2-5-4, Suido, Tokyo 112*

In Greece: Please write to *Penguin Hellas Ltd, dimocritou 3, GR-106 71 Athens*

In South Africa: Please write to *Longman Penguin Books Southern Africa (Pty) Ltd, Private Bag X08, Bertsham 2013*